W9-AVS-504

By Elizabeth Lowell

DEATH ECHO
BLUE SMOKE AND MURDER
INNOCENT AS SIN
THE WRONG HOSTAGE
WHIRLPOOL
ALWAYS TIME TO DIE
THE SECRET SISTER
THE COLOR OF DEATH
DEATH IS FOREVER
DIE IN PLAIN SIGHT
RUNNING SCARED
MOVING TARGET
MIDNIGHT IN RUBY BAYOU
PEARL COVE
JADE ISLAND
AMBER BEACH

ELIZABETH LOWELL

DEATH ECHO

AVON

An Imprint of HarperCollinsPublishers

Hardcover and mass market editions of this book were published June 2010 and February 2011, respectively, by William Morrow and Avon Books, both Imprints of HarperCollins Publishers.

AVON BOOKS
An Imprint of HarperCollins*Publishers*
10 East 53rd Street
New York, New York 10022-5299

First Avon Books digest printing: February 2011
First Avon Books mass market printing: February 2011
First William Morrow hardcover printing: June 2010

10 9 8 7 6 5 4 3 2 1

To Jan and Bill Croft
And the inimitable
Dong Shui

Prologue

You must believe me. St. Kilda Consulting is our best hope."

Ambassador James Steele pinched the bridge of his nose and wished he had never met the woman who now sat opposite his desk. "Alara . . ."

"I'm no longer called that."

Steele blew out a hard breath and wheeled his chair back from his desk. Very few people on earth could make him uncomfortable. The woman no longer called Alara was one of them.

And one of the most dangerous.

"Just as I no longer work for the government," Steele said.

"We established that years ago." Alara smiled almost sadly. Her silver hair gleamed, hair that once had been as black as her eyes. "In the shadow world, St. Kilda Consulting has made quite a reputation for itself. Trust is rare in any world. Even more so in the shadows."

"You're asking him to break that trust," Emma Cross said, speaking up for the first time in fifteen minutes.

Steele and Alara turned sharply toward Emma, telling her what she'd already guessed—they had forgotten she was there.

All emotion faded from Alara's expression. It was replaced by the frightening intelligence that had made her a legend within the nameless, anonymously funded government agencies whose initials changed frequently but whose purpose never changed.

"I came in soft," Alara said coolly, "requesting, not threatening. I don't have time for games with disillusioned children." She looked at Steele. "According to our intelligence, America could lose a major population center in less than seven days. We need St. Kilda to prevent that. We will have what we need."

Without looking away from Alara, Steele said, "Emma, summarize the facts as they were presented to us."

Emma's light green eyes watched her boss for a moment. Then she began speaking quickly, without emotion. "As given to us, no questions asked or qualifications offered. Ms. Alara's department or departments have been following various overseas entities. One of those entities is suspected—"

"Known not suspected," Alara cut in.

"—of stealing and reselling yachts," Emma continued without pause. "One of the stolen yachts was specially modified to hold contraband—chemical, biological, and/or radioactive. Motives, whether the actors are state or non-state, weren't part of Alara's presentation, which will make finding and stopping who or whatever is the enemy before time runs out just this side of impossible." She looked at Alara. "No surprise the bureaucrats and politicians want to dump this steaming pile on St. Kilda's doorstep."

Steele almost smiled. Emma Cross had a pretty face and a bottom-line mind.

"The excuse for said dumping," Emma continued, turning back to Steele, "is that St. Kilda has an agent who has been investigating missing yachts for an international insurer. The yacht, *Blackbird*, which I have been tracing, is a dead ringer for the stolen, refitted, and purportedly dangerous yacht pursued by Alara's department. Or departments. The person, group, or entities responsible for theft of the nameless yacht weren't identified. At all."

Alara's still-black eyebrows rose, but she said nothing about Emma's coolly mocking summary. The older woman simply sat in her crisp business suit and pumps, looking like an employee of a middle-management team, back when women were called secretaries rather than administrative assistants.

"Satellite tracking and other intel confirm that a yacht believed to be *Blackbird* will be off-loaded from the container ship *Shinhua Lotus* at approximately fifteen hundred hours Pacific Coast time," Emma continued. "According to St. Kilda's investigation, an unknown transit captain will pick up the boat in Port of Seattle. We have no assurance that the yacht aboard the container ship is the same one that originally was loaded aboard the *Lotus*. We won't have that assurance until someone finds a way to get aboard either the container ship or the yacht. I'm sure our would-be 'client' has the resources to covertly conduct that search."

"Had," Alara said. "Past tense."

"You have a leak," Emma said bluntly.

"Always probable," Alara said. "St. Kilda has carefully and repeatedly distanced itself from any traceable connection with any U.S. intel agency. The targets won't be looking for you. They sure as bloody hell are looking for us. We don't have anyone on the ground who isn't being followed."

Emma kept her mouth shut because she hated agreeing with the other woman. Nothing personal. Just past experience. The officers and agents she had worked with all over the world had been decent people . . . at the lower levels. The further she went up the food chain, the less trustworthy the bosses became. Again, nothing personal. Just the Darwinian facts of survival in a highly politicized workplace whose rules changed with every headline.

"Do you have anything else you can tell St. Kilda?" Steele asked.

"Not at the present time," Alara said.

Emma made a rude sound.

Steele didn't bother.

"You aren't required to help," Alara pointed out.

"But it sure is hard to do business in the U.S. when everyone who works for St. Kilda is audited quarterly," Emma said, "when St. Kilda personnel are stopped at the border, or their passports are jerked, or their driver's license is revoked, their spouse fired, and every business that approaches St. Kilda is warned not—"

Steele held up his hand.

Emma swallowed the rest of her rant and waited. Steele knew how harassment worked. Good old Uncle's bureaucrats could hound St. Kilda to death. Literally.

"That's the price of living in a society you can't fit around a campfire," Alara said to Emma. "Cooperation is required in reality if not in law. Ambassador Steele knows this. Why don't you?"

Emma hoped her teeth weren't leaving skid marks on her tongue. She really wanted to unload on the older woman.

Because Alara was right.

"Reality is a bitch, and she is always in heat," Alara said. "When all else fails, you can count on that." She glanced at her watch. "In or out?"

Steele rolled his chair to face Emma. "You're off the hook on this one. Be prepared to brief another St. Kilda employee in less than an hour."

"No," Emma said. "I'm in."

"I don't want someone whose head isn't in the game," Alara said.

"No worries." Emma's smile was thin as a knife. "I've learned to use my head, not my heart. I'm in unless Steele says otherwise."

"You're in," Steele said.

"Seven days, which began counting down at midnight," Alara said, coming to her feet. "When the time is up, be prepared for panic and chaos. If we're lucky, the deaths will be under ten thousand." She looked at Emma with cold black eyes. "Be smarter than your mouth."

1

Emma Cross gripped the round chromed bars of the pitching Zodiac's radar bridge as it raced over the Puget Sound, twenty miles beyond Elliott Bay. St. Kilda Consulting had assured her that the boat driver was capable. But Joe Faroe hadn't mentioned that the dude called Josh didn't look old enough to drink.

Was I that young once?

Yeah, I must have been. Scary thought. You can make some shockingly dumb, entirely legal decisions at that age.

I sure did.

Josh must have, too. His eyes are a lot older than his body.

She had seen too many men like him while she worked as a case officer in places where local wars made headlines half a world away, innocents were blown to bloody rags, and nothing really changed.

Except her. She'd finally gotten out. Tribal wars had been

burning long before she joined the CIA. The wars were still burning just fine without her. World without end, amen.

Until Alara had dropped into St. Kilda's life.

She has to be wrong, Emma told herself. *God knows it wouldn't be the first time intel was bad.*

But if she's right . . .

The thought sent a chill through Emma that had nothing do with the cold water just inches away.

Seven days.

Automatically she hung on as the Zodiac bounced and skidded on the wake of a ship that was already miles behind them, headed for Elliott Bay's muscular waterfront. She pulled her thoughts away from what she couldn't change to what she might change.

Emma tapped the driver and shouted over the roar of the huge outboard engines. "Shut it down."

He eased off the throttle. The boat slid down off plane and settled deeply in the steel-colored water. Like a skittish cat, the inflatable moved without warning in unexpected directions.

"You okay?" Josh asked.

"As in not wanting to hurl?"

He smiled crookedly. "Yeah."

"I'm good."

He gave her a slow onceover filled with obvious male appreciation and nodded. "Sure are."

She laughed. "Thanks, darlin', but no thanks."

Josh looked at her eyes for a moment, nodded, and waited for his next order. No harm, no foul.

Emma wished she could say the same about her own job.

Shading her eyes against the bright afternoon overcast, she looked west, toward the Strait of Juan de Fuca. Swells from the distant Pacific Ocean, plus choppy wind waves, batted at the twenty-foot-long Zodiac, lifting and dropping the rubber boat without warning. Some of the waves had white crests that streaked the gray water.

"We good?" she asked. "That wind's kicking up."

"We can take three times the blow, easy."

Land looked real far away to her, but she'd learned to trust expert judgment. For all the pilot's fresh-faced looks, he was utterly at home with the inflatable and Puget Sound.

"Let me know if that changes," she said.

Even as Josh nodded, she switched her attention back to the western horizon. Ten minutes earlier, she'd spotted her target when it was only a dark blob squeezed between the shimmering gray sky and the darker gray sound.

Now the target was a huge ship plowing toward them like a falling mountain. Dark engine smoke boiled up from funnels behind the bridge deck. The deck cargo was a colorful collage of steel shipping containers stacked seven high. The boat was close enough that she could make out its white bow wave.

"That her?" Josh asked.

She lifted binoculars, spun the focus wheel, and scanned quickly. On the Zodiac's shifting, uncertain platform, staring through unstabilized binoculars was a fast way to get seasick.

The collage of colors leaped forward and became a random checkerboard of blue and white and yellow and red and green, toy blocks for giants playing an unknown game.

"Meet the container ship *Shinhua Lotus*," Emma said, lowering the glasses. "Standard cruising speed close to thirty knots. One hundred and eighty thousand horsepower. Her hull is steel, a thousand feet long. She's stacked with more than fifteen thousand steel freight containers. One hundred and sixty thousand tons of international commerce at work."

"Gotta be the most boring job in the world."

She glanced quickly at him. "What?"

"Driving that pig between ports. Tugs do all the fun bits close in. The ship's captain mostly just talks on the radio."

She looked at the little boat that had carried her out to meet the *Lotus*. Twenty feet long, six feet wide and powered by two outboard engines. She touched the fabric of the Zodiac's inflated side tube. It was only slightly thicker than the rubberized off-shore suit she wore. All that supported the boat was the breath of life, twenty pounds per square inch of air pressure.

And one of the biggest ships ever built was bearing down on them, carrying bad news in the shape of a yacht called *Blackbird*.

She lifted the binoculars again. The huge ship overwhelmed her field of view. Everything was a fast-forward slide show. Stacks of shipping containers in various company colors. The windshield of the bridge deck. The hammerhead crane next to the forward mast.

The black-hulled yacht perched in a cradle on top of stacks of steel boxes.

Hello, Blackbird. *So you made it.*

If that's really you.

"How close can you get to the *Lotus*?" she asked.

"How close do you need?"

She pulled a camera from the waterproof bag at her feet. Unlike the binoculars, the camera had a computerized system to keep the field of view from dancing with every motion of the boat.

"I have to be able to see detail on a yacht sitting on top of the containers. A two-hundred-millimeter lens is the longest I have."

That and intel satellite photos, courtesy of Uncle Sam. Too bad I don't really trust Alara.

For all Emma could prove, the photos St. Kilda had been given could have been taken on the other side of the world a year ago. Or three years. Or twelve. Not that she was paranoid. It was just that she preferred facts that she'd checked out herself. Thoroughly. Recently.

"Two-hundred-millimeter lens." Josh whistled through his teeth and narrowed his eyes. "And the lady wants details."

"What's the problem?"

He held up one finger. "That great pig up ahead is throwing a ten-foot bow wave." A second finger uncurled. "The Coast Guard patrol boats would be on us like stink on a cat box. After 9/11, they lost their sense of humor about bending the rules."

No news there for Emma. "You saying it can't be done?"

"Depends. How bad do you want to swim or go to jail?"

"Not so much, thanks." She let out a long breath and reminded herself that impatience was a quick way to die, and she was chasing nothing more dangerous than luxury yachts.

At least she had been, until Alara appeared like a puff of darkness.

"I can wait until the tugs are nudging that 'great pig' against a dock," Emma said.

"If you're working on a really short clock," Josh said, "I'll be glad to take a run at the *Lotus* right now." He grinned suddenly. "It beats my usual gig—hauling seasick tourists out to chase whales."

She thought about it, then shook her head. "It's not life or death."

I wish.

She laughed silently, bitterly. That was why she'd quit the CIA and taken an assignment from St. Kilda to investigate yacht thefts. No alarms with this job. No adrenaline exploding through her body.

No blood.

No guilt.

And best of all, no corrupt politics.

Guess again, she told herself. *Then get over it.*

"Back to shore?" Josh asked.

"Not yet. Keep the *Lotus* in sight while you give me a sightseeing tour of the famous and beautiful Elliott Bay."

"Legal distance maintained at all times?"

"Until I say otherwise."

2

Standing on top of seventy-foot-high stacks of containers, with only the unforgiving steel deck below to catch him, MacKenzie Durand wrestled with the cargo sling that would lift the yacht off *Shinhua Lotus*. He looked up to the glassed-in cab of the deck crane, where the operator was waiting for directions.

Hope he knows what he's doing, Mac thought as he held up his right hand and made a small circle in the air. Sign language for giving more slack to the cable that held the lifting frame.

The operator dropped the frame six inches at a time until Mac's hand clenched into a fist.

The cable stopped instantly.

Damn, but it's sweet to work with professionals, Mac thought as he began positioning the sling on the yacht's black, salt-streaked hull. The man in the cab might be a miserable son of a bitch who beat his wife and was an officer in the most corrupt labor union on the waterfront, but when he was at the controls of his pet hammerhead crane, he could be as sure and gentle as a mother cradling a newborn.

Mac manhandled a wide strap into position just ahead of the spot on the hull where twin prop housings on *Blackbird* thrust out like eggbeaters. Lift points were crucial in controlling a vessel that weighed almost thirty tons.

Besides, if anything went wrong, he was going to be splat on ground zero. He'd been there, done that, and vowed never to be there again. He'd been the lucky one who survived.

At least he had been told that he was the lucky one. After a few years, he even believed it. During daylight.

At night, well, night was always there, waiting with the kind of dreams he woke from cold, sweating, biting back howls of fury and betrayal.

Long ago and far away, Mac told himself savagely. *Pay attention to what's happening now.*

When he was satisfied with the position of the lifting strap, he signaled the crane operator to pick up cable. The frame went from slack to loaded. The aft strap was in front of the propellers and the forward strap was even with the front windshield. Both straps visibly stretched as the overhead cable tightened.

Just before *Blackbird* lifted out of its cradle, Mac clenched his fist overhead. Instantly the crane operator stopped bringing in cable.

Mac checked everything again before he scrambled up the ten-foot ladder that stood against the swim step at the stern of the yacht. When he was aboard *Blackbird*, he gave the crane operator a palm-out hand signal with fingers spread.

Take a break, five minutes.

The operator nodded and reached for a cigarette.

A *Lotus* deckhand appeared and took the ladder away from the yacht's swim step.

Mac opened the salon door and went inside. He had been a professional transport skipper for five years. He was regularly dropped on the deck of a boat he had never seen before and was expected to take command of immediately. Since he didn't plan on going down with any ship, he had developed a mental checklist as rigorous and detailed as an airline captain's.

He liked the idea that if he died, it was his own screwup, not someone else's.

The engine hatch was on the main deck, just behind the pilot seat and the galley. He opened the heavy, sound-proofed hatch and secured it.

The engines were at the stern, leaving an open area below waiting to be used for storage of extra equipment, parts, whatever—a real luxury on a forty-one-foot boat. He walked quickly through the anteroom to the engines. He had to duck a bit, but it was a lot easier access to the engines than he was accustomed to.

The first thing on his mental list was the big batteries. He snapped on their switches and checked the output. They had kept enough charge on the ten-day trip from Singapore to start the yacht's engines and operate its various systems.

Next, he opened the seacocks that supplied saltwater to the cooling systems of the two shiny new diesel engines that drove the boat. Oversized engines, a special order that made for a cramped engine room.

Gotta love those yachties with more money than sense, Mac told himself.

Quickly but thoroughly, he checked the hose clamps on the through-hull fittings to make sure none had vibrated loose at sea. Cooling water was required. Gushers of saltwater in the bilge weren't.

The through-hull fitting that normally supplied cooling water to the generator had been left open to drain rainwater or ocean spray out of the yacht during the voyage. Mac closed the seacock so the yacht wouldn't sink minutes after it touched the waters of Elliott Bay.

He checked the through-hull fittings for the septic and water-maker systems, then the fuel lines that fed the two six-cylinder diesel engines. He had been assured there was enough fuel aboard to make Rosario, sixty miles to the north, but he was suspicious by nature.

It had saved his life more than once.

A shipping crew in Singapore, where the yacht had begun its voyage, could make hundreds of dollars by shorting the fuel tanks. Mac didn't want to come into the Rosario rigging yard at the end of a tow line.

The sight gauges for both fuel tanks showed less than an inch of fuel.

Ah, human nature. All for me and screw you.

The good news was that the diesel fuel in the feed lines from the tanks looked clear. The bad news was that he would be visiting the fuel dock on the Elliott Bay waterfront.

With quick, economical motions he checked both fuel filter housings for water.

All good. At least the greedy sucks put in clean fuel.

What there was of it.

He looked carefully around the engine room. Salt water was as corrosive as acid to metal parts and systems. Even with the best care and maintenance, time and use and the sea would mark the yacht. But right now, she was bright and clean, shining with promise.

Mac loved taking a new boat on its first real cruise. It was like meeting a really interesting woman. Challenging. That was where the reward came—getting the best out of himself and an unknown boat.

No one else at risk, no one else to die, no one else to survive alone and sweat through nightmares the same way.

When Mac had finished his checklist, he climbed the inner steps back up out of the engine compartment into the salon. Plastic wrapped the upholstered furnishings and protected the narrow, varnished teak planks that were technically a deck but were too beautiful to be called anything but a floor. When he closed the hatch, it fit almost seamlessly into the floor in front of the sofa.

Opposite the sofa was another, bigger, L-shaped sofa. Nestled in the angle of the L was a teak dining table, also protected by plastic and cardboard. Polished black granite curved around the galley. It was tucked underneath wrappings. Everything was, except the wheel itself. Varnished teak gleamed with invitation.

Mac opened the teak panel that concealed two ranks of

electrical circuit breakers and meters. He noted a scratch on the inside of the door. Cosmetic, not a problem. He checked each carefully labeled meter and breaker, going down the ranks, engaging breakers and energizing the circuits he expected to need.

The last two breakers he threw were marked Port and Starboard Engine START/STOP. When he engaged them, two loud buzzers signaled that the diesels in the engine room were ready to go.

With a final check of the batteries, he went back through the salon, into the well, and up the narrow six-step stairway to the flying bridge. He checked the switch settings on bridge controls, then lifted his hand and twirled his fingers in a tight circle.

The overhead crane operator smoothly picked up five feet of cable, lifting the yacht up and out of its cradle. The fresh afternoon breeze off Puget Sound tried to turn *Blackbird* perpendicular to the container ship, but the operator had anticipated the wind and corrected for it. The overhead crane arm swung the yacht toward the huge ship's outside rail.

For a second Mac felt like the boat was adrift, flying. This was the part of the job he didn't like, when he had to trust his life to the crane operator's skill.

He looked out over the waterfront toward the Seattle skyline beyond. The restless sound, the rain-washed city, the evergreen islands. The beautiful silver chaos of intersecting wakes—container ships, freighters, ferries, tugs, pleasure boats zipping about like water bugs.

One of the water bugs seemed to be fascinated by the

process of off-loading the yacht. Mac had seen the Zodiac while he waited for the *Lotus* to be nudged into its berth. The little rubber boat had weaved through the commercial traffic, circling ferries and tugs, taking pictures of everything, even the Harbor Patrol boat that had barked at it for getting too close to the *Lotus*.

Sightseers, Mac thought, grateful that he no longer lived a life where the little inflatable would have been an instant threat. *Sweet, innocent civilians.*

He did a quick check of the water near the container ship, where he would soon be dropped into the busy bay. A small coastal freighter, freshly loaded with two dozen containers destined for local delivery, pushed west toward the San Juan Islands. Two Washington State ferries, one inbound to Seattle and the other headed across to Bainbridge Island, were passing one another a few hundred yards to the north. A City of Seattle fireboat was making way toward its station at Pier 48, and a dozen pleasure craft of varying sizes were crisscrossing the heavily traveled waters in the afternoon sunshine.

The black rubber Zodiac with two people aboard lay about a hundred yards offshore, bobbing and jerking in the wakes and chop. The open craft had a shiny stainless-steel radar arch and the logo of a local tour outfit. The captain and single passenger wore standard offshore gear to protect them from wind and spray in the open boat. The passenger was busy with the camera again.

The round black eye of the long-distance lens made the fine hairs on Mac's neck lift.

Too many memories of sniper scopes.

He shook off his past and watched as the crane operator delicately lowered *Blackbird* into the water. Mac signaled for a stop. The operator held the boat in place in the cradle, afloat but not adrift. Mac checked his instruments once more, then touched the port start button on the console.

Beneath him, he felt as much as heard one huge engine rattle and cough. He held the switch closed while he glanced over his left shoulder toward the stern quarter of the boat. Black smoke belched, then cleared and belched again. The stuttering sound of engine ignition smoothed out into a comforting, throaty rumble.

The starboard engine started more easily and leveled out instantly. He went to the stainless-steel railing aft of the bridge and checked. Both exhaust ports were trailing diesel smoke. Beneath it, he could see the steady flow of cooling water.

Good to go.

He signaled thumbs-up to the crane operator. The yacht slipped down a few more inches until the water took the full weight of the boat. Moments later the slings went slack. Then the operator let out enough cable to ease the lifting frame far enough aft that the yacht was free.

The big power pods took over as Mac put the engine controls into forward. She felt solid. Clean. Good. A grand yacht doing what she had been designed to do. He left the joystick controls alone and worked with the old-fashioned throttle levers. Testing himself and a new control system in the busy bay was stupid. He'd try the joystick out later, when he was away from the crowds.

Mac idled away from the container docks. He purely

loved the first instants of freedom, of being responsible only for himself. Grinning, he glanced over his shoulder to check the wake.

The black Zodiac was moving with him. No faster. No slower. Same direction. Same angle.

The hair on Mac's neck stirred again in silent warning.

This time he didn't ignore it. He got his binoculars out of the small duffel he always carried, and took a good, long look from the cover of the cabin.

You're being paranoid, the civilian part of himself said.

The part of him that had been honed to a killing edge years ago just kept memorizing faces, features, and boat registration numbers.

3

Put me ashore there," Emma said, pointing at the dock next to the Belltown Marina.

"Isn't your car back at—"

"My problem, not yours," she cut in.

While Josh headed for the dock, she stripped off the red Mustang suit and secured the camera in her backpack. They had wallowed behind in *Blackbird*'s wake for fifteen minutes, long enough for Emma to realize that solo surveillance on the water was even trickier than on city streets. Joe Faroe would be flying in as soon as he could, disguised as a tourist. Any more obvious backup for what was supposed to be an insurance investigation would send off warning bells in the wrong places.

All she could do was pray that Alara had some trustworthy people on the ground.

Or not.

Leaks were something Emma didn't want to share.

Josh brought the Zodiac up to the hotel dock, cutting his speed at the last moment and killing all momentum with a short burst of reverse power. Emma stood poised, one foot on the black rubber gunwale, and stepped off just a second before the Zodiac touched the dock.

"Call me if you want a different kind of tour," Josh said, watching her hips.

With a cheerful wave, Emma went quickly up the ramp that led to Western Avenue. As she walked, she pulled out St. Kilda's version of a sat/cell phone. The parts she most appreciated were the long-lived battery and built-in scrambler.

When she hit speed dial, she glanced over her shoulder. The Zodiac had backed out into open water and was now heading south, toward its dock next to the ferry terminal.

Blackbird had turned into the marina four hundred yards to the north and disappeared.

"Where are you and what are you doing?" her cell phone demanded.

It had become Faroe's standard greeting when one of his operators called in. As operations director of St. Kilda Consulting, he had a lot to do and no time to waste doing it.

"*Blackbird* is on the wing," she said, "headed for Belltown Marina."

"For the night?"

"That's what I'm going to find out."

"Get aboard somehow. Before our guy in Singapore vanished, he left a scratch on the inside of the electrical panel cupboard. Given the dither factor on the satellite beacon, it's a low-tech way to be certain that we're talking about the same boat."

Emma called up the interior of *Blackbird* from her mental file, located the panel, and said, "Will do."

"Any bogies?" Faroe asked.

"So far, so good."

"Said the skydiver as he reached for the ripcord."

Weaving her way through herds of tourists, Emma half-smiled at the gallows humor. Vintage Faroe.

"If *Blackbird* is what we're told it is," he continued, "somebody is keeping tabs on her. Could be the man running her. Could be the man behind the tree. Find out."

"Still getting the pings?" she asked.

Faroe covered the phone and said something she couldn't hear.

Holding on to her backpack strap, Emma checked over her shoulder as she walked north. Old professional habits. She'd thought that quitting the Agency would strip away her professional paranoia.

It hadn't. Maybe just being a woman alone in modern cities kept the reflexes alive. Maybe it was simply who she'd become. Whatever. It was part of her now, like dark hair and light green eyes.

Faroe's voice came back to her ear. "Lane says the locator beacons are still coming through. The government dither must be turned way up on the satellites, because the beacon on the container ship and the one on *Blackbird* aren't showing enough separation to set off our alarms."

"The yacht is getting farther and farther from *Shinhua Lotus*. God, what if we have the wrong one?"

"That's why the scratch is there. What's the transit captain's name?"

"On my to-do list."

Faroe grunted. "Description?"

"I'll get back to you on that along with the name."

"Soon."

The phone went dead before she could say anything. She flipped it shut and tucked it into the holster at her waist without breaking stride. She didn't notice the people around her unless they looked at her for more than a passing glance. Then she memorized them.

Nobody stood out—front, side, or behind.

So far, so good.

Belltown Marina was guarded by a gate with a coded and keyed entrance lock. Given enough time she'd be able to get the combination. But on an unusually warm October day, all she had to do was be a little lucky. People would be coming and going from their boats.

When she spotted two yachties walking up the long ramp from the water, she moved into position. As the gate opened, she caught it, holding it for the couple.

"Great timing," Emma said. She tapped her cell phone. "I was just going to call my husband to let me in."

The male looked her over, as if trying to decide whether she really belonged to the boating fraternity that might tie up to the most expensive overnight docks in Seattle.

Smiling, Emma pointed toward *Blackbird*, which was motoring at dead slow speed down one of the marina fairways, headed for the fuel dock. "We just got her delivered. Isn't she a beauty?"

"Yeah," the male said, still looking at her.

Emma's smile stayed bright, even though the man's eyes had come to a full stop on her breasts. She had dressed to emphasize her assets and lower a male IQ. Tight jeans, tight crop top, and the toned body to make it work. She wasn't movie-star material, but she was plenty female.

And she'd learned a long time ago that men remembered breasts much better than faces. Telling questioners that the woman they're asking about had a nice rack didn't help anyone trying to find her.

"Hap, for God's sake, get out of the way," his companion said. She, too, was dressed to catch the male eye.

"I just wanted to make sure she wasn't some street person."

"She may be a street person, but not the kind you're worried about."

Emma slid through the gate and shut it behind her, leaving the couple to their practiced bickering. When she reached the interconnected docks at the water, she stopped, caught by the sight of *Blackbird* maneuvering in close quarters. Next to the container ship, the yacht had looked dainty, almost tiny. In the crowded fairways of the marina, she looked big.

Slowly, elegantly, the yacht turned in its own length. The man running her seemed almost motionless, but she could tell he was fully in control of the boat. She enjoyed watching that kind of skill at work.

Quickly she closed the distance to the fuel dock. Even if it hadn't been her assignment, she would have been intrigued by the grace and restrained power of the black yacht.

And the captain. He was a big, rangy male with a saltwater tan and a dark, closely cropped black beard. His hair was equally short beneath a battered baseball cap. A faded black T-shirt tucked into his close-fitting, worn jeans.

For all his threadbare clothes, he was perfectly at home on the obviously expensive *Blackbird*. He touched the controls on the flying bridge with calm expertise, nudging a throttle for a second, then tapping it back to neutral and waiting for a moment to gauge *Blackbird*'s momentum and direction. He brought the yacht parallel to the fuel dock, letting the residual thrust slowly take the flared starboard bow over the edge of the dock without brushing the hull against the heavily tarred wood and rub rail.

The dockhand grabbed the mooring line that was draped over the yacht's bow rail. She took a turn of the line around the steel cleat, and nodded up at the man on the bridge.

A propeller kicked for a second, then quit. The stern slid sideways and eased toward the dock. The inflated fenders dangling protectively from the yacht's rails barely kissed the dock before *Blackbird* was at rest. The dockhand made a "cut it" motion with the side of her hand over her throat as she walked quickly back to the stern line.

Bounced, really. She wasn't old enough to drink, but she wasn't jailbait, either. Tight shorts and T-shirt aside, she knew exactly what she was doing on the fuel dock.

The engines stopped.

Emma knew just enough about boats to be impressed with how easy the captain made docking the big boat look. Even a lightweight aluminum rowboat had a mind of its own. The mass involved in a yacht *Blackbird*'s size was measured in tons. A lot of them.

The captain climbed down the steep fly-bridge stairs like a cat and vanished into the boat's salon.

Swiftly Emma sorted through available strategies. She decided to stick with the IQ-lowering crop top. The lace inset between her breasts was a bigger tease than bare cleavage. The oldest approach in the world might be a hip-swinging cliché, but it was still around because it still worked. She tucked the left earpiece of her sunglasses into her cleavage, pulled out the colorful band that held her hair in a ponytail, shook her hair free, and sauntered forward.

Time to brighten the captain's day—and get an invitation aboard.

4

DAY ONE
BELLTOWN MARINA
AFTERNOON

Mac stepped out of the cabin and walked to the stainless-steel fuel plate that was flush with the deck. He went down on one knee to open up for fueling. Two prongs of the metal tool he held fit into indentions in the flat, circular fuel plate. A hard twist loosened the big, stainless-steel screw. While he turned the plate on its threads, he glanced at the fuel dock.

The lithe woman strolling down the ramp was older than the bouncy little line catcher who'd been hired by the fuel dock as eye candy for the yachting set. The woman with the small backpack over one shoulder moved with easy confidence. He liked that in a person, male or female.

But he wondered if he'd like the reason why she was interested in *Blackbird*.

Stop being paranoid. Yachties love to look at what's on the water. Just because her hair is the same color as the woman's on the Zodiac, there's no reason to be wary. Lots of women have dark hair long enough to be pulled back in a ponytail or left free to fall to their shoulders.

And nice breasts. Real nice, not a bra line in sight.

His neck hairs ignored sweet reason and kept on voting for paranoia.

"That's one beautiful yacht," the woman called out to him.

Mac looked at her. There was only appreciation in her voice and in her expression. No reason to get upset. *Blackbird* was indeed a fine boat.

And the female wasn't bad, either. Not fat, not skinny, with a spring to her stride that came from some kind of athletic activity. She was probably a few years past thirty. Her eyes were clear, light, and direct. Everything he liked in a woman.

Too bad she's the one from the Zodiac.

It was in the line of her jaw, the curve of her ear, the narrow nose and full mouth. Dark hair now ruffled by the wind. The lacy gap in her top should have been illegal.

He didn't know the game, but she was one intriguing player.

"Thanks," Mac said, standing up. He braced his arms on the railing, looked down, and drawled, "She's very responsive."

Her head tilted up toward him. She could have been friendly. She could have been measuring him for a coffin. Her eyes were a green that reminded him of the color of big ocean waves in the midst of breaking over the bow. Clear. Light green. Powerful. A warning a smart man listened to.

Oh, I'm listening.
Looking, too.
Damn, she just might be worth the trouble.
And Mac knew she was trouble.

"You handle her well," she said. "Have you had her long?"

Hell. She's the wrong kind of trouble. She knows just how long I've been aboard this boat.

He glanced at the dock girl. She was waiting with a fat fuel hose. The nozzle was green.

"Diesel," he said. Double-checking.

She nodded.

He took the nozzle and lifted the heavy fuel line aboard. The area around the deck's fuel tank feed was protected by a white square of absorbent padding. He had cut a hole in the center to allow fueling. When the nozzle was in place, he looked at the dock girl.

"One hundred in each tank," he said.

"One hundred diesel each," she said, walking back to the pumps. "Fast or slow?"

"Fast."

Emma watched the fueling process and chewed over the fact that she'd made a mistake. Obviously he'd seen her aboard the Zodiac, and taken a good enough look through binoculars to know her even without her ponytail and Mustang gear. His dark eyes had gone blank the instant she asked how long he'd owned *Blackbird*.

He enjoyed her crop top, but it didn't affect his IQ. A hard man in every way that counted.

Time for Plan B: Honesty.

Yeah. Right.

"So much for light conversation," she said clearly. "I'm Emma Cross and I've got a qualified buyer for *Blackbird*."

"She's not mine," he said without looking up from the diesel nozzle. "I'm just delivering her."

"So the owner is in Seattle."

Mac didn't answer.

"News flash," Emma said crisply. "Being rude will just make me more pushy. I have a job to do and I'm going to do it, with or without your charming help."

Mac almost smiled. "Charming, huh?"

"Yeah. Bet no one has ever accused you of that."

This time Mac did smile. "No bet."

Emma almost stepped back. The difference between this man with and without a smile was enough to make a woman think about doing whatever it took to keep the smile in place.

"Wow. You should try smiling more often, Mr. Who-ever."

He shook his head and decided he was going to find out just what kind of trouble this woman was. Give her enough rope and she might just tie herself up.

Now that was an intriguing thought.

"MacKenzie Durand," he said. "If you want me to answer, call me Mac."

"One hundred!" called out the dockhand.

Mac loosened his grip on the nozzle, replaced the tank cover, and walked around the stern to the tank on the other side. The dockhand leaped forward to feed more hose aboard.

Emma looked at the thick hose, stepped behind the dockhand, lifted a few coils to help, and almost staggered.

Heavy. Who knew yachting was hard work?

Silently she revised her estimate of the captain's physical strength. He was handling the stuff like it was garden hose. That rangy frame of his was deceptive.

"Hey, no need to get that cool top dirty," the dockhand said. "I can handle it."

"That's what washing machines are for," Emma said. "Do you do this all day?"

"Every day. The other dockhand quit. But I'm making a lot of money toward my degree."

"In what?"

"Engineering."

"That's a lot of hose hauling," Emma said.

"Beats waiting tables. I love being outside with boats."

"Ready," Mac called from the other side of the yacht.

"Coming on," the dockhand said as she flipped a lever on one of the pumps. The dial began to spin, fast.

Another smaller yacht nosed in behind *Blackbird*. The dockhand went quickly to catch the lines.

Emma watched the dial on the fuel pump for a time. She was just reaching for the shutoff lever when the dockhand appeared, turned off the pump, and went back to feeding hose to the second boat.

"One hundred," Emma called to Mac.

Moments later he appeared with the nozzle and heavy hose trailing. "New job?" he asked Emma.

The dockhand teleported into place, took the nozzle, then began dragging hose back and coiling it out of the way.

"Just a helping hand," Emma said. "Poor kid has her work cut out for her." She rubbed her hands on her jeans. "Permission to come aboard?"

"I'm on a short clock, but I can spare a few minutes." He called out to the dockhand. "Go ahead and take care of the other boat. I can wait for the fuel ticket."

She waved and looked grateful. The other customers were fishermen, eager to get out on the water.

Short clock.

Emma noted the military phrase as she headed for the stern of the boat. She grabbed the yacht's stainless-steel rail, felt the grainy residue of salt spray, and lowered herself to the swim step. Her weight was nothing compared to that of *Blackbird;* the boat didn't bounce or jerk as it accepted her.

Yet she sensed immediately the difference between dock and deck. *Blackbird* was alive with subtle motion.

Years peeled away and she was ten again, fishing with her father on the Great Lakes. She shook it off and concentrated on the mission.

"You aren't staying in the marina?" she asked Mac.

He'd already decided to tell her the truth, because she could easily find it out anyway. Nothing like appearing helpful to catch someone off guard.

"I'm a transit captain," he said, waving her toward the steps leading up to the deck. "I'm being paid to deliver this boat to the commissioning yard in Rosario."

She walked onto the deck and looked around. "What's a commissioning yard?"

"The hull and most of the interior of the boat is built in Shanghai. The navigation electronics, water maker, satellite linked chart plotter, TVs, radar, computer uplink, speakers, dishwasher, washer-dryer, stove, microwave, refrigerator, freezer, CD, DVD, and all the other expensive toys are added in the commissioning yard."

She glanced at him. "So what kind of navigation system are you using to get to Rosario?"

"Paper charts and experience."

He gestured her into the main salon.

"How long will the final work take?" she asked, looking around at the covered furniture—and the open panel on the breakers.

He shrugged. "Depends on how jammed up the commissioning yard is. Why?"

Emma stuck to the role she had developed over the last year on her St. Kilda assignment. "Have you ever worked for someone really, really, really rich?"

"No."

"That kind of money makes people impatient," she said. "My client wants a yacht like *Blackbird* and he doesn't want to wait a year or more for it. That's how long the list is. A year, minimum, no matter what kind of money you have."

"So he's going to make the owner an offer he can't refuse?"

She rolled her eyes. "Nothing that physical. Just a lot of green. Bales of it."

Mac decided it was barely possible that her story was true. "Nice finder's fee for you?"

"You bet." She wandered toward the open panel. "The boats I've handled have been from one to eight million."

"Relatively modest, for the kind of wealth you say your employer has."

"He has five other boats," Emma said, running her hand

over the beautiful teak wheel. The cover story came easily
to her lips. All those years of lying for a living, people dying,
everybody lying, and no one gave a damn. "His wife saw a
picture of a boat like *Blackbird* in a yachting magazine and
decided that she had to have it. Yesterday."

"Why?"

"*Blackbird* is small enough for the two of them to handle
alone. Roomy enough for a captain if she changes her mind.
And luxurious to the last full stop. You can get bigger boats
for the money, but you can't get better."

Emma crouched down, rubbed her hand over the glorious teak, and glanced casually at the electronics panel.

The scratch was right where it should be, which meant
Blackbird's twin was still missing.

Good news or bad?

Both, probably. Luck seems to go that way.

Mac said nothing while Emma straightened and moved
on to the galley. He decided he could get used to watching
her.

"I doubt that *Blackbird* would go for much more than
two, maybe three million after she's commissioned," he
said. "Depends on the electronic toys and the demand in
the marketplace."

"And on how stubborn the present owner is about selling." She shrugged, then faced Mac. Nice wasn't getting the
job done. Time for something else. "Price isn't my problem.
Getting the boat is. So just who owns *Blackbird* and how do
I get hold of him? Make my life easy and I'll see that you
get paid for your time. That's what you do, isn't it? Sell your
time?"

Her eyes were clear, green, patient, cool.

Stubborn.

Mac's smile was thin. He knew all about stubborn. He saw it in his mirror every morning. The razor edge of her tongue didn't bother him. He'd been insulted a lot worse for a lot less reason.

But it meant that he didn't have to play the amiable and easy game any longer.

"Yeah, that's what I do," he said, smiling. "Sell my time."

This smile was different. It had Emma wishing the gun in her backpack was in her hand.

"How much time do you have on your clock?" she asked.

Blackbird moved restlessly, responding to a gust of wind. Mac didn't have to look away from Emma to know that the afternoon westerlies had strengthened. The overcast was now a faint diamond haze.

Time to get going.

"I'm delivering the boat to Blue Water Marine Group," Mac said. "Today."

"In Seattle?"

"Rosario. San Juan Islands."

That could be checked. And would be.

"Is Blue Water Marine Group a broker?" she asked.

"Sometimes."

Emma throttled a flash of impatience. "Do they own this boat?"

He shrugged.

"Do you have their telephone number?" she pressed.

"I use the VHF. That's a radio."

She told herself that she didn't see a gleam of amusement

in his nearly black eyes, but she didn't believe it. She hoped he couldn't see the gleam of temper in hers. She felt like a dumb trout rising for pieces of indigestible metal.

"I'd like to go with you to see how *Blackbird* rides," she said evenly. "I don't want to sell my boss a pig."

"I'd like to have you along." He shrugged again. "No can do. Insurance only covers the transit captain."

"I'll risk it."

"Blue Water Marine Group won't."

Emma knew a wall when she ran flat into it. She pulled her sunglasses out of her crop top and put them on. "Is there some way I can contact you?"

"I'm right here."

She flashed her teeth. "So am I. I won't be for long. How do people who aren't standing on your feet get hold of you?"

"I move around a lot," he said. "That's the life of the transport skipper."

"But you have a cell phone, right, one that rings almost anywhere?"

Mac decided that baiting wasn't going to get him anywhere with this woman. She had a temper, and she kept it to herself. So he pulled out one of the stained business cards he always carried in his jeans.

She took it and slid it into her backpack as she walked to the swim step. "See you around, Captain."

Mac didn't doubt it.

Nor did he doubt that someone would be running his fingerprints soon. She had handled that card almost as carefully as a crime-scene tech.

5

Taras Demidov leaned against the sturdy pipe railing that kept careless pedestrians from falling fifteen feet into the waters of Belltown Marina. Part of him was amused by the railing. It summarized the difference between Russia and America. Russia believed citizens should watch out for themselves; if they got hurt, it wasn't the government's fault. America's citizens believed the state should take care of them like children. Russia accepted a world of good and evil. Americans believed only in good.

Demidov enjoyed working with a culture that believed in God but not in the Devil. Americans were so genuinely surprised when flames burned through their flesh to the bone.

Unfortunately, the world wasn't made up of Americans. The so-called nations of the Former Soviet Union understood about the reality of evil. Some of them contributed to it at every opportunity.

A movement in the marina caught his eye. He lifted his camera again, bracing the long lens on the railing. A light touch of his finger and the automatic focus homed in on the brunette who had reappeared from the cabin of *Blackbird*. Even though he knew that he wouldn't be able to identify her at this distance, he took a series of quick pictures. Digital cameras were useful for fast transmission of images, but they just didn't have the resolution of a good, slow film camera.

But tourists carried digital cameras. As long as he appeared to be a tourist he could vanish among the crowds. He was pushing it by having a long lens on the digital frame, something few tourists had. He wasn't particularly worried. People saw what they expected to see. If anyone asked him a question, he would answer it in genial American English.

To the crowds around him, Demidov was just one more sightseer enjoying Seattle's long summer days.

That startling, useful naïveté about strangers hadn't changed since Demidov had first come to the U.S. many years ago, as a young commercial attaché in the Russian Consulate in San Francisco. He had been amazed then at his freedom of movement from city to city, state to state. He was still amazed. His movements were unwatched, unmarked, anonymous. As long as he stayed away from any Russian Federation consular buildings, he didn't have to worry about FBI counterintelligence watchers.

All he had to do was wait for Shurik Temuri to appear and claim *Blackbird*. Unless the sullen old wolverine was disguised as a supple brown-haired female, Temuri was staying hidden in the background. Shadow man in a shadow world.

As was Demidov, who tracked the woman through the

camera lens. She walked like an American, open and confident. Maybe she was the captain's "friend." Maybe she was a player. If she got close enough to the camera, he would find out if Moscow had any record of her.

Like a hunter slipping from blind to blind, Demidov tried to take pictures of the woman as she approached. If the crowd around him moved, he went with it. He was careful never to be alone against the sky. That could attract attention. Attention was the death of many a careful plan. And man.

He lined up for another attempt. She was almost close enough for a useful shot. He held his breath, waiting, waiting. . . .

At the last instant the woman turned away, attracted by the white flash of a seagull diving for food thrown by laughing tourists. Turning away like that was a trick experienced agents had, an instinct that made them duck.

Or it could be what it looked like. Coincidence.

Demidov swore silently and turned in another direction, giving her his back as she reached the top of the ramp and slipped into a group of pedestrians. Like the woman, he didn't want to give away his identity to strangers.

When he turned back, camera and hands shielding his face, he couldn't find the woman. His mouth flattened. Thinking quickly, he took more pictures of nothing. He could follow her or follow *Blackbird*.

Demidov turned back to Belltown Marina. If the woman was a player, she would reappear when the yacht was delivered in Rosario. If not, it didn't matter.

All that mattered was *Blackbird*.

6

Emma pulled off at a rest stop and sat for a few minutes, pretending to talk into her cell phone. The people in the two cars and one long-haul rig that had followed her off the freeway got out, went into various restrooms, walked dogs, and stretched out cramped muscles. Everyone piled back into the same vehicles and left.

She watched her mirrors and told herself to stop being paranoid.

Herself didn't listen.

She blew out an impatient breath and punched two on her speed dial. The outgoing call to St. Kilda was automatically scrambled, just as incoming calls from St. Kilda were automatically decoded by her phone, which could use either satellite or cell connections. All of St. Kilda's field agents carried the special phone. In a pinch, it could double as a camera, still or video, with or without sound.

"Faroe's phone," said a woman's voice. "Grace speaking."

"Emma Cross. Is he around?"

"Annalise has her daddy in a chokehold. Anything I can do for you?"

Emma laughed. "I'd like to see that."

There was a brushing sound, then Faroe's voice said, "Where are you and—"

"I'm north of Seattle, heading for a Puget Sound waterfront town called Rosario," Emma cut in. "The captain is about six foot two inches, rangy, stronger than he looks, unusual coordination, maybe thirty-five, very dark brown eyes, short black hair and beard, no visible scars or missing digits or teeth."

"Name?"

"MacKenzie Durand, called Mac, no 'k,' according to his card."

"Impression?" Faroe asked.

"Warm smile, cold eyes. Very smart. In the right situation, I bet he'd be damned dangerous."

Faroe grunted. "Somebody wasn't happy to find out that *Blackbird* is the same vessel that left Shanghai."

"Somebody will have to be happy with the radiation patch and business card I passed off in Seattle."

"Somebody is never happy."

"Yeah, I get that. The *Blackbird* is either owned or brokered by Blue Water Marine Group in Rosario," she continued. "I'd like a fast run on them from research. Mac is a transit captain. Is the research in on him yet?"

"Still pulling threads. Stay on him and watch your back."

"How carefully?"

"How many backs do you have?"

Emma closed her eyes. "Right."

"If research turns up anything useful, it will appear on your computer or as a text on your phone."

"Faroe . . ."

"Yeah?"

"I'd swear I was being followed when I left the Belltown Marina."

"Description?"

"That's the problem," Emma said. "I never saw anyone. I just had this feeling I was being watched. I did all the standard things for dumping a tail, both on foot and after I got in my rental. Nothing popped."

"How are you feeling now?"

"A little foolish for wasting time, but I'd do it all over again."

"The dumping tail thing?" Faroe asked.

"Yes."

"Keep it up. Everyone who ever worked with you at the Agency mentioned your good instincts. Some folks didn't like what you found with those instincts—"

"I'm shocked," she cut in.

"But that's why St. Kilda hired you," he continued. "We're not politicians. All we want are answers. Get them."

Faroe disconnected before Emma could say anything.

She sat, staring at the phone, drumming her fingers on the steering wheel, thinking.

I left the Agency because I got tired of shadows within shadows within darkness. Every shade of black and gray.

And now all my instincts are twitching like I'm in Baghdad. Bloody hell.

She snapped the phone shut, started her rental Jeep, and headed north on Interstate 5.

7

Mac Durand slid the black-hulled yacht through the narrow channel at dead idle. By dark or sunlight, Winchester Passage was beautiful, distracting, something he didn't need while single-handing a complex new boat in the ever-changing waters of North Puget Sound. The long-lasting twilight made everything difficult—seemingly clear but actually not.

Yet Stan Amanar had insisted that *Blackbird* be in Rosario tonight, even if it meant running after dark.

Mac didn't like it. Deadheads—logs that had been soaking in the saltwater so long they floated straight up and down, exposing only a few inches of themselves above the water—were a constant danger. More than one twin-prop boat had met a deadhead and limped into the nearest port on one prop. Unlucky single-prop boats were towed or came in very slowly on a small kicker engine.

Some of the boats sank.

Never underestimate the sea.

Or a woman.

Mac smiled slightly. He was looking forward to seeing Emma Cross sometime soon. It would be interesting to find out what her game was. Or to get her out of her clothes, depending.

He didn't get naked with crooks.

He picked up a channel marker a half-mile ahead and checked the paper chart spread out on the helm station in front of him. He would turn to port when the marker was abeam on his starboard side. Then it was a straight shot in two miles of deep water to the lights that marked the channel into Rosario.

Mac set aside the joystick controller and returned to the throttles, nudging them forward. Speed had its risks. So did going too slow and feeling his way in the dark. Without radar or an electronic chart plotter, he was cutting things close. Sight navigation in full darkness was a good way to be surprised to death.

Mac made his turn at the markers and brought the speed up more. The diesels purred and the wake boiled out behind the transom, a pearl fan spreading over the black water. He headed for town at what he estimated was the most efficient rate for both speed and fuel use—about fourteen knots. Engines like the ones in *Blackbird*'s belly could push the hull at more than twice that speed.

Two hundred yards outside the breakwater, he cut the throttles back to reduce his own wake. The marker at the outside end of the alley was flashing red against night-black water.

He picked up the hand-held VHF he had brought aboard. *Blackbird* wouldn't have any proper electronics until after she was commissioned.

"Blue Water Marine, Blue Water Marine, Blue Water Marine, this is *Blackbird* outside the breakwater."

The response was immediate.

"*Blackbird*, this is Blue Water Marine, switch and answer on six-eight."

He twisted the channel selector and punched the transmit button. "Blue Water, this is *Blackbird*. You have somebody down there to catch a line?"

The man-made marina looked calm in the deceptive light, but tidal currents could be a bitch.

"With those pod drives, you won't need help," Bob Lovich said, "but we're coming down to watch."

Whatever, Mac thought impatiently, and punched the send button instead of answering. *The worst part of this job is owners who don't know as much as they think they do.*

No matter what the spec sheet said, *Blackbird* was an untried boat. It took a lot of arrogance, plus a full helping of stupidity, to assume that the spec sheets were the same as the actual boat in the water.

He pulled the engines out of gear, flipped off the engine synchronizer, and stepped out onto the main deck. Quickly he coiled bow and stern lines and placed them on the gunwale where someone on the dock could reach them. Because he was cautious, he put most of the weight of the lines on the inside half of the gunwale. If something went wrong, the lines would slide to the deck, rather than into the sea, where they could tangle with the props and cripple the boat.

Caution was also why he tied fenders on the dock side of the boat. He didn't want sudden wind or current to push him against the dock and mar *Blackbird*'s hull. Salt washed off. Scrapes didn't.

As he stepped back into the cabin, he heard the radio's impatient crackle.

"Stop wasting our time playing with fenders, Mac," Lovich said. "That boat can dock herself."

Only if the captain knows the drill. Even a pod drive isn't idiot-proof.

Yeah, the worst part of his job was the owners.

Mac knew that *Blackbird* was equipped with the latest and greatest pod drives, but he didn't want to rely on a system he'd never used in the close quarters of a marina. He knew what the boat would do if he used the twin throttles for maneuvering. He couldn't say the same about the joystick for the pod drives.

Mac glanced around the deck, planning his moves, and then stepped back to the helm station inside and put the engines in gear. Dead-slow, he passed through the slot in the breakwater and entered the boat basin at a crawl. Using throttles and helm, he cruised down the outside alley, stopped and pivoted between two docks that were crowded with moored boats.

The Blue Water dock was flooded with light, more to discourage theft than for safety reasons. Mac saw three men waiting at a gap between a fifty-two-foot sailboat with tall

aluminum masts and a smaller pleasure boat with a square
stern and long, overhanging bowsprit. He recognized two
of the men, Bob Lovich and Stan Amanar, owners of Blue
Water Marine Group. The third man was a stranger.

On the approach, Mac kept going in and out of gear to
keep his speed down. The gap awaiting him at the dock left
him maybe two feet to spare on bow and stern.

Hoohah, this should be fun.

The tide was on a steep ebb. Beneath the glittering dark
surface of the water, heavy currents pulled and shoved. He
came out of gear and let *Blackbird* drift to a stop parallel
with the gap where the three men stood, impatiently waiting for him.

Immediately Mac felt currents work on *Blackbird*, pushing it away from the dock. He stepped out and called to
Amanar.

"You sure you want *Blackbird* in this spot? I'd hate to put
a mark on your new boat."

"Ever play video games?" Amanar asked.

"I'm male, what do you think?"

Lovich laughed.

The stranger didn't change expression. Though he
looked about Mac's age physically, his eyes were older than
the first sin. Mac's instincts started crawling over his neck.
He'd seen men like this stranger before, usually on a killing
field.

"Forget the wheel," Amanar said. "Use the joystick. It's
just like a video game."

Mac didn't hide his skeptical look.

"Go ahead," Amanar said. "We won't charge for scratches."

"Your boat, your money," Mac said.

It's a good thing I don't have to like someone to work for him. I'd go broke otherwise.

He went back to the helm, checked that the joystick was powered up, then cautiously tapped the upright stick toward the nine o'clock position.

More quickly than he had expected, *Blackbird* moved sideways toward the dock. The short burst of power cut off the instant he released the joystick, but the boat continued to move slowly sideways.

Huh. It works.

He switched the stick toward the three o'clock position for half a second. It was enough to cancel the portside drift and bring the boat to a halt.

"Be damned," Mac said softly.

He repeated the sequence, nine, then three. *Blackbird* edged regally sideways, then stopped. He pushed a little longer toward nine. The boat sucked in toward the dock.

Mother of all miracles. It really works.

Some of the pod drives he had used were clumsy. This one was sweet.

He checked forward and aft. The anchor mounted on the overhanging bowsprit of the powerboat ahead of him would whittle his margin for error down to inches, so he pushed the joystick toward six o'clock. *Blackbird* slid a few feet out from under the threat. He pushed toward nine again, twice. Each time the boat moved sideways, against the current, as though on rails.

"Really sweet," he said, loud enough for the men on the dock to hear.

Amanar and Lovich laughed.

The stranger showed the emotions of a cement slab.

Mac nudged the black hull closer and closer until he felt the fenders touch the rail of the dock.

"Just punch the button that says 'Maintain,'" Amanar called.

Mac did. The twin propellers took over automatically. *Blackbird* held nearly motionless against the dock.

Amanar took the bowline, then the stern line, and secured *Blackbird* to the dock.

Mac leaned on the rail and looked down. "You're going to put me out of business. Nobody will need a captain anymore. A baby could do it."

"Have to be a damn rich baby," Amanar said. "Pod drives ain't cheap. Shut it down. You're good."

Mac stepped back to the helm long enough to shut down the big engines.

Lovich said something to the stranger.

Mac watched the third man, a heavy-set male with a wide Slavic face, black eyes, shoulder-length brown hair, and a well-combed mustache. He looked a lot younger than Lovich and Amanar, who were well advanced on the downhill slide to fifty. All in all, despite the longer hair, the stranger could have been Lovich's nephew.

And he was colder and more confident than anyone Mac had ever met outside of a sniper reunion.

He caught a word or two of a language that could have been Eastern European or even Russian. Mac couldn't be sure. Languages hadn't been a specialty of his. He had been the backup medic and sniper for his team.

Memories stirred in him, black and red, screaming. He shoved them down and bolted the hatch.

Lose the replay, he told himself roughly. *Long ago, far away, and nobody cares about it but you.*

Mac shoved a line through one of the midship hawse-holes. As he bent to tie the line to a dock cleat, he deliberately brushed against the stranger.

Beneath the soft brown leather jacket there was solid muscle.

"Sorry," Mac said. "Just need to get this line."

The man stared at him with blank, black eyes.

Lovich murmured something in the stranger's language.

The man watched Mac.

Suddenly the night was quiet, only the gentle lapping of water against the boats and the faint ringing sound of a loose stay hitting the mast on a nearby sailboat.

The third man said something.

Lovich nodded.

"Let's go aboard," Amanar said, looking at his partner.

Mac watched the third man move. Though he had an athlete's coordination, slight hesitations and adjustments in balance told Mac that the man wasn't used to the transition between land and water. Yet his confidence was superb. He catalogued his surroundings with a few sweeping glances.

"You're working late," Mac said, glancing at his watch. He still had plenty of time to go to Tommy's place for the promised drink.

Unfortunately.

Drinking and talking about the good old days weren't Mac's favorite ways to spend time.

Amanar hesitated, then said quickly, "We want to get a good look at her tonight. There's going to be a rigging crew all over her soon. We have to turn her around fast."

Mac nodded toward the dark stranger. "Is this your new owner?"

Amanar didn't answer.

"If he is, tell him I know how he might double his money overnight," Mac added.

The stranger stared at him rudely. He was a few inches under Mac's height and perhaps forty pounds heavier. Muscle, not fat. He seemed to resent the English conversation.

Lovich quickly translated.

The stranger squinted at Mac, as though weighing him.

"There's a woman who got all wet and bothered over *Blackbird* the first time she saw the boat," Mac explained casually, talking to the third man while Lovich translated. "She's a qualified buyer with money sizzling in the pockets of her very tight jeans."

Lovich was a good translator. He accompanied his words with hand gestures that outlined a shapely female butt.

The third man answered with a sharp string of words that took the smile off Lovich's face.

"He says he's not interested in selling."

"Are you going to be around for a few days, or do you have another job?" Amanar asked Mac.

"I'm getting my boat ready for a cruise. I'll be around."

"Great. We don't have anything right now, but you never know."

Mac heard what wasn't being said: *Now get lost.*

"You have my cell number," Mac said. "I'd like my check. I've got some bills to take care of."

"Stop by tomorrow morning," Amanar said. "The book-keeper is gone now."

Mac nodded, not worried. Blue Water Marine Group had always paid him on time.

As he started to gather his charts and stow his gear in a red canvas duffel, the three men disappeared down into the engine room. He could hear their murmured conversation. All were speaking the third man's language.

Mac heard someone rap a piece of metal on the side of the heavy, sheet-steel fuel tank on the port side. Then Amanar muttered a single word. If his tone could be trusted, it was praise rather than curse.

Duffel in hand, Mac stepped onto the dock. The marina parking lot was full of empty cars. The nearby streets had the usual traffic for a small town on a working night.

And Mac felt like he was being watched.

Shove that along with the memories.

The back of his neck didn't listen.

He paused at the top of the marina ramp and looked around, trying to find a reason for his unease.

It wasn't the cement-cold stranger. He was still below decks with the owners of Blue Water Marine.

Mac swept the front ranks of the parked vehicles on the marina lot, searching out spots where someone could see without being easily seen. There were pickup trucks, a few panel vans, and plenty of rusted-out urban beaters worth less than the gas in their tank. Nothing unusual.

Except the hair on his neck wouldn't lie down.

Get over it. You're in the good old U. S. of A., not on a mission. You promised Tommy you'd meet him. Quit looking for excuses to stay in town.

But I need a shower. Fact, not excuse.

His own boat was docked on the other side of the marina, a mile closer than the little house he owned. Mac cut across a corner of the parking lot, punched in a code at another gate, and vanished down the gangway.

8

Ambassador Steele turned away from the wall of television screens in his office/home. A quick push with his hands sent his wheelchair humming across the polished tile floor. He had a motorized wheelchair but preferred the modest exercise he got rolling himself around his large office.

He hit the button blinking on his phone and spoke so that the microphone could pick up his voice. "Steele."

"Emma Cross, as requested."

"Thank you, Dwayne."

In the next room, his assistant transferred the call and went back to talking in a low voice into the headset he wore.

"You requested information on MacKenzie Durand, called Mac," Steele said, forcing himself not to look at his watch.

"Yes."

"I'll tell Grace as soon as we're finished, but I wanted you to know right now that Durand could be a valuable ally or a lethal enemy. Until five years ago, he and his Special Ops team were deployed into some of the world's nastiest places. On the last op, he was the only survivor. He quit and never looked back. Rumor is that the CIA hung his team out to dry with bad intel."

At the other end of the line, Emma drew in her breath and stared out over the marina parking lot. "Mac wouldn't be the first that happened to."

"Or the last. The political back-stabbing among American intel agencies is St. Kilda's biggest recruiting boost. That and the built-in lack of competence that comes from political hacks being appointed to high office."

Emma wanted to laugh, but it hurt too much. "Amen. Been there, got screwed without being kissed, didn't go back for seconds."

Steele's laugh was as unexpected as sunrise at midnight. "As I said, St. Kilda is more than happy to pick up the talented survivors. You're one of them. Durand is another. As much of his background as I could get without ringing alarms is in a file waiting to be downloaded to your computer."

"Thank you, sir."

"I want you to recruit Durand. You have all the skills."

Emma blinked. She indeed had been trained by the Agency in recruiting locals. She had been very good at it.

And she had hated it.

"What if he doesn't want to be recruited?" she asked.

"Buy him."

"From what I've seen of him, I doubt that would work. He's too self-confident, not needy or greedy."

Steele let the silence lengthen before he said, "If *Blackbird* leaves port, you'll have to follow. Durand is a transit captain. Connect the dots."

"Yes, sir," Emma said through her teeth.

Steele laughed again. "Why am I hearing echoes of 'screw you, sir'?"

"Good ears?" she asked dryly.

"Don't be surprised to see Grace and Annalise with Joe."

"Family vacation," she said. "Always heartwarming."

"Joe loves the Pacific Northwest when it isn't raining," Steele said. "Ask anyone who knows him."

"Fickle man. I hear it rains a lot here. That's how it got so green." But Emma understood what hadn't been said—Faroe was traveling with his wife and daughter under cover of a vacation.

"Research is still digging," Steele said. "We'll get back to you."

He broke the connection.

Emma rubbed her forearms, feeling chilled. She hoped it wasn't her grave St. Kilda was digging.

She settled into the cold Jeep, booted up her laptop, and began reading—keeping one eye out for Mac to reappear. Living aboard a boat was illegal at the marina.

According to Mac's file, he had a little cottage in town.

All she had to do was freeze her butt off waiting for him to go home.

9

Taras Demidov shifted in the plastic lawn chair he had put in the back of the beat-up van. He had purchased the vehicle for $850 cash and driven it off a dead lawn in front of a badly kept house. The panel van was a long way from the bulletproof limos and high-tech listening posts once available to Demidov, but he accepted it as he had accepted other changes.

Survivors adapted.

Demidov had survived by making himself as useful to the twenty-first century's political/criminal oligarchs as his father once had been to unashamed dictators. Information never went out of style. Neither did extortion and execution. Demidov was adept at whatever had to be done.

The van fit in well with the ragged assortment of vehicles in the marina parking lot. Hidden by the interior shadows of the vehicle, taking care to stay well back from the windshield and the lights of the parking lot, Demidov scanned the gate closing off the Blue Water Marine Group gangway.

Nothing moving.

Even the feral cats had vanished into the shadows. He'd last seen one of them chasing a rat around the big refuse bins at the edge of the parking lot, right next to the portable toilet that had been set out for marina visitors. Like the animals, the visitors had disappeared into the night.

The captain, who had docked *Blackbird* with admirable economy, had climbed the Blue Water ramp, crossed the parking lot, and disappeared into another arm of the marina. The view straight through the van's windshield didn't tell Demidov if the captain had stayed wherever he had gone.

He could get a better view by moving to the front of the van, but that would reveal his presence to anyone walking by. Better to limit both his exposure and his view to the top of the Blue Water ramp. In any case, the captain wasn't his assignment.

Shurik Temuri was.

Perhaps I'll just kill him now and end the game.

A pleasant dream, but Demidov knew it was unrealistic. His employer wanted to catch Temuri with enough evidence to thoroughly discredit him. Temuri dead was worth five thousand dollars. Temuri caught with his pants down was worth more than a million dollars in a bank on the Isle of Man.

That kind of math wasn't hard to do. Even in the modern world of recession and inflation, a million dollars was a good payday.

Demidov sighed and set aside the glasses. The van stank

of the slops bucket he used rather than revealing himself by crossing the open parking lot to a portable toilet each time he needed one. He ignored the ripe smell just as he ignored the uncomfortable lawn chair set behind the driver's seat. An ear bug in his right ear monitored the Blue Water office. He monitored the VHF channel to the marina with his portable radio. He would eat, doze, and watch from the van until Temuri appeared.

Standard surveillance—exhausting, boring, and risky for a man working alone. At this point Demidov didn't have a choice. He must wait, watch, and collect information. Information was his weapon of choice, although he preferred a silenced pistol for close work.

The bug he had put in the Blue Water office before it closed was transmitting nothing but static.

I should have bugged Lovich.

It had tempted Demidov, but the risk wasn't worth the reward. The office of Blue Water Marine Group gave him much of the information he needed. If and when that changed, he would consider the problem again.

Until then, he would watch *Blackbird* more closely than a hen with one chick.

As he had every thirty minutes, Demidov checked his cell phone for a text message from his employer.

Nothing.

He switched screens to check on movement. The upper lat/long numbers hadn't changed. The lower set reflected the location in Rosario.

He settled in for a long, uncomfortable night.

10

Carrying a bottle of bourbon in a paper bag, Mac climbed to the top of the marina gangway, pushed open the gate, and headed for the old pickup he used when he was in town. Marina parking was too expensive for anyone but tourists. He always left his truck in a lot a few blocks away, close to the commercial docks favored by fishing boats. As a rule, commercial boats didn't play well with private marinas and yachties.

Before Mac got a block away from Blue Water Marine Group, he heard a car engine start up in the parking lot he'd left behind.

Just someone going home late, he told himself.

He turned right and headed for his truck. A minute later he stopped to fiddle with one of his shoes—and look over his back trail.

A white Jeep idled in the mouth of an alley. The headlights weren't on, but the streetlight glanced off the wind-shield and grille, giving away the vehicle's location. A shadow figure sat behind the wheel. The driver had been forced to expose himself in order to keep Mac in sight.

Okay, not someone going home late.

Mac stood and walked briskly toward his pickup truck. If someone was dying to talk to him, he'd take care of it after he saw Tommy. Until then, it would be easy enough to lose a watcher among the heaped seine nets and crab traps that stood watch over the commercial docks.

The dark hulls of fully rigged fishing boats tied off at the docks closed in around Mac. He moved lightly down another ramp, took a spur dock, and climbed back to the parking lot via a third ramp. Nobody noticed him. The fishermen who slept aboard were already deep in their dreams of nets filled with seething silver wealth.

When Mac surfaced at the parking lot, there was no sign of the white Jeep. He waited anyway, taking a long look at the shadows surrounding his truck. The only sound was his own heartbeat and the sudden scream of cats fighting or mating in the rough boulders that lined the working marina's waterways.

Mac unlocked his truck. No light came on when he opened the door. He had spent too many years dodging bullets to ever feel comfortable about spotlighting himself when he climbed into a vehicle at night.

No headlights showed up in the parking lot. No lights came on in any of the moored boats. No one walked or waited near the parking lot exit.

Good to go.

Mac started the truck, wincing at the noise. But there was no help for it. A diesel engine was one loud son of a bitch. Not to mention the whine of a water pump that he should have replaced by now, but he had been too busy driving yachts for Blue Water and other brokers to manage any truck work on his own.

After a last look around, Mac put the truck in gear and headed across the lot, headlights off.

No car lights came on in front or in back of him.

He drove slowly through the jumble of cars, work trucks, crab and prawn pots, gill and seine nets, and the large metal drums designed to pull and store nets during the fishing season. He didn't vary his speed, easing his way through the obstacle course without flashing his brake lights. He entered the street the same way. When he turned onto a more heavily used street, he flipped on his headlights and began driving like a regular citizen.

There wasn't much flash and glitter in Rosario to distract Mac as he drove. It was a blue-collar, sweat-stained working town. Or it had been. Those glory days were more than a half-century gone, but the town refused to adjust to the new reality of tourists and boutiques. It was a battle that had been fought through the city council and mayor's office for as long as Mac could remember.

As far as he could tell, about everyone lost. The fishing was gone, the forests logged out, the crabbing unpredictable, the town itself too poor to pave some of the streets within the city limits. People who lived in Rosario drove to nearby towns to shop for anything more durable than groceries and beer.

Through all the years, smuggling was the only Rosario industry that had truly thrived. Cigarettes north and marijuana south, a round trip that could net thousands or end in gunfire, prison, or death.

The smuggling was run by the Eastern European immigrants who had been fishermen and smugglers in their homeland. There had been no reason to change a winning combination when they emigrated to America a century or more ago. With each generation or each old-world conflict, their ranks grew. Overseas cousins, second cousins, relations by marriage, and relatives no American bothered to count fled to the New World when the Old World became deadly.

Once, Mac had thought of joining the local smuggling industry. A close friend of his had been Ukrainian, another was Salish Indian, giving him an entrée into the closed worlds of Rosario's immigrant and native communities. Mac had been seventeen and too full of testosterone to put up with the small town of his birth. But after a few smuggling runs, he got smart, left town, and joined the navy.

His best friend died two months later, simply vanished during a smuggling run. Tommy still survived, if anyone called living as a barely functioning alcoholic on the rez survival.

Most of the time Mac thought he'd made the right choice in leaving Rosario and smuggling behind. If he had any doubts, all he had to do was visit Tommy.

My own personal penance.

Yet Mac couldn't figure out what he was paying for. He'd got out, Tommy had stayed, and life went on either way. Yet somehow Mac felt guilty, as if whatever life he'd enjoyed had come at Tommy's expense. It was stupid, but there it was. Guilt for being born white in a time and place where non-whites were considered second class.

The distant flash of headlights in the rearview mirror shook Mac out of his bleak thoughts. There wasn't much traffic out late on a weeknight. The people who had families to support were asleep. The people with habits to support had either scored or gone home with the shakes. The drinkers were wrapped up in their favorite bar, huddled protectively over their poison of choice. They wouldn't move until they passed out or the bars closed.

God, I hate this town.

But I love Puget Sound.

The headlights in the rearview mirror jiggled again as the vehicle went over a rough patch of pavement. The state highway that headed out to the federal freeway always needed repair. Eventually the state highway would get what it needed, after the densely packed voters in Seattle got what they wanted. Simple math and electoral politics.

Mac slowed so he could turn onto Tribal Road without hitting his brakes. No point in making it easier if someone was following him. Since his white guilt had taken him many times to see Tommy, Mac knew the way. He could have driven without headlights, but he didn't want to run over stray animals or people.

He watched in the rearview mirror as the headlights that had been behind him passed the Tribal Road's turnoff.

So much for paranoids having real enemies, he told himself.

Tribal Road skirted the edge of tidal mudflats for several miles before heading into the scrubby, fourth-growth forest that bordered the tidal zone. The road was in the open until Mac reached the trees. He kept glancing at the rearview and side mirrors.

Brake lights glowed on the highway as a vehicle slowed, then made a U-turn and came back toward Mac. The vehicle turned onto Tribal Road.

Score one for paranoia, he thought unhappily.

He killed his headlights, accelerated hard, and prayed the tribal cops were drinking together. He didn't lift his foot until he reached the bend in the road. Fifty yards later he turned and coasted onto twin dirt ruts that bored into the scrubby forest. The tires skidded a little in the shallow muck before they bit in. He kept coasting until he saw the old cedar stump. It was twelve feet high and wide enough to hide a truck behind, a leftover from the nineteenth century when big trees were cut off where the trunk finally began to narrow, no matter how high up that was. The fifteen- or twenty-foot-high stump was left behind to rot. With cedar, it took a long time.

He tucked behind the stump, turned the engine off, and yanked on the emergency brake. An instant later he was lowering the window.

A slight breeze. The scent of moldy forest and evergreen and salt. No lights anywhere. No sound but the irregular ticking of the truck's engine as it cooled.

And the mosquitoes. It took them about ten seconds to realize there was fresh food available.

Chow down, he thought. *I hope I poison you.*

He heard a vehicle approaching from the direction of the highway. It was still several hundred yards away and closing fast.

Mac got out and eased the door shut behind him. From the dense shadow of the forest, he watched the narrow opening onto Tribal Road that was the only sign the rutted, partially overgrown track existed.

A car flashed by the cramped opening.

Pale. Could be white.

Could be a Jeep.

And it could be a tired driver returning to the rez after a long day on the water or working at the casino.

As the sound of the speeding car faded, Mac jogged toward Tribal Road, swearing at himself for being paranoid but not about to change. He hesitated in the shadow of the forest just long enough to be certain there wasn't any traffic heading his way. When he was sure he was alone, he scuffed out the fresh tire marks he had left in the peaty mud when he had turned onto the nameless, overgrown dirt lane. Soon there was no clear sign of his recent passage.

To make doubly certain, he broke off a cedar branch as long as his arm and messed up the tire tracks even more. Then he threw the bough back into the woods and scattered some old forest debris over the lane. He'd just finished when he heard a distant engine. He pushed deeper into the forest and waited.

He didn't wait long.

Score two for paranoia.

A car was coming back down Tribal Road, heading for the state highway. The vehicle's high beams were on and it was moving slowly. A flashlight speared through the open driver's side window and probed the dark roadside.

The skin on the back of his neck tingled.

Mac was close enough to the road to recognize the body shape of the Jeep when it went by. But no matter how hard his paranoia worked, he couldn't figure out even a stupid reason for someone to follow him.

Yet there it was as big as life, a white Jeep whose driver was shining a flashlight over every opening along Tribal Road, looking for him.

Mac wasn't particularly worried about being found. He had been trained in escape and evasion by experts. He could vanish in bare desert at high noon. Nighttime in the forest was easy.

Mosquitoes sung nastily in the darkness.

He resigned himself to being fast food for bloodsuckers.

Headlights and the flashlight flickered through the woods as the prowling car slowly approached. The Jeep stopped at the far end of the tunnel. The beam of the flashlight ran over the shoulder where Mac had brushed away his tracks. As the driver studied the ground, the light twitched back and forth like a hunting cat's tail.

The driver's door opened.

No overhead light, Mac thought sourly. *I wish that surprised me.*

Without getting out, the driver bent over and held the light almost parallel to and only inches above the ground. The raking beam of light revealed more details than a light held at ninety degrees to the ground would have.

Someone has been trained in the basics of tracking. Mac

breathed slowly, shallowly, making no sound. *This just keeps getting better and better.*

The light raked over the dirt lane. Mac hoped that he'd done a good enough job cleaning up.

Should have been more careful. Been a civilian too long.

At least he hadn't left parallel lines in the muck with the branch. Not all of his training had been forgotten or ignored.

After a long minute, the flashlight snapped off and the Jeep drove on down the road.

Mac didn't move until the sound of the Jeep's tires had faded. Then he reached up and rubbed away the mosquito that had been drilling down into his neck. A second insect had already come and gone from his cheek. He could feel a welt rising there.

Damn. I'll itch for hours.

But he kept standing in the night anyway, waiting, listening, waiting some more.

11

After walking deeper into the forest for about half a mile on the dirt track, Mac came to the edge of a clearing. Waist-high weeds, several rusting wrecks, and one ancient flatbed truck piled with corroding crab traps landscaped the area around the old trailer house.

He paused in the shadows as he always did. And, as always, he felt like he was back in a war zone.

Maybe that's why I hate coming here.

He shifted the bottle of bourbon and wished it was that easy, but he knew it wasn't.

Tommy was all tied up with Mac's own past, the wild times from child to man, running free when someone should have hauled him up by the scruff and shaken some sense into him. He'd been the youngest of three. His father had hit the road just after Mac's birth. His mother hadn't left physically; she'd just quietly drunk herself into an early grave. Hard work, but she'd kept at it until she reached her goal.

Tommy was headed down that same early-grave road. It wasn't alcohol that would get him there, though it was certainly greasing the way. Tommy's reckless rage was what would kill him, his certainty that someone or something had stolen everything worth having, leaving him with a double handful of dog shit.

Once, Mac had felt the same way. Then he'd grown up, taken responsibility for his choices, and clawed his way out of a life that should have destroyed him the way it had his mother and two older brothers.

He didn't even know if one of his brothers was still alive. The other had died in a single car rollover on the highway outside Rosario an hour after the bars closed.

Maybe that's why I visit Tommy. He's all that's left of my childhood.

Pathetic.

Both of us.

Get over it, he told himself grimly. *That boat sailed and sank a long time ago. Looking back is just another way of drowning.*

The breeze shifted, bringing with it the stink of a trash fire smoldering in a fifty-five-gallon fuel drum. The rank odor of an overflowing outhouse lay heavily beneath the smoke. Light from a bare bulb gleamed weakly through the dirty window in the front of the trailer. Heavy metal music from his and Tommy's childhood hammered through the darkness, making the mold-streaked trailer vibrate.

Mac walked swiftly across the clearing and pounded on

the front door. "Yo, Tommy. You still awake? I brought the bourbon you said I owed you."

It was the kind of bourbon Tommy couldn't afford but knew he deserved.

Mac pounded harder. "Tommy, it's Mac. You in there or did I make the drive for nothing?"

Part of Mac hoped that Tommy was gone. A big part.

The music stopped.

"Who's there?" The voice was hoarse, wary.

"Mac."

"Dude! It's about time. I thought you forgot me and sucked down the righteous booze alone."

The door opened, framing Tommy's narrow body in light. The smell of rancid takeout pizza rolled over Mac, competing with the other rank odors of the night.

"A whole bottle?" Mac said, shaking his head. "I never could drink like that."

"Yeah, true fact. You're a white pussy. Don't just stand there looking stupid. Bring that bottle in."

Mac walked inside and saw that it was still the maid's year off. Even for a bachelor sea captain, the place was a mess.

Tommy opened the bourbon bottle and took a long swig. "Damn, but that's primo. Just in time, too. I'm broke and tired of being straight."

"I hear crabbing is really down," Mac said.

"You hear right." Tommy took another swig. "But I got me a sweet gig coming."

"Good," Mac said quickly, not wanting to hear more about any *sweet gig* Tommy might have.

Too late. Tommy was already talking.

"Gonna get rich, richer than the ass clowns that run the casino."

Mac nodded and kept his mouth shut. He'd heard it all before, and if he came back to the rez, he'd hear it again.

"Yeah, yeah," Tommy said. "I know you don't believe me. Nobody believes me."

"If getting rich was easy, there would be a lot more rich people," Mac said mildly.

"If they can't see the way, too bad." Tommy took another long swig and sighed. "Better than a woman, not as good as crank."

Mac frowned. "Thought you gave that crap up."

"Did. Ran out of money. Did some deals." Tommy shrugged his thin shoulders. "But now I'm goin' for the gold. Just like a fuckin' athlete."

Laughter that wasn't quite sane filled the small trailer.

Mac snagged the bottle and took what looked like a drink. It wasn't. He planned on driving home. Soon. Obviously Tommy was riding the ragged edge of the shakes.

Coming off crank was a bitch.

Tommy grabbed the bottle again and flopped into an overstuffed chair that was held together by duct tape. A lamp with a bare bulb sat on the small table nearby. It cast his grinning features in stark angles, dark hollows, too many lines and not enough teeth for a man who hadn't seen the other side of forty yet.

"Remember when we ran that load of cigarettes to Vancouver?" Tommy asked, swiping hair out of his face with a dirty hand.

"Long time ago. We were young and stupid."

"Sweet money." Tommy drank and swallowed, drank and swallowed, his Adam's apple working like a piston. "That's smart."

"Karl died."

"Lucky Karl. He didn't have to live rat-turd poor on the rez."

Neither do you. But Mac kept that truth to himself. A man in Tommy's shape could teeter from normal to enraged in a heartbeat.

"But I'm getting out," Tommy said after another long drink. "Gonna take my money from my next job and head for white man's land. Live like a fuckin' sheik."

"Sounds good." *As always.*

Too bad it never came through.

The half bottle of booze that Tommy had bolted hit him suddenly. He shook his head and slumped back into the chair.

"Just the beginning," Tommy mumbled. "And here I thought old Granny was just a mama's boy. Turns out he's a big swinging dick. Got rich friends." Tommy frowned. "Mean bastard." A shiver shook his wiry frame. "Goddam, he's one mean son of a bitch."

Mac frowned. Tommy wasn't making any sense. He looked close to panic, eyes wide, sweating although the room was cold.

"You okay?" Mac asked.

Tommy took another long gulp. "Nothin' wrong that a bottle of good bourbon won't cure."

Mac kept his mouth shut and wished he'd gone straight home from the marina.

Like the old saying—no good deed goes unpunished.

Before Tommy could swig again, Mac retrieved the bottle.

"Careful, buddy," Mac said. "That's a load of alcohol hitting your system all at once."

"Ain't no pussy."

"Somebody say you were?" Mac asked.

"A pussy wouldn't take *Blackbird* out. Bad shit going down. Really bad. Gonna be rich. Gimme the bottle."

Mac pretended to drink. Anything to keep the bourbon out of Tommy's reach. He always had loved booze, but at the rate he was drinking, he was going to kill himself tonight.

"So when does your job begin?" Mac asked, trying to keep Tommy out of the bottle.

"What job?"

"The one that's going to make you rich."

"Need a drink."

"Wait your turn." Mac pretended to drink. The good news was that Tommy was going down fast, floating facedown in a bourbon sea.

"They been smuggling forever. Even before they got here."

"Who?" Mac asked.

"Granny's kind."

Lovich, Mac realized, understanding.

Grant Robert Lovich, known as Bobby to his cousins and Granny to the kids who hated him in school. Like his father and grandfather and great-grandfather. Outsiders to the whites and Indians alike. Determined outsiders.

"Thought we agreed a long time ago that what our parents believed was bullshit," Mac said.

"Then how come they own Blue Water and I don't have nothing? Only crooks make out in Rosario."

The sullen cast to Tommy's face was more warning than Mac needed.

Time to go.

"Gimme the bottle," Tommy snarled. "Fuckin' foreigners. We was here first, now we got dirt."

And casinos.

And smuggling.

The kind of hopeless existence that destroys souls.

Mac went to the sink and poured out all but a taste of the bourbon. He gave the bottle to Tommy and walked out into the night.

Mac hoped whoever was following him caught up again. He felt like hitting something.

12

Emma hated parking in the open for a surveillance, but there wasn't any choice. The Blue Water marina parking lot didn't have so much as a leaf to hide behind. The best she could do was wedge the Jeep between two rumpled pickups and pretend not to be there at all. The puddles and mud she'd deliberately taken the Jeep through helped it to blend in. She was no longer driving a shiny white rental.

And she had a lovely view of *Blackbird*.

People wearing tool belts were swarming over the yacht. A man whose picture was on the billboard advertising Blue Water Marine Group was overseeing, shouting and waving his arms. If the billboard could be trusted, it was Bob Lovich himself giving orders. Another man stood nearby—above medium height, stocky build, wraparound sunglasses, and a coat cut to fit over a shoulder holster. He didn't look like

Stan Amanar, also featured on the billboard, but he might have been.

If Stan had dyed his hair recently. And grown a mustache.

Plastic sheeting and other protective materials had been yanked out of *Blackbird* and piled up on the dock. Colored wires were coiled on the deck and what looked like electronics were stacked in boxes inside the cabin.

She lowered her small binoculars and remembered what the elusive Mac Durand had said about expensive toys and yachts. It looked like *Blackbird* was being wired to the max.

Her cell phone vibrated against her waist. She looked at the ID window and almost groaned.

Faroe.

All she had for him was nothing. Oh—and a sore back from the motel bed. Hey, that was something, right?

Too bad it wasn't anything useful.

"Cross," she said, answering the phone.

"Where is he?"

"Who?"

"Durand."

"Good question," she said. "I'll get back to you with the answer."

"Soon."

"Which is primary—*Blackbird* or MacKenzie Durand?"

"Both."

"Then you better send more bodies," she said. "I can only be in one place at a time."

"Lost him, huh?"

Emma took a deep breath and a better grip on her

temper. "Yes. He ditched me out on the rez last night. There are multiple exits on the rez, so I got a motel room near the marina and had a bad night's sleep keeping an eye on *Blackbird.*"

"Did Durand make you?"

"Define 'make.' "

"ID," Faroe said impatiently.

"Doubt it. The Jeep, quite probably. Me, no."

"Steele is on my ass like a rash."

"Try baby powder."

Faroe laughed. "We're flying in to meet Durand personally. We'll be there tomorrow. Sooner if we can manage it without tripping wires and alarms."

This going in soft is too damn slow, Emma thought, but didn't say anything. Faroe knew the time limit as well as she did.

"Have you read Durand's file?" Faroe asked.

"Three times." And she'd wondered if Mac Durand had the same kind of nightmares she did.

"Steele wants him. So do I."

"A hard man is good to find," she shot back. "I'm working on it. That man you're interested in is a ghost. He flat vanished into the rez. Early this morning I went by the address in his files. A nineteen-twenties cottage. His truck was in the driveway. By all external signs, he was sleeping at home like a good citizen. Now, I can cover MacKenzie or *Blackbird,* take your pick."

"Long night?" Faroe asked.

Emma made a disgusted noise. "Yeah."

"Anything happening on *Blackbird* right now?"

"She's swarming with technicians."

"So she won't be leaving the dock in the next hour or two," Faroe said.

"It looks that way. Want to bet on it?"

"For an hour or two, yes. Go track down Durand and make your pitch."

"You're the boss."

She closed the phone and reached for the ignition key.

The passenger door opened. MacKenzie Durand slid into the seat next to her.

"Breakfast or lunch?" he asked. "You're buying."

13

The vibration of a cell phone against his ribs woke Demidov from his doze. Without moving anything but his eyelids, he looked around. It was hard to see out through the smoked windows in the front of the van, and the rear door windows were even darker. Demidov approved. People had an even harder time looking in than he did looking out.

The parking lot had tourists and boat owners coming and going. At the moment, nobody was walking nearby.

Most important, *Blackbird* was still at the dock.

People were still busy ripping things out of the yacht and putting other things in. Binoculars had told him that everything being installed on the boat came from a legitimate commercial source.

The bug in Blue Water Marine Group's office had told him the same thing. Even so, he'd checked every name on the boxes. His computer told him that each was a common supplier for Blue Water boats.

His ribs vibrated again.

Demidov reached into his jacket pocket and pulled out the cell phone. Since only one man had this number, he knew who he would be talking to.

"Yes?" he said in quiet Russian.

"I need more time. Get it for me."

"How much?"

"The boat can't leave until after tomorrow, at the earliest."

"Nothing of interest has been put on board yet," Demidov said. "Even at night, when you would expect it. They have the ship lit up like a stage. It would take a fool or a very, very clever man to sneak by while anyone could be watching. Temuri is not that clever."

"My source tells me the exchange will be made in Canada."

"Where?"

"If I knew that, fool, I wouldn't need you to follow the ship. Make sure *Blackbird* does not leave until Thursday. Friday would be better."

Demidov bit back a curse. He was safer working alone—no one to betray him—but being alone on a job this complex wasn't easy.

"Then I will sabotage the boat so—"

"No! Too unpredictable. *Blackbird* must fly. Later than Saturday isn't acceptable. Earlier than Thursday isn't acceptable."

The connection ended, leaving Demidov alone in the sun-struck, stinking van. He didn't notice the smell or the heat or the random Blue Water Marine Group office noise bleeding through his ear bug. Like a computer programmed to find certain words, he wouldn't focus on the bug until it said something interesting.

Thinking of various ways to make certain the *Blackbird* didn't leave the dock until Thursday, Demidov dozed, cat-like, both resting and alert. For a man working alone, death was the most reliable way of carrying out a mission. The only question was whose death would get the job done.

14

Emma drove into the casino's parking lot in the same silence she'd maintained since Mac had invited himself into the Jeep. She still hadn't decided whether to slug him for his attitude or hug him for making her mission easier.

She turned off the engine and faced him.

"Dealer's choice," she said. "For now, you're the dealer."

Mac smiled slowly. "You decided that two seconds after I opened the door. Why the silent treatment?"

"Poor baby. Are you used to nervous chatter?"

"I won't get that from you, will I?"

"I'm told the food is edible here." She opened the door and got out. "Breakfast or lunch."

Mac slid out and faced her over the top of the Jeep. "Food is better at the bowling alley."

"A local's place?"

Mac nodded.

"I don't do local when I'm working a small town. I don't fit in."

He nodded again, as though he'd expected the answer.

"I haven't been to the casino," she said, "but I'm guessing I won't be all that unusual."

"Good-looking women are always noticed."

Emma took a mental inventory of herself—jeans, a loose T-shirt, rugged sandals that would have been at home on a hiking trail—and said, "In this outfit, I'll pass without a second glance."

"Probably. I liked the crop top better."

Ignoring him, she locked the Jeep and headed toward the casino entrance, leaving Mac to follow or not, his choice.

He followed, smiling to himself. Ms. Emma Cross didn't like having the initiative taken out of her hands. He could understand that. He felt exactly the same way.

Mac caught up with her before she reached the casino's double doors. Unlike Nevada casinos, this one lacked the clamor and clang and razzle-dazzle of slot machines. Without that kind of relentless, come-and-bet-your-life atmosphere, the casino echoed like the nearly empty warehouse it was. The only action was at the poker machines, where retirees old enough to know better and too bored to care fed the electronic monsters.

"How can they take the excitement?" Emma said under her breath.

"Clean living and constant prayer."

She smiled in spite of herself. "Good to know."

"Two," Mac said to the unsmiling hostess.

The woman waved her hand toward ranks of empty tables. "Sit anywhere you want. Someone will be over to take your order."

Mac led Emma to a corner and chose a seat next to the wall. She selected a nearby chair and moved it slightly, keeping an eye on the entrance.

"Talk," she said to him.

"After you."

"What do you want?"

"Why are you following me?" he countered.

Emma sighed. She'd guessed he wouldn't make it easy. That didn't mean she liked being right.

The server appeared and said, "Coffee."

It was a take-it-or-leave-it kind of offer.

Emma looked at the server. She had the same dark, expressionless face and bad hair that the hostess did, plus all the welcome of a No Parking sign.

"Coffee," Emma said.

The server started to leave.

"Coffee and menus," Mac said.

The woman walked off without a word.

"Are they always this friendly or is it a special effort?" Emma asked.

"They're tribe. They won't be fired."

Emma glanced at her watch. The time she could safely ignore *Blackbird* was ticking away. Since Mac kept pushing the ball into her court, she'd take it and ram it down his coy throat.

"My boss would like to hire you," she said.

"The boss with more money than sense?"

"Have you ever heard of St. Kilda Consulting?" she asked calmly.

Mac frowned and searched through his memory. "Civilian. Private. International. Kidnap security."

"Among other things."

"What do they want me to do?"

Emma looked at Mac's clear dark eyes and wondered why she kept thinking he was laughing at her.

"You'll have to ask Joe Faroe," she said.

"What do you do for him?"

"You can ask him that, too."

"I'm asking you," Mac said.

"Do you know if or when *Blackbird* is leaving port?"

"No."

"Can you find out?" she pressed.

"Why?"

"Why not?"

Then she closed her eyes and took a better grip on her temper. She knew how to recruit someone.

This wasn't the way.

"Sorry," she said. "Perhaps I should—" She stopped abruptly.

The server showed up with coffee, splashed it into their cups, and dropped two menus on the far side of the table.

Emma picked up the coffee, sipped, and grimaced. "Colder than the hostess. Pass the sugar, please."

Mac's smile was the warmest thing in the casino.

She enjoyed the vision, then smiled herself.

"If you're interested in making some honest money," she said, "I'll put you in touch with Joe Faroe. Whatever St.

Kilda wants from you will be legal in whatever country you do it in." *So far, anyway.* "They don't play politics, they've been honest with me, and they pay on time."

"Do they work for the good guys or just anyone who pays?"

"Find me some good guys and I'll let you know," she said. Then she met Mac's dark eyes. "They're more trust-worthy than the government."

"Faint praise."

"In this world, that's as good as it gets."

His expression changed. "I left that world."

She laughed, as much at herself as at him. "Sorry, babe. It's the only world there is."

"If you can't tell me what you're doing for St. Kilda, I'm not interested in talking to Joe Faroe."

Emma decided quickly. As long as her existing cover got the job done, she'd stay with it. "Missing yachts."

"Piracy?"

"Not yet. Just yachts that are made in Asia and 'fall off the ship' before they get here."

"They go through Vladivostok?"

Though Emma's expression didn't change, Mac sensed that she had come to a point.

"How did you know?" she asked.

He shrugged. "Anything that transits through the FSU is fair game for the local strongmen. Think of it as paying a toll."

"The insurance company is tired of that game."

"What can I do about it?" he asked. "I'm not in Vladi-vostok."

"A year ago, a black-hulled, forty-one-foot boat—the exact twin of *Blackbird*—disappeared in transit from Asia."

"It happens," Mac said.

"Somehow only the multimillion-dollar yachts fall off in transit."

"Shock and awe."

"We've been watching *Blackbird* since Singapore," Emma said, ignoring his sarcasm. "We want to keep on watching it until—" She stopped abruptly.

The server strolled up. "You ready to order?"

"Hamburger and fries," Mac said without looking away from Emma. "Salad with blue cheese."

"The same," Emma said. It wouldn't be the first cold hamburger and fries she'd eaten.

"There's a fish special," the server said.

"I smelled it first thing," Mac said. "I'll stick with the cow."

"Whatever. You want beer?"

Idly Emma wondered if they served the beer as warm as the coffee was cold.

"Coffee's fine," he said.

"Same here," Emma said.

The server turned and walked off in sneakers so old they fit like slippers. No socks.

When they were alone again, Emma said, "—*Blackbird* is delivered to its owner. Then the insurance company is off the hook."

The continuation of a previous conversation didn't throw Mac.

She hadn't expected it to.

"What if the owner isn't in Rosario?" Mac asked.

"I'll need a captain and a boat to follow *Blackbird* until the owner appears and signs off."

"A thousand a day, plus fuel."

"Tell it to Faroe." She held out her cell phone. "Punch two."

Using his index finger, Mac nudged the phone away. "I don't work for anyone I haven't had face time with."

"You're going to love Faroe. He feels the same way."

"When do I see him?"

"Tomorrow, unless he gets lucky and gets here sooner."

"Here?"

Emma looked around the casino. "Right here? Doubt it. Probably at his motel in Rosario."

"Which one?"

"You'll know when I do."

There must have been a replicator in the kitchen, because the server appeared with two plates of food and two small bowls of salad. She dumped them on the table. French fries leaped onto the cloudy surface. The salad was too heavy with dressing to scatter.

This so won't be worth the calories, Emma thought.

But she needed fuel. It would be a long day and a longer night.

She picked up her burger and bit down. Not quite as cold as the coffee. Definitely warmer than the fries.

"Ketchup?" Mac asked, holding out a plastic squeeze bottle to Emma.

"Good idea."

The server dug in her pocket until she found a piece of

paper. She dropped the bill on the table and walked away to talk to the hostess.

Emma finished slathering ketchup over her food before she looked at the bill. Without a word she dug a ten and a twenty out of her wallet and put them on the check.

"I can make change," Mac offered.

"No need."

He lifted black eyebrows. "Fine tip for lousy service."

"Her ankles are swollen."

He bit into his own hamburger, chewed, and swallowed. "I think I like you."

"Same goes." She lifted a limp, ketchup-drenched fry. "I think."

Mac's slow smile transformed his face. "Get back to me when you know for sure."

"I'll have to find you first."

"I'll be nearby." He looked at her expression and knew she wasn't happy. Fair enough. Neither was he.

He couldn't wait to see what a sober Tommy had to say for himself.

15

As Mac turned onto Tribal Road, he kept watching his mirrors. Apparently the intriguing Ms. Cross was more interested in hanging out at the marina than she was in following him. All he saw behind him was the glorious blue sky and whipped-cream clouds of a San Juan Islands autumn.

The air flowing through the open truck windows was cool, silky, and rich with the smell of intertidal mud flats. The state highway leading past the casino and gas/liquor store deeper into the reservation was lightly, if carefully, traveled. The few vehicles that were out had no interest in anything but getting wherever they were going without getting tagged by the state, county, city, or tribal speed teams that haunted the area.

When he turned off the highway, Mac set the cruise control to equal the ridiculously low posted speed limit on the rez. Zero tolerance for outsiders was the rule. Just one more way of getting even.

Or getting respect, depending on which side of the rez blanket you were born and raised.

Mac turned off onto the rutted, overgrown dirt lane that led to Tommy's trailer. The truck's water pump was making the kind of unhappy mechanical noises that told him he'd be lucky to get home without a tow truck. He hoped everything would hold out until tomorrow, when the much-needed water pump would finally be in stock at the Rosario auto supply store.

All around the truck, alder and big-leaf maple competed with cedar for a place in the wet earth. In the mixed forest, twilight was pretty much an all-day thing. He parked behind the old cedar stump, locked up, and walked deeper into the trees. When he reached the clearing, the trash fire and outhouse still flavored the air, telling him that Tommy was probably still around.

"Yo, Tommy! You there?" Mac called.

"Who cares?" Tommy called back, opening the front door a crack and peering out.

"Hey, it's me," Mac said. Tommy looked a little wild-eyed, but it could just be a hangover.

Hope it isn't crank. He's snake-mean on that poison.

"Thought you might like food and a beer, my treat," Mac said. "We didn't get much time to talk last night."

The broken screen leaned drunkenly, halfway covering the front door. Tommy kicked the bent frame out of the way.

"Last night?" Tommy stared and shook himself hard, like a dog coming out of water. "You here last night?"

"That bourbon really tanked you."

Tommy blinked, rubbed the dense beard shadow on his face, and blinked again. His hazel eyes began to clear. With his chestnut hair, Tommy looked less Native American than Mac did. They used to joke about it.

These days, Tommy didn't have much sense of humor.

"Oh. Yeah. You were here." Tommy cleared his throat. "Guess I had a little too much." He looked behind Mac. "You alone?"

Mac nodded and wondered why Tommy cared. He was giving off a deadly-edgy kind of vibe.

"You tweaking?" Mac asked.

"Nah. Got any more bourbon?"

"They have beer at the bowling alley."

"Can't leave," Tommy said roughly.

"Problem with the town cops?"

"No. Just waiting. Got a job coming down. Supposed to be tomorrow, but could be sooner. Dude's going to pick me up here. I have to be ready to roll."

"It won't be today." Mac watched Tommy without seeming to. "*Blackbird* is still being fitted out."

Tommy flinched and looked away. "What the hell you talking about?"

"Your job. Blue Water Marine Group wants a boat moved. The boat's name is *Blackbird*."

"Who told you about that?" Tommy snarled, flushing. "They told me they'd beat the crap out of me if I—" He stopped abruptly. "They wanted it real quiet, you know? How'd you find out?"

"I brought *Blackbird* from Seattle."

It wasn't really an answer, but Tommy nodded.

"You want it quiet," Mac said, "it's quiet."

Tommy made a visible effort to calm himself. He dug a limp cigarette out of his T-shirt pocket, lit it with a match, and took a long draw.

"Quiet. Yeah. Dead quiet." He laughed wildly, then looked around the dark clearing as though expecting people to be listening behind every tree. "Let's go inside. Better there."

Mac doubted it, but followed Tommy into the trailer. Mac didn't know if the man's paranoia was a side effect of tweaking or based in reality.

"You never used to worry about Stan," Mac said easily.

"Screw him." Tommy slammed and locked the door. "It's his buddy I worry about."

"His cousin?"

"That pussy?" Tommy waved his cigarette in dismissal. "Nah. The other one. Temuri. At least I think that's the bastard's name. Blood brother to a shark."

Mac filed the name and went back to fishing for information. The instincts he had tried to leave behind in Afghanistan had taken a single look at Temuri and come to a quivering point.

That was one stone killer.

"Wonder why Bob and Stan got in bed with someone like that," Mac said.

Tommy went to the window, stood to the side, and looked out. "Money, dude. What else?"

"Are they hurting?"

"Isn't everyone?" Tommy kept squinting out the window,

searching the dim forest. "Besides, I heard Stan talking about it in the inner office with Bob. The Temuri dude is a prick, but he's some kind of family."

Mac shrugged. "So long as they pay."

"Oh yeah. Half up front. Half on delivery. Forty big ones. Supposed to go tomorrow. Having trouble with some of the electronics. Wrong size or some such crap."

"Forty thousand American?" Mac asked, black eyes narrowed. That was a lot for the kind of short-haul transit the other man did.

Tommy nodded, making his lank hair jerk.

"Sweet," Mac said. "Want another hand aboard?"

Tommy turned on him with a snarl. "No. And you never heard of the job, hear me?"

"Sure," Mac said easily. Unless Tommy was taking the boat across the ocean to Vladivostok, it was an outrageous payday. "Long trip, huh?"

Tommy took a hard drag on the cigarette. "Don't know."

Mac didn't push it anymore. "You hear anything from Jeremy?" he said, asking after the last of the wild ones who once had run together as a teenage pack.

"What do you care?"

"Shove the attitude. It's me, Mac, the dude you used to steal crabs and boost beer with. Sometimes Jeremy went along, remember?"

Tommy blinked, seemed to refocus. "Sorry, man. I'm a little tweaked, waiting for this job. I really need it."

"I get that."

"Jeremy's pulling pots for some white guy."

"Thought crabbing was closed."

Tommy lit another cigarette. "The white guy's a sport crabber."

Mac didn't need to hear the details. If Jeremy got caught—unlikely, given that the fish cops couldn't afford to put gas in their boat—he played the Indian card. White courts couldn't touch him. Tribal courts wouldn't.

"It's a living," Mac said.

"Pays shit."

"And all the crab you can eat or sell on the side."

With a jerky movement, Tommy flicked ash onto the floor of the trailer. "It's still shit. That's all we ever get. Fucking whites."

"Present company excepted," Mac said neutrally.

"Huh?" Tommy blinked, focused again. "You know I don't think of you as white."

"And I don't think of you as not white. Ain't we the rainbow pair."

Reluctantly Tommy smiled, then laughed, the kind of laugh that reminded Mac of all the good times they'd had as kids, running wild in a ragged land. They hadn't been innocent, but they hadn't believed in death.

If that isn't innocence, what is?

He and Tommy had come a long way since then. They hadn't ended up at the same place.

16

The Learjet turned in the late afternoon sunlight and lined up for its final approach to the asphalt strip at the Lopez County Airport. The co-pilot stuck his head through the open cockpit doorway.

"Short-runway landing coming up," he called back into the cabin. "Come and get this sweet little thing before she ends up as part of the electronics."

"I'm on it," Joe Faroe said before his wife could get up.

He put aside his laptop and went forward to grab his daughter, who was examining every ripple and shadow on the plane's floor. He swung her up easily into the crook of one long arm.

"Did you find any yummy cigarette butts or globs of things better left unidentified?" he asked her.

She drooled and patted his mouth.

"Haven't you ever heard of don't ask, don't tell?" Grace said without looking up from the computer on her lap.

"Don't you listen to her, sweetie," Faroe said. He lowered Annalise into the special airline seat and fastened her restraint. "You always want to come to Daddy and tell all, especially about boys."

Grace shook her head. "You just keep dreaming, darling. You're cute."

Faroe stretched, then sat in the seat next to Annalise and fastened his own seatbelt. "You're the only one who thinks so."

She flashed him a look out of dark eyes that made him wish he was alone with her. In bed.

"That's because I know you so well," Grace said.

He smiled slowly. "I love you."

"Same goes. And the light of your life is chewing on her restraint."

He looked over at Annalise. "Gumming it, actually."

"Bleh."

"Good for her immune system," Faroe said.

Grace rolled her eyes. "Give her a cracker."

"She'll just turn it into mush and smear it over everything in reach, including her loving daddy. They'll bill us extra for cleaning the plane. Why don't they make kids' chewies as tough as the ones for dogs?"

"Do you know what dog chewies are made of?"

"Pig ears."

"And bull pizzles."

"What?" Faroe asked.

"Penises. From male bovines."

"Tell me you're joking."

"Not."

"Cover your ears, sweetie," Faroe said to Annalise as he reached into the bag beneath her seat. "Your mama's talking dirty. Here you go, beautiful."

Chubby fingers wrapped around the thick cracker Faroe held out. She shoved a corner of it into her drooling mouth and gummed blissfully.

"You strapped in?" he asked Grace.

"The instant I got back from the head." She finished the document page and went on to the next as the pilot announced the upcoming landing. She had one more recommendation to file before she could devote her full attention to the brushfire presently burning St. Kilda's ass. "Someone should just blow that place to the darkest reaches of hell."

"Which place?"

"*Silnice hanby.*"

"The Highway of Shame," Faroe said.

"Where young girls sell themselves to old men and sadists for a handful of rotten food," Grace said wearily. "Then there are all the weapons, nuclear and otherwise, that trundle along that freeway to hell. Not to mention the traffic in children destined for foreign whorehouses."

Faroe looked at his daughter and silently vowed it would never happen to her.

"It's why we keep working bad hours," Grace said, understanding her husband.

"It's never enough."

"No," she agreed. "It's never enough. But it's all we have."

"I still want you the hell away from Seattle."

"We've been over this so often I feel like a digital recording. If you're here without me and Annalise, it's news to anyone who's watching you. Deal with it, Joe. A lot of bad people care about where you are and what you're doing."

"But—"

"As the unforgettable Alara said, if we go in soft, we have a fallback position."

"I don't like it having you and Annalise here. If Alara is right, it's too damn dangerous."

"You think I like having Annalise here?" Grace looked at their sleeping child. "But liking it doesn't matter." She let out a long breath. "I believe in St. Kilda. So we do what we can do. If that goes to hell, we do something else."

"Fast," Faroe muttered.

And pray that fast was quick enough.

17

Emma kept one eye on her watch and the other on *Black-bird*. It was still crawling with techs, but there were a lot less boxes waiting on the dock to be installed on the boat.

Damn it, Mac. Where are you?

She sensed he was out there, somewhere, watching as she was watching. But she couldn't keep an eye on *Blackbird* and MacKenzie Durand at the same time.

I'll be nearby.

She grimaced as she remembered his words. *Yeah. Right. We have an appointment, big boy. You don't know where or when.*

Her cell phone rang. Faroe. She picked it up.

"He's not here," she said.

"But he kept his promise," Faroe said. "He's nearby. You can't see him from where you are. I can. Come toward the second marina ramp. He's talking with the lady in the shrimp shack. Which is a boat. When Captain Di of the *No*

Shrimp is lucky, she sells fresh prawns off the back deck to locals who know how to find her. You're going to buy some."

"You're telling me to leave *Blackbird* uncovered."

"Grace can see into the marina from our motel room. Annalise is sleeping like the innocent she is. We're covered."

"See you at the shrimp shack."

Emma disconnected, got out, locked the Jeep, and walked across the parking lot toward the second marina ramp. As she went down the ramp, she discovered that the "shrimp shack" was indeed a scow tied off just below the ramp. The idea of eating fresh, never-frozen, never–chemically altered shrimp made her stomach growl.

"I hope Captain Di was lucky," Emma said, licking her lips as she walked up to Mac.

Mac watched her tongue and decided prawns were the least he could do for her.

Captain Di's laugh was as big as she was. It echoed up the ramp. "Mac there has a hungry look about him."

He smiled. "Nothing better than prawns. Well, almost nothing."

The woman laughed again, grabbed a small net, and headed for the live tanks at the stern of her boat. "How many pounds?"

"Coon-stripe or spot?" he asked.

"Spot."

"Two pounds." Mac looked at her. "I'll cook aboard the *Autonomy*."

"Make it four," Emma said in a low voice. "I crave prawns after days of fast food. And there will be at least one more eating with us."

"That explains why I've been feeling like I have cross-hairs on the back of my neck," Mac said, his voice equally soft. Then, in a carrying tone, "Make it a heavy four, Captain Di. The lady is hungry."

The sound of Di's laugh covered any noise Faroe might have made coming down the marina ramp. Mac turned around anyway, warned by the vibration of the dock beneath his feet.

Faroe nodded at him, but walked right past toward the *Autonomy*. Without hesitation he swung aboard Mac's boat.

"He has his own boat," Emma said softly.

"Looks like it."

"Is your boat locked?"

"Would it make a difference?"

She almost smiled. "Probably not."

She walked back on the dock until she was even with the stern of *No Shrimp*. Captain Di was weighing and wrapping prawns. Their bodies snapped and rustled against the clear plastic bag. Emma recognized the tails, but the whole animal was something she hadn't seen alive. She paid for the prawns and walked back to Mac carrying dinner squirming in a plastic bag.

"Modern woman," Captain Di said, nodding and pocketing the cash with approval.

"You have no idea," Mac said.

Captain Di's laughter followed them down the dock.

"Does that mean you'll clean them?" Mac asked. "Or are we eating them Asian style?"

She raised her eyebrows in silent question.

"Whole," Mac said.

"Forget it. I'll help clean them."

"Ever done it before?"

"No. Is it tricky?"

He glanced at her. "Basically, you just rip their little heads off."

"I think my skill level is up to that."

"How about your stomach?"

"Beats eating them whole."

Mac was still trying not to laugh as he helped Emma aboard the *Autonomy*. When he opened the salon door, Faroe was sitting at the shadowed banquette, watching the readout on a palm-sized electronic device.

Nobody spoke until Mac closed the door.

"Boat's clean," Faroe said, coming to his feet. "So are both of you." He held out his hand to Mac. "Joe Faroe. Sorry about the informality."

Mac looked at Faroe, shook his hand, and said, "Usually I dump people over the side when they come aboard without permission."

Faroe nodded. "It's the same on my boat. The *TAZ* is my own private place."

"*TAZ?*" Emma asked.

"As in Temporary Autonomous Zone," Faroe said.

She looked at Mac. "I sense an area of agreement here."

"Autonomy," Faroe said. "Nice thing to have."

"Or to think you have," Mac said neutrally.

Faroe's smile made him look younger, less like a man you wouldn't want to meet in a dark alley. His intense green eyes gleamed with humor. "Like she said, an area of agreement."

"We'll see." Mac took the plastic bag from Emma. "Why

don't we clean these while your boss explains why I shouldn't treat him like a big prawn?"

"Rip his head off?" she asked.

"Yeah." He took her to the galley and emptied the prawns into the sink.

She looked at the seething, snapping mass, like Halloween with ebony eyes and countless orange bodies. "Now what?"

"Grab the head in one hand and the body in the other and twist, like wringing a washrag," Mac said. "But be careful. Spot prawns have pointy parts that draw blood."

"So does Joe."

Mac remembered Faroe's relaxed yet fully balanced moves as he boarded the boat. "That's why I'm cleaning prawns instead of him."

"Good choice."

Faroe looked from one to the other and shook his head. "Grace was right about you."

"Who?" they said simultaneously.

"Move over," was all Faroe said. "I'll help rip heads."

"Keep your hands clean and open one of the New Zealand whites I have in the fridge," Mac said. "Glasses are in the cupboard next to the sink." To Emma he said, "Put the tails in the blue plastic bowl to your right."

"This is going to be interesting," Faroe said, opening the tiny fridge.

"What?" Mac asked.

"You like to give orders. So do I. Could be interesting when we work together."

"If, not when."

Faroe ignored him.

Before they had cleaned half the prawns, Faroe had the wine opened, poured, and was rummaging through the galley for a big pot to heat water in. While the water came to a boil, the men finished cleaning dinner and talked about the joys and drawbacks of boat ownership.

No one mentioned *Blackbird*.

Emma left the men to sizing each other up, took her wounded fingers to the head, and washed them thoroughly. The flesh of the prawns looked like translucent pearl, but the "sharp bits" protecting the succulent flesh drew blood and stung like the devil. She dried her hands and rejoined the men.

They both cleaned prawns with an efficiency she could only admire.

After a bare taste of the crisp white wine, she set the table and tore up the salad makings she had found in the fridge. A loaf of fresh bread with butter rounded out the meal.

When they sat down to the very fresh, just-barely-cooked prawns, she looked at her fingers ruefully.

"I'm still oozing," she said.

"Told you they were sharp," Mac said.

"Don't hire him," she said to Faroe. "I hate the 'told you so' kind of man."

Faroe ignored both of them. He savored the succulent delicacy. When he took a break to breathe, he praised the lines and workmanship of *Autonomy*.

Despite himself, Mac began to relax. There was little that he liked better than sharing his love of his boat.

Making small, throaty sounds of pleasure, Emma went

through the prawns like a quick-fingered lawn mower, leaving nothing but small pieces of shell behind. Then she wiped her hands, took her plate to the galley sink, and drank her fifth sip of wine while she finished her salad.

"It's getting too dark to watch *Blackbird* from the motel window," she said, reaching for her small purse. "Unless you brought night-viewing equipment?"

"We're on vacation," Faroe said. "But if you need it, I'll get it. So far they've kept the dock lit up like opening night."

Mac said, "Don't worry about *Blackbird*. She's not going anywhere until tomorrow."

"How do you know?" Faroe asked.

"Common sense. And her transit captain told me."

Faroe didn't move, didn't shift his expression, but suddenly Mac was the sole focus of the other man's attention.

"Why?" Faroe asked.

"I've known him since first grade," Mac said. "The common sense took a lot longer." He wiped his hands as he met Faroe's hard green eyes. "And I pushed."

"Are transit jobs usually secret?" Emma asked.

Both men said, "No."

Emma waited.

Faroe asked, "Is he smuggling?"

"Why would I tell you?" Mac said. "I've barely known you for an hour."

She watched them exchange level looks and wondered how badly this "interview" was going to end.

"If it's weed or cigarettes," Faroe said, "I'll kiss your friend on all four cheeks and wish him bon voyage."

Mac looked at him for a moment longer, then nodded. "Tommy didn't mention smuggling to me. That doesn't mean he isn't carrying hot cargo. It just means he didn't talk about it with me."

"Would he?" Emma asked.

Mac shrugged and looked at her. "Usually, yes. He always talks about his next run like it will be the answer to all his problems."

"It never is," Faroe said. Not a guess.

"No, it never is." Mac sighed and ran his hand over his short hair. "Damn, I don't want to get Tommy into any more trouble than he's found all by himself."

"St. Kilda isn't looking to hang the errand boy," Faroe said. "We don't fish for minnows."

"Not even to use as live bait for bigger fish?" Emma asked, thinking of her own childhood.

Mac looked at Faroe and waited.

"We work very hard to limit any collateral damage," Faroe said. "But we're not perfect."

"Nothing human is," Mac said. "But some things sure are more imperfect than others."

"You want to investigate St. Kilda before you sign up?" Faroe asked. "If we talk long enough, we'll find people who know people who know other people."

"I already did. 'Merry' Marty Jones sends you this." Slowly Mac raised the middle finger of his right hand.

Faroe almost fell off his chair laughing. "Good to know the son of a bitch is as mean as ever. If he wasn't pushing eighty, I'd harass his ass into signing on with St. Kilda." Then Faroe's smile vanished. "You in or out?"

"I've got a few more calls that I'm waiting to be returned."

"Don't wait too long," Faroe said bluntly. "This op has a real short clock on it. Call the instant you decide."

Mac gave Faroe a long look before he nodded curtly.

Faroe headed for the door, with Emma right behind him. She paused at the open door.

"What if we have to contact you?" she asked Mac.

"I have your cell phone number."

Emma bit back what she thought of Mac's response, turned on her heel, and followed Faroe. They had a lot of intel to go over together and damn little time.

There was never enough time.

18

A stiff breeze blew through the mixed forest, making needles whisper and leaves rattle. Demidov was just another shadow moving among shadows, sliding between the scrubby trees with an eerie kind of grace. It had taken him an hour to discover the overgrown dirt lane leading into the forest. The "address" he'd found in the Blue Water Marine Group's office was more of a general direction than any specific guide.

The reservation reminded him of the farthest fringes of Vladivostok, where cart roads became footpaths that unraveled into the wild, ragged land, places where somebody's location was a matter of spirited discussion among natives.

The wind helped Demidov find his destination. He followed the odor of feces and burning trash to the moonlit clearing where bottles and plastic bags studded the wrecked vehicles in bizarre decoration. Again, it reminded him of

Vladivostok. Even the can of kerosene he carried brought back memories.

There was one light burning in the sagging trailer at the far side of the clearing. Demidov circled the trailer once, then again, before he climbed carefully up the broken steps at the back door. After listening for a minute, he caught the stem of the handle in a pair of grip-lock pliers, and twisted. The lock came apart with the small whine of inferior metal.

He slid back into the shadows and waited. One minute. Two.

Ten.

The trailer remained quiet, motionless but for the occasional quiver beneath the rising wind.

Demidov waited some more. If he was a religious man, he would have prayed, but his only god was power, so he simply waited, listening.

No noises came from inside the trailer.

Quietly he skimmed over the broken steps and through the door, a shadow dancer taking his place on a shabby stage. Any small noises he made were simply part of the performance, the night and the wind and the forest dancing together.

The inside of the trailer smelled like the clearing, with an overlay of sour pizza and beer. His target was facedown on a lumpy couch, snoring into the crook of his arm. Crushed beer cans lay scattered on the floor like a fallen house of cards.

A loaded, cocked pistol waited among the cans.

This becomes more like Vladivostok with every moment, Demidov thought in wry disgust. *Fear makes them drink. Too much alcohol makes even the smartest of them a fool.*

Easy.

Demidov had planned to question the target, but experience told him that even intense pain couldn't cut through some alcohol stupors. He set the kerosene can aside, picked up Tommy's gun, and frowned.

A man would have to put this .22 caliber toy up a target's ass to make any impression.

Worse, my silencer won't fit this barrel.

Damp salt air magnified sound like a megaphone. Demidov wanted to be off the reservation and out of sight before any alarm went out. He put the little pistol out of reach without bothering to wipe it. There was no chance of fingerprints; his thin, black driving gloves covered all manner of problems.

Demidov reached into his long leather coat and pulled out one of his own guns, an SR-1 Vektor. Eighteen rounds, quite reliable as long as the safety was put out of commission with thin tape. With the correct ammunition, the Vektor was capable of penetrating body armor, cars, walls, and light armor plate.

But tonight he was loaded for a much more fragile target.

Swiftly, silently, Demidov walked forward. Habit, not necessity. The target's snores were louder than the wind. With his gloved left hand, he reached between Tommy's legs, found his testicles, and squeezed hard. Sometimes a sudden, brutal shock of pain could wake up even the most sodden drunk.

Tommy made a sound rather like that of the back-door lock giving way, but his eyelids didn't open.

Demidov gave another crank, twisting as he squeezed.

With another whine, Tommy tried to curl protectively around himself. His body didn't respond. He was under too deep.

His eyelids quivered and stayed closed.

I don't have time for this drunken shit-eater.

With a word of disgust, Demidov released the other man's slack flesh. He knew men who would have enjoyed trying to wake Tommy up, but Demidov wasn't one of them. To him, torture was a means to an end, like kerosene or a silencer. A tool, not a pleasure.

If he had been worried about misleading the authorities, he would have simply poured kerosene and let them decide if it was accident, suicide, or murder. But all he was concerned about was making sure the job got done. Once, such a weapon as his had been rare outside of Russia, too distinctive to use overseas. The modern weapons trade had changed that. Using a Vektor was no longer like leaving his name written on a corpse.

Demidov took out his 9 mm pistol, pulled a sofa pillow over the target to limit the back splash of gore, and shot Tommy twice in the head.

Moving quickly, Demidov poured kerosene on and around the body. He lit it with matches the dead man had dropped. When he was sure that the fire would take hold, he went out the same way he had come in, a dark dancer moving through the forest.

19

The sirens had already awakened Emma. She was just getting back to sleep when her cell phone vibrated and warbled on the motel's end table. With an impatient movement she snagged the phone.

"What," she snarled.

"I'm out front in your Jeep," Mac said. "In three minutes I leave without you."

"I have the keys."

"I don't need them."

The line went dead.

Emma had slept fully clothed—shoes, socks, jeans, and a black pullover—too exhausted after her turn watching *Blackbird* to care about undressing. She grabbed her purse and a jacket and ran out.

Twenty seconds after Mac had hung up on her, she was in the parking lot of the motel.

Sure enough, he was sitting at the wheel of her Jeep. Wires dangled from the console. She got in the passenger seat, threw him the keys, and shut the door very quietly when she really wanted to slam it.

"Is it *Blackbird*?" she asked as he drove out of the parking lot without benefit of headlights.

"Not directly."

He went down a side street, turned onto an eastbound feeder street, and flipped on the lights.

"Where's your truck?" she asked.

"Crapped out, waiting for a new water pump."

Silence.

Emma turned toward him. "You have about ten seconds to tell me what the hell is going on. If I don't like what I hear, I'm going to reach into my girly purse, pull out a Glock, and turn you into splatter patterns."

Mac gave her a sideways look and started talking. "I have a police scanner at my house. There was a fire on the rez. They're talking about arson. One crispy critter in the ashes."

She grimaced. She'd seen—and smelled—enough of that kind of death in Iraq to last her a lifetime.

"I don't know how firemen stand it," she said.

Mac didn't have to ask what she meant.

"Some of them turn vegetarian for a while," he said. "Then they get over it and go back to rare beef."

"Glad to know I wasn't the only one."

"Where?" he asked.

"Baghdad. You?" she asked, wondering if he would lie. Or if his file had.

"Afghanistan," he said shortly, accelerating onto the highway, "well beyond any city."

"Out with the tribes?" she asked casually.

"Not much else out there but rock. Got a lot of that, all of it standing on end."

"How long were you there?"

"Why do you care?"

"Call me curious," she said.

"Call me classified."

Behind them an official vehicle came on fast, light bar flashing and siren screaming the need for speed.

Mac pulled over like a good citizen.

The sheriff's car blew past them into the darkness.

"Guess he's late to the barbeque," Mac said.

She grimaced, thought about calling Faroe, and decided against it until she knew more. There was no point in waking her boss up to share the ignorance.

"I'll wait until the sheriff's car is out of sight," Mac said. "Then I'm going to speed like a dirty bastard. Every official in a twelve-mile radius will already be at the fire."

Mac hit the accelerator hard. Being a rental, the Jeep took its time getting up to eighty.

And that was all it had. Eighty.

"What a piece of crap," he muttered.

"Wheels need alignment or balancing," Emma said. "Or both."

"What it needs is another engine."

"That, too. Sweet thing is, the mileage really sucks."

Mac almost smiled. Emma was that rare find in a partner, male or female—easy to be with.

Especially when she pulled a Glock from her purse and checked it over with the motions of someone who knew which end of a gun bit and which didn't.

"Think we'll need that?" he asked.

"I think I'd rather be ready than point my index finger and say 'bang.' " She put the weapon back into her purse.

They drove in silence until they rounded the long curve half a mile from Tommy's lane. Instantly Mac lifted his foot off the accelerator and began losing speed fast.

At least sixteen official vehicles were parked on both sides of Tribal Road, light bars wheeling. The lane to Tommy's trailer was choked with more vehicles. Their lights stabbed through the woods in flashes of blue and red and spotlight-white.

Wary of making a loud screeching noise, Mac slowly engaged the emergency brake.

"Tommy's place," he said.

"How did you know?" Emma asked tightly, reaching for her cell phone. "Was the address on the scanner?"

"Not in so many words. But even on the rez, most people have addresses. The place that burned didn't." He glanced at her phone. "Don't bother waking Faroe up yet. We don't know what's going on."

Dead slow, the Jeep bumped along the verge of the road. After about sixty feet, Mac stopped, reversed, cranked the wheel, and started backing up. Once there had been another nameless lane here, but someone had moved on or died and everything was completely overgrown now.

As the Jeep backed in, it bent brush and small saplings away from the vehicle. Branches shivered and scraped. Most of the undergrowth sprang back upright after the Jeep passed.

When they were invisible from the road, Mac turned and looked Emma over, taking in her outfit.

Before he could open his mouth, she started removing her watch and small earrings, things that could reflect light, giving away her position. It had been years since she had been trained in covert ops, but it was coming back to her. Along with a wave of adrenaline.

"Any mud nearby?" she asked.

"I don't think I'll need it for camouflage. I don't want to get that close."

"If you think I'm staying here, you're not smart enough to sign on with St. Kilda."

Mac had been expecting that since he'd seen the Glock. He didn't waste time arguing with her. He just fished around on the floor and tossed her one of the black knit caps he had stuffed under the seat.

"Pull it on," he said, reaching down again for his own cap.

"You carrying?"

"Knife," he said. "Quieter than a gun."

"Range bites."

His lips quirked. "I've got a good arm."

Together they eased out into the night. Emma followed him as he angled through brush and around bigger trees, always holding his course to the same general direction. When the moonlight was bright enough, she could see the faint line of the overgrown trail Mac was following. She tried to make as little noise as he did, but it had been a long time since she'd gone through night training.

They walked for ten minutes before they began to catch the smell of burning excrement and garbage, bitter and foul and disgusting, like a trash fire jacked on steroids. Through a screen of trees and brush, they saw flashes of bright red lights on emergency vehicles and the steady white spears of headlights parked at all angles.

Emma didn't need Mac's signal to freeze and drop. She was already on her belly, wriggling as close as she could. A hand on her ankle halted her. Mac slithered along her left side and breathed into her ear.

"Eyes."

For an instant she didn't understand. Then it came back to her in a rush of memory and knowledge. She nodded. She wouldn't get close enough to the action that her eyes reflected light.

What remained of the trailer was a sullen, stinking pile of twisted wreckage. Firemen circled it in turnout gear. They called back and forth, kicking at rubble and bent metal, looking for anything that still was hot enough to produce flames. Occasional bursts of water from their hoses added to the stench.

She leaned close enough to Mac's ear to feel the heat of his body. "Overgrown wreck," she breathed. "Two o'clock."

Eyes narrowed, Mac judged the possibilities. His face looked grim in the pulsing light from the clearing. His black gaze switched to hers, then vanished as his lips brushed her ear.

"Wait here. You're out of practice."

She went stiff, then relaxed. When it came to slithering through the woods, he was better than she was. A lot better. She'd been trained for city work, recruiting rather than recon.

She signaled for him to go. Then she got as close to the pungent forest floor as she could and still peer through the undergrowth into the clearing.

Mac set off at an angle to a place where there was a group of rez types talking and gesturing. They were so engrossed by the grisly scene that Mac could have walked right up to them.

He didn't. He just got close enough to eavesdrop.

" . . . was always looking for trouble."

"Sure found it." The man spat on the churned ground.

Mac saw the glint of a badge at the man's belt and recognized him as a tribal cop.

"Arson. Damn." The smaller man almost danced in place with excitement. "Wonder who did it?"

"Half the rez hated Tommy's ass." The cop spat again, as though the taste of the air was getting to him. "Besides, he might be out on a boat. Might be someone else was sleeping in his trailer."

Mac hoped the cop was right but doubted it. Tommy hadn't had any other place to go while he waited for *Blackbird*.

And he'd been scared.

Floodlights from two fire engines played back and forth over the lumpy, twisted rubble like stiff white fingers combing the wreckage.

"There," called one of the firemen.

The floodlights paused, then converged on a corner of the ruins. The wind swirled, increasing the unmistakable odor of barbeque gone wrong.

Ugly memories drenched Mac, men burning, dying, dead. Long ago, far away, and as fresh as the bile rising up his throat. He'd hoped never to smell that particular kind of death again.

"Jesus Christ," the fireman said. "Half his skull is gone. I mean, just flat gone. What the—"

"Knock it off!" said a woman's voice. "This is a crime scene."

Mac understood the words that the woman was too well-trained to say: *Civilians around. Shut up.*

The woman who spoke wasn't from the rez, but people gave way to her just the same.

Silence descended as she strode into the harsh light of the clearing.

She was on the downhill side of forty-five and didn't give a damn. Her blond-gray hair wasn't dyed and she wore no makeup. She was dressed in a pale windbreaker and dark slacks. As she walked up to the firemen, the floodlights caught three large block letters on the back of her jacket.

FBI.

Hold your ankles and brace yourselves, boys and girls, Mac thought bitterly. *This just became an official Mongolian goat-fuck.*

He eased back into thicker cover and silently, quickly made his way to Emma. A curt signal had her wriggling backward. When he was certain her retreat hadn't attracted any attention, he followed.

Once they were well back into the forest, hidden by the night and the restless wind, he signaled for her to stand. Silently he led the way deeper into the trees. Neither of them spoke until they were in the Jeep and had driven down the road, out of sight of the cluster of vehicles. He flipped on the headlights.

"You okay?" Mac asked.

"Swallowing hard," Emma said tightly.

"Tell me if you need to pull over."

"Tough guy, huh? The smell didn't get to you."

"You learn not to throw up. Too much noise will get you dead real quick." His hands flexed on the wheel, as hard as his voice. "FBI was on the fire scene."

Emma's head hit the back of the seat. "This just gets better and better."

"Let's go wake up Faroe. I'm signing on."

20

Mac, Emma, and Grace Silva-Faroe sat at a small dinette table in the motel suite Faroe had rented. Nobody spoke while Mac read and signed the papers that would make him a contract agent for St. Kilda Consulting, assigned to missing yachts in general and one called *Blackbird* in particular.

From a nearby bedroom came the pealing laughter of Annalise Faroe as her daddy took her for a shoulder-high tour of the suite. His "Shhhh, sweetie, let the civilians sleep" was ignored by Annalise.

Grace watched out the window toward the Blue Water Marine Group. People were still crawling over *Blackbird*. But not as many. Empty boxes went up the ramp much more often now than full boxes went down.

She had been as relieved as Faroe when Mac turned up at their door in the middle of the night. With a silent sigh, she stacked papers Mac had signed and handed him a St. Kilda sat/cell phone.

"You'll continue working with Emma," Grace said. "She'll be the senior partner."

"Except if we're on a boat," Mac said. "I know more about the water than she does."

Grace looked at Emma.

"No problem," Emma said. "If it floats, I'm junior partner."

Grace stashed the papers in her briefcase and looked at Mac. "What do you know about Bob Lovich and Stan Amanar?"

"They're descended from a long line of hardworking fishermen and part-time smugglers."

"Arrests?"

Mac shook his head. "You have to understand how it is in Rosario. There are three major factions. One is the Eastern European immigrants and their descendants who still speak the mother language. Or languages. They're a hard-headed, suspicious clan. Damn few marry out, especially if you're talking about the smugglers."

"Common enough for immigrant communities," Grace said. "Particularly those who make a living outside the law."

"Like the Sicilians," Emma said.

Grace nodded. "Or the Asian tongs."

"The second faction is the white businessmen who have been here long enough to own the mayor and city council," Mac continued. "They have a lot of the official, legal power, but they don't mess with the immigrants and their ways. The white power structure ignores nearly all the smuggling, gambling, prostitution, after-hours bottle clubs, and the like."

"What about the police?" Emma asked.

"Anyone who tries to do real cop work finds himself out of a job pretty quick." Mac shrugged. "Basically, the police keep the streets clean for the businessmen and yachties."

"Again, pretty standard," Grace said.

"Except for the murder rate," Mac said. "This sweet little town holds the highest U.S. record for unsolved murders per capita."

Grace lifted her dark eyebrows. "Like the one on the rez tonight?"

"Most aren't that obvious. Just people who go missing when there's a shift in the immigrant power structure. Low-level smugglers, usually."

"You were one of them, weren't you?" Emma guessed.

"I ran away when I was seventeen," Mac said. "Hated the ever-stinking guts of this place. One of my best friends died in a 'fishing accident' after I left. The body was never found. He was moving cigarettes north and weed south in a small, hell-fast boat. Tommy was, too, but he survived. Until last night."

"The rez is the third faction?" Grace asked.

"Yeah. There's some pushing and shoving at the smuggling trough between the rez and the clan, but nothing like between the Sicilians or the Asian tongs or the Russian *mafiyas* in our big cities."

"Where do the Mexicans come in?" Grace asked. "I've seen more than a few since we got here."

"The ones who are illegal keep their head down," Mac

said. "The legal ones invest in Mexican food joints, the mayor, and the city council."

"In other words, the Mexicans are pretty much ignored, except to be milked," Grace said.

"They came too late to the Pacific Northwest to have much traction in local crime," Mac pointed out.

"Unlike the southern border states," Grace said wearily. "Nice to know that the Pacific Northwest is holding up its end of the twenty percent of world Gross Domestic Product that is the result of crime."

"Also known as the shadow economy," Emma said. "Does anything ever change?"

"I can't fix the world," Grace said. "But I can fix what I trip over." *Or what is shoved down my throat.*

Faroe passed the dinette, stroking Grace's cheek on the way by. Annalise was blissfully slack in his arms. Laughing one minute, sleeping deep the next. A look passed between man and wife. He shook his head in answer to the unspoken question and vanished into Annalise's room.

Grace looked at Mac. "You've given me a general picture. What about Bob Lovich and Stan Amanar in particular?"

"First cousins," Mac said. "Closer than most brothers. When their ancestors emigrated, it was from the part of Russia we call Georgia, with a lot of Ukrainian cousins thrown in. Close cousins."

"No love for Russia," Grace said.

"Not as tsarist Russia, the U.S.S.R., or the new Russia," Mac agreed. "Don't get me wrong. Rosario's immigrant community isn't awash in old-country nationalists. They wear the ancestral costumes and cook the food and speak a dialect of the home languages, but all they really care about is the clan here and now in America."

"So they don't have much contact with the Old World?" Emma asked him.

"They're still bringing over cousins and cousins of cousins, especially after the Wall fell, but if there are dodgy business contacts in the Old World, I don't know about them."

At the back of her mind Grace listened to the soft sound of the door to the other room closing. When Faroe's big hands settled on her shoulders and began to work on knots, she sighed in relief. She hadn't realized how tight she'd become.

But nothing showed on her face when she said to Mac, "Tommy was *Blackbird*'s transit captain. What are your chances of being tapped as his replacement?"

"Pretty good," Mac said. "I do a lot of work for Blue Water Marine. So do a few other captains. I don't know who's in port now."

"If they go with someone else, are you ready to follow *Blackbird* right now?" Faroe asked quietly.

Mac went through a mental checklist in his head. "*Blackbird* is fast for her size. If they run above fourteen knots, I'll have to make it up at night."

"If it comes to that, we'll rent you a faster boat," Grace said.

"Fuel tanks are full on my boat," Mac continued. "Water tank is full. Engine is good. Oil is good. Electrical is solid. So is the generator. Rations are adequate for a week. I was going out if no new job turned up."

"Adequate for two?" Emma asked.

"It won't be fancy," he said, looking at her.

"And here I was dreaming of fresh prawns and champagne."

Grace smiled tiredly. "Emma will check out of her room immediately and move aboard. Joe will organize our watch times."

Faroe stroked his hand over Grace's head and said, "I'll take it until six. You haven't slept well since you met Alara."

"Who could?" Grace asked under her breath.

Faroe looked at Mac. "You've signed on, so we can tell you why we're after *Blackbird*. You can access Emma's computer for facts, guesses, estimates, and updates about this whole nasty cluster, so I'll give you the short form."

Mac measured Faroe's grim expression and braced himself.

"*Blackbird* is a dead ringer for *Black Swan*," Faroe said. "That yacht went missing somewhere between Vladivostok and Portland a year ago. Yet *Blackbird* was built from the hull up in Singapore after that and shipped safely to Elliott Bay."

Mac waited.

Faroe almost smiled. The more he was around Mac, the better he liked him.

"A woman who is no longer known as Alara," Faroe said, "came to St. Kilda and requested in the most forceful possible way that we assist Uncle Sam in following *Blackbird* and finding out whether her hidden or intended cargo is biological, chemical, or fissionable."

Mac closed his eyes as his breath hissed out in a savage curse. "So this Alara woman has a network full of leaks and a stinking rose she wants pinned somewhere else. She pass along any other helpful little hints?"

Grace smiled. "Ambassador Steele was right. You have a top quality, bottom line mind. She gave us seven days. This is day three."

"And after seven?"

"We risk losing a major city," Emma said.

Mac didn't ask which one. No matter where this dirty deal went down, civilians would die. A lot of them. The fact that they were innocent wouldn't make them any less dead.

Seven days? Christ. Seven months wouldn't be enough.

But Mac didn't say anything aloud. Complaining about the huge serving of shit on your plate just wasted time. All you could do was grab a spoon and start eating.

Fast.

"I'm going to be spending a lot of time with your computer," Mac said to Emma.

"While you do," Faroe said, "she can work on learning how to handle boat lines, fenders, and other matey stuff."

Emma made a startled sound.

With a dark-eyed smile, Grace said, "If I can learn how to be a first mate to my snarling Captain Joe, you can learn from sweet, gentle Captain Mac."

"Sweet? Gentle?" Emma glanced sideways at Mac.

He tried to look sweet and gentle. Given the information he'd just received, it wasn't possible.

"Tell me lines aren't as heavy as fuel hoses," Emma said.

"They aren't as heavy." He lowered his eyelids to half mast. "And I can be very gentle."

She shook her head. She'd walked right into that one.

"Emma has her cover story," Grace said, no longer trying not to yawn. "Mac came with his intact. As for why you're suddenly joined at the hip, I suggest going with the tried and true."

"Sex," Emma said, grimacing.

"Sex," Grace agreed. "Start practicing snuggling and snogging in public."

Mac and Emma looked at each other and said simultaneously, "Snogging?"

"Look it up," Grace said. "It will grow on you."

21

Timothy Harrow ignored the inbox marked Urgent on his desk. Pragmatically speaking, it was a low designation of priority. Everything that came across his desk was urgent. The only question was of degree.

At the moment, he was frowning over an email that was a good deal more than urgent. Somebody's ass was going to get burned. His job was to make sure it didn't belong to the Deputy Director of Operations, his immediate boss. Hopefully he could save his boss by putting the fire out. If that didn't work, some serious finger-pointing was going down.

And if the op blew up . . .

Don't think about it. Just make sure it doesn't happen.

At the highest levels, politics was a blood sport.

Harrow hit the intercom button. "Duke? Got a minute?"

"Make it fast. I have to brief the DO over the mess in Caracas in five and then brief his boss on the uncivil war heating up between the narcos and elected Mexican politicians. You have anything that's going to make my life easier?"

Harrow sincerely doubted it. "You told me to keep you current on anything coming out of Rosario, Washington, state of."

"What's up?"

"An Indian on the rez bought it, execution style. Half his head blown off and his trailer burned down around his dead ears."

"So?"

"Weapon was an SR-1 Vektor. Silenced, from the condition of the bullets. Less deformation that way. Either the victim or the killer—or both—had ties to the item we discussed Sunday."

"Sometimes I wish that Berlin still had a wall," Duke said. "I'm told this job was a hell of a lot easier back then. How good is your source?"

"FBI. They get called in on major rez crimes."

"You trust an FBI agent?"

Cooperation between the two agencies was a minefield filled with back-stabbing, misdirection, and agent eat officer.

Politics as usual.

"The agent owed me a favor," Harrow said. "Even if he didn't, he's reliable."

"Stay on top of it," the DDO said. "If it moves off the rez to Canada, somebody will stick us with the ticket."

"Then I'm praying it doesn't."

"No shit."

Neither one of them wanted to testify before the kind of political investigation committees that would be formed if the op that wasn't quite the CIA's went south.

22

Shurik Temuri trimmed his fingernails with a very sharp Japanese folding knife. The big, wedge-shaped blade hadn't been designed for manicures, but Temuri didn't care. He simply wanted to flash the lethal knife as he browbeat the two stupid Americans.

Once the knife appeared, any Georgian with balls would have pulled his own knife and begun working on fingernails or other body parts. But it seemed that Lovich and Amanar had lived a soft life too long to recognize the old-country insult of an unsheathed knife.

It was the same problem with the language the cousins spoke—an outdated, corrupt form of what any proper Georgian would speak.

"So what did your informant tell you?" Temuri asked Amanar.

"Don't call him an informant," Amanar said unhappily.

"He's the chief of police. He briefed me along with other members of the city council, that's all."

"Policemen are always informants to politicians." Temuri shaved off a piece of nail. "Unless they're the politician as well as the policeman."

"Look, I keep telling you that you aren't back in the old country," Amanar said. "This system is different."

"What is it Americans say? Shit of the bull?" Temuri waved the knife. "Police and politics are the same everywhere. What did he say to you?"

Blank faced, Lovich looked out the window. He wanted no part in this conversation.

Amanar started to argue with Temuri, then shrugged. The Georgian simply didn't grasp the nuances of American politics. Or maybe the other way around. Whatever.

Either way, *Blackbird* needed a captain.

"I was told that the Indian was shot twice in the back of the head," Amanar said. "Then the murderers doused the trailer with kerosene and lit it off. Any real evidence was destroyed in the fire."

"Murderers? More than one?" Temuri asked.

"Uh . . . that's what the police chief said."

Another crescent of nail shaving hit the carpet. "One child with balls could have executed the Indian and burned the place down."

"Look, I'm just telling you what I was told."

Temuri grunted.

Amanar kept talking in his out-of-date dialect. "The body was almost burned beyond recognition. The assumption is that it's Tommy. Considering that he isn't answering his cell phone and can't be found, we're going with Tommy as the corpse. Even if he's alive and running, we can't count on him anymore. My cousin and I are really, really unhappy with how this is turning out."

"Yeah," Lovich said in English. "This talk about an execution isn't making me feel the love."

Temuri gave him a hard look for speaking in English. Then he turned his attention back to Amanar. "Is there a problem?"

"The chief didn't say anything about any execution," Amanar said. "He thinks it was some kind of ongoing, uh, argument about fishing rights or something among the Indians."

"Why, then, is your Federal Bureau of Investigation involved?" Temuri demanded, his dark eyes glittering with temper.

"They always investigate crimes of violence on reservations. That's what the chief said, anyway."

Temuri spit on the rug.

Amanar winced but didn't say anything.

"Amateurs," Temuri said.

The knife flashed so quickly Amanar couldn't see much beyond a metallic blur. He swallowed hard and didn't ask just who the amateurs were that Temuri spit upon.

"You are telling me a cheap murder on a tribal reserve that is mostly scrub timber and blackberry bushes is worth the attention of no fewer than fifty federal agents," Temuri said with a deadly lack of inflection.

"Fifty? Are you sure? The chief never said anything about that many feds." Amanar shook his head in disbelief. "How did you find that out?"

"I drove by the tribal headquarters building and counted the shiny four-door sedans parked there. That is called intelligence work. I know Chechens who can drive by a Russian barracks and tell you within five men the number of soldiers housed there. It is how we determine the number of bullets issued to our freedom fighters."

Amanar started sweating. "I don't like this talk about soldiers and attacks. You told us this was a simple smuggling operation, like dope or cigarettes. That's all we signed on for. We're Americans, not freedom fighters or terrorists."

"Yet you smuggle the *narco* to sell to children and addicts?"

"It's not the same," Amanar said impatiently. "It's just a game. Dope doesn't hurt anybody. Guns do. My cousin and I don't want anything to do with anyone else's wars."

Temuri stared at him, then tested the edge of the knife on Lovich's wooden desk.

Lovich worked hard on ignoring him.

"What of the people of yours who disappeared at sea years ago?" Temuri asked. "Was that all part of the game that hurt no one?"

The two boat brokers traded startled glances.

"You stupid son of a bitch," Lovich said in English. "Why the hell did—"

"I didn't tell him," Amanar said in the same language. "Now shut up. He knows more English than he lets on."

Sullenly, Lovich returned to staring out at the bay.

"Look, I don't know who you've been talking to or what they've been saying," Amanar said. "We never killed anybody. Accidents happen, especially when you're in a small boat on big water."

"I know precisely what happened and why," Temuri said. He carved another groove in the desk. Wood shavings fell on the rug next to neat slices from his nails. "So would your police, if they ever decided to investigate. Yet death at sea is a federal matter, is it not? I am told death has no limitation in the United States."

Amanar got the point: Temuri knew that the statute of limitations on murder had no end date.

"And then the monies owed—taxes, yes," Temuri said. "Is there a limitation on them?"

Amanar and Lovich exchanged a long look before Amanar gave in, turned away, and asked the question whose answer neither cousin would like.

"What do you want?" he asked Temuri.

"A captain for my *Blackbird*. You have until tomorrow at dawn."

Neither Lovich nor Amanar asked what would happen if they failed Temuri. They really didn't want to know.

23

Taras Demidov swallowed the last of three hamburgers, squeezed the final drops in the tenth packet of ketchup over a pile of fries, and took a sip of the surprisingly awful coffee. No amount of sugar smothered the bitterness.

But it did take the smell inside the van off his tongue.

Eating fries, Demidov listened through his ear bug while the two cousins continued arguing over possible replacements for the Indian who had been taken out of the game. Demidov didn't bother to sort out the voices. Only the topic mattered to him.

"And I tell you, your wife's nephew isn't up to a boat that size."

"Stupid shit deserves to die. He knocked up his own cousin."

"Second cousin."

"Still a cousin. I say we use Durand."

"Too risky."

"Who'd miss him? No family, no friends except maybe Tommy, not even a regular hump in town."

"Tommy was stupid. Durand isn't."

"If Durand's so smart, why ain't he rich?"

Demidov laughed soundlessly as he stood and walked the few steps to the slops bucket. The cousins came from families that had lived in America so long they had absorbed the culture whether or not they wished to.

"Temuri wants Blackbird *out of here by tomorrow at dawn, no later. None of the other captains we use are available right now. You want to drive that boat yourself?"*

"Fine. Whatever. If no one else can take the job by this afternoon, I'll call Durand. Temuri won't like it. He didn't take to Durand."

"So let Temuri drive the boat."

"He'd make us drive it. Better we get Durand. He doesn't have kids."

"You don't know anyone's going to die."

"You want to bet your life on it?"

Listening to the cousins wrangle, Demidov shook off the last drops and zipped up. It was time to message his boss and make him smile.

Blackbird wouldn't be going anywhere today.

24

f I tie any more ropes—*lines*—to this cleat," Emma said, wiping sweat off her forehead, "I'm going to yank it out of the dock and put it where your sun don't shine."

Mac hid his smile by reaching into the grocery bag and pulling out a chocolate bar. "Truce?"

"You have a sandwich to go with that?"

"And chips."

"Truce." She jerked the line tight, leaving two neat, secure figure-eights of line lying on the cleat. "Is it always this hot in October?"

"No," he said. "It won't last. You want to take a turn at the computer?"

She looked at him blankly. "Did something, um, new come in?"

"I'm talking about the other computer. You know, chart-plotting and navigation and—"

"No, thanks. Knock yourself out."

She stretched her back muscles. Handling fat lines and big fenders—always at strange angles that increased the stress of leverage on her body—used more strength than she would have guessed.

"After lunch, then," he said.

She looked at his expression and knew she was going to learn more about boat handling than she'd ever wanted to. At least Faroe and his magic electronic machine had been by before dawn, assuring them that *Autonomy* was still without bugs. They could talk freely, if carefully.

"Sure," she said, concealing a sigh. "Can't wait."

Mac took her hand, drew her close, and nuzzled her neck. "You've got to learn enough so that if I'm out of commission you'll be able to do whatever has to be done. Both our lives could depend on it."

"I hear you." She bit his ear. "Now feed me."

"Tongue sandwich?"

She laughed, hugged him hard for anybody who might be watching, and was tempted to take him up on his offer.

So she did.

He tasted fine, coffee and salt air and man. A lot of man, covering her from lips to knees, settling in for a good long kiss. She told herself she wanted to pull away, then gave up lying and returned as good as she got. Everywhere she touched him he was hot, way too hot. From the feel of the erection pressing against her stomach, he felt the same way about her.

Hot.

Slowly, very slowly, they separated.

"Whew," she said against his lips. "That should have melted anyone's binoculars."

"Sure set my jeans on fire."

"I noticed." She smiled. "I'd show you how much I appreciate it, but we'd get arrested."

Her stomach growled.

He laughed and shook his head. "Lunch? Normal kind?"

"Lunch," she agreed. "Boring kind."

Emma followed Mac inside, grabbed the local newspaper out of the grocery bag and sat at the banquette.

It was that or grab Mac right where his jeans fit so well. *Down, girl. Think work. Work. WORK.*

She skimmed the headlines while he unwrapped sandwiches and took out bottles of iced tea. Nothing new on the rez fire. Not that she expected anything. Once the feds got involved, usually chatty sources took a vow of silence.

St. Kilda hadn't been a whole lot of help in the information department either. Reams of Alara's background briefings had appeared on Emma's computer along with conclusions that varied from bureau-babble to useless. A lot of words wasted when two words would do it: We're trying.

Very trying.

Mac wedged more fresh vegetables into the small fridge and folded the paper bag for reuse. Between the check from Blue Water Marine Group and St. Kilda's "petty cash" advance, he wasn't worried about paying for his next meal.

He made a point of not noticing that Emma was back to wearing one of her eye-candy outfits. Her short shorts and tight crop top told him what he already knew—playing her lover was going to be hard on him. Literally.

Get your mind out of your pants and into the game.

Good advice. He was trying hard to take it.

Hard. Really hard.

Sex was easy to ignore only when you were getting some regularly. Having Emma close by reminded Mac that he'd been on short rations recently. He shut the fridge door.

Hard.

Warily, Emma watched him from the corner of her eye. The waves of testosterone were thick enough to float on. Problem was, she was tempted to dive right in.

Hey, at least I don't have to worry about the temperature of the water, she thought wryly. *It would be hot.*

She took a bite out of her ham sandwich, chewed, and wished she was sipping on him rather than on iced tea.

Mac settled onto the bench seat opposite her, unwrapped his sandwich, and said, "Anything new?"

Emma opened her bag of chips. "Not in the last half hour."

"Tell me more about *Black Swan*. Damn little was on your computer."

"Blue Water Marine Group franchises yacht dealerships," she said, "mainly on the West Coast. The hulls are laid in Malaysia and the fancy teak work is done there. The boats are mostly finished by the time they go on a container ship."

Mac took a big bite from his meatball sub.

"Several other high-end boat names also have the major work done in Malaysia," she said. "Costs less and the craftsmanship is better than good."

He nodded. "I've picked up more than one overseas boat in Seattle for Blue Water."

"There's one you didn't pick up. About a year ago, there was a yacht called *Black Swan*."

He waited, chewing an oversize chunk of meatball sub.

"We don't know where it was hijacked off the container ship," Emma said. "Irkutsk or Vladivostok are most likely."

"Was *Swan* really identical to *Blackbird*?"

"In every way we've been able to confirm."

Mac chewed on that for a while. Then he opened his tea. "St. Kilda has been working this for a year?"

"Investigating yacht thefts? Yes."

"Are the thefts tied together?"

"No pattern has been found beyond the fact of the luxury yachts themselves. Every major American shipbuilder in Malaysia has been hit. If one of the Russian *mafiyas* is running the scam, we can't find names. *Black Swan* was the loss that pulled the pin on the patience grenade of the insurance arm of IYBC—that's International Yacht Builders Consortium to non-native speakers."

"Were all the missing boats about the same size?" he asked.

"So far, nothing smaller than forty-one feet or bigger than seventy-three has been hijacked. The smaller boats are the really high-end ones."

Mac nodded.

"Within that size range, the estimates are that at least two yachts a year have been lost in the last decade from container ships departing Malaysia. It adds up to a lot of millions, and that's just from the boats covered by the Consortium's insurance program. Other insurers have losses as big or bigger. They're all tired of paying without really playing."

Mac ate and turned over pieces of the puzzle in his mind. "Unless you dupe in a bunch of undercover agents along various waterfronts, the insurers have a hard slog ahead. All a hijacker needs is one crooked shift on harbor duty and a big-ass hammerhead crane."

"That pretty much describes any of the big ports along Malaysia and the Pacific coastline of the FSU. Excuse me, Russian Federation. Wonder what they'll be called a year from now?" She shrugged. "But I'd lay good money on hijacked yachts being used to shuttle *mafiya* brass around the Caspian Sea. When it comes to bare-assed naked thievery, I'll put the *mafiyas* against anything the globe can offer."

"How did the insurance claims explain the losses?"

"Rogue waves. Each and every one of them."

Mac raised dark eyebrows. "With all the satellites in orbit measuring changes in height of the ocean surface, and the amount of traffic in the shipping lanes, there should be plenty of warnings on the air about rogue waves in the containership transit zones."

"You'd think," Emma agreed wryly. "But, damn, those sneaky mountains of water just keep rushing up and washing really expensive yachts into the drink. Nothing cheap, mind you. No wannabe yachts need apply."

"Is there a chance that the Consortium is some kind of stalking horse for the opposition?" Mac asked.

"If they are, St. Kilda couldn't find it. And yes, we looked. We're real picky about our clients."

When we have the choice.

For a few minutes there was nothing but the small sounds of lunch being devoured.

"Is *Blackbird* going to the same owner who commissioned *Swan*?" Mac asked.

"Not on any documents we could find. *Swan* was on her way to Portland, Oregon. Owner was a really pissed-off class-action attorney whose bouncing buddy spent just *hours* on the boat's design. *Hours*, I tell you. Getting a black hull and matching swim step cost buttloads of money. *Buttloads*, I tell you."

Mac smiled. "Bent your ear, did she?"

"He," Emma said. "Before I was assigned to the case, he chewed on insurance agents while his lover threatened class-action suits in all possible venues, known and unknown."

"Class action for yachties?" Mac shook his head and laughed over his vanishing sandwich.

She smiled. "You and Faroe think alike."

"I know those yacht hulls come off the production line like big cars, only in much smaller numbers," Mac said. "But what are the chances of two rich yachties going to Blue Water Marine Group franchises in two states and insisting on identical interior design and black on the hull and swim step? And throwing in whacking great oversize engines just for kicks and giggles?"

"Same questions Faroe asked. Their son is still trying to calculate the odds, and Lane is some kind of math-computer guru."

Silently Mac finished his sandwich, took a big swallow of iced tea, and rapped his knuckles slowly, gently, on the table.

Emma could tell when a man was thinking hard. She shut up and waited.

"If it wasn't for the built-alike thing," Mac said finally,

"I'd say that the thefts were probably done by unrelated gangs in various Malaysian and FSU ports that were lifting anything they could get a sling under."

"The identical-twin thing is why I was assigned up close and personal to *Blackbird*. Faroe really hates coincidences."

"Smart man."

"Very. People who believe his easygoing, howya-doing act deserve what they get. Then there's the name of the first ship."

"*Black Swan?*" Mac shrugged. "I know the term— something that is believed to be impossible until it happens."

"The name got popular after the World Trade Center was brought down by terrorists. We were like the Europeans who had never seen a black swan until they discovered Australia. Black swans were an event impossible to forecast, therefore impossible to prepare for."

"Like winning a lawsuit based on the fact that people who drink coffee are too stupid to know that coffee is hot?" Mac asked dryly. "Could be the lawyer who ordered the yacht has a really twisted sense of humor. A name like that deserves hijacking."

"I know. But I just . . ."

"Don't like it?" Mac finished.

She shrugged. "Sort of like a raised middle finger."

"Like I said. Twisted. And yes, I read a book called *The Black Swan*. Along with about a million other people in the U.S."

"Pretty much what St. Kilda said." She sighed. "Wish Blue Water would call and hire you."

"Don't like your little bunk?"

He'd offered to share the stateroom with her, but she'd had an attack of common sense and taken the tiny second cabin with its cramped bed.

"I don't like waiting," she said. "I'm used to it, but I'll never enjoy it."

Before Mac could answer, his cell phone rang. He looked at the incoming message ID: Blue Water Marine Group.

"Your wait just might be over," Mac said.

25

Demidov watched Temuri pace the dock, his very presence driving the techs to work faster. Temuri was a muscular, silent shadow ensuring that no one slacked off or lifted a few expensive electronics for individual profit.

Watching Temuri was like looking in a mirror.

Once, we would have worked together, Demidov thought. *Now . . .*

The world had changed. Temuri was on the other side of a deadly divide running through the Russian Federation like an earthquake fault. So far the pushing, shoving, strutting, and killing among former satellite regions had stopped short of outright civil war.

Demidov's job was to see that didn't change.

Temuri's job was the opposite.

Since Blue Water Marine had lost their captain, Temuri

was pushing to finish the installation of the same electronics he'd been willing to leave ashore before Tommy died.

Demidov smiled. Temuri was making the best of a situation he didn't really control. More than once, Demidov had done the same. It was called surviving in a game whose rules changed without warning or apology.

Now that the delay his boss had wanted was accomplished, there was little left in Rosario to interest Demidov. Mentally he went through his pre-departure checklist. It had come down to a simple choice. He could go north now and wait for *Blackbird*, or he could stay here and watch *Blackbird* leave. Then he would chase her northward sea passage, but he would be on land. Roads wound around mountains and bays and waddled through towns. The course over water was as the crow—or seagull—flew.

When presented with the choice of staying or leaving, Grigori Sidorov's message had been terse.

Go north.

Demidov put a lid on the bucket, changed all of his ID to that of a Canadian national who had been stamped through U.S. customs eight days ago, and drove out of the parking lot. He dumped the bucket in a vacant lot, left the van in long-term ferry parking, and effectively vanished.

Until Sidorov ordered otherwise, he was headed north.

26

Ready?" Mac asked, squeezing Emma's shoulder and pulling her closer to his side.

She slid her left hand into his left back jeans pocket and leaned into him. The radiation patch he had in his jeans poked her finger. "More than."

Just a game, Mac told himself.

Yeah. Right.

He settled Emma's lithe body closer against him, and envied the patch she wore inside her bra.

I'll enjoy the fringe bennies of our cover, Mac thought. *But not too much.*

That's my story and I'm sticking to it.

Emma rubbed his butt lightly.

"Watch it, woman," he muttered.

She tilted her head back and glanced down to where her hand was in his pocket. "Worth watching."

Mac set his back teeth.

She pinched him. "Loosen up, big guy. We're supposed to be friends, remember?"

"Friends?" he retorted.

"With benefits."

She gave him a look that made his jeans feel tighter. But then, she always made him feel that way.

"You're good at this," he breathed into her ear. "Too good."

"You make it easy. The last dude I had to play the benefits game with was twice my age, four times my weight, and had breath like a donkey fart."

Mac fought it, but he laughed.

And relaxed.

She stood on her tiptoes and breathed in his ear. "Much better. When you smile, it's easy to see how you hooked up so fast with a woman who doesn't have donkey breath."

Still smiling, Mac punched in the marina gate code, ushered her through, and let the metal gate clang loudly shut behind them. Down on the dock, Lovich and Amanar looked up and waved.

The third man just stared at them.

Mac dropped a nibbling kiss on Emma's bare neck. "Watch Stoneface. He's murder on two feet."

"Got it. I'm all big eyes, big smile, and tiny mind."

"Keep your mouth shut and they just might believe that."

Making like Siamese twins, Mac and Emma strolled down the gangway.

The three men waiting for them were the only people

on the dock near the *Blackbird* who weren't moving fast. A half-dozen technicians and riggers swarmed over the boat like pirates on a prize. On the flying bridge, two men shoved electronics leads down through the stainless-steel tubes of the radar arch. A flat ten-mile radar antenna and domes for satellite television and telephone were already in place. Inside, at the helm, a tech installed the multipurpose screen for a chart plotter, radar receiver, and depth sounder.

"You meant it when you said you were in a hurry," Mac drawled as he looked at the controlled frenzy.

"The boat's gotta sail tomorrow," Amanar said. "First light. We've already been delayed by losing a captain. We asked for more time and didn't get it. We've been running double shifts and then some, but she'll be ready. You'll have to do sea trials along the way."

Mac didn't point out that he hadn't been hired. All he said was, "New owner must have lots of green if he'll underwrite that fast a commissioning."

"The perfect customer," Lovich said. "Cost is no object." He ran his hand over the close-cropped, graying beard on his chin and looked around. "Let's go to the office."

"Whatever," Mac said mildly, even as he slid in the knife. "We're in kind of a hurry ourselves. Taking my boat out for a week or so."

Let Amanar chew on that.

Frowning, Amanar looked at Emma. He started to say something, then shrugged and led the way up the ramp to the Blue Water dealership office. Lovich followed.

Stoneface watched them from the dock.

Both brokers were unusually quiet until they were inside the office with the door closed behind them. Amanar stood behind the desk, keeping an eye on the activity on the dock. Lovich pulled the tabs on three cans of light beer. He set one each in front of Amanar and Mac, then took one for himself.

Apparently Emma was invisible.

"Thanks," Mac said, pretending to drink. He hated light beer. "Getting *Autonomy* ready is thirsty work."

He tilted the can toward Emma. She sipped, made a throaty noise, sucked, and licked her lips like a porn star with a bratwurst.

"What's on your mind?" Mac asked Amanar.

Amanar looked over Mac's latest girlfriend.

Emma admired her freshly painted fingernails. She'd learned that the ropes—*lines*—ate manicures, but there was the image thing to uphold. A dumb piece of ass without scarlet finger- and toenails? Ain't happening.

"We want to talk business," Amanar said curtly. "Lose the candy."

"Her candy is my business," Mac said. "She knows when to close her mouth."

"Over your cock," Lovich muttered.

Emma leaned harder into Mac. The tension snaking through his body reminded her of just how strong he was. It also told her that he didn't like her being the target of trash talk.

"Are they talking cash?" she asked Mac, just loud enough for the other two men to overhear.

He looked at Amanar and Lovich. "You talking cash?"

The cousins looked at each other. Neither liked it, but they were getting the game plan. Play with the candy or play without a captain.

"Yes," Amanar said. "Twenty thousand, up front. Twenty on delivery. Expenses are on you."

At that pay rate, Mac wasn't surprised. "How long, which boat, where, and when?"

"*Blackbird*. Tomorrow before dawn. You head up the Inside Passage toward Broughton Island. You've got five days to get there. If the buyer can't take it over somewhere along the way, you'll get more instructions."

Mac lifted his black eyebrows. But he didn't say anything. The brokers knew just how unusual the cash assignment sailing to nowhere specific was.

Amanar's lips thinned when Mac didn't grab the money and kiss him on all four cheeks.

"The new owner is involved in negotiations to sell one of his businesses. His schedule is hour-to-hour, so yours has to be, too," Amanar said impatiently. "That's why the boat will be in your name, in case things fall through and you have to bring *Blackbird* back here. It all depends on the negotiations. The money's good, so what's your problem?"

"I was looking forward to some time off," Mac said easily. He tucked Emma closer to his side. "But we can take a ride on your boat instead of mine."

The broker snatched up a colored pencil and started drumming the end on the desk blotter.

"Look," Amanar finally said, "just drive *Blackbird* north,

follow directions, fly home when the owner takes over, and then take your pussy cruise."

"If money was all I wanted out of life, I'd be working another job," Mac said. "See you around, boys."

Holding Emma close, Mac headed for the door.

"Hey, ease up," Lovich said quickly. "You want to take some cock-rider along, we don't care." He stared at Amanar. "Do we?"

"C'mon, Mac," Emma said, pouting. "I have a passport. I'm between jobs, between husbands, between everything. I just want to finally have a little fun."

"Your family won't mind?" Amanar acted like he had just noticed that Emma was in the room.

"You talking to me?" she asked.

"Am I looking anywhere else?" Amanar retorted.

"Babe," she said, smiling and stretching slowly, "I'm here because I don't want a steady man, don't want a steady job, don't want two kids, and don't want a white picket fence in the 'burbs. You feeling me?"

The two cousins looked at each other. They spoke quickly in the old-country language.

All Mac understood was the word Temuri, because it was repeated several times, in a louder voice each time.

A curse? A name? Stoneface, maybe? Mac wished he knew, but languages hadn't been his area of expertise.

Emma looked bored, but the tension in her body told Mac that she was listening to every word. He hoped she understood more than he did.

"I hear you," Amanar said finally to his cousin, "but I don't like it."

Lovich nodded and looked at Mac. "You in?"

"If you're smuggling anything to Canada, tell me now," Mac said.

His voice said that this demand wasn't negotiable.

"Nah," Lovich said. "We leave that to the Indians."

"Bullshit," Mac said. "I grew up here, remember?"

"Hey, we changed," Lovich said. "Money's not as good, but we sleep a lot better."

"If I find any extra cargo," Mac said, "it's going to the bottom."

"*Blackbird* is clean," Amanar said. "You want to go over it, you'll have plenty of time before you hit Canadian waters. How you use your time is your problem."

Mac thought about it, then nodded. "I want twelve thousand now, eight thousand when we board tomorrow. For expenses. I'm not signing off on any fuel slips for a yacht I don't really own, haven't chartered, and haven't been hired as a transit captain on."

Amanar smiled at Lovich, who headed for the office safe.

"Cash is smart," Amanar said. "The new owner is the eccentric kind. Wants his privacy. So don't be hitting the bars tonight, bragging about this job."

"Men in bars are looking for women," Mac said. "I've got mine."

Emma stretched up and nibbled on his ear. "Sure do, babe."

Mac returned the favor, with interest, as Amanar counted out the money Lovich had fetched. While Mac counted bills, Emma went back to her invisible act.

The bills were hundreds. Nonsequential, used hundreds, anonymous as dirt and a lot more valuable.

The hell they've cleaned up, Mac thought.

But he kept his mouth closed, finished his own counting, and stuffed twelve thousand dollars in hundreds into his front jeans pocket. After the round of mutual nibbling, it was a tight fit.

When he was done, Mac put his arm around Emma, her hand returned to his back pocket like a homing pigeon, and they headed for the door as a unit.

"Before first light tomorrow," Amanar said.

"Eight thousand on the dock," Mac said.

"Don't count it until you're inside," Lovich called out.

"If you think I'm that stupid," Mac said without turning around, "you're a dickhead for hiring me."

The door closed behind them.

Voices erupted in the office.

"Walk slower," Emma said, nibbling on his ear. "It's hard to hear."

"You understand that racket?"

"Enough to get words here and there. Sounds like bastard Russian of some kind. Almost a dialect. For sure those yutzes haven't been to Moscow lately."

Slowly, nibbling between every other step, Emma and Mac walked out to the parking lot. The more she heard, the less she understood.

It can't be the same Shurik Temuri. Last I saw a bulletin about him, he was selling arms to a separatist splinter group in the Ukraine.

Nobody had known which side of the war games Temuri

had been on. All they knew was that he was making a lot of money playing.

"What's wrong?" Mac asked softly.

"I don't know. But I know something is."

"We knew that already."

"There's knowing and then there's *knowing*," she said. "Let's move. If Faroe hasn't already taken a surveillance photo of Stoneface, it just went to the top of St. Kilda's must-do list."

27

Tim Harrow glanced idly around the tapas bar. It was small, plush, and preferred by congressmen meeting lobbyists for a little off-the-record monkey business. Just one of the many open secrets of Washington, D.C., that the press corps never got around to "discovering" until one of the congressmen pissed on some editor's private crusade for truth, justice, and headlines.

Don't ask. Don't tell.

Happy hour begins at 10:00 A.M.

Although Harrow's expression didn't show it, he was annoyed at being there. Usually his contact was happy with coded emails or black-box telephone calls.

Maybe she was looking for a little action.

The thought eased a lot of Harrow's irritation. Carin Richards was as good on her knees as she was in back-channel communications.

The beveled glass and mahogany bar door opened. A woman dressed in the D.C. uniform—good quality business suit in a subdued blue, leather briefcase, short dark hair, medium heels, and simple jewelry—walked through the crowded bar area to the quiet booth where Harrow waited.

No one hit on her. She wasn't dressed for it, wasn't swinging her ass for it, and wasn't looking around for it. Just one more lobbyist having a drink after a long day.

Except this lobbyist was an FBI agent and an old friend. With benefits.

Harrow smiled as she slid into the small booth opposite him. She toasted him silently with the drink he had ordered for her. As she did, she leaned forward and said a name.

"Shurik Temuri."

Harrow's expression didn't change.

"Mean anything to you?" Carin asked.

"In what context?"

"Rosario, Washington, state of."

"The rez murder?" Harrow asked.

"Big coincidence otherwise."

Harrow sipped his neat Scotch. "As far as we're concerned, that's not a familiar context for him."

"No shit. My boss—and his boss, and the one above, all the way up to top of the mountain—is stroking out over the fact that your people didn't warn them that your good buddy is on U.S. soil. Where you, by the way, are specifically not permitted to act under the laws we all know and love. This is an unofficial warning. The official one will land as soon as my people can speak in language fit to print on a memo. We want Temuri. Bad."

"How certain are you of the identity?" Harrow asked.

"Ninety-three point six probability, based on a surveillance photo that came through back channels. And yes, we trust the source."

Harrow sipped when he wanted to hurl the heavy glass into the booth across the bar. "I'll look into it."

"You do that. Real fast." She waved a server over. "I'm hungry. How about you?"

He'd just lost his appetite, but he knew he might as well eat. He had a long night of work ahead. Silently he damned all informants who couldn't be trusted to stay bought.

Not that anyone with two brain cells expected Temuri to do anything but what he was best at. Betrayal.

"Knock yourself out," Harrow said. "I'm buying."

"You bet you are. My expense account gets maxed out at a soda machine."

28

Showtime.

Emma took a long, hidden breath and walked next to Mac. Both of them were carrying a duffel and wearing wind jackets. It might be one of the rare, almost warm dawns the Pacific Northwest got after summer, but experience told her that the water was always cooler than the land. Direct sunlight was different. She planned on a little sunning on a sheltered part of the yacht. No reason she couldn't read files outside.

Mac pushed a marina cart filled with enough food and water to get them to Campbell River in a day. It would be a long haul and a fast way to determine if *Blackbird* had any kinks to work out, especially with all the electronics that had been wired in by harried techs.

The bulkiest item Mac had was a box of paper charts that covered the Inside Passage all the way to southeast Alaska.

The twelve thousand in cash was in St. Kilda's care. Mac wouldn't leave until he had a fresh eight thousand for his pocket. In Canada, fuel was priced like liquid gold. He wanted to be certain he had plenty of cash for the ride, no matter how fast he pushed *Blackbird*.

The only thing lacking in their equipment was any kind of radiation detector, chemical sniffer, or even a bug detector. St. Kilda didn't want to risk tipping off anyone that the transit captain suspected this was more than a somewhat dodgy delivery.

Better to assume they were bugged and act accordingly.

The radiation patches they had worn to the Blue Water office yesterday had showed zero exposure above the expected norm. No one in the Blue Water office had unusual exposure, so they hadn't been handling fissionable material. Chemical and biological were still on the suspect list, and would stay there until there was a reason to cross them off.

There weren't any room lights on in any of the motels that serviced the marina. Emma didn't need that kind of signal to be certain Faroe or Grace was watching.

She had turned her gun over to Faroe. A girlie .22 purse pistol might have been explained away as a city girl's paranoia, but the Glock? Way too much firepower. Illegal to carry in Canada, too.

Mac had kept his knife. Male necessity, apparently, expected and accepted by all but the airlines.

A restless night in separate beds hadn't done either of them any good. Today Mac kept watching her, catching himself, and looking away.

It will be even more fun aboard Blackbird, she thought. *Sharing a bed. God. Never saw that one coming.*

Faroe had. So had Grace. They had told her—and Mac—to suck it up and do the job.

Mac had made it clear he would rather do Emma.

It was mutual.

While she waited, he punched in Blue Water's code at the gate. The techs were gone, but portable work lights set up on the dock still flooded the yacht. A cool breeze rose with the distant dawn, ruffling the marina's polished black surface.

Lovich waited for them at the bottom of the ramp. Silently he passed keys and a thick envelope to Mac, ignored Emma, then followed them aboard *Blackbird.* Heavy privacy screens shielded the salon. Light gleamed faintly through various cracks.

Mac opened the stern door into the salon. When he saw that someone was waiting for them, he shouldered Emma aside and went in first.

A blunt-faced man with dark shoulder-length hair and a darker mustache was seated on one of the salon sofas. Even in the filtered light, his black eyes glittered. He had no expression.

"Are you going to introduce us," Mac said to Amanar, "or should I just call him Stoneface?"

The third man said something that sounded rude, crude, and insulting. Then he gestured bluntly toward the cargo they had carried aboard.

Amanar's face seemed to flatten, but he did as he was told. He searched everything Mac and Emma had carried onto the boat, including the seams of the duffels. He found nothing unexpected.

Stoneface grunted and gestured.

"Sorry," Lovich said in a low voice. "I have to search you. Mr. Paranoid over there thinks you might be wearing a wire."

Score one for Faroe's own paranoia, Mac thought. *A great big one.*

Without Faroe's mandate that they go in as soft as possible, they would have brought along something that could detect bugs, radiation, and certain chemicals.

And they would have been busted before they even left the dock.

"No problem," Mac said calmly, holding out his arms. "But you touch her and you'll be eating your own hands."

Amanar said something quickly to Stoneface.

Stoneface looked at Emma and said something.

"Um . . ." Amanar cleared his throat. "He says it's not optional."

Calmly Emma began stripping.

Four men stared at her, not knowing what she knew— she'd worn her string bikini under her clothes. Though there were clouds racing across the stars, she had hopes of sitting on a sunny deck.

When she was done removing clothes, she lifted her hair off her neck with both hands, pirouetted, and then stood with her hands on her hips in unsubtle female challenge.

If she was wearing anything but skin, it would take more than a strip search to reveal it.

"Put your clothes on," Mac said gruffly.

She gave him a real slow smile. "You sure, big guy?"

Mac's eyelids lowered. "Babe. You need spanking."

She licked her lips and lowered her eyelids right back at him. "Works for me."

He forced himself to look at Stoneface. "You feel more like a man now?"

Lovich cleared his throat, went through Emma's clothes like they burned, and threw them at her.

She wiggled into her jeans, slid into her snug black pullover and ignored the wind jacket. She clipped on her cell phone and smoothed everything in place with slow hands as she waited for orders like a good little girl.

Or a really bad one.

Mac didn't know whether to cheer or strangle her. She'd taken what could have been an ugly situation and turned it into a farce. He glanced over at Amanar. The yacht broker's cheekbones were flushed. With jerky motions he searched the stuff they had brought aboard. Toothbrushes, toothpaste, floss, condoms, clothes, cooking supplies.

Emma watched indifferently. She knew there was nothing more deadly than hot sauce in the provisions.

Stoneface saw that Emma and Mac both had computers and fired off fast questions.

Lovich asked, "Why the computers?"

She rolled her eyes like a four-year-old. "Same reason I have a cell phone. Just because I'm on vacation doesn't mean I'm unplugged. How else can I keep up with the latest Hollywood sex swaps?" Before Lovich could ask, she added, "Mac uses his as a backup nav system. He's real cautious."

Lovich translated.

Stoneface let them keep the computers. And the camera

Emma had brought with her. Their cell phones drew a look, but he didn't touch them. In the modern world, cell phones were like oxygen, a required part of living.

Silently Mac kept counting the money he'd been given. Accurate to the last rumpled bill. Nice to work with professional crooks. They paid up front and on time, in cash.

"Sorry about the search," Lovich said roughly. "He's from the old country. Doesn't even trust his reflection in a mirror."

"I'm surprised he has a reflection," Mac said. "We finished with the party games now?"

"Uh . . ."

Stoneface got to his feet and stalked out the door. Seconds later he reappeared on the dock. With smooth, powerful strides, he went up the gangway and vanished.

Both cousins let out a silent breath.

"The fuel tanks are full," Amanar said to Mac. "When you get to Campbell River, top up the tanks. Then motor north like you're going to the Broughton Archipelago. You'll hear from us if and when we want you to change course. You have five days to get to the Broughtons, max. The owner could be ready to pick up even sooner."

"Weather permitting," Mac said neutrally.

"That boat will take anything the Inside Passage can dish out," Amanar said.

"That *boat* hasn't had a shakedown cruise. You know as well as I do that something will go wrong. Likely more than one thing. Just a fact of life and complex electronic and mechanical systems."

"Yeah. Whatever." Amanar glanced quickly at his cousin,

and just as quickly away. "Get going. Don't spare the fuel—you're sure as hell being paid for it. You'll hear from us."

Mac stuffed the money into the front pocket of his jeans. "Any preferences in Campbell's fuel docks or is it captain's choice?"

Emma swallowed laughter. She hadn't known Mac long, yet she had no doubt that he was pissed.

"Uh . . . no," Lovich said. "All the documentation you need for crossing the border is in that ring binder," he added, waving a hand to the wide, padded pilot's bench.

Mac picked up the binder, read through the documentation, and looked up. "Anything else I need to know? Radio codes, rules of the sea, Canadian nav markers?"

Amanar's mouth flattened at the unsubtle mockery. "You're being well paid."

"Did I complain about the money?" Mac asked.

Lovich grabbed his cousin's arm. "C'mon. I'm ready for breakfast. It will be good for what ails us."

With a final glare at Mac, Amanar allowed himself to be led out the door.

Emma was careful not to say anything she wouldn't mind having overhead. "What a dickhead."

"Amanar?"

"Him, too.

Mac smiled. "I'll start the engines. You pick up all the lines that are loose."

"Loose."

"As in not under tension holding the boat against the dock."

"Oh. Yeah. Sorry. I'm still back with dickhead."

"Come here a minute and put those sexy lips to work."

She gave him a startled look, but did as he asked.

His mouth brushed over hers, lingered, then he breathed against her ear, "You did good, partner. Real good. Nice bathing suit. Now get that beautiful butt out on the dock."

"I like your butt, too."

Mac laughed out loud.

Smiling, Emma sauntered out the door and onto the dock. She heard various buzzers, bells, and engine noises while she picked up two of *Blackbird*'s four dock lines. By the time she got the loose lines coiled and tossed onto the deck, the engines had farted happily and settled in to a muscular purring.

She ignored the three men watching from the top of the gangway.

Mac signaled for her to pick up the forward spring line and toss it aboard. When she was finished, he stepped out on deck with a portable joystick controller.

"Leave a half-loop around the cleat on the aft springer and hand me the line," Mac said.

Emma had already gone over this maneuver several times before on *Autonomy*. She understood that the loop was backup in case something went south with the joystick or the engines. She passed the line up to him and hopped aboard via the black swim step and stern gunwale gate.

He gave the joystick the lightest of nudges. *Blackbird* tugged against the line. He nudged the stick in the opposite direction, nodded to Emma, and handed her the line. She flipped it off the cleat and brought it safely aboard while Mac maneuvered the big boat away from the dock and into the fairway. With a wary eye to wind and current, he turned

Blackbird in its own length and motored slowly out of the marina.

"Where to, besides north?" Emma asked.

"James Island. We'll put down a lunch hook and give everything a going over."

"Ah, sure thing." She leaned close and murmured, "What's a lunch hook?"

"Get a wind jacket and come up to the bow. With this toy," he waved the joystick at her, "I can hang out up there and see everything on the water."

And not be overheard by any salon bugs.

"Gotcha," she said, grabbing her wind jacket.

When both of them were on the bow, Mac began talking to Emma without looking at her.

"A lunch hook is a small anchor with a short scope," he said, pointing to the smaller of the two anchors resting on the bowsprit. "In other words, short work for a short stay."

She fought against a smile. "Not asking what a short scope is. Guys get unhappy talking about duration or length or heft."

Mac shook his head and laughed. He didn't want to like Emma. He just wanted to get the job done. But she made being together easy.

Too easy.

"Did you see the look on Lovich's face when you stripped?" Mac asked.

"I was too busy watching Amanar swallow his tongue."

"You enjoyed that, didn't you?"

"Hey, I was stationed way too long in cultures that spent so much time ignoring and suppressing sex that a man couldn't breathe air within ten feet of a woman and not get hard." Emma shrugged. "If they're thinking about tits and ass, they're not thinking about the job, are they?"

"What about me?"

"You have enough wattage to do two things at once."

"Babe, I hope so," he said, blowing out a breath. She had looked way too edible in a bikini. "What does a captain have to do for a cup of coffee?"

"Let me think about all the delicious possibilities."

"Make coffee while you think."

"You like yours with sugar or salt?" she asked.

He grabbed her, kissed her hard, and growled, "Sugar on the side."

"Not touching that," she said, retreating hastily.

"That's what they all say."

She muffled a laugh. "Should I toss the galley while I make coffee?"

"Only if you're bored. We'll have plenty of time at James Island."

Mac didn't look away from the water until he heard the salon door close. Then he let out another long breath and forced his mind back to the job at hand. It was hard.

Way too hard.

Faroe, are you nucking futz? She's too much woman for this game.

Then Mac thought of Grace. That, too, was a lot of woman. And it didn't get in the way of her brains one bit. Or Faroe's.

Count backward by sevens.

Ninety-three, eighty-six, seventy-nine . . .

29

Grace Silva-Faroe leaned back on the uncomfortable motel couch. Annalise lay in her arms, drooling on her momma's dark green blouse, blissed out and blowing bubbles.

Faroe scrambled eggs in the kitchenette, sent the toast on another round trip, and watched the computer he'd set up next to the tiny stove. Information scrolled by at a speed that would have made a lot of people dizzy. Faroe just read, absorbed, and made breakfast. When there was a break in the information stream, he looked over his shoulder.

"Nice work, *amada*," he said, grinning at Grace and his relaxed daughter.

Grace just smiled and stroked Annalise's silky, wild mop of hair.

"Will she sleep long?" he asked.

"Should be out for hours," Grace said. "She spent most of yesterday and last night exploring for forbidden fruit."

"I like her priorities. Want to snuggle her some more or should I put her in the playpen?"

"Did the long-distance shot you got of the dude yesterday morning—what's his name—the guy with the cousins get any hits?"

Faroe fielded the change of subject without hesitation. "Temuri. Research ran it through St. Kilda's magic computers. Because he's playing nice, Steele sent a digital copy to Alara and the FBI as soon as we knew."

Grace's lazy stroking of Annalise's relaxed body stopped. "The FBI? What did Alara think about that?"

"No backwash that I know of. Hell, she probably did the same herself. Think of it as a bit of polite ass-covering. The FBI is still doing push-ups over that rez execution. Since St. Kilda just happened to be here on a different matter, we felt duty bound to point out to the FBI a possible connection with the new killer in town."

The judge that Grace had once been couldn't help pointing out, "We don't know he's a killer."

"I'll take Mac's word for it. That boy has the training to sort out the wannabes from the shooters."

She sighed and didn't disagree. "What did research find on Temuri, under all spelling variants?"

"His first name is Shurik—street name of Sure to his fellow thugs who happen to speak some dialect of English. He's a snake-mean son of a bitch who appears in the top fifteen of nearly all the international shit lists."

"Good thing your daughter is asleep."

Faroe smiled. "No matter how much we shelter her, her

peers will tell her all the forbidden words by the time she hits first grade."

"In several languages," Grace agreed wryly. "Anything useful on Temuri, besides his likelihood of going directly to hell?"

"He's either Georgian or Ukrainian, depending on if you're talking about his mother or his father. Like a lot of men who made fortunes in the wild economic frontier of the former Soviet Union, he comes from a long line of former KGB turned businessmen/crime bosses."

"I'm shocked," Grace said, kissing her daughter's soft cheek.

"Me, too. Daddy Temuri picked the wrong side of the Putin/Georgian wars, so son Temuri got an early start in the killing business. He's good for seven hits that we know of, and suspected of a whole lot more. Did I mention that he's as smart as he is deadly? Rich, too, with enough cash in offshore accounts that if/when Russian tanks start rolling into Georgia, he'll be positioned to disappear or become a nuclear thorn in Russia's flesh. Dealer's choice, and the guys with the nukes do the dealing."

"In other words, one more region with a grudge backed up by thugs with nukes. Sweet. How did he get his radioactive toys?"

"Probably the usual way—theft from failed Soviet-era nuclear installations and/or purchase on the international arms black market. Ditto for chemical and biological weapons. Anyone who thinks all those goodies are under lock and key is living on Planet Denial."

Grace sighed. Time to leave Denial and reenter the other world, the one beyond the warmth of her family. She gave her daughter's hair a final stroke.

Before Grace could shift to her feet, Faroe gently scooped up their daughter, put her in the portable bed/playpen, and covered her with her favorite snuggly blanket. She sighed and blew bubbles into the fuzzy, zebra-striped cloth.

"If Temuri's family had swung the Putin way," Faroe continued, "Shurik would probably be in the top tier of Russian government or industry or crime. Same thing, a lot of the time."

Grace went to the tiny dinette table. "What are two homeboys like Lovich and Amanar doing hanging out with that kind of international weight?" she asked between bites.

"Business," Faroe said, sitting next to her. "The black kind."

"Big duh moment. Is Alara still 'helping' St. Kilda with information?"

"Reams of it, from every U.S. intelligence agency, named and unnamed, plus a few that Steele hadn't heard of until now. Problem is, she isn't giving us much that we couldn't have found out on our own, even in the time we have."

Grace shrugged. "We knew she would hold back. Or have people holding back from giving her necessary intel until the last possible instant—if they give it away at all."

Faroe wished he could argue with her, but he couldn't. He'd gone to jail for a politician's photo-op. Nothing personal. Just the way things were. Until there was no other choice, politicians and bureaucrats would rather bury the dead and have live-broadcast Senate committee investigations of nothing useful than put their own assets on the line.

Public theater, the politicians' way to get around campaign spending limits. Ring the publicity bell with TV and Internet instant coverage, all in the name of public service, of course.

"I gave Lane the go-ahead to enter some closed databases," Faroe said as he loaded eggs onto his own toast. "We should know more soon."

"Sometimes I worry about what we're teaching our son."

"You mean what *I'm* teaching him."

"You, Steele, me, and now he's got a thing for Mary."

"St. Kilda's Mary? Our very own long-gun specialist?" Faroe asked.

"Aka sniper," Grace said.

"Really? Since when?"

Grace gave him a startled look. "Earth to Joe. Mary has been St. Kilda's sniper since before I—"

"No, I meant Lane. Since when?"

"Since she's been training him on the gun range."

"Huh."

"She says he's a natural shot. Steady hands, great eyes—yours, by the way. Hands, too, come to think of it."

Faroe grinned. "That's my boy."

"Has your temper, too."

"Nope. Can't take credit for that one. I'm even tempered."

Grace gave him a dark, sideways look. "Yeah. All bad, all the time."

"It's a miracle you married me."

She smiled over her coffee cup. "It's all in your hands."

"All?"

"With our daughter in the room, I only talk about your hands."

"You finished with breakfast?" Faroe asked.

"Almost. Why?"

"Got some handwork I want to show you."

Grace smiled and ate faster. In this world, she had learned to take her desserts whenever they were within reach. Life's only guarantee was that no one got out alive.

30

Mac fired up the winch and lowered the small anchor into the dark, restless water. When the sun made a swift appearance among the low, racing clouds, fir trees were reflected in rippling green lines on the surface of the water. In the background, the engine-room blower whined as it cleared heat away from the big diesels.

When he was sure the anchor would hold for as long as it had to, he turned his attention back to Emma, who had been watching closely his every move. If she had to, he'd bet that now she could do a creditable job of setting a lunch hook.

"So Stoneface—Temuri—doesn't think a lot of you?" Mac asked softly.

"Pretty much," Emma said, her voice as low as his. There were other boats nearby on the water, and sound carried way too well. "To call me female plumbing with two feet and three openings comes close."

Mac made a choked noise.

"But his accent is different from his cousins'," she continued. "Much more modern Russian, with a solid whiff of breakaway Georgian when he's angry."

"You must have a really good ear."

"That's what every language instructor I ever had said." She shrugged. "To me, it's like breathing, only easier."

"My team's language tech was like that. Spooky."

"As in CIA?"

"As in scary good," he said.

"The CIA isn't good?"

"Their political games killed every man on my forward recon team," Mac said with a deadly lack of inflection. "Took me three months to get out of the hospital." He bent over to secure the windlass chain. "The CIA are miserable shits."

"Guess that makes me a former miserable shit."

Mac went still, then straightened hard and fast. "You're Agency?"

"I was. I taught English as a second language in some really ugly places while I recruited and ran covert agents. I understand eight languages and am fluent in five. Or used to be. Hard to stay on top of your game when you're not practicing daily." She turned toward him and looked up, her expressionless face only inches from his chest. "Is that a problem for you?"

"Were you ever in Afghanistan?"

"No."

"Then there's no problem."

After she studied him for a few moments, she nodded. "Are we searching for bugs or contraband?"

"Both. If it's a voice-activated bug any idiot would have found, it goes to the bottom. Otherwise we leave it until we figure out a believable, 'accidental' way to get rid of it."

"Considering the ambient noise level of those diesels," she said, "plus the wind gusting and the water splashing and whatever that pump is that runs half the time—"

"Refrigeration unit," Mac cut in. "If it was the bilge pump, we'd be in deep water."

"What with one thing and another," she continued, "I'd be surprised if any voice-activated bugs are aboard. Or if they are, they're pretty much useless unless we're right on top of them."

"Good point. I'm so used to the background sounds, I don't notice them unless something goes wrong."

"If I was the one in charge of this op," Emma said, "I'd stick in a locator bug or three and let the chatter go."

"Contraband aboard now?"

"I'll take money on either side of that bet."

"So will I. C'mon. Let's go treasure hunting."

He led the way to the engine hatch in the middle of the salon. When he opened it, residual heat from the diesels poured out. Blower noise tripled. He latched the hatch open.

"We'll do forward quarters first," he said against her ear. "Engine room is pretty warm right now."

"Another reason not to put a voice-activated bug down there. Touchy electronics. Too hot? Too many vibrations? Paff."

"Locator bugs are a lot tougher."

"Since they often get stuck inside an engine compartment or under a vehicle chassis, they have to be."

Emma searched the obvious hiding places—clothes lockers, cabinets, drawers, under the mattress, inside the pillows, in the anchor locker—while Mac quickly, methodically searched the odd spaces only someone accustomed to boats would think of using. She watched in growing amazement while he unscrewed what looked like solid panels to reveal storage areas or wiring races in the walls and floor. Ceiling tiles shifted to reveal a small safe. Empty. Stairway treads opened to more storage beneath. There was another small safe in the floor of the head. Empty.

The galley, pilot's seat, storage lockers, chairs, cushions, second bedroom, and everything else inside were exactly what they appeared to be. Harmless.

The outside deck storage areas were equally bare of contraband. Same for the flying bridge. The inflatable boat resting on its upper-deck chocks was as innocent as a baby's smile.

The water tank and the fuel tanks were next on the list.

Emma's stomach began thinking about breakfast. Coffee and a muffin didn't get it done when she was working. Or maybe just being on the water made her appetite sit up and beg.

Or it could be that searches were almost as boring as stakeouts. It made watching trees grow look exciting.

Mac opened the fill ports up on the deck, unfolded a telescoping measuring rod, and probed the water tank.

"Can't you just check it visually down in the hold?" Emma asked.

"Tank is opaque."

"Well, that's dumb."

"Gotta love tradition. Wipe this down, would you?" he asked, handing the wet rod to her.

"How clean?"

"Just don't want it dripping water in the fuel tanks."

Emma yanked out her pullover, wrapped the hem around the rod, and began wiping. By the time she finished, he had closed the water fill port and opened one fuel port. She handed over the rod.

"If you think I'm going to wipe diesel off this, you're nuts," she said.

"Did you see where the fuel rags were?"

"In the back deck locker. But they weren't rags. They were absorbent white squares, some kind of paper. You used them in Seattle."

"You're more than just a pretty face."

She gave him a disgusted look. "If you're just figuring that out, you're a lot dumber than I thought."

Smiling, Mac probed the starboard fuel tank. The bottom was right where he expected it to be. Same for the port tank.

"No false bottom," he said. "Both tanks are the same, but I'd already guessed that from the trim. Fuel tanks are baffled, though, so it's possible that matching compartments are either equally full or equally empty."

"Trim? As in fancy bits?"

"Trim is how the boat rides in the water."

"We're still floating."

"Always a good sign," he agreed. "But if the boat is badly loaded or designed—or if one fuel tank is holding something that weighs more or less than diesel—the trim reflects that."

"Considering how heavy *Blackbird* is, you'd have to be smuggling gold to tip it one way or another."

"Or have a solid gold keel."

Her eyes widened. "Do people still do that?"

"Not so much now. Ounce for ounce, diamonds are worth a lot more."

"That's what I thought. Now what?"

"Engine room."

Her stomach growled.

"I'll check out the black-water tank and the tool room while you make something to eat. Sandwiches work for me."

"Anything edible works for me." She skirted the open engine hatch, glanced down into the dazzling white tool room, and went to the galley.

Mac went below, through the nearly empty tool room and into the engine room. The big diesels crowded the space, telling him what he already knew: some idiot had ordered more power than the boat was designed to handle efficiently. As a result, the engine room was unusually cramped. No matter how careful he was, every single time he changed position he bumped his head, elbows, or knees.

As he worked his way through the mess, he thoroughly cursed the size of the engines.

Emma stuck her head into the hatch. "Need any help?"

"I'm beating my brains out just fine all by myself, thanks."

"All I found was cheese and the hard rolls we brought aboard."

"Bring it on." He wiped sweat off his face. "I'll grill it on an engine."

"Water?"

"In a minute. Right now I'm on my knees thanking God that I don't have to change the zincs on this bastard."

"Should I ask what zincs are?"

"No."

Mac wiped his eyes with his T-shirt, and looked around the engine room. When it came time to change the zincs, frustration would be the order of the day. With those big diesels crowding the space, even something as simple as checking fill levels on various tanks required a contortionist.

The only good news was that the black-water tank had a clear stripe to let everyone know when it was getting close to time to pump out. He checked the other tanks as best he could, tapping and listening and tapping again.

The first locator bug was attached to one of the colorful wires snaking from the various subsystems to the breaker board.

The second beacon was stuck to the back side of the water tank.

A third was in a toolbox that held spare fuses.

A fourth was taped to the bottom side of the duckboards that covered the bilge.

Talk about redundant systems and overkill, Mac thought as he found a fifth locator bug. *Someone really wants to know where this bucket is at all times.*

He pulled out the cell phone that Faroe had given him, took photos of everything, and sent them to St. Kilda. Wiping his eyes again, he hoped that he'd found every bug. He really doubted it, but a man could hope.

And keep his weapon handy.

31

Ambassador Steele frowned at one of the many electronic screens that filled all but the doorways and window walls of his oddly shaped office. His silver hair gleamed in the room's full-spectrum lighting.

"Is research saying that all of these bugs came from different sources?" Steele asked.

The ruby in Dwayne's pinky ring gleamed with each movement of his elegant, dark hands over the computer keys. The digital photos Faroe had sent weren't museum quality, but they got the job done.

"Not all of them," Dwayne said. "The one we planted on *Blackbird* in Singapore came from the good old U.S. of A. The others didn't. Of course, someone could have bought any or all of the bugs at some second-world spy bazaar or first-world swap meet. Two of those trinkets are almost old enough to vote."

Steele looked at him sharply.

"Joke," Dwayne said without looking away from his computer. "The bigger they are, the older they are. One of these is downright clunky. Of course, it will still work when the newer, thinner, more finicky models go dead."

"Basically," Steele said, "anyone could have planted the bugs on *Blackbird* at any time since the engines and tanks were put in place."

"Pretty much."

Steele muttered something in Urdu.

Dwayne winced. When Steele started talking in tongues, some asses were going to get chapped.

"I'll let you tell Joe Faroe how little we have," Steele said.

One of those chapped asses would be Dwayne's. Faroe never had taken failure with grace.

32

Activate sleeper.

Only two words had been texted to Taras Demidov's cell phone. Two words that conjured a world long lost, when only two powers ruled the planet.

Or seemed to.

And nothing was ever as it seemed.

Demidov erased the text message and drove his small white Japanese car off the Horseshoe Bay ferry at Nanaimo, Vancouver Island. His wallet was thick with Canada's modestly colorful currency, his pockets clanked with one- and two-dollar coins.

Best of all, the last time he had checked the locator numbers, he was still ahead of *Blackbird*. The cautious captain apparently had done everything but dismantle the yacht to reassure himself that there was no contraband aboard.

Demidov crawled in a line of vehicles until he got onto

the bypass around Nanaimo. He drove north toward Lantz-ville, a small coastal community that had been buried under the sprawling waves of housing developments and malls surging out from Nanaimo. His destination was just beyond Lantzville, in an undeveloped area overlooking Nanoose Bay.

When he held down the accelerator, his small rental whined. Reluctantly the car increased speed. In the old days, he would have traveled under diplomatic immunity in a powerful black Mercedes. He still had the diplomatic passport—and the connections to make it stick—but he preferred using the fake Canadian identity.

It was more anonymous.

As a Canadian, his cover would probably hold for the return trip into the United States, where he would disappear back into the loose diplomatic community representing the Russian Federation. Such ease of movement was difficult for people with foreign diplomatic credentials, particularly those from nations who might be unfriendly to the U.S. Unfriendly diplomats were required to seek formal permission to travel more than twenty-five or fifty miles from their consulates or embassies.

Demidov amused himself by thinking about the multiple copies of his itinerary he wouldn't be filing.

Even if he had to blow this cover, he could slip back into the U.S. through the woods east of Blaine, Washington, and return to Seattle with its consular protection. Russian security officers paid professional marijuana smugglers for current maps of the sensors and guard posts on the American side. Despite the Homeland Security Act, illegal passage between Canada and the U.S. was easy. Only legitimate citizens had difficulty and long waits.

He switched screens on the cell phone he'd left on the passenger seat. Nothing unexpected.

His target was being slow, if predictable. After a delay in American waters, *Blackbird* had resumed its northerly course. But if the big American had found the bug that had been put aboard in Asia, he hadn't disabled it. Moscow Center was locked on *Blackbird*'s locator signal. Everything was on track.

Demidov was locked on the location of a sleeper who had been under so long he wondered if she still spoke Russian. To find her address, he followed the electronic maps on a device attached to the dashboard. It was amusing to have so much accurate, on-the-ground information about local roads at his fingertips. Even where the technology existed in Russia, his country wasn't nearly so helpful to visitors.

Some things never changed. Paranoia was one. Staying alive was another. Demidov understood the necessity of the first for the second.

The colorful little display panel on his dashboard directed him to a small, weather-beaten house in a grove of cedar and alder trees overlooking Nanoose Bay. Demidov lowered the window, turned off the ignition, and simply sat, letting the sounds of the place wash over him.

Birds.

Whisper of sea breeze edged with salt and cold.

Engine ticking.

More birds.

Silently he got out, eased the door shut, and looked

through the trees toward the saltwater. A big, gray-hulled service vessel with a large white number painted on its side slid through the chain of islands at the mouth of the bay. There were other boats on the water, smaller boats, civilians rushing around, ignoring the official naval installation that had become an accepted, if sometimes irritating, part of their daily lives.

The sweeping view on the cliff was the reason for putting a sleeper in place at this spot. The ships coming and going were mostly Canadian naval vessels, with regular visits from U.S. vessels for joint actions in Whiskey Gulf. Each ship that paid a visit to the wharves tucked into the blind end of the bay had to pass beneath the wooded bluff. The sleeper logged the movements and duly reported to her homeland.

Or she once had. The reports had stopped a few years after the government stopped sending payments to her Hong Kong account.

Demidov walked to the other vehicle that was parked beneath the trees. He touched the hood of the car. Cold.

He listened for a time and finally picked out the sound of a radio or television underneath the natural sounds. It was coming from the cabin. Swiftly, silently, he walked up the overgrown path and knocked on the door.

Footsteps approached. The door opened.

The trim, aging woman with the unlikely red hair wasn't the same as his memories, but there was no doubt of her identity. The female wearing a gray fisherman's sweater and lightweight wool pants was the same agent he had put in place a lifetime ago.

The world had changed a lot since then. But not enough

to free Galina Federova, known to her Canadian friends as Lina Fredric.

She stared at him for a long three count. Understanding—and a deep current of wariness—darkened her blue eyes.

"Galina," Demidov said. "Invite in an old friend."

She started to slam the door. Then she noticed his left hand deep in his jacket pocket, sensed as much as saw the deadly weight his fingers were wrapped around. Fear streaked through her, followed by anger.

So many years.

So many, and still not enough.

She had finally believed she was free. And now he stood in front of her, holding a weapon hidden in one pocket.

"And what do you have in your other pocket, Taras?" she asked coldly. "Money? Another weapon?"

"A different kind of shot, Galina." He smiled, deepening the lines in his face. "Vodka. Much preferred, yes?"

"My name is Lina."

"But of course. Let me in, Lina."

The dark hair she remembered was steel gray now, thinner, but the deadly grace of the man himself hadn't changed. In a physical confrontation with him, she would lose.

Without a word she turned her back on him and walked into her small house, leaving him to stay or follow as he wished.

It is always what he wishes, she thought bitterly. *So much changes, but that never changes.*

Damn Taras for the devil he is.

Demidov shut the door and followed his unhappy hostess down a short hallway into a living room with three big picture windows that faced out onto the water. The gray ship entering the harbor was in the middle of the view.

"I see the Americans are still using the torpedo test range," Demidov said.

He walked over to a telescope on a tripod that was set up by the big window. Turning his back to her, he closed one eye and looked through the eyepiece. The point of focus wasn't the channel where big ships came and went, but a small island perhaps a mile offshore where fir trees clung to rocky outcrops. The biggest fir's storm-twisted crown held the immense weight of an old eagle nest.

Nobody home.

Gone fishing.

Demidov's mouth curved in amusement and envy. Once he had loved to fish Kamchatka's wild lands. Once, a lifetime ago. He could hardly remember that boy now, only his young enthusiasms and savage ambition.

"The ships come and they go," Lina said. "Destroyers and submarines and patrol boats from the Canadian forces, as well as games with American ships. I quit paying attention after the deposits stopped coming to my account at Bank of Hong Kong." Her hand made a dismissing movement. "There are other ways to survive than spying. I found one that worked for me."

Demidov adjusted the focus on the telescope. Though decades old, the instrument was still good. Fallen feathers and unwanted boney bits leaped into focus, debris of a predator.

"So you resigned in place," Demidov said.

Silence answered.

He glanced at the woman who stood, arms folded across her chest, staring out at the water.

"Don't you think it would have been wise to turn in your equipment?" he asked, his voice mild. "This house is in your name but it still belongs, technically, to the Russian people. Just as it did when your predecessor lived here."

Lina's smile was a grim curve. "I took my share of the state's assets, just like everybody with any sense. Why do you care? You're too smart to be working for a fallen regime. Everyone who originally hired us has long since turned to civilian pursuits. Much more profitable, if equally violent."

Demidov watched her smallest movement. They had been lovers once, a lifetime ago, when the world was different and people were the same. Maybe she had better memories than he did of those times. She had always been more of a romantic than he was or ever would be.

Like the generations of eagles that had built the huge nest, he survived. And like the eagles, when he became too old for the hunt, he would die.

Soon. A handful of years, maybe more. Maybe less.

In the end, luck rules.

His great-grandfather had lived to be one hundred and four, but he had been a peasant, a grass-eater. His great-grandson was a predator.

"I take my satisfaction from doing my job well, not from my paycheck," Demidov said.

She shrugged. The movement was tight, impatient, almost a flinch. "So you stayed with the spiders in the KGB web, waiting for your blood meals to come trembling to you."

He laughed softly. "Still the romantic. What have you

done to occupy your clever mind since the fall of our great and noble Soviet Union, followed by the rise of capitalist Russia?"

"Old history. All of it. I'm no longer a part of that."

"I'm disappointed, Lina. I trained you so . . . thoroughly."

She gave him a sideways look that hadn't changed through all the years.

"You taught me to be a wise little spider, alert for the tiny vibrations at the edge of my web," she said. "That kind of teaching doesn't fade. Nor does the teacher. You know what I've been doing as well as anyone does."

"From spy to licensed fishing guide," Demidov said. "Quite a good one, I hear. I'm impressed."

"Stop pretending to be an old friend. What do you want?"

"You have a fast boat. When it doesn't carry summer fishermen, it carries other cargo. B.C. Bud, yes? Marijuana. Illegal in your adopted country as well as in the country you smuggle it into."

Lina closed her eyes. It had been many years since she had smuggled British Columbia's premier cash crop, but time didn't matter. Demidov knew enough about her to crush the small, fragile world she had built for herself from the wreckage of empire.

And he would do just that if she didn't obey him.

Fear left her along with choice. She would do whatever he wanted. All that remained was waiting for orders.

"I was raised on the water," she said. "That's why I was given this assignment. As for the rest, a woman alone does what she must to survive. The training passed on to us from

Lubyanka Street was rather useful in my new life, at first. Today, my boat isn't a racehorse. I chase salmon, not outrun police."

Demidov reached into the pocket of his jacket and pulled out the bottle of Grey Goose that he had purchased in the duty-free shop on his ride north. He held the bottle by its neck with his thumb and forefinger. In his other fingers he held a fan of photos. They showed a modified trawler-style boat with a black hull.

"If you would just produce two glasses, my old love," Demidov said, "we will toast one another as we used to do. So much more civilized. Then I will tell you why I request your help."

Lina stared at him for a long time, seeing the young wolf beneath the older, harder exterior. If anything, he was more dangerous than he had been so many years ago.

"You're very good," she said. "I almost believe my cooperation is a voluntary matter. Almost."

Demidov waited, one hand holding out the vodka and photos, the other in his pocket holding a knife.

"Two glasses," she agreed. "I prefer vodka to blood."

33

Timothy Harrow hadn't personally met the FBI agent in front of him until two minutes ago. That didn't keep the man from chewing out Harrow's ass.

"—bad enough, don't you think?" the agent demanded.

Harrow didn't have a chance to answer, because the agent kept on speaking with hard, clipped words.

"No, you had to go and keep Temuri's presence on U.S. soil from us, when you bloody well knew we've been chasing him for seven years!"

Harrow told himself that he wouldn't show his impatience by fiddling with his pen, his notebook, or anything else on his desk.

The ranting FBI agent was wearing a sports jacket, open-necked shirt, jeans, loafers, and an expression of acute irritation. He looked like he'd been hauled in from the relaxed West Coast through a wormhole and then plugged into a live electrical socket.

Harrow felt the same way, but hid it better. Old School versus New Wave.

"We've been chasing Temuri ever since we busted a shipment of vials headed for Afghanistan," Harrow said evenly.

"Vials? Biological stuff? Not nukes or chemicals?"

"He's an equal opportunity vendor," Harrow said. "You need it, Temuri will deliver it. For a price."

"What he is or isn't selling overseas is no excuse for not telling the FBI that Temuri was in the U.S. where he could be detained and questioned!"

Harrow looked at the younger man. Still eager. Still a believer. Every agency and bureau needed them, but Harrow just didn't have time or patience for the dance right now.

The interoffice phone buzzed, reminding Harrow of his next appointment—a senator fishing for a headline to shove up the present administration's ass. Harrow's boss hadn't decided whether to play or pass, so effusive stalling was in order. Harrow could do that half-asleep. In fact, he often did.

After the interview he was packing for a fast trip to western British Columbia, Canada. At least, he hoped it would be fast.

Slow would mean the end of careers and lives.

"Your department will have a formal apology as soon as I find the proper security clearance for it," Harrow said.

"That's not—"

"The op," Harrow cut in, "has moved out of the U.S, as your boss already knows. It has been turned over to us. If we discover anything we can share, you'll be right behind Congress on our show-and-tell list."

In other words, you've been cut out of the game.

The agent got the message. It was one he had passed out a lot on his own turf. That didn't mean he liked getting it.

Vibrating with anger, he stalked out of the office.

When the senior senator from Minnesota walked into Harrow's office, passing by a tight-lipped FBI agent, Harrow was mentally plotting various approaches to former CIA officer Emma Cross.

It would help if he knew what the soured op had been about, but all Duke had told him was to be prepared to fly out on a moment's notice.

Harrow rose to his feet, smiled, and greeted the senator.

34

Emma sat in a swivel armchair on the flying bridge next to Mac. She watched the radar sweeping over the electronic chart on the computer's wide screen. Nothing—land, boat, or seaplane—was close enough to worry about, yet Mac's dark eyes kept probing the blue water ahead.

"What are you looking for?" she asked.

"Floating debris, logs, deadheads, clumps of seaweed, anything that can put a dent in my day."

She frowned and looked out at the water. "Is there a lot of that going around?"

"It's worse in spring, when the melt comes and scours the riverbanks and vomits out dead forests to clutter up the sound. But we've been having big tides, the ones that lift centuries-old logs off beaches and send them out in the currents to play with anything else that floats."

She glanced at the various boats within sight. "I can see

why the ferry and the big freighter aren't worried about a few random chunks of wood, but why are all those pleasure craft racing around? And I do mean racing."

"Some of the captains are playing the odds. Most are watching as carefully as I am. Even then," he shrugged, "shit happens. That's why pleasure boats don't run at night out here, unless they have a steel hull and skegs protecting their props. Pod drives like ours just have to take their chances."

"No protection?"

"We have skegs, but no guarantees. Like commuting on a freeway—sooner or later there will be a wreck. You just hope it's not yours, because you have to keep on driving to make a living."

"The waterhole theory of life at work," Emma said.

He looked at her in silent question.

"Think of grazers approaching a waterhole at the end of the day," she said. "They know lions are lying in wait, but there's no choice. Water is just behind oxygen in our drive for life. So the grazers sweat and snort and shy and sidle closer to the water, knowing an individual blood sacrifice must be paid so that the rest of the herd can drink. Can survive."

Mac smiled like a hungry lion. "And everybody's hoping it isn't his turn to die."

"Yeah." She frowned and rubbed her hands over her arms. "I just wish I didn't feel like *Blackbird* is a floating sacrifice for the good of the human herd."

He didn't argue with her, which didn't make her feel better.

"So, we won't be running at night?" Emma asked.

"Not unless we have to. Take the controls. Let's see how much you learned. And be grateful you already knew how to plot a course on paper."

"Basic training," she said. "Like riding a bike. Never goes away."

Unfortunately, knowing how to plot paper courses and run the boat's computer and understanding the theory of throttle movements wasn't the same as actually driving all those tons of yacht on a fluid, shifting, unmarked road.

"Pod drive?" she asked hopefully. She'd played more than her share of video games.

"Too easy. Better you learn the hard way so you can appreciate the easy way."

She grimaced. "You sure? Theory is one thing. . . ."

"You'd rather practice with me dead on the deck and bullets screaming around?"

"God, Mac. You should write a book on sweet talk."

"Tell me that tomorrow morning."

She looked at his dark, dark eyes and felt like she was soaring off a cliff, flying high, no land in sight.

She liked it.

He said something under his breath, gestured to the controls, and slid out of the wheel seat.

Steering the boat suddenly seemed safer than looking in Mac's eyes. Emma took the controls and concentrated on something besides the unnerving pulse of heat in her blood.

He watched silently, letting her learn firsthand the difference between driving a car and a boat. Once she caught on to correcting for tide and currents, he told her to plot a point ahead and lock it into the autopilot. She touched the screen quickly, answered the computer's prompts, and let go of the wheel.

Blackbird sailed on, correcting its course via satellite, uncaring whether it was under human or electronic control.

"You're a quick study," Mac said.

"I've had to be." She smiled suddenly. "Besides, I like challenges."

Mac wished he could take this challenging woman down to the master suite and see what each could teach and learn.

Bad time.

Right woman.

"We'll be crossing over the international line in an hour," Mac said, looking at the computer.

"What's our border protocol?"

"In the old days, we'd call Canadian customs, give them our stats, and hope the waterhole theory holds."

"Meaning?" she asked.

"Meaning they would log *Blackbird* into their computers, give us an entry number to stick in the window by the pilot seat downstairs, and we would sail on without a pause."

"Old days, huh? Would that be pre-9/11?"

"Pretty much."

"And today?" she asked.

"The lion always pounces."

"Meaning?"

"Technically we probably should go through the closest customs," he said. "But what we're going to do is take the protected run through the Gulf Islands to Nanaimo, and get inspected there. For going to Campbell River, it's quicker."

It definitely was a smoother ride. Until he knew more about how Emma's stomach took rough water, he'd stick to the easy route.

"How detailed is the inspection?" she asked.

"Depends on how nice the U.S. is feeling toward Canada, and vice versa. If we've been giving Canadian yachties a special look-see at our border, we get the same in return. Or if the Canadians are miffed about a U.S. import tax on their lumber, they squeeze tourists. Same for our side. There can be any number of reasons for dicking with border crossings that have zero to do with anyone's security—except the politicians'."

"How unsurprising," she said.

"Yeah. Humans."

In silence Mac watched Emma handling the boat, altering course on instruction, entering waypoints into the plotter, checking tides in Nanaimo at various possible arrival times, watching gauges for problems, and doing all the other things that added up to driving a boat.

In return, Mac watched the radar screen that overlaid the charts, his eyes alert for anything that followed their course, random alterations included.

"And?" she asked after he had studied the radar a particularly long time.

"Nothing that makes my neck tingle."

She watched *Blackbird* cut through blue water to the imaginary but very real international line in the water. When their radar showed the boat entering Canadian territory, Emma looked at Mac.

"How long does inspection take?" she asked.

"Normally it's just a courtesy," Mac said. "You show passports, get a number, put the number on both sides of the front cabin, throw out whatever fruits are in season, and you're good to go. Fifteen minutes on a busy day."

"Friendly, in a word."

"Anything to grease the flow of commerce and tourism—as long as someone isn't suffering from short dick syndrome."

She nodded. "Okay. I'll go back to learning to drive."

To get a feel for manually steering the boat under different water conditions, Emma took off the automatic navigation and guided *Blackbird* through the choppy waters that marked the fluid boundary between sovereign nations. The motion of the boat changed and the speed dropped.

Tidal line, she thought, remembering Mac's explanations. *Or currents. Maybe both together.*

Gently she nudged the throttles up until they were making about nineteen knots again.

Mac watched for a few moments, then said, "Push it to the max. Let's find out what these big engines are really made of."

And how Emma's stomach was.

35

Ambassador Steele rolled his chair from one workstation to another, talking through his headset the whole time. He stopped rolling long enough for his fingers to fly over a computer keyboard. One of the wall screens blinked and showed a close-up of a dirty village whose open sewers festered among glorious mountain peaks.

Dwayne glanced over. The name on the bottom of the screen was Ecuador. But for that, the village could have been in any mountainous country where poverty and villages prevailed.

"The op is compromised," Steele said. "Evac is on the way to primary location. You have less than ninety minutes to extraction." He paused. "Good. And if you see that lying toad on the way out, step on him."

Dwayne winced. Steele was at his most lethal when his

voice was neutral. A click told Dwayne that his boss had disconnected.

"Did we get the kidnap victim out in one piece?" Dwayne asked.

"I'll tell you in ninety-one minutes."

Dwayne pursed lips that more than one woman had openly lusted after. He blew out a long breath that was also a curse. "So the government was in on it after all?"

"Crotch-deep and still sinking." Steele sped toward another station, another screen. "That's why factions are useful, though slippery. It's the ones that aren't getting a cut of the ransom money that get chatty."

"And then they go to another faction and sell the same information." *Sell us out.*

Steele shrugged. "If we can buy someone, we can be assured that someone else can and will. Just a matter of who gets to the finish line alive. Has Alara returned my call?"

"Twice." Dwayne glanced at a bank of lights on his desk. Number Four was still blinking. "Transferring line four to your headset."

Before Dwayne had finished speaking, Steele was.

"Alara. Thank you for getting back so quickly. What have you discovered?"

The voice on the other end of the line was as clear and precise as Steele's. "Somebody in the FBI stuck a screw-you flag on *Blackbird*'s name in the Canadian customs' computer system."

"Any reason, other than the usual?"

"An inter-agency pissing contest."

"That would be the usual," Steele said.

"The FBI was quite unhappy that they weren't made aware of Temuri's presence within U.S. jurisdiction."

"According to Joe Faroe, Temuri left Rosario shortly after *Blackbird* did."

"The FBI was notified as soon as Temuri's car turned onto Interstate 5, heading north or south," Alara said blandly. "Our informant couldn't be certain of the direction. In fact, he wasn't certain that it was Temuri's car until we traced the plates back to a rental agency. As soon as we were certain, one of my co-workers shared the information with the FBI."

"Pity it was too late to catch him," Steele said, his voice deadly neutral. "Any sign of other computer tags on *Blackbird* or its crew?"

"None."

"Any new information?"

"I've sent many files to your computer," Alara said.

"My dear, if I were a farmer, I would be ecstatic at the amount of fertilizer you've given to me."

Alara beat Steele to the disconnect button.

36

After being at full throttle, or even at sixteen knots, four to six knots was a yawning crawl. Emma felt like giving back the controls to Mac, who had let her take over as soon as they were through Dodd Narrows.

She wouldn't have touched the controls in the narrows. The current had been running at six knots and the slot looked like a churning, foaming invitation to disaster.

Mac had brought *Blackbird* through without hesitation.

"Are they serious?" Emma asked, looking at the "speed limit" sign floating at the beginning of Nanaimo Harbor.

"Very," Mac said. "Enjoy the slow-motion scenery."

She shook her head, but didn't argue, just kept easing off the throttles. After some time at *Blackbird*'s controls, she was more relaxed, if no less alert to the hazards on the water.

She spared the scenery a few admiring glances. Nanaimo was a surprising gem set about halfway up to Campbell River on the east side of Vancouver Island, right in the middle of boating paradise—green and blue and white, rocky islets, whipped-cream clouds, and picturesque shore-line. The water was alive with workboats and cruisers, water taxis and the single- and twin-engine seaplanes of three different airlines. Not enough commerce to totally destroy the ambience, yet enough to sustain a small city.

Except . . .

"That smell," she said.

"Pulp mill," Mac answered. "Used to be the perfume of the Pacific Northwest, the engine of growth. Now, so few lumber operations are active that the smell is almost nostalgic."

"Nostalgic." She cleared her throat. "That's one word for it. I suppose you get nostalgic over the odor of fish canneries."

"Me? No. But a lot of old men who used to provide a good living for their children and grandchildren sure would."

"The world still eats boatloads of fish."

"Processed by factory ships on the high seas, ships fed by trawlers clear-cutting the ocean bottom far away from shore," Mac said. "Out of sight, out of mind, the way clear-cutting forests used to be."

As he spoke, he kept a wary eye on a nearby sailboat struggling with the Pacific Northwest's famously fickle winds. But he couldn't decide if it was the on-and-off wind or the captain's inexperience that was causing the bigger problem.

Then there were the young kayakers larking about in chunky, wide-bottomed plastic craft, ignoring shouted directions from the leader of their colorful little flock.

Not to mention the aluminum workboat that thought

speed limits were for tourists. It was leaving a wake steep enough to capsize a careless or inexperienced kayaker.

Emma had also noticed the sudden complications of her life as newbie captain. Trying to figure out where the sailboat, kayakers, and speeding workboat would/might intersect with *Blackbird* gave her a headache.

"I just surpassed my pay grade," she said. "The wheel is yours."

"Sure?"

"Positive. It's not an emergency, so I'm outta here."

She switched places with Mac.

After a few moments she got twitchy. To everyone else, she and Mac looked like a couple on an autumn vacation, but they weren't on vacation. The gap between appearance and reality kept smacking her in the face. She just wasn't used to the double game. Or triple. Maybe more.

"When I was in training," she said, "we spent hundreds of hours preparing for border crossings. Potentially, they're always the most dangerous part of any operation."

"You aren't crossing from Casablanca to Lisbon, sweetheart," he said, doing a reasonable impression of Humphrey Bogart.

She smiled in spite of her restlessness. "You're saying the natives really are friendly? Even after Steele's heads-up call?"

"Oh, we'll probably get tossed, thanks to the FBI ass clown who put a flag in the Canadian customs' computer." Mac's dark eyes checked gauges. "But I doubt if it will be a rubber-hose experience. America as a nation may be genially despised, but our money is always welcome."

"If the government isn't the problem, why did Lovich and Amanar send you on *Blackbird*? Why didn't they just take the boat themselves?"

"Same question Faroe asked. And I asked," Mac said.

"And the answer is?"

He shrugged and adjusted the throttles so that the sailboat and the most foolish kayakers could get tangled up without him. The workboat was little more than a frothing, receding wake, throwing small craft around like wood chips. Somehow the kayakers had managed to stay human side up.

"I think Blue Water wanted to establish an unremarkable profile for *Blackbird* in Canada," Mac said.

"New owner and new girlfriend taking new boat for a cruise?"

"Pretty much. Nothing special. Nothing different. Nothing unexpected. Absolutely nothing to notice."

"Amanar didn't expect the FBI to say that we're smuggling in enough champagne for a party of two hundred," Emma said, thinking about Steele's call. "If we don't get through Canadian customs . . ." She hesitated. "I can't figure out if that's good or bad. It's certainly a game changer."

Mac eased through the kayakers without upsetting anyone. The sailboat had lowered yards of flapping cloth and gone back to good old diesel power.

"But since we don't know what the game is," he said, "we don't know if this is opportunity knocking or an IED ticking by the roadside."

She winced. "I don't suppose Alara gave any hints to Steele. Beyond the champagne charade."

"You don't suppose correctly."

She started to say something, then looked at him. "Was that grammatically possible?"

"Did you understand me?"

"Yes. Frightening, but true."

"Then it was possible."

Laughing, enjoying his quick mind, Emma put her head against Mac's shoulder. And bit him.

He gave her a look that went from startled to smoky in one second flat.

"Shouldn't we go through the border protocol again?" she asked as though nothing had happened.

"There are a lot of things I'd like to do. Doubt that they're in the protocol manual."

"You'd be surprised. The manual is very . . . thorough."

"Some day you're going to read it to me," he said. "Thoroughly."

Emma thought of all the dreary paragraphs and subparagraphs. "You'd fall asleep."

"Try me."

She wanted to. Really wanted to.

"Border protocol," she said.

"Nothing we haven't covered. You help me dock—"

"That's a whole different thing we haven't talked much about."

"—then get back aboard immediately," Mac said, ignoring her interruption. "I take our passports and *Blackbird*'s papers to the official on duty. He runs them through the computer, asks a few questions, and decides to search the boat or not. Either way, you don't set foot on the dock again until the official tells you to, or I have an entry number, or we're told to take our ugly American selves back south."

She nodded.

"Are you worried that we won't get the magic number?" he asked.

"I'd be surprised if we got turned back," Emma said. "The FBI isn't stupid. They'll get in the CIA's knickers just to remind everyone to play nice, but they won't intentionally blow an op."

"Unintentionally?"

"It happens. Too many agencies. Too many secrets. Too little real cooperation, because budgets depend on delivering departmental success stories. Partial gold stars for taking part in joint operations doesn't get you as many points as getting a job done within your own department."

"Sounds like branches of the military fighting over whose elite ops get used in a high-profile rescue," Mac said, disgust clear in his voice. "None of the brass cares about the poor sucks caught behind enemy lines, just who gets the glory for saving the day."

"The really good news is that our enemies are the same."

"Yeah?"

"Oh, yeah. Petty, jealous, kiss-up, shit-down humans."

"Huh," he said. "Never looked at it that way."

"Feel better?"

"I don't know."

She smiled rather grimly.

"Makes the amount of cooperation between Canadian and American border guards all the more impressive," Mac said. "And I don't mean the tit for tat of international politics. I mean that the Canadians and the U.S. exchange information on boats crossing the border. The entry number you get from Canada is logged in right next to your return number when you check back into the States."

"I'm guessing that's post-9/11," she said.

He nodded. "Even with 'heightened security,' most of the yacht traffic between countries doesn't get more of a look-over than a car full of tourists at the land border crossings."

"Probably because the terrorists everyone is worried about don't use expensive yachts for transport. Neither do smugglers. If you're caught with contraband, it's not worth the price of losing a multimillion-dollar yacht. Not cost effective."

"But yutzes with small, fast boats and smaller brains . . . real cost effective," Mac said.

"Cannon fodder."

"What would a barbecue be without hot dogs?" Mac asked bitterly.

Emma remembered the reservation and wished she'd kept her smart mouth shut.

37

Demidov looked at the lower set of latitude and longitude numbers on his cell phone, the ones that were direct from the locator aboard *Blackbird*. Reassured, he turned back to the charts of the water between Vancouver Island and the mainland of Canada. He had the charts spread over Lina's small living room floor. Every time the breeze shifted the window curtains, the big charts fluttered.

"I'm surprised this isn't all on a computer," he said.

In the daylight pouring through the front windows, Lina's red hair was younger than her skin. She tossed stray locks behind her shoulder with the practiced moves of the flirt she'd once been. But her blue eyes didn't tease. Their color was a bit faded and a whole lot harder than it had been back when she was an untried agent assigned to Taras Demidov.

"I have a chart plotter and sonar on my boat," she said. "It's all I need for fishing."

Demidov didn't bother saying that it wasn't enough for him. He checked the numbers again, then nodded abruptly.

"What?" she asked.

He glanced at her, then back to the charts.

Blackbird wouldn't be sailing up the Inside Passage right away. The yacht had gone into Nanaimo harbor, to check in with Canadian customs. Even if it was the usual cursory inspection, there would be time for him to set up the interception. After that . . .

After that, it depended on *Blackbird*'s captain.

"Taras?" she asked. "Is something wrong?"

"Something is always wrong. It's just a matter of finding out what and where and when," Demidov said. "Your boat. Is it ready to use?"

"Always. That's how I make my living."

"Come, you will show me about this living."

"Now?"

"Now."

38

Mac let the boat idle for a moment, feeling what the tidal currents and the wind were doing to *Blackbird*. The brisk northwest wind was strong enough that even the yacht felt its push and pull. The customs dock and its claustrophobic modular shed waited for them. It didn't look like there was anyone in the small office yet, but someone was strolling down the long ramp that went up and away from the water to much larger headquarters.

Mac tapped the battery-operated headset he wore. The microphone was the size of a bumblebee hovering just beyond reach of his lips. Low tech compared to what he'd used in war zones, but it got the job done.

Ate nine-volt batteries, though.

"Ready?" he asked.

"No, but I'm awaiting detailed instructions."

Though they couldn't see each other, the headphones

they wore made it seem like they were standing side by side.

"You have your PFD cinched tight?" he asked.

Emma fingered the straps of the flat life vest she wore. It wouldn't inflate unless she hit the water, which she really didn't want to do.

"I'm good," she said. "The lines are all coiled and ready to go."

"This landing is going to be different," Mac said. "Bowline first, then stern, then forward spring line. Don't worry about pretty or efficient. Just get it done. Step off onto the dock when I bring her alongside. Ready?"

Frowning, she thought through the steps.

"Unless you want to take the controls?" he invited.

"Pod drive?"

She'd learned to like it in the few minutes he'd let her play with it before they got into real traffic near the harbor. Then he'd made her switch to old-fashioned throttles for control. The pod drive was sexy and easy, but it wasn't something he really trusted.

"Nope," Mac said.

"Then it's all yours," she said.

After a few moments he heard her counting, "Three, two, one—I'm on the dock."

He saw the flash of colorful shirt and long legs as Emma took the bowline and brought it partway back on the dock before she went to tie off. Using a wooden bull nose to tie off on rather than a big metal cleat threw off her rhythm, but she secured the line with the double half-hitch knot Mac had taught her.

"I like cleats better," she said, tugging hard on the line.

"So do I. Easier on the lines. But when in Canada . . ."

"Do as the Canadians," she finished.

Despite the headset that kept wanting to fall into the water every time she leaned over, she got the bow tied off.

"Secure, Captain," she said.

Wind gusted across the dock, catching Emma by surprise.

"Yikes," she said. "The wind is trying to shove me off the dock. You, too. The boat's butt—stern—is too far away for me to reach that line."

"It won't be."

The bow came up against the line that was already tied off to the dock. Gently Mac applied the throttle. Despite the wind and tide, the stern swung majestically back in line with the dock. He didn't even bother to use special thrusters. He wanted to know how *Blackbird* would act if some of the fancy electronics cut out.

As Emma watched the big boat snuggle against the dock, she had a gut understanding of the multiple forces at work, and the elegance of Mac's skill. He could have used the pod drives so that he could hold the boat against the dock and handle the lines himself.

But he loved the feel of the currents and wind, weight and momentum, the sound of line creaking as it took *Blackbird*'s weight and brought the stern back to kiss the dock.

"Beautiful," she said.

His grin was a flash of white against his dark skin. "Don't forget the stern line."

"Oops." She sprinted to the stern, grabbed the line, and tied it off without losing her headset.

Mac walked back to the stern and looked over the rail. "Good work."

"I just had a gut insight that *Blackbird* always lives at the intersection of two huge forces, water and atmosphere, and we hope to control it all with a third force called the engine. Plus momentum, did I mention that?"

He gave her an unnecessary hand getting aboard.

"Kind of like us," she said, "sliding around between forces we can't really control, only staying afloat for as long as we can. And docking, coming to stasis with all those forces? Whole other thing entirely."

He looked at her, traced her mouth with his thumb, and said, "Stay aboard until you're told otherwise."

She nodded.

He switched off his headphones, handed them to her, and stepped onto the dock carrying various papers in his big hand. There was a short ramp up to a modular building that had suffered a severe outbreak of official signage. In its earnest desire not to favor the English language over French—which was spoken by a minority of citizens in the eastern provinces—Canada had doubled the paperwork of the government bureaucracy.

Mac wondered if Canada would make the same accommodation for the big, and rapidly growing much bigger, population of Chinese in the western provinces. Somehow he doubted it. Forced parity seemed reserved for those of European descent living along the Atlantic Coast.

The dark-skinned customs clerk walked past Mac and unlocked the door to the cramped modular. He stood behind the counter, looked at Mac with the dispassionate eyes of a loan officer or a hit man, and spoke English oddly mixed with a Bombay lilt and British precision.

"Papers, please."

Mac presented his passport and Emma's, along with the newly issued U.S. Coast Guard documentation for *Blackbird*.

The clerk, whose nameplate said he was Singh, Edward, left the counter and went to a computer, whose screen was angled away from the counter. Singh's fingers raced over the keyboard. He yanked the mouse across the desk like he was drilling down through a multilevel secured website.

Singh read, then reread the screen message, then deliberately killed it and came back to the counter.

"Where is this boat, exactly?" he asked.

"Right outside, sir, tied to the dock."

"Superintendent!"

Singh gathered up the documents like he was afraid Mac would snatch them back. The clerk marched stiffly toward an office beyond the end of the counter.

A balding Caucasian male in a uniform shirt with epaulettes and extra patches appeared in the doorway of the office that had seemed empty from the dock. Singh briefed his boss in hushed tones. As he spoke, both men glanced over at Mac from time to time.

Mac kept his game face on and cursed the flag that the FBI had tucked into the border-watch computers.

After a moment, the boss issued a clipped set of orders and turned away. Singh walked back smartly, grabbed a uniform hat from beneath the counter, and came through the swinging gate.

"Your boat must be inspected," he told Mac without meeting his eyes. "Come with me now."

Like Mac had a choice. "Sure."

As he followed the small bureaucrat, Mac cursed the FBI's middle-finger salute. Wasted time.

They didn't have it to waste.

Deliberately Mac didn't do the math in his head, the countdown to disaster that beat in his brain and blood and heart. He did the only thing he could do at the moment, which was to follow a Canadian border bureaucrat down the short ramp to *Blackbird*.

Emma was standing in the cockpit, talking on Mac's phone. She took one look and ended the call with a terse, "Later, babe."

"You are the passenger?" the inspector demanded. He consulted the two passports in his hand. "Emma Cross?"

Emma nodded. "Yes, is—"

"Come with me," he interrupted, leading the way off *Blackbird* and down the dock. When Mac started to follow, the inspector stopped him with one hand. "I wish to speak with her alone."

She looked at Mac, shrugged, and stepped onto the dock to follow the inspector. As she walked, she quickly organized her thoughts for a more formal interrogation than they had been expecting. Agency training had focused on border crossings and customs inspections because those were the areas that most often tripped up agents and handlers. St. Kilda had already composed a backstory of her relationship with Mac that told the truth whenever possible.

Emma approved of that. The truth was much easier to remember than an intricate web of lies.

"Miss, uh, Cross," the inspector began, checking her face against the photo in her passport. "Where do you live?"

"Seattle, Washington," she said.

Though she had an address memorized and documented, thanks to St. Kilda, she didn't offer any more information because Singh hadn't asked for it.

Truth and lies, separation and balance.

Survival.

"Where are you going in Canada?" he asked quickly, watching her eyes and body language for signs she might be lying.

"I don't know. It was one of those spontaneous things. We're just heading north up the Inside Passage for as long as it works for us."

"What is your relationship to"—he checked the other passport in his hand—"Mr. Durand?"

Emma wanted to make a smart remark about Adam and Eve, but she knew better. "He's the captain. I'm training to be a first mate."

"How long have you known Mr. Durand?"

She smiled like a woman remembering a satisfying, steamy night. "Not long. We met at a fuel dock in Seattle, liked what we saw, and decided to hook up as long as it lasted."

The inspector's eyes changed. He gave her an up-and-down look that suggested he might enjoy hooking up with her. Then he blinked and his training kicked in.

"Are you bringing any alcohol or firearms with you?" he asked.

She frowned. "I haven't seen any, but you'll have to ask Mac. He's the owner. I'm just along for the ride."

"I saw you handling the lines when you arrived at the dock. You seemed too competent for a recent 'hook up.'"

"Mac is a good teacher," she said with a slow smile. "He doesn't yell or anything. I'd never even been on a boat this size, but he makes everything easy. All I have to do is listen and follow instructions."

Again, the truth . . . as far as it went.

"Wait here," Singh ordered, handing her passport over.

He marched down the dock to confront Mac and, undoubtedly, ask the same questions all over again.

Emma examined her manicure, which was being rapidly deconstructed by handling lines. She didn't worry about what was happening at the other end of the dock. Mac was a solid partner. In an odd way, they were closer than if they were simply vacation lovers. They clicked under pressure, anticipating one another's moves like cops in a squad car.

She shoved her passport into one hip pocket and pulled her cell phone out of the other. She dialed into the St. Kilda secure network. Faroe answered on the first ring.

"How's it going?" he asked.

"Hey, girlfriend. I told you not to worry. Mac's one of the good guys. Even if we have to stand on the dock for a few hours while they look for whatever we shouldn't have on board."

"Girlfriend?" Faroe made a sound that could have been a laugh. "So the customs dude is still hassling you?"

"You know Canada's motto: Good government and plenty of it."

"Given that one of you is supposed to be a rich yachtie, you probably won't get a body cavity search."

"Aw, that's so sweet," she said, making sure she was loud enough to be heard at the other end of the dock.

"Obviously you've never had one," Faroe retorted.

"Wanna compare notes?"

"No," he said. "We found out from back-channel sources, not Alara's, that, among other no-nos, Temuri is an active member of the suitcase nuke trade. Especially in the last three years."

"Gee, where have I heard that before?"

"And you didn't want to go back to hearing about portable nukes. That's why you quit the Agency."

"April Fool on me," she said, watching Mac and the inspector from the corner of her eye.

Neither one looked upset.

"The same source that mentioned suitcase nukes floated the idea that you'd never really left Uncle Sam."

Emma got the point very quickly. Someone was trying to separate her from St. Kilda, in trust if not in fact.

"You have to stop believing the Internet gossip sites," she said. "Pretty soon you'll believe that Elvis was Michael Jackson's son."

There was a beat of silence, then swallowed laughter. "Um, I think you have that the wrong way around."

"Actually, I think the sites do."

"I know they do. St. Kilda backs their people, Emma. All the way to the wall."

"And if you find out you're wrong?" she asked cheerfully, smiling at Mac.

"We bury our mistakes under that wall."

"I hear you, girlfriend. Sounds good to me."

Mac and the inspector went aboard *Blackbird*.

Emma stopped calling her boss girlfriend. Turning so that no microphone or lip-reader could gather information, she spoke quickly.

"If the Agency thought there was a radioactive threat moving through Canada to the U.S.," she said, "they'd add as many layers of deniability as they could, and then they'd flat clean house, no matter which side of which border."

"That kind of robust foreign policy is out of favor right now."

"Only in public."

"Alara mentioned something about that," Faroe said drily. "She's outmaneuvered the FBI for now, but they really want Temuri. Alara is more polite—"

Emma snorted.

"—but she'd like Temuri's ass on a spear. Steele said Temuri's ass didn't interest him, but if St. Kilda's operatives got hurt by any of Uncle Sam's players, he'd air some political underwear that would make Watergate look like a potluck at a small-town Lutheran church."

"Okay, I'm impressed. St. Kilda's version of nuclear détente. Mutual annihilation."

"You're quick. So is Alara. She's no longer kicking our butt every half hour. And she's sending less bullshit files. The Cover Your Ass part of the program is over."

"So the bloodletting begins," Emma said under her breath.

"Pretty much. Our job is to make sure it's the bad guys who bleed."

"Which ones?"

"If they get in our way, they bleed."

39

The windows of Steele's office were guaranteed bullet-proof, eavesdropping proof, and weatherproof. He liked staring through the oddly tinted glass at the hive below. The surge and stall of traffic, the amoebic warfare between pedestrians and Yellow Cabs, the frustration of sirens wailing and wailing and not moving at all—the whole metropolitan mess amused and bemused him. So much change since humans first painted cave ceilings in reverence and hope.

Change, yes.

But progress?

Steele doubted it. Just as he doubted the phantom, piercing pain from his nerveless legs would evolve into something useful, such as a precursor to true feeling.

It had been a long time since he'd walked, even in his dreams.

"The woman formerly known as Alara is waiting outside your office," Dwayne said, his voice rich with irony. "You're forty-seven seconds late for her appointment. And counting. Should I let her in, or should I leave you wallowing in your whither-humanity moment?"

Steele smiled and looked toward the man who knew him better than his starry-eyed, change-the-world parents ever had. "Wallowing is one of the few human activities that doesn't require legs."

Dwayne frowned. "You're in pain. I'll call Harley."

Harley, the big bodyguard-nurse-caregiver, was as much an extension of Steele in private as Dwayne was in public.

There was barely a hesitation before Steele shook his head and said, "This one is too important."

"They all are."

"Yes." Steele sighed. "But this one *is*. Show Alara in. Then, perhaps, some music, a nap."

"Food."

Steele shrugged. "Let her in."

Dwayne wanted to insist, but knew it wouldn't do any good. His boss didn't have energy to waste chewing out a stubborn employee who was also a friend.

Tight-lipped, Dwayne went to the locked door of Steele's office, opened it, and ushered Alara inside. She was wearing one of her old-school dark suits, dark pumps, dark blouse against dark-toast skin. If her straight, short hair hadn't been silver, she would have been a study in darkness.

"Coffee, tea, water, soda, something stronger?" Dwayne asked.

"Water, thank you. And privacy."

"We've been through this before," Steele said. "Unless you know something about Dwayne that I don't—and have proof—he stays."

In silence, Alara took a seat across from Steele's desk and waited until he wheeled into place opposite her. Dwayne put a bottle of water in front of her, refreshed Steele's water supply, and went back to his own office, which was an extension of the main office whose heavy doors could be shut if Steele required privacy. Steele had made it clear that he didn't.

Two of the five phones in front of Dwayne showed calls on hold. All three of his computer screens showed message alerts. He put on his headset and went back to work.

Alara listened to the low murmur of Dwayne's voice and the muted, hollow clicks of his computer keyboard.

"It is a dangerous luxury," Alara said.

"What is?"

"Trusting your assistant."

"Again, we have had this conversation before. If you have nothing new to add, I have calls waiting."

She raised her eyebrows at Steele's unusually curt manner. She almost asked if he was in pain, then stopped herself. The bullet that had taken Steele's legs so long ago still echoed through other lives.

So many things that might have been.

But are not.

"Do you have anything new for me?" Alara asked.

"Did I call you?" Steele countered.

She nodded once, conceding the point. "Like pulling hen's teeth."

"To pull teeth, there must be teeth to pull."

"Exactly. Shurik Temuri is a member of Georgia's most secret government security agency," she said evenly. "A very high-ranking member."

"Is his trade in death and destruction private and personal, or an aspect of state business?"

"Unknown. However, most men in his position within the Russian Federation have lucrative quasi-personal sidelines—drugs, extortion, human traffic, and so on."

"That would complicate, rather than simplify, this matter," Steele said. "At the very least, it adds a layer of deniability to Temuri's employer if its employee is caught with his hand in the wrong cookie jar."

"I noted the same thing."

"And?" Steele asked.

"Nothing. Just one more piece added to the puzzle we must solve."

"Delightful. No wonder I anticipate your visits." He drank from his water glass. "Anything else?"

"Where is *Blackbird*?"

"In Canadian customs, being vetted."

She hissed with impatience. "Idiots."

Steele didn't ask if she was referring to Canadian customs, the crew of *Blackbird*, or the FBI agent who had whispered suspicions into an international ear. There was more than enough idiocy to go around.

"Time is wasting," she said.

"Tell me something I don't know."

"I loved you once."

In the sudden silence, the hollow tapping coming from Dwayne's office sounded like ghostly Morse code.

Alara stood, her smile caught between sorrow and amusement, and said huskily, "It was a long time ago. Call me when *Blackbird* sails again. We must find those teeth to pull."

40

The northwest wind had gone from gusty to full-time blow. The only clouds left were those clinging to the mountain peaks on Vancouver Island and the mainland. The radio in *Blackbird*'s cockpit spit static and a small-craft wind warning. Ten to twenty knots with occasional gusts up to twenty-five.

Emma looked outside doubtfully. If the wind got much worse, the Strait of Georgia was going to be more white than blue or gray.

Mac listened to the radio, looked at the computer, measured the state of the water beyond the sheltered marina, sensed the muscular rumble of big diesels beneath his feet, and remembered Amanar's confidence that *Blackbird* could take anything the Inside Passage could dish out.

Easy to say when you aren't on deck.

But it would be much better to find out in twenty-five-knot winds than in forty-five.

"Stand by, Emma," he said through the headphones when she reached for the stern line. "I'm calling my special weather guesser."

The door to the customs modular slammed hard behind Singh. The wind-assisted closing made the small building shudder.

"Standing by," Emma said.

Mac flipped the mic away from his mouth as he punched the speed dial of his cell phone. The call was answered immediately.

"Faroe here. Where are you?"

"Nanaimo customs dock," Mac said, "getting ready to leave."

"I hear a 'but' in your voice."

"The wind is kicking up. Small-craft warning just went out for Nanaimo on south. I'm holding *Blackbird* against the dock with the pod drive as we speak."

"Bad?"

"If I knew *Blackbird* better," Mac said, "I'd already be heading north with a grin on my face. But we really haven't had a shakedown cruise."

"You pushed her to get to Nanaimo so fast. Had to be doing more than twenty knots," Faroe said.

"Nothing came loose. But the water was pretty much glass."

All Mac heard for a few moments was silence infused by the rush of wind over the cell phone's small microphone.

"Is it dangerous if you go now?" Faroe asked.

"If I thought it was, I wouldn't have called. I'd have found dock space in one of the marinas. But it could get dodgy if something cuts out because a cap or a screw or a fitting wasn't tightened down."

"As you said, shakedown cruise. Any worries with her on the way up?"

"No, she's a really sweet boat. I'm tempted to sail off into the sunset with her, because I sure never could afford to buy a ride like this."

Faroe laughed. "What does your gut say about going north?"

"I trust *Blackbird*. It's the weather-guessers I'm iffy about."

"How's Emma doing?"

"She's a first-rate first mate," Mac said.

"Say that ten times fast without stumbling and I'll know you haven't been drinking."

"I don't drink when I'm working, unless it's a cover. And then it only looks like I'm drinking."

"One of the things I really like about you," Faroe agreed. He paused, swore under his breath, and said, "Alara visited Steele again. Temuri not only has criminal connections, he's a top member of Georgia's secret service."

"This is getting all the earmarks of a really grand cluster."

"Yeah."

"We've wasted a lot of water time in Nanaimo."

"Alara said the same thing."

"What did Steele say?" Mac asked.

"He hires people he trusts. When it comes to sailing conditions, it's your call, Captain."

"We're going north. If the wind drops the way it should, we'll be in Campbell River well before dark."

"If not?" Faroe asked.

"We'll get to see how Emma likes being aboard *Blackbird* when its plowing into the wind at speed."

"Let me know."

Faroe ended the call.

Mac flipped the headphone mic back into place and signaled Emma to release the line. He watched her leap lightly onto the swim step, stern line in hand. He eased off the pod drive and waited to see if the yacht would respond as expected to the twin forces of water and wind.

The wind peeled the bow away from the customs dock. The stern followed, but not so quickly that the swim step banged against the dock. The wind was doing more pushing sideways than turning the boat.

Mack took a quick look around the marina, making certain that nothing had popped up on the water that hadn't been there the last time he looked.

"Clear," Emma said calmly into the mic.

He stepped into the cabin and let the boat drift until he was certain that turning the bow more wouldn't slam the stern into the dock. Then he shut off the joystick, picked up the throttles, checked that the engines were in sync, and put them in gear.

"Pick up all the lines and fenders and stow them the way I showed you," Mac said. "If you need help—"

"No help. Just time."

"—let me know," he finished.

He divided his attention between the course and Emma. She worked over the four lines, only had to coil one of them twice, tied each off neatly, and stowed them in an on-deck locker. Then she began dragging fenders into another area and hanging them out of the way by their own lines.

Mac had handled a lot of fenders. He knew that they were heavier than they looked, especially when you were holding them at arm's length half the time. It would have been easier if there had been fender holders on the rails, but there weren't.

Emma had caught on fast to the role of first mate. She didn't question why he wanted the deck clear of lines and fenders now and not on the way to Canada, or why he did things one way and not another. When she'd said that he was the boss on the water, she'd meant it.

Mac saw the blinking yellow channel light that warned of a floatplane coming in or taking off. He stepped out long enough to get a visual, then went back into the cabin.

Emma looked up when the roar of a small plane drowned out everything else. She could see the pilot as he thundered by, floats barely forty feet overhead.

Another plane came a minute behind the first. Since she knew what the sound was now, she ignored it and continued wrestling with cold fenders and cranky lines. As she did, she tried to imagine what it would be like doing the job on a heaving deck in a sleet storm.

I'll pass, thanks.

She made a mental note to ask Mac if sleet was in their immediate future. She didn't think her deck shoes were up to that kind of traction.

By the time Emma was finished with first-mate duties, she was ready to add layers to her eye-candy outfit. She went into the salon, hurried past the pilot station, and ducked below to the master stateroom with its big bed, closet, and drawers, all built into the hull. She could walk around three sides of the bed, which Mac had assured her was a real luxury. When she thought about making a bed with only one open side, she had to agree.

The clothes she'd brought in her duffel didn't fill up a tenth of the space allotted to the "first mate." She swapped shorts, boat sandals, and crop top for jeans, a T-shirt, and boat shoes with socks. She yanked a black sweater over her head, pulled her hair out from under the collar, put her cell phone on her belt, and called it good.

When she climbed the short stairway up into the galley, Mac was watching the electronic chart with unusual attention. She looked out the window and saw why. The big harbor had vanished. There was a tiny island off their right—*starboard*—side that looked close enough to touch. The miniature marina on the port side wasn't nearly as close.

Instead of asking why they were scraping an islet when there was plenty of water on the other side, she studied the chart and their projected course.

"Yikes," she said.

"Yeah, it's a narrow channel out of the north end of the harbor, but it saves time and dodging ferries coming in from the strait."

Silently she looked through the windows, comparing the electronic chart to what she could see. Nearby, just off the bow, a bright buoy swung in the current at the end of its anchor chain.

"What's that?" she asked. "A weird channel marker?"

Mac punched a button, zooming in on the chart symbol for the buoy.

She leaned in to look at the chart, then looked outside, and listened to Mac. She could learn from books, but she'd discovered long ago that she was what was called a "directed" learner—if she experienced it physically as well as intellectually, she learned much faster.

"That marks Oregon Rock," he said. "At low tide, it's only a few feet below the water, right at the entrance to the Nanaimo Yacht Club," he said. "There's another rock forty yards north. I could run us over it—"

"No thanks," she cut in.

"—but I'd like to stay afloat."

"Good plan."

On the islet that crowded the narrow channel, trees bent to the wind. Watercraft of all sizes poured into the far end of the channel, chased off the strait by the growing wind. She stood on tiptoe, peered into the water, and saw a shadow beneath the surface. The buoy was connected to it by a slimy green chain.

"I prefer deeper water," she said, measuring the size and closeness of the hazard. "And plenty of it."

Mac's smile flashed beneath his short beard. "I hear you."

"You'd think an ohmygod-rock like that one would be marked with bells, whistles, bonfires, and brass bands," she said.

"The farther north you go, the less bells and whistles there are. You have to pay attention to your charts and whatever nav markers exist. Go far enough north, and you're lucky to find nav markers in a harbor, much less away from it."

"Are the electronic charts as good as paper?"

"Mostly. Often better. But like paper, it's all information that someone on the ground—or water, in our case—has supplied."

"Good intel, good result," she said. "Bad intel, or none, and you're hung out to dry."

Mac went still, fighting memories. It took a few moments to shove the bloody past back into the basements of his mind.

"Nice thing about paper charts," he said, "is they don't go down if a circuit trips."

"Where is the paper chart of this channel?"

"In my mind. I've done this a few times," he said.

"What if I have to do it by myself?"

"Top chart." He pointed.

She went to the pile of folded charts that were to the left of the galley sink, took the first chart, and started to orient herself. Since the electronic chart was on the "heads-up" mode—whatever was on the chart in front of the triangle that represented the boat was also what was visible beyond the bow—she turned the chart until it showed what was in front of her, rather than true north.

The channel looked even more narrow on paper.

"Tell me this is safe," she said.

"What is?"

"Shoving this whacking great boat through the eye of a small damn needle."

"Bigger boats go through without problem."

"Knowing there are bigger fools on the water isn't comforting."

Mac laughed. "Have I mentioned that I like you, Emma Cross?"

"That's me, Ms. Congeniality."

But she smiled at him before she stared at the water swirling around the nearly exposed tip of the second rock in the channel. She told herself that it was all good. If Mac wasn't worried, she wasn't worried. And he wasn't worried.

Alert, yes. Worried, no.

The second shadow slid by beneath the water, chained to another buoy. She let out a relieved breath when the channel opened up in front of them. They dodged through the flotilla of small craft running for harbor.

As soon as they were out of the lee of the islet, the wind whooshed over the yacht and the water changed, becoming rougher. Out in the strait, whitecaps were turning over.

"In a few minutes we'll be using the fourth chart," Mac said. While she replaced the chart she'd been looking at with a new one, he stepped close to her and added, "Faroe passed on a blast from Alara. Temuri is very well connected to Georgia's most-secret service."

Her hands stilled as he stepped back to the wheel.

"About all this sweet talk, Mac. I don't think my heart can take it."

But even as she spoke, she was running possibilities in her mind. It was one of the things she did best. None of the possibilities made their life easier.

"Bloody hell," she said as she smoothed out the chart.

"Yeah."

"Mac . . ."

He looked at her.

She closed her eyes for an instant, then met his dark glance. "I'd rather have dealt with international crime lords."

"Why? Killers are killers."

"With crime, motivation is a lot easier to discover. Money is the primary mover. Everything else follows, including power. If you know motivation, you know your enemy's weak point and can plan accordingly. But politics is like building something on the tip of a flame. Every breeze changes the lay of the land. Motivation follows the breeze."

The curve of his mouth changed. "Pretty much how Faroe and I feel about it."

"God, I hate politics and politicians. Give me a gang-banger any day. How good is Alara's intel?"

"Your guess is better than mine. You were in the business more recently than I was," he said, coming up on the throttles.

Open water lay ahead.

She fiddled with her phone. "Has Steele put Alara through research?"

"I didn't ask."

Emma hit speed dial.

"Got a problem?" Faroe asked by way of greeting.

"What do St. Kilda's data banks say about Alara?"

"Nothing you couldn't get by searching a few very academic magazines and some former State Department types who have online blogs."

"What does the gossip side of research say?" Emma asked.

"Twice divorced, various lovers at various times, never married a third time, three children, eight grandchildren, career government in departments whose names mean nothing and whose funding isn't questioned by Congress. Retired nine years ago."

"Someone's file needs updating."

"Someone didn't retire," Faroe agreed.

"What did Steele tell you?"

"That she's one of the shining ones still left playing a tarnished game."

"Huh."

"Yeah, huh. Grace thinks that any ambitions Alara has are related to making sure her grandchildren don't inherit a world where every balcony has a dictator with a suitcase full of secondhand nukes."

Emma let out a slow breath. "Then we have the same goal."

"Now pray that you have the same path to that goal."

41

Lina Fredric, who wanted very much to forget that she had started life as Galina Federova, watched Taras Demidov from the corner of her eye. Though the water was choppy, headed toward outright rough, the motion didn't appear to bother his stomach.

But of course, Lina thought. *Nothing short of a nuclear blast would upset that man.*

At least he is paying me well. Quite well.

It could have been much worse. Whether in the "free world" or the FSU, money and violence talked very clearly. She preferred money. So far, Demidov seemed to share her preference. If that changed . . .

Mentally Lina shrugged. Even though she had learned that he carried a knife rather than a gun, she didn't fancy her chances against Demidov in physical combat. She'd grown soft over the years. He hadn't.

The static and snatches of words from the VHF radio made a familiar background for her thoughts.

" . . . *Sun Raider*."

"*Sun Raider to XTSea 4EVR, switch to channel . . .*"

The only good news about the shifting weather was that the clouds were being blown out by the northwest wind. Clear skies were nice but the price was wind, which meant rougher water, especially when the tide changed and the wind pushed against the flooding water.

A gust of wind, a small trough, and the *Redhead II* lurched beneath Demidov. Though he was sitting down, the sudden motion jerked him like a puppet. He muttered a Russian curse, lowered the binoculars, and rubbed his eyes. With barely veiled impatience, he switched his attention from binoculars to his special cell phone. Relieved not to be viewing a world that jumped about like water drops in a hot skillet, he keyed in a number.

After a few moments, two sets of latitude and longitude numbers appeared on the small screen. A cold, thin smile stretched his lips as he checked, then checked the lower numbers again.

Blackbird was out of Canadian customs and working her way north from Nanaimo.

North, where Demidov lay in wait.

42

When Emma glanced up from making a late lunch in the galley, she was glad she'd ditched the eye-candy look. The waters north of Nanaimo were colder somehow, even though the temperature reading on *Blackbird*'s many gauges had shifted only a few degrees down after leaving the harbor.

"Brrrr," she said.

Mac gave her a fast look. "Brrrr? The temperature inside the cabin hasn't changed that much." He half-smiled. "I'll turn up the heat if you go back to the tube top."

She shook her head. "Men."

"That would be me."

She laughed and sliced cheese. "It's just that the water seems different out here. Like the whole world is colder."

"Until now, we've been pretty much sheltered by either the San Juan Islands or Canada's Gulf Islands. The Strait of Georgia is long enough and wide enough for the wind to work the water. It's a good fetch from Campbell River to the Gulf Islands. The wind is free to play. So it does."

Emma measured the increasingly choppy water. The whitecaps that had looked so tiny from the harbor weren't all that small—they were riding the backs of steep-sided, wind-stacked waves that looked to be three feet high.

"Is it always like this?" she asked.

"It can be calm as a cup of tea. It can be six-foot razor waves. It can be like now, two or three foot waves with some wind chop on top. A little snotty, but hardly noticeable on a boat the size of *Blackbird*."

"So what happened between here and Nanaimo. Just the wind?"

"Partly wind, partly the water itself, and a good bit that we're heading right into it," Mac said. "The tide is pushing to the north and the wind is shoving to the south. Irresistible force meets immovable object, and we're caught between."

She reached for crackers, braced herself against an unexpected motion, and waited. The next motion was equally unexpected.

"There's no rhythm to the waves," she said.

"We're in the strait, not out on the ocean. The period between waves is shorter in the strait, less rhythmic. Unreliable. Makes for a spine-hammering ride if you're in a small boat."

Carefully she stacked crackers, cheese, celery, and sliced sausage on a plate with a rim around the top and a rubber ring on the bottom. Then she looked through the windows at a world of water, wind, and sky.

"You don't think of *Blackbird* as small?" she asked.

"Compared to a ferry or a containership, yes. Compared to most of the pleasure craft on the water, no. We're big enough that we're officially allowed to decide if we want to play in gale force winds, which would make these winds look like a baby's breath."

"Pass," she muttered.

"Me, too."

She looked at him, surprised. "It wouldn't be safe?"

"Safe ain't the same as fun," he said. "I'd rather be tied up snug in port listening to rigging lines slap and sing than out hammering my spine through a storm. On my own time I'm a pleasure boater, not a masochist."

A few of the waves that broke against the bow sprayed over the decks and dotted the windshield with saltwater. Emma was aware of a change in motion, but she didn't feel any need to hang on to things when she moved around the galley.

Yet.

"Will it get rougher?" she asked.

"If the wind doesn't drop, yes. It's supposed to fall off as we go to the north. That's why we're running for Campbell River."

"What if it gets worse?"

"Depends," he said.

"That's an all-around, universally unsatisfactory answer. You want tea?"

He gave her a sideways glance. "Depends."

"I'll take that as a no."

"Yes."

"Yes to the no?"

"No."

Laughing quietly, she put a bottle of iced tea in a holder near the wheel and gave him the food.

"Have you eaten?" he asked.

Watching the water, she shook her head.

"You work on this plate," he said, handing over the wheel. "I'll make more after I take a bio break."

"Um . . ."

Before Emma could think of an excuse, she was left with the wheel and her doubts about steering *Blackbird* in anything but calm water.

"Put it on auto if you want," Mac called over his shoulder as he disappeared below with a handheld VHF radio. "Just make sure you stay well outside those rocks and islands."

"What rocks and islands?"

"Zoom out on the chart. You'll see what I mean."

She zoomed out on the computer screen, saw what he meant, and frowned. Going around the various small islands would take longer. But then, going *aground* would waste even more time.

Mac's voice floated up from below. "If you're nervous, I can keep an eye on things while I pee off the stern."

"Great, I'm stuck on a boat with a flasher."

"Flashers are used with downriggers. For trolling. Wanna see how it's done?"

"MacKenzie, just pee!"

Laughter, then she was alone with *Blackbird* and frisky water. She thought about putting the controls on auto, then decided to try learning the rhythms—if any—of boat and water.

With her hands on the wheel, *Blackbird* became a living presence caught between external forces and its own nature. The balance between vessel and water shifted continually. At the edges of her concentration she heard the sounds of the head flushing and the static of a VHF radio. Mac was talking to someone.

She was too busy to wonder who or why. She oversteered a few waves, overthought a few more, and was surprised by several. The waves seemed steeper than they had been.

At least some of them did. The problem was, she couldn't tell which ones until it was too late to do much but stagger on through.

"Different when the water is choppy," Mac said cheerfully as he climbed up from the lower deck.

Emma's hands were clenched around the wheel. She stood in front of it, stiff-legged, her face tense.

"A lot more motion," she agreed curtly.

"Ever ride a horse with a western saddle?"

"Yes."

"Move with the boat as you would a horse," Mac said. "Loosen your knees. Let your spine flex. Fighting against the motion just tires you out."

She looked at him. He was relaxed, balanced, his legs apart and his knees loose.

He looked good. Edible, even.

Blackbird took advantage of her lack of attention. The bow slid off the heading, pushed by the quartering waves.

"You'd better grab it," Mac said.

He moved closer as he took a cracker and a slice of cheese from the plate by the pilot station.

Emma turned the wheel too hard. She knew it even before the boat's bow went past centerline.

"Damn," she said under her breath as she swung the wheel hard the other way.

Too far.

Again.

"Give the helm a chance to respond before you crank on the wheel again," he suggested.

"I know," she said, remembering his instructions when she took the wheel on and off during the run to Nanaimo. "I'm just not doing it. The choppy water makes everything different."

"Relax. Have a cracker."

He fed one to her before she could object.

She chewed through the cracker and cheese, forced herself to slow down, and handled the helm more gently. To her relief, the boat responded. The motion evened out.

"Good," he said. "Now, look at the compass. Try to steer a course of 340 degrees."

She studied the compass dial beneath its glass dome and identified the 340-degree mark. It danced slowly with each motion. She tried to make tiny corrections on the helm to keep the alignment exact.

"Remember what I told you before?" he asked calmly, picking up another cracker. "Five degrees on either side is fine. It all evens out on the water. *Blackbird* isn't suspended like a race car, where every little twitch from the driver results in a big change in the car's direction."

Emma loosened her grip on the wheel and eased the tension from her shoulders and legs. She quickly realized that if she didn't try to anticipate every little motion of the boat, she felt more relaxed.

Not more in control, just less unhappy about it.

"Check the compass heading from time to time and save your real attention for watching the water ahead," Mac said. "You can't avoid the waves, but you can dodge rafts of seaweed and logs."

"Yikes." Emma narrowed her eyes and stared out at the water. "I'd forgotten about the logs."

"Seaweed will shut down your cooling system real quick. Hot engines freeze up. Bad luck all around."

"God, Mac. All the sweet talk. Don't know if I can take it."

Smiling, he crunched into another cracker, this time with a slice of sausage and cheese.

As water rolled on beneath the hull, *Blackbird* and Emma reached a wordless understanding. She didn't crawl all over the controls and the boat settled into doing what caused the least motion while still sticking to a route that would lead eventually to Campbell River. Like a horse trained to the western style of riding, *Blackbird* responded best to a light hand on the reins.

Mac reduced the plate of food to random crumbs before he looked up. "Did you eat?"

"The cracker you fed me."

He stepped over to the galley, sliced, assembled, and threw in some potato chips and cookies for variety. Celery tasted fine when you'd been out on the water for a week and fresh greens had been scarce. But celery the first day of a trip? Not if he had a choice.

Mac went back to stand next to Emma and started feeding her crackers and cheese. He told himself that there was nothing sexy about giving a woman food from his fingers. Nothing sexy about watching her tongue lick away crumbs. Nothing sexy about the accidental touch of her lips. Nothing . . .

The hell with it.

He'd never been real good at lying to himself.

"Mac?"

"Yeah?" he asked absently, watching her tongue.

"This marked-off area . . ." She pointed to the computer chart.

"Whiskey Gulf," he said without looking at the chart. "A Canadian naval firing range. I just called, and they're not active until dawn tomorrow, so we don't have to go around. Keep on this course until I tell you otherwise."

"Okay. Er, aye, aye, Captain."

Mac wondered if she'd take orders as well in bed. Or give them.

Hold that good thought until we—

The primary VHF radio resting in a holder by the wheel came to life with an update of the past weather report. Emma tried to listen, steer, and keep the speed up in the face of rapidly changing wind and water.

And eat.

When the radio stopped spitting words, she swallowed half-chewed food and said to Mac, "Translation?"

"Small-craft warning has been shifted to include Campbell River."

"Meaning?"

"If I was in a small boat, I'd come about and run back

to Nanaimo, just like them." He pointed to their port side. Miles away, two small white boats raced along the shore.

"But we're a big girl, right?" she asked, lightly turning the wheel, anticipating the next action of boat and water.

"You sure are." He popped a chocolate cookie into his mouth.

Blackbird rose to meet the choppy waves, slid through, and lined up for another round of whatever the strait delivered.

"Good," he said simply. "You're a natural on water."

She looked pleased. "Thanks. Eat more cookies. It improves your sweet talk."

"I'm not sweet-talking. People can learn navigation and rules, but a feel for the water can't be taught. It's there or it isn't."

"Like languages."

"Or shooting." He crunched into another cookie.

"About that sweet talk . . ."

"I'm practicing," he said. "See? I'm eating cookies."

"And I'm thinking it would take more than cookies to sweeten your tongue."

"If we were on calm water, I'd prove how wrong you are."

She looked at him, knew what he meant, thought about how good he'd felt when she petted him in her arm-candy mode. She took a breath and reminded both of them, "We're not on calm water. Damn it."

Then she shut up and concentrated on handling the boat instead of its captain.

43

Lina felt the increasing strength of wind in the action of the water. A meter high and occasionally higher, the steep-sided, unevenly spaced waves broke over whichever part of the *Redhead II* was handy. Even seated, with the wheel to hang on to, the open cockpit of the boat was an uncomfortable ride.

Wet, too, despite the cloudless sky.

Her only consolation was that Demidov had to be more miserable than she was. He wore the cheap slickers she used for clients who didn't bring their own. She was in a medium weight Mustang suit and wore warm, waterproof boots. He didn't. She was accustomed to being on the water. He wasn't.

Never know it from looking at him, she thought sourly.

Driving in circles waiting for Demidov to do something

was even more boring than trolling in circles waiting for a salmon to bite.

"Where are they?" she finally asked him.

Despite her intentions, her voice came out sharp, demanding.

Demidov glanced at the small, bright screen of the cell phone. "Head five degrees more to the southeast."

She looked at the compass, then at water.

"I'll have to tack back and forth on that heading," she said, "or I'll take on too much water over the stern. My boat isn't designed for following seas."

"Just get us five degrees to the southeast."

When Lina put the boat into a turn, she made certain he was the one who got whitewashed by the waves. A petty triumph, but with Demidov, she took what victories she could.

Why wasn't he murdered? So many others were.

But Taras Demidov was still alive. She was stuck with the devil himself until he had no more use for her.

Rather distantly, Lina hoped he left her alive when she no longer served a purpose.

Kill him yourself. Shove him overboard and leave him for the crabs.

She rejected the thought almost as soon as it came. Even in rough water, scanning the strait through binoculars, Demidov had the balance and predatory awareness of a cat. It was unnatural. Unnerving.

If anyone went overboard, it would be her.

It infuriated Lina that she had grown older while he had

grown more dangerous, but she wasn't stupid enough to act on her emotions. In that, at least, she was his equal.

"That's far enough," Demidov said abruptly. "Turn off the big outboards and get on the little one."

"Are you talking about the *kicker*?"

"Is that the small engine?"

"Yes," she said.

"Then do it."

Lina bit back her objections. Her gear would keep her dry from the neck down—she hated hats and only wore them when the temperatures dropped below freezing. If she got a saltwater face wash and cold water down her back today, she'd still be more comfortable than the devil who had commandeered her boat.

She cut the big outboards and staggered back to the stern, thrown off-balance by the choppy, unpredictable waves. Not for the first time, she wished she'd replaced the little kicker with a bigger one that had an electronic starter. But she hadn't. She would pay for that now.

As she reached for the pull rope to start the kicker, water slammed into the boat and spray slapped across her face. She yanked the starter rope once, and again, then again. On the fourth try the small outboard shuddered, belched a cloud of unburned gas and oil that wind swept back into the boat, and died.

Demidov looked sharply at her.

She ignored him and yanked on the starter rope again. This time the engine not only caught, it held. Bracing herself on the stern gunwale, she steered *Redhead II* with the kicker.

It wasn't easy, but it could be done.

Barely.

Rather savagely she hoped that Demidov appreciated the uneven, sloppy, stomach-churning ride.

At least it isn't raining, she thought. *It shouldn't take long for* Blackbird *to spot us.*

44

Emma was comfortable enough with the wind and water that she had hopped up into the pilot's seat behind the wheel. More a loveseat than a simple chair, the cushion was big enough for two to use. Once she sat down, the riding-a-horse analogy was even more apt. She let the motion of the boat go through her spine in an invisible wave.

Mac settled on the padded bench seat next to her, close enough for her to feel his warmth. She liked that almost as much as the fact that both of them were relaxed with the silence and one another.

The multitude of pleasure boats that had cluttered the water near Nanaimo had disappeared. The few boats she could see were well off in the distance, much closer to land, leaving white streaks on the water as they slammed from wave-top to wave-top in a run for whatever safe anchorage was within reach.

"How often do they change the weather report?" Emma finally asked.

"Depends."

"On the weather?" she asked sweetly.

"On how bad they missed the forecast the first time."

"I don't know much about weather, and less about water, but . . ." Her voice faded into the hiss and smack of waves against the hull.

"Yeah." Mac looked at the whitecaps, measured how much spray lifted into the air. "The wind looks closer to twenty than fifteen, much less ten. The gusts are at least twenty-five."

"Still want to go to Campbell River?" she asked.

"Is your stomach kicking?"

Emma looked surprised. "No. Should it be?"

"Some people get seasick on a floating dock."

"Guess I'm not one of them."

"We could take a lot more wind than this and be perfectly safe," Mac said. "Unless you're uneasy—"

"As in puke green?" she said, smiling.

"Yeah."

"I'm not."

"So kick the throttles up a notch and keep going."

"How much is a notch?" she asked.

"Take it up to twenty knots, more if the motion doesn't bother you. We've got time to make up."

"Aye, aye, Captain," she said, and hit the throttles.

The sound of the diesels deepened. The wake behind the boat churned out even more white. Surprisingly, the ride didn't change much, neither smoother nor rougher. The fuel consumption sure shifted, though.

"We're filling up the tanks in Campbell, right?" she asked.

"Yes. Why?"

"We eat a lot more diesel at this speed."

"Wait until you see it above twenty-four knots. Sucks diesel like water flushing down a head," he said.

"Expensive."

"If you can afford *Blackbird*, the cost of the fuel it takes to run her is small change."

As Mac spoke, he reached across Emma for the binoculars that were held snugly in a grip near the pilot station.

"Looking for logs?" she asked.

"If I have to use glasses to find them, the logs are too far away to worry about."

"Good to know. I've been wondering."

He grunted.

After a moment Emma straightened in the seat and leaned over the wheel, staring into the water ahead.

"Is that a boat out there?" she asked. "Just to the left of the bow."

Mac was already watching the shape through the binoculars. "Twenty-eight-foot motorboat. Red gunwale stripe. Fisherman's special. You want to see something suck fuel? Try opening the throttles on those two big Yamahas strapped to the stern of that boat. Probably go twenty-two knots, maybe twenty-four. Hell of a butt-breaking ride, though. Especially in this chop."

"Is that why the boat is going so slow? It's barely moving."

"I noticed."

Mac refocused the glasses.

Redhead II all but disappeared as a wave broke against its side. Someone with wild, wet red hair was hunched over the steering arm of the kicker, getting whitewashed as often as not.

The boat wallowed like a half-beached log.

"They're on the kicker but no fishing gear is out," Mac said. "Steer an intercept course."

Emma started to ask about kickers and fishing gear, but Mac leaned across her and lifted the radio microphone out of its cradle. Before he could use it, the radio crackled to life.

". . . calling the black-hulled yacht off Nanoose," said a man's voice. "I have a visual of you."

"*Blackbird* here. I didn't catch your name. Switch to six-eight."

A few seconds later, on the new channel, a man's voice said, "*Blackbird*, we're having trouble with a fuel filter or the electrical system. Hard to be certain in this water. Can you assist us?"

It wasn't a request Mac could or would refuse. He was the only boat within sight, he had the skill and the means to aid the smaller boat, and the weather was going downhill. Marine law—and simple decency—insisted he do what he could to help.

He focused the glasses on the stern of the pitching boat, where her name was written in bold script.

"*Redhead II*," he said, "stand by for assistance. Can you turn her into the wind?"

"I think—yes, the captain says we can."

"That will make it easier. Stand by on six-eight, please."

"Thank you."

Staring at the boat ahead, Mac held the microphone, then said, "I'll take it from here."

"Good."

Emma shot out of the pilot position. The thought of steering *Blackbird* close to another boat in this water was enough to lift the hair on the back of her neck. Mac, on the other hand, seemed to take it for granted.

"Call Faroe," Mac said as he took the wheel. "Have him check the registration on a Canadian pleasure boat, about twenty-eight feet, called *Redhead II*."

Maybe it's not the idea of getting close to the boat that's making my neck tingle, she thought.

"Are you suspicious?" she asked.

"Aren't you?"

"Now that I'm not busy running the boat, yes."

"If you can, get a photo of both people on *Redhead II*," he said, easing back on the throttles.

"Dumb arm-candy taking shots for the folks back home?"

"Better that no one catches you and wonders why you're taking pictures."

"My camera's zoom will be a snotty bitch to use out here."

"I have faith in you."

Emma wanted to roll her eyes. Instead, she punched Faroe's number on her phone.

A voice answered immediately.

"Hi, Emma. This is Lane. Dad and Mom are on other lines. Since you didn't roll over to Steele, he's busy, too."

Emma looked at her phone. "You sound just like Faroe. Can you take a message?"

She heard a swivel-type office chair squeak and rattle across a tiled floor.

"Sure," Lane said. "Ready."

"Are you up north pretending to be on vacation?"

"Nope. San Diego. I've got university classes, but not today." His voice said just how much he loved being left behind.

Quickly she relayed Mac's request, and added, "I'll be sending jpgs ASAP and will want the people in them identified double-ASAP."

Lane grunted, sounding so much like Faroe that she couldn't help smiling. If she could have a kid like Lane . . . well, the idea of a family suddenly appealed. She wondered idly how Mac felt about it.

"Processing boat ID as we speak," Lane said. "Want me to call back with the info?"

She looked out over the bow of *Blackbird*. They were closing quickly with the smaller boat.

"Only if it's in the next two minutes," she said. "After that, send to my computer. Or Mac's. Whatever. Just get it to us."

"Gotcha. Dad's line just opened. If he has any questions, he'll call in the next two minutes."

The connection ended with an abruptness that reminded her of Faroe all over again.

"Faroe's son is running the boat's name for us," Emma told Mac.

"He any good?"

She stared at him, then realized he'd been part of St. Kilda for only a few days. "He's as good as our researchers. And that means really good."

All Mac said was, "Get your camera and be ready to shoot through the window. If that isn't close enough, show yourself. They might not like it, but they can hardly object. If they're legitimate."

Emma went to the canvas purse she had brought aboard. While Mac cautiously maneuvered closer to the other boat—and then closer still, until Emma held her breath—she turned on her camera. She felt like a witness watching two trains slide toward collision.

Silently she hoped Mac was as good as she thought he was. Otherwise it was going to get ugly for the little boat.

Not to mention unhappy for *Blackbird* and its crew.

She stood in mid-cabin and focused through the least spray-washed window she could find. The figure of a woman braced next to the small outboard jumped and jittered in the focus.

Emma switched to the electronic motor drive, hoped her battery could take the hit, and did her best to keep one or another of the two people in the field of focus. The clicking sound that told images were being taken came so close together it was like a single ripple.

She switched off motor drive, braced her feet farther apart, and reviewed the photos. No single one was good, but there were enough separate parts in focus with all the shots that a good ID program should be able to work its electronic miracle among St. Kilda's huge databases.

"I'm sending the jpgs," she said.

"Make it fast. I may need you on deck."

"Making it fast, Captain, sir!" she shot back.

He grinned.

With practiced motions she plugged her camera into her computer, created a new file, downloaded the photos, and sent them *MOST URGENT* to St. Kilda. In the background she heard Mac try—and fail—to raise the *Redhead II*.

"What's wrong?" she asked, closing up the computer and putting away the camera.

"They're not answering."

"Maybe the electronic problem took out their radio."

Mac made a sound that could have meant anything. "You have your good deck shoes on?"

"Yes."

"See if you can shout across to *Redhead II*." A wave sprayed against the port windows. "Unless you'd rather sit here holding station with *Blackbird*?"

She looked at the scant yards separating the gunwales of the two boats and said, "No, thanks. It's all yours."

"You'll need a jacket."

"I'll be fine, Mom."

Mac shut up and concentrated on keeping enough, but not too much, separation with the other boat. He could have used the joystick. Probably should have. He just preferred the old-fashioned way. New toys meant new problems as well as new solutions. For now, he'd take the devil he knew.

He opened the pilot door to let Emma out. The outside air was beyond fresh and bracing. It was cold. The damp edge of salt spray didn't help.

Emma ignored the temperature. She braced herself on

the railing, remembered her arm-candy role, and called out, "What's up with your radio?"

The woman steering with the kicker said nothing, simply looked at her companion. The man stepped up to the rail of the *Redhead II*. For the first time Emma got a clear look at his whole face.

I've seen him before, she thought. *Or someone who looks a lot like him. Mug shots? Long-distance surveillance?*

"What I have to say to you is too sensitive to be put out over a public radio," he said.

At first Emma thought she hadn't heard correctly. Then she knew she had.

Mac had really good instincts.

"What?" she yelled.

"Follow me to calmer water. There we will discuss Shurik Temuri, Stan Amanar, Bob Lovich, and the extreme danger you are in."

She gave Mac a do-you-get-this-dude look through the open cabin door.

He caught the other captain's eye and made a wind-it-up motion with his hand.

The woman staggered from the kicker to the cockpit and fired up the big outboards.

Mac gave *Redhead II* plenty of room before he followed.

Emma came back into the cabin. "It's not like we have a whole lot of choice. Shurik Temuri is someone we have to know more about."

"Yeah. An opportunity we can't refuse."

Mac hoped they were doing the right thing. Because the wrong thing was a fast way to die.

45

DAY FOUR
ROSARIO
3:04 P.M.

"Good work, Lane," Faroe said over the phone. "Thanks."

"I told you I'd be more useful if I—"

"Get a degree," Faroe cut in. "Your mother and I both agree on that. Emphatically."

Lane groaned or growled. It was hard to be certain.

"I'll let you know if I find anything else useful," Lane said.

Grumbled, actually.

Faroe was glad he wasn't on visual. He didn't have to hide his smile. He'd felt just like Lane when he was young.

And Faroe was determined that Lane wouldn't make the same mistakes his daddy had.

"Just don't tell Steele that I whispered through a couple of his databases," Lane added.

Faroe came to a point. "You did *what*?"

"I'll make a patch before class tomorrow. When I give it

to Dwayne, I'll tell Steele. No one will be able to use that route again."

"I'm impressed. Frightened, actually."

Lane snickered. "I had help."

"Your 'swarming' buddies?"

"One of them. She's über."

Faroe hesitated, but couldn't help saying, "She'd damn well better be über quiet."

"I didn't tell her anything that would point to St. Kilda Consulting. We give each other puzzles all the time, then race to see who gets there first, and how. If it will make Steele feel any better, she found the same way in that I did. Usually there are two or three paths, at least."

"You'll be the first to know Steele's mood. Get that patch made yesterday and talk to him yourself."

Faroe hung up and rubbed his eyes. "This 'vacation' is going to be the death of me."

"What now?" Grace shut Annalise's bedroom door behind her and hoped their cranky daughter would take a nap. Her sleep schedule was all over the place.

Sort of like her parents'.

"Lane hacked into one or more of St. Kilda's databases," Faroe said.

"Mother of God."

"That's one way of looking at it," he agreed dryly. "Father of Satan is another. But Lane's making a patch to keep other hackers out, so I'll give the honors to Mom rather than Dad. Lane sent the information he got to Emma's computer. And mine."

Grace sat down next to him on the couch and sighed.

"Have I told you lately that I love you and don't know how I would have handled Lane alone?"

Faroe set aside the computer, pulled Grace into his lap, and nuzzled her neck. "You would have done fine, but thanks for sharing him with me. And Annalise. If we survive them, we can conquer the world."

Laughing, she settled closer, letting her husband's warmth sink through to her bones. "Flip you to see who talks to Steele next."

"Tails," Faroe said as he smoothly flipped Grace out of his lap and onto her back on the couch. Head up. "You lose."

Her arms tightened around his neck. "Two out of three?"

"Think she'll sleep that long?"

"Let's find out."

46

Lane got us a lot of stuff," Emma said, frowning at her computer screen.

"Anything useful?"

"Do you read Cyrillic?"

"Enough to make out road signs," Mac said. "Maybe."

"It's been a long time since I've read more than memos. It's coming back, but slowly. Apparently Lane didn't think to translate it."

"So he's a Russian agent?" Mac asked.

"Lane?"

Mac gave her a look. "Demidov."

"He was a Russian agent. Supposed to be freelance now, though he still has active Russian Federation diplomatic credentials."

Mac made a sound that said he was listening.

"He's most often known to the English-speaking world

as Taras Demidov," she said, "though he has several other aliases. I have to assume he has all the necessary documentation to back up those identities," she added. "He's certainly in a position to get whatever papers he needs."

"Welcome to the post-Wall world, where no one works for the name signing his paycheck."

"And no one has the same name as the dude cashing it." She laughed curtly. "I don't like that world. For all the good it does me."

"Now you know why ostriches prefer sand. Much more comfortable."

"Until somebody kicks your feathered butt."

"Yeah," he said, "that's the downside."

Emma looked up from the computer. "The water is a lot calmer."

"We're in the lee of a small island. Soon it will be quiet enough to safely take a passenger aboard, which I'm not wanting to do, even if we lock down our cell phones and computers. I'm hoping he'll settle for shouting across the water."

She skimmed content faster, deciding nuances could wait until there was more time. "Demidov is a shooter."

"Sniper?" Mac asked.

"Is that professional interest I hear in your voice?"

"I used to keep track of the ones that got away. Otherwise they had a nasty habit of turning up in my rearview mirror."

"Sorry I asked," she said. "And no, Demidov is an executioner, not a sniper. Close work. Really close. He has nine confirmed kills and three times that many suspected."

"Nice dude."

"Yeah," she said absently. "Just what every mother dreams of for her little girl."

"In a lot of places in the world, you'd be exactly right. Having the protection of a *mafiya* type beats starvation or selling your daughter into the skin trade."

Emma let out a long breath. There were aspects of the modern world she really despised.

Not that things had been much different a thousand years ago.

At least most places have laws against slavery now, she told herself tiredly. *That's something.*

"Anything about the female, or is she a local hire?" Mac asked.

"The woman aboard *Redhead II* is Lina Fredric, born Galina Federova. She's the registered owner of the boat."

"Sleeper?"

Emma frowned and skimmed as quickly as she could. "If she's a sleeper for Russia, she's been in place so long she's put roots down and grown moss. No dings on her record. Naturalized Canadian citizen, pays all taxes on time, doesn't speed, doesn't get in bar fights, ekes out a good-enough living taking fishermen after salmon. Once rumored to hang with drug runners, but never caught with so much as a whiff of anything contraband."

Mac thought of the time when he'd driven a fast boat flat-out in the dark, sure that he'd live forever.

"A young man's game," he said. "Fool's game."

"I'll take your word for it." She scanned quickly. "If the birth date is correct, Lina aka Galina just turned fifty."

"Demidov?"

"He's fifty-seven, if we can trust the stats. And the chances of him just choosing Lina Fredric from one of the what-to-do tourist pamphlets on a Canadian ferry are zero and negative."

"So . . . a sleeper rather than a shooter?" Mac asked.

"Until we have a reason to think otherwise, yes."

"Anything else we should know before *Redhead II* finds a quiet place to chat?"

"I'm looking."

Mac bit back an urge to tell her to look faster.

"Demidov often works for a *mafiya* head turned philanthropist. At least, that's what some sources say. Others say he's a kingmaker rather than a rainmaker."

"Demidov?"

"His boss," Emma said. "Name of Sidorov, according to one source. Others say it's Lubakov, or his son or brother-in-law or nephew. All names could be aliases. Could be ten other people. The players change too often to keep a scorecard. Whatever, Demidov climbed the ranks by playing brass-knuckle hardball, with extra innings of shoot, shovel, and shut-up."

Mac smiled unwillingly. "Demidov and his boss probably work for the national government or the higher ranks of the crime lords."

"Often the same people," she said. "One-stop shopping at its finest."

"Lock down the electronics. *Redhead II* slowing." Mac gave her the code on his computer and locked his cell phone himself.

Emma hit keys quickly on her computer, did the same

for his, and went below to shove both computers under the mattress in the master stateroom. Not proof against a real thief, but all she wanted was to minimize the chances of "accidental" discovery by a guest on the boat.

By the time she came back to the main cabin and locked down her cell phone, Mac had turned on the joystick and was inching closer to *Redhead II*. The water was almost as calm as a backyard swimming pool—with teenagers performing cannonball dives. But much nicer than the open strait.

"Lee of the island," she said, sighing. "I think I'm in love."

"Would you rather handle the talk or the joystick?" was all Mac said.

She decided that the water wasn't all *that* calm. "Talk."

"Put out fenders on the starboard side so that they'll protect us from the *Redhead II*." Without looking away from the other boat, he handed her one of the headsets. He was already wearing the other.

She yanked the headset into place and turned it on. "You there?"

"Yeah."

"With Demidov, I'm going for total arm candy with just enough brains so a man knows the difference between me and a blow-up doll," she said.

"Can't wait for you to try out that act with me," was all Mac said.

"That way, I have a fallback position," she added. "With him, not you."

She put four fenders overboard in record time before she looked up to check their position.

Redhead II was breathtakingly close.

"Good god. Why don't I just throw him a headphone?" she muttered under her breath.

"We may need it later," Mac said. "If you can keep him off the boat—"

"I'd rather drown him than let him aboard," she said quickly.

"Get his info first, then do whatever you can get away with."

She laughed. "I knew there was a reason I liked you."

"Yeah, yeah, yeah, just what every mother wants for her daughter."

"No. Just what every daughter wants for *herself*."

Emma stepped outside.

Like Mac, Lina was at the wheel, working to keep the two boats close enough, but not too close. Demidov was standing on the port side, waiting. He had his hands in the pockets of his jacket, staring across to *Blackbird*.

At that moment, Emma believed every word in the files about Demidov that she had just scanned. Her pulse jumped, but not in a happy way.

That is one really hard piece of work, she thought. *If you're fooled by the gray hair, you're dead.*

She moved her microphone a few inches to the side. No use shouting in Mac's ears. This way, he might be able to hear both conversations.

"Hi, I'm Emma," she said, pitching her voice to reach across the boats. "Who are you?"

"I would rather come aboard to talk," Demidov said.

His face was angular, lean, fined down like that of a

ballet dancer still trying to hold center stage with dancers half his age.

It made him look all the more dangerous.

Discipline, experience, and talent all in one package, she thought unhappily.

Then she got down to work.

"The captain told me he would rather talk over the sides. Gunwales?" she asked, going for nautically clueless. "Is that what you call them?"

"I wish to make a business proposition," he said, ignoring her attempt to engage him in getting-to-know-you chatter.

"That's the captain's department," she said. "I'm just a first mate in training. But I know he doesn't like strangers on board. He's really touchy that way."

If Demidov was surprised or angry, it didn't show in his body language. "We don't need to be strangers."

Emma pretended to be listening to her earphones. "Babe, I can't follow two people at once," she complained. Then she glanced at Demidov. "I didn't mean you. I'm listening to Captain Babe."

A strangled sound came through her earphones—Mac trying not to laugh out loud.

"All right, all right, I'll ask him," she said with a whiny edge in her voice. A few seconds later she looked back to Demidov. "Captain Babe wants to know if coming aboard is, uh, required." Then she held up her hand before Demidov could answer. "Captain Babe says he'll waste some fuel out of curiosity, but he won't risk the boat."

Demidov thought about it for two seconds. "Shurik Temuri may be a covert actor, but he is not one of ours."

Talk about cutting to the chase, Emma thought, but she kept her game face on. "Is that supposed to mean something?"

"To you?" Demidov's upper lip almost curled. "No. To your Captain Babe, yes."

She looked blank. "Uh, he wants to know who 'ours' is." She shook her head and asked Demidov, "Does that make sense?"

This time the Russian didn't bother to conceal his contempt. "I work for the Russian Federation. Shurik Temuri is Georgian."

"Georgia?" she asked. "As in really yummy peaches? Shurik doesn't sound like a Southern name. I'm getting confused, here."

Mac made another strangled sound in her ear.

"What?" she whined into her microphone. "Everyone knows about Georgia peaches."

"Quit teasing him or he'll demand to come aboard," Mac said.

"Can your captain hear me?" Demidov asked impatiently.

"Can you?" she asked the mic.

"Yes."

"He says he can." Her voice was doubtful.

"Excellent," Demidov said. "Then you will shut up and let us talk."

"Well, that's just rude," she said.

"Emma," came through her headphones.

"Oh, fine, just see if I handle your lines again," she said into the microphone. Then she waved at Demidov. "Talk. Captain Babe is listening."

Demidov looked past her and pitched his voice to carry

into *Blackbird*'s cabin. "Temuri was once a citizen of Russia. Now he is its enemy."

"And the captain cares . . . because?" she muttered.

"Good question. Why do I care?"

Demidov waited.

Emma pushed. "He said, why should he care?"

"That is something he shouldn't discuss through an intermediary," Demidov said.

His expression told her that he had a much less polite word than intermediary in mind. Whore, probably. Or worse. Temuri certainly had been creative.

She turned to Mac, silently questioning.

"I want to get to Campbell River tonight," he said, covering his mic.

"He says—"

"I heard him," Demidov cut in. "Shurik Temuri is a relative of Stan Amanar and Bob Lovich."

Very quickly Mac came out on deck, holding the joystick. Emma gave him a look and stepped back, well out of the way.

"Keep talking," Mac said. "Tell me why I wasted fuel on you."

"Have you told your so-called first mate that she is a party to smuggling?"

Emma let her eyes go wide. "Über kewl! What kind?"

Both men ignored her.

"No contraband is on board," Mac said. "I made sure of it. The Canadians double-checked."

"You are only on the first leg of the smuggling trip."

Mac waited, watching the Russian with no expression.

"I hadn't taken you for a fool." Demidov glanced toward Emma. "But that would account for your companion."

"I don't screw her brain," Mac said. "What am I supposed to be smuggling if the owner doesn't show up—"

"He won't," Demidov cut in.

"—and I take *Blackbird* back to the States?"

"You'll be smuggling death," Demidov said.

"In what form?" Mac shot back.

"Temuri trades in weapons, whether biological, nuclear, or conventional."

Mac shrugged.

"You don't care about your country?" Demidov asked sharply.

"Why do you?" Mac asked.

"Temuri is a traitor."

"To Georgia?"

"If he was, I wouldn't be here," Demidov said. "He wants to hold an American city for political ransom. Or worse."

Emma was glad she had already talked to Alara. Otherwise she would have jumped over the railing and landed on Demidov with both feet and a sharp knife, demanding information.

He spoke the words so calmly, as if terrifying and then wiping out a large city was a perfectly normal way to go about international politics.

"Why?" Mac asked, nudging the joystick.

Demidov hesitated, shrugged. "My people—"

"The Russian government?" Mac cut in.

"Yes. We assume Temuri plans to blame the entire episode on Russia." Demidov connected the dots for Emma.

"Then the U.S. would side with Georgia more forcefully on the Russian-Georgian border disputes."

"If we lost a city, we'd probably do a hell of a lot more than take sides," Mac said.

"If you could prove guilt, yes. Or perhaps, no. International politics is never what it seems."

"No shit." Mac nudged the joystick, waited to see the result, and asked, "What do you want from me?"

"We don't know all of Temuri's plot, just his goal, but we are certain that *Blackbird* is key to the matter."

Where have I heard this before? Emma thought. *When even the bad guys don't know who's on first, the game is beyond lunatic.*

But she didn't so much as glance at Mac to find out how he'd taken the non-news.

"So where do I come in?" Mac asked.

"It's quite simple," Demidov said. "I will transfer fifteen thousand dollars to whatever bank account you give me. In return, you will tell me when you are contacted and what you are told to do. At that time, I'll transfer another fifteen thousand dollars to your account. That will more than cover any loss you have from Lovich and Amanar."

Mac thought about it. "Do Lovich and Amanar know what's really going on?"

"Unlikely. They are too soft."

Mac hated to agree with Demidov, but he did. "What if I take your fifteen thousand and blow you off?"

"I will kill you."

"Figured that," Mac said.

"Do we have a deal?"

"Keep talking."

47

Dwayne tapped on the door of the suite that was part of Ambassador Steele's top-floor offices and residence.

Harley opened the door instantly. Behind him Manhattan blazed across the windows like a 3-D light show.

"Alara is here," Dwayne said very softly.

"He just got to—" began Harley.

"I'm awake, Harley," Steele called from the darkened room. "Help me into my chair."

Dwayne winced. Steele must be really tired. Usually he only needed Harley's help with stairs or narrow doors. Steele might be retirement age, but his arms and chest were strong from hauling the rest of him around.

"Has he eaten?" Dwayne asked Harley in a low voice.

"No."

"Bring some omelets and fruit, toast, crackers, cheese, whatever. And tea. You could try herbal—"

"You'd end up wearing it," Steele interrupted impatiently.

"On Harley it would look good," Dwayne said. He watched as the big, muscular, bodyguard-nurse walked to Steele's bed. "Is your partner still out of town?"

"Yes." Harley bent and lifted Steele easily. "His mother is sick, so he stayed in Kirkland to help her."

"Washington?" Dwayne asked.

"Isn't that close to Seattle?" Steele asked at the same time.

"Right next door, why?" Harley said.

Steele hesitated.

"When your partner gets back," Dwayne said quickly, "let me know. My girlfriend likes you better than she's liking me lately. We'll have both of you for dinner."

"She cooking?" Harley asked, carefully settling Steele into his wheelchair.

"If both of you come," Dwayne said, "you'll get Cajun guaranteed to smoke your eyeballs black."

"Stop," Steele said. "I'm drooling like Pavlov's dog."

"I'll get the recipe, boss," Harley promised. "Meanwhile, I'll start cooking those omelets."

"Thank you," Steele said. "On nights like these, you're better to me than I deserve."

"I'll be sure to bring that up around bonus time," Harley said mildly. "Do you want your tie back?"

Steele straightened the collar of his dress shirt. "No. Just a sweater. It's a bit chilly tonight."

Dwayne and Harley exchanged a glance that Steele didn't see. Harley went to the closet, took a soft charcoal pullover from the top shelf, and handed it to Steele.

A few moments later, Steele rolled his chair out to meet Alara.

"It would be terribly convenient to communicate by phone," he said by way of greeting.

"As I told you the first time you brought it up, for some communications I don't trust phones or computers," Alara said crisply. "They're too easily compromised. My hotel room has been bugged four separate times in the past few days."

Steele made a sound of disgust, then shifted to ease the legs he wasn't supposed to feel. "If only our various government agencies would stop fighting one another and concentrate on the designated enemy."

"That will happen about the time lions become vegans."

Steele would have smiled if he wasn't so tired.

"We agree with the ID of Taras Demidov as a Russian shooter," Alara continued. "The woman, Galina Federova, is one of the many abandoned sleepers gone to earth beyond the shores of former empire. She was a minor player. Demidov ran her along with his other numerous agents. The files are so old, they should be classified as historic rather than active."

"So should we, but we live on anyway."

Alara's smile was swift and real. "Demidov may or may not know what Temuri is smuggling."

"I hope you didn't leave your hotel just to tell me what I already know."

"Temuri's family is Georgian and Ukrainian, raised in Russia. He works for whichever side pays him best."

"Did you learn anything new?" Steele asked bluntly.

"Ah, old friend, you are in pain."

"That's how I know I'm alive. Answer my question."

"The sum of fifteen thousand dollars has been transferred from an account funded by one of the many arms of Russian intelligence to a St. Kilda Consulting account. Demidov has the connections to move very quickly, as apparently the order came through barely an hour ago."

Steele's black eyebrows rose. "Impressive. Your connections, as well as his."

"Thank you."

"So Demidov is indeed working for some aspect of the Russian government."

"They are paying him," Alara said. "It isn't always the same thing. You will tell me immediately if your agent calls about contact by or from Shurik Temuri."

Steele waited for several beats, then nodded. "As we agreed. Speaking of which . . ."

Alara waited, poised like a falcon ready to fly.

"Since when are Russia and the United States working the same side of the street?" Steele asked. "Did I miss the memo? Or is it the usual case of politics making ridiculous bedmates?"

"We have cooperated with Russia in the past, when both parties had the same goal."

"Do you trust Demidov?"

Alara laughed in genuine amusement. "Do you?"

Steele rubbed the bridge of his nose. "Have Demidov and Temuri ever worked together in the past?"

She looked thoughtful. "Possible, but unlikely. Demidov is of another generation, political not criminal. Temuri came up through the *mafiya*. His family is rabidly against Russia. Temuri is simply rabid."

"He has a lot of competition," Steele said.

"That is the nature of life among the ruins. It suits Temuri. The most recent intel we have puts him with Chechen separatists, many of whom draw support from Wahabbi fundamentalists in the Middle East. Money, to be precise. A great deal of petro dollars."

"Is Temuri selling them nukes?" Steele asked.

"Not the finished product. Not yet. Fissionable materials only. More suited to blackmail than to bombs. He is the middleman for more ordinary weapons, as well. We also believe he is responsible for at least one of the outbreaks of bubonic plague that have occurred on the fringes of former empire. One instance of plague served to keep the Russians out of a strategic area."

"What if we take Temuri alive?"

"The Russians have offered a million dollars American to anyone who turns him over to them alive," Alara said. "Dead? Perhaps he would be useful to Russia as fertilizer, nothing more."

"Does Uncle Sam have any preferences about Temuri?"

"We would . . . enjoy . . . talking with him. But it is not required. Proof of death is. He has several rewards on his head. In fact, he is worth more dead to us than alive to Russia."

"I'm not a bounty hunter."

"Yet St. Kilda has collected bounties in the past."

"Any bodies on our ticket were made on the way to a different goal," Steele said. "Did you trace the telephone number Demidov gave our agent as a contact?"

"Useless. The phone was probably recently purchased and won't be in anyone's electronic files for a week or so. Too late to do us any good."

"Do you know any more about what is actually at risk than Demidov does?"

Alara's mouth tightened. "No. We are unhappy to find out he knew that much. It means there are more loose ends than we thought."

"And the time limit?"

"Unchanged." She stood up. "I wish your agents luck. We all will need it."

48

Blackbird rose on the breast of the creaming wave. Wind combed salt spray from the sea and dashed it over the windshield. Hands light on the wheel, Emma held the yacht's bow into the weather, enjoying the swell and rush of water. Mac was at the dining table, awash in charts. He kept them corralled with a casual ease she envied. She was just learning to be at home on the restless strait.

He *was* at home.

Her phone rang.

"I'll get it," Mac said, reaching into her purse. "It's Faroe."

"So talk to him. I'm busy."

Mac answered the phone. "We're about an hour south of Campbell. Where are you?"

"Hello to you, too," Grace said.

"Sorry. I was expecting your husband. Hello, how are you, how is Annalise, and why are you calling?"

"Faroe is looking at reports from various Canadian marine weather stations on his computer. He's making unhappy noises."

"We're fine. *Blackbird* may be beautiful, but she's not just a pretty face. She's built for this part of the world."

"How is Emma taking to it?"

"Fish to water," Mac said. "Quick and smart. You may not get her back."

"Thinking about keeping her?" Grace asked, amused.

"Yes."

"What does she think about it?"

"No screaming yet," Mac said.

"Give yourself time. It doesn't always happen for new lovers the first few rounds."

Mac made a choked sound.

"Joe wants to know if you're going to run through the night," Grace continued.

"No. Even if the water was calm and my first mate had all the appeal of moldy concrete, I wouldn't run in the dark past all those coastal log yards unless something bigger and meaner than me was closing in fast."

"See any cruise ships?" Grace asked.

"Four of them so far, but none are headed toward Campbell. You expecting trouble from a bunch of retired folks on their dream vacations?"

"No. I just always wanted to see a cruise ship from a distance. All those lights and glamour."

"Only at night. Close up in daylight, at the end of a season, cruise ships look like hookers after a hard night."

"You and Faroe. Not happy unless you're captain. Let

us know if anything changes. We'll do the same. Hello and good-bye to your first mate."

Mac closed the phone and answered the question Emma hadn't asked. "Faroe is following the weather up here and got nervous."

"Is this the kind of water you call snotty?" Emma asked.

"Getting there," Mac said. "If I want to use the electronic charts, are you happy steering by compass for a few minutes?"

"Better that than autopilot. It doesn't correct fast enough for this kind of water."

"Told you."

"Yeah, yeah," she said without heat. "So I'm a slow learner."

Suddenly she felt his heat and sheer bulk along the left side of her body. The warm, slightly rough surface of his fingertips traced from her left cheekbone to her jaw, her throat, and lingered on her pulse. Her heart stopped, then beat double time. His breath brushed her ear.

"Emma-love, you are anything but slow."

She plucked at her sweater and let out a long breath. "Getting hot in here, Captain."

Teeth closed gently on her earlobe. "If the water was calm, it'd be a whole lot hotter. But I want to be in Campbell before dark, so medium warm is as good as it gets for now. Hot comes later."

She cleared her throat. "You keep nibbling like that, you're going to distract me."

"My hands are in my pockets," he pointed out.

She moved her head quickly, caught one of his fingertips,

and sucked it into her mouth for a thorough tasting. She released it slowly, enjoying the flush of color high on his cheekbones.

"My hands are on the wheel," she said.

He took a long breath, then another. "Point taken. Damn it."

She laughed softly and moved aside so that he could get to the chart plotter while she steered. "All yours, Captain."

"Promises promises."

"I keep mine," Emma said.

"So do I."

She cleared her throat. "So . . . good. I won't have to date myself tonight." She shook her head hard, trying to clear the haze of lust. "God, Mac. Is it something you were born with, or did you take classes?"

"In what?"

"Sexual heat."

He blinked, then smiled slowly. "I'm learning from my first mate. One hell of a teacher. Can't wait for night school to begin."

She blew out her breath and ignored him. It was that or jump him, and *Blackbird* really did need a guiding hand. Two hands, actually. The waves were building with the wind. And the wind had teeth in it, forewarning of the cold autumn gales Mac had talked about.

"Is this weather as bad as it looks?" she asked after a time.

Mac didn't even glance up from the electronic chart plotter he was putting through its paces. "Not for us. If we were in a small boat, yes, I'd already be ashore or real close to it. Out here, size matters."

"Not touching that."

"Ever?" he asked.

"Not hearing you. La la la la. Not a single tempting word."

Mac laughed and quit teasing her—and himself—for the moment. He checked the boat's position, the tide, the currents, and the time to Campbell River. It would be an interesting ride. They were right on schedule for a beating from the steep tidal currents just south of Campbell River. The wicked water would slow them down, but they should make Campbell before dark.

Mac could hardly wait.

But he kept at work on the chart plotter, trying out various possibilities for the next day of running. The beauty of a boat like *Blackbird* was that speed opened up so many choices that a six-knot boat didn't have. The downside was that choices led to more opportunities to screw up.

That's how you learn, Mac reminded himself. *And along the learning way, you try real hard not to make the kind of mistakes that are fatal.*

Not to mention praying that somebody else didn't make those mistakes for you.

49

The front door closed behind Timothy Harrow with a weighty restraint that whispered of money. As he walked down the echoing marble foyer, he pulled off his suit coat, yanked his tie loose, looked at the muted gleam of bottles in the home bar, and sighed.

He'd rather have a woman. Unfortunately, his wife—soon to be ex-wife—had discovered that sometimes any woman would do for him. It wasn't anything against her, certainly nothing personal. It was just the way he was.

He looked around the suburban home that had become a house with the divorce decree and decided all over again that his career was a relationship killer. He should have stuck with serial affairs. Or found a wife who understood the demands of his career. Marrying a beautiful, ambitious lawyer had been a head-banging mistake, one he'd be making payments on for the rest of his life. Unless the clever bitch remarried.

And speaking of clever bitches . . .

He picked his cell phone off the table and looked at his contacts, searching for the personal number of his FBI contact. Information or a hookup, either would be fine with him. Both would be better. But before he could find the number, someone knocked at the front door.

Harrow locked and set aside the phone before he pulled out the drawer in the end table by his chair, saw that his pistol was in its usual place, and picked it up. He checked the load and flicked the safety off. Holding the weapon more or less out of sight along his right leg, he went to the security screen at the end of the foyer leading to the front door.

The surveillance camera showed Duke standing at the front door, but far enough back to make ID easy. What everyone hoped would be the final heat wave of the year had left Duke's expensive suit wrinkled and his bald head sweating in the porch light.

He was alone. Even his driver-bodyguard wasn't in sight.

Suddenly the Scotch looked more likely to Harrow than a hookup. With a subdued curse, he opened the door and let his boss into the mechanically cooled air of the house.

"You look like you could use a drink," Harrow said.

Duke ran a palm over his head. "You alone?"

"Yes." Harrow put the safety on his pistol and led the way to the living room.

"Nice place," Duke said.

"It will be Pam's in a few weeks." The end table drawer shut with emphasis.

Duke grunted. "Yeah, she's a shark."

"And a bitch. You want some bourbon?"

"No time."

"What's up?" Meaning: *What's too hot to talk about over the phone?*

"I don't know."

Harrow didn't ask any more. Whether Duke didn't, wouldn't, or couldn't share wasn't the point. The point was that something had sent a jolt through intelligence networks, a shot hot enough to burn some very important butts.

"How can I help?" Harrow asked.

It was the question that had taken him very near the top of the pyramid at an age when most people were still wondering what they would do when they grew up.

"One of Shurik Temuri's aliases entered Canada through Blaine," Duke said. "That's on the northern border of Washington State."

Harrow made a sound that said he was paying attention.

"By the time we got someone on Temuri, he'd ditched the rental. We're going through the records of nearby car rentals as fast as we can get to them, but it will take time. We don't have time."

The Scotch looked more like nectar with every word Harrow's boss spoke.

"Is there anything I've missed in Temuri's file?" Harrow asked carefully.

"No."

"But we're upset that he's in Canada."

"Yes. He's on our ticket, now," Duke said.

Says who? Harrow thought. *Nobody told me about an op, especially good old Duke.*

Harrow didn't say anything out loud, just waited, hoping his boss would say something useful.

Duke was an old hand at the silence game.

Harrow gave up and asked, "What's the op?"

"It's an old sting that went south," Duke said. "A few years back, a political golden-boy decided that it would be useful to catch a well-connected Russian dirty in the U.S."

It was a time-honored way to recruit double agents. Nothing new. Certainly nothing to send Harrow's boss roaming wealthy D.C. suburbs when he should be home having a drink.

"What was the contraband?" Harrow asked.

"A hundred million in counterfeit cash."

Harrow didn't bother to hide his surprise. "That's a lot of dirty to set someone up with. A million would have been more than enough."

Duke shrugged. "It wasn't my op. It was political from the get-go. Politicians don't notice a million here or there. Not anymore. To make a splash in the headlines you need a splashy amount of money, plus the threat of levering a corner of the U.S. economy off the rails, which would yank the rest of the economy down into the train wreck, one financial sector at a time. People are still goosey about 2008."

"Old news."

"Not to the politicians who were voted out and went back to mowing lawns for a living," Duke said. "They won't forget until they die. Neither will their children. Hell, the last thing my grandpa said to me was 'Don't trust banks or the stock market. Don't forget the Great Depression.' Turns out he had wads of cash buried in the rose garden."

Harrow's interest in Scotch turned into the stabbing of a migraine beginning behind his right eye.

"Anyway," Duke said, "Temuri somehow made off with the really good-looking bad cash our side had used to set up the sting. Temuri is getting ready to run it into the U.S."

This just gets better and better, Harrow thought unhappily, *heading toward a grade-A cluster.*

He rubbed his right eyelid and asked bluntly, "Is Emma Cross a willing or unwilling participant in all this?"

"Unknown. Personally, I suspect she's former Agency with an ax to grind. Think how bad we'll look if it's revealed that we helped a foreign national get hold of a hundred million in good-looking fake cash."

"I thought this was a political ploy, not one of our ops."

Duke gave him a disgusted look. "It's all politics, boy. Thought you'd figured that out by now."

Harrow grimaced. "So do you want the bad money or Temuri or Emma Cross?"

"All three would be gravy."

"What's the meat?"

"Get that money any way you can," Duke said. "Destroy it. No money, no headlines. No headlines, everyone goes back to playing in their own national sandbox."

"Where's the cash?"

"Hidden aboard a yacht called *Blackbird,* which is somewhere in British Columbia. Campbell River is what we were told. Somebody up the line has a locator on the boat and is keeping a watch."

"How soon can you get me there with a good, quiet team?" Harrow asked.

"The team is already in place. As soon as the storm along Vancouver's east coast dies down, we'll fly you on recon. Once you ID the boat, you get the team and find a way to take the boat. Then you find the money, destroy it, and everybody goes home. Questions?"

"Are you worried about witnesses?"

"Go in soft," Harrow said. "No need to worry. And if you go in hard . . ."

Shoot, shovel, shut up. Everybody's favorite fallback solution when money and threats don't work.

Harrow's right eyeball felt like it was being gouged out of its socket. "Does Canada know?" he asked.

"No."

"Am I using my own name?"

"She's going to recognize you anyway, right?" Duke asked.

The headache shot through Harrow's right eye socket and along the back of his skull. It didn't take a bureaucratic genius to see that he'd been nominated the sacrificial goat in this game of tin gods.

"The team I got you is really good," Duke said. "They won't talk no matter what goes down."

Harrow just looked at him.

"Shit." Duke sighed. "I'm sorry. I tried to take it myself. They said no and then switched my bodyguard. I'm locked down." He looked at his watch. "In two minutes my new 'bodyguards' will drag my ass out of here. I'll do everything I can to help you. I'm sorry, Tim. Really sorry."

So was Harrow.

50

DAY FOUR
CAMPBELL RIVER
8:15 P.M.

The thirty-five-knot wind ripping through Campbell River's Discovery Harbor made *Blackbird* flinch and her fenders rub against the dock. The water in even the most protected fairways sported small whitecaps. All through the marina, loose stays rang against masts, keeping an odd sort of time with the wail of rushing air. The docks were filled to capacity, a man-made forest of metal masts and small boats leaning away from the wind.

Emma felt the seat give as Mac slid in next to her on the couch behind the dining table.

"Anything new on the weather?" she asked, glancing up from her computer.

"General consensus is that the wind should die down around dawn."

"If it doesn't?"

"We go out against the floodtide," he said. "That way

the wind and the water will both be moving the same way."

"Which means less wind chop?" she asked.

"And more fuel expenditure. Fortunately, we can afford it."

Emma made a sound. "I'm still in shock over what it cost to fill this baby up. Both tanks."

"They're cross-connected, so that you end up drawing down both." The leather banquette seat creaked as he moved closer. "The generator runs off the starboard tank."

She felt his body heat and automatically moved to give him more room. When he took that, and more, she smiled. And stayed put.

"You get through to Faroe?" Mac asked, glancing at her cell phone.

"By way of Grace, who had to pry a cooing Annalise from her daddy's arms."

Mac grinned. "Gotta admit, watching him with that little charmer makes me smile. A really unlikely combination."

"You and smiling?" she asked, wide-eyed.

He leaned close enough to nip her ear. "Someone as deadly as Faroe with a drooling, cooing, cracker-smeared toddler in his arms."

She gave him a nip right back. "Grace and Faroe both agreed that Demidov could have been lying."

"From hello to good-bye and most spots in between," Mac agreed, watching her lips.

"He probably was telling the truth about his government's relationship with the former Soviet Socialist Republic of Georgia," she said. "They've been at one another's balls since the Berlin Wall came down."

"And the U.S. has been playing 'Let's you and him fight' for just as long," Mac said. "What doesn't make sense is that Georgia would sponsor an attack of any sort inside the borders of its most powerful ally, the U.S.A. That moves straight down from stupid to suicidal."

"You know that because you're intelligent and you follow international news from time to time. I know the truth about the Republic of Georgia for reasons that national security prevents me from listing."

Mac stole the last sip of coffee from her cup.

She ignored him and kept talking. "But how much would the average transit captain/dope smuggler and his arm candy know? Demidov made an educated guess that we're as self-centered and internationally ill informed as the average American. For Jack and Jill Average, the Caucasus Mountains are a long way from anything meaningful, like finding a parking place or paying the bills."

Mac wished he could disagree, but he couldn't. Too many citizens were happily uninformed about the larger world.

For a moment, Emma looked wistful. "I wanted to be Jill Average. That's why I quit the Agency."

"And I hoped to be Jack."

Mac put his hand on top of hers on the varnished teak table. She wove their fingers together.

"I guess that makes us stupid," she said, sighing.

"Foolish."

"Same difference."

"Not always." He lifted their joined hands and sucked one of her fingertips into his mouth. "I've decided I'll take foolish over lies. Rather than lie, I'll be blunt. I want you, which under some circumstances could be really, really stupid."

Her eyes met his. "What if I want you, too?"

Mac felt his pulse increase. "Then we're only foolish."

"Foolish," she said neutrally.

"Isn't that supposed to be what happens when you combine business and pleasure? Foolish?" he asked.

"Under some circumstances, yes," she said. "Now, what would be stupid is trying to get naked while stuffed behind this dining table. Makes the front seat of a sports car look like a limousine."

Mac's slow grin transformed his face. "I like a woman who doesn't lie."

"Prove it."

He slid out of the banquette, pulling her after him. "Your condoms or mine?"

"Yours. I had to guess at size."

He gave a crack of laughter and headed for the master stateroom with long strides. "Not going to touch that."

"No problem. I'll take care of it for you," she said slyly as they went into the stateroom.

With a swift movement he lifted her and stretched her out on top of the bed. Then he looked at her.

Just looked.

"Mac?" she asked uncertainly.

"I'm trying to decide where to start."

"That's easy. Take off your clothes."

"I wasn't thinking about my clothes," he said.

"I was." Her hands worked at his jeans.

His fingers returned the favor on hers.

Despite side trips for kissing and laughing and tasting, they managed to get naked and locked together from tongues to tangled legs.

"You taste good," she said, when her mouth was free.

His tongue circled the tip of her breast, making her breath break. "Same for you. Really good."

"Yes," she gasped.

"Yes, what?"

She wrapped her hand around his erection. "Yes, *this*."

She rubbed the drop of moisture around his hard tip, making him lose track of their game of words. Her hand slipped down, then up, then down, until all he wanted was to be inside her, feeling all of her closing around him at once.

"Good thing we're using your condoms," she said huskily.

"What?" he managed.

"I was always told the bigger the man, the smaller the package. I was told wrong. If I'd stuffed you into the kind of condom I bought, you'd have been singing falsetto."

Laughing, groaning, Mac made a blind grab for his condoms in the bedside drawer. She straddled him and leaned down, giving him a full-body kiss, dragging her nipples through his chest hair. Then she replaced her hand with the wet ache between her legs. Slowly, she slid up, then down him, enjoying every bit of what she could reach.

"You're not—helping," he said, breathing hard, working the condom box open one-handed.

"Am I doing—something wrong?" she said, her voice as breathless as his.

"No. That what's wrong. Unless you want me going commando inside you in about three seconds, help me with this damn thing."

After one long, slow, reluctant glide, she shifted to take the condom package from him, opened it, and rolled it down him. Then her fingertip traced him from tip to root.

"Glad this thing fits one of us," she said.

His eyelids went to half mast. "We'll fit."

"Sure?"

"Yeah." He flipped both of them over and pushed slowly into her. "See?"

Her breathing unraveled. "I love a man of his word."

He smiled, kissed her, tasted her, felt her tasting him. Their hands learned the feel of muscle and softness, cool hair and hot skin. He looked at her eyes, stormy green, and she laughed, biting his shoulder, sucking on him.

Then it was too late for words or for anything but the steamy slide of flesh over flesh, the rushing climb and dizzying fall into satisfaction.

When they recovered, they began all over again, slower, learning about themselves and one another and the kind of pleasure that created a whole world from two interlocked bodies.

51

Stan Amanar hung up the phone and concentrated on breathing past the rage and fear in his throat. When he no longer felt like he was at the dark end of a long downward spiral, he punched in his favorite cousin's phone number.

"What's cooking?" Bob Lovich asked when he picked up the phone.

"Our asses."

Lovich yawned into the phone. "Look, we've been pulling too many back-to-back shifts for games."

"This isn't a game. Is Janet home?" Amanar asked. "And the kids?"

"Yeah. What's up with you?"

Amanar let out a long breath. "Good. Good. Throw some clothes in an overnight bag and meet me at the public dock. A seaplane will pick us up in half an hour."

"Are you drunk?"

"No, and you better not be."

"Stan? What's wrong? Is Susie okay? The kids?"

"They're fine. And they'll stay that way as long as we meet that plane in thirty minutes."

"You're not making sense," Lovich said.

"Shurik Temuri, you remember him?"

"Hell, yes. I was never so glad to see the back of a dude as when he left for—"

"Shut up and listen," Amanar shouted. "Listen good. The lives of our families depend on it!"

"What the—"

"*Shut the fuck up.*"

Lovich took a harsh breath.

And shut up.

"I got a call," Amanar said. "Don't know who. He had an accent like Temuri's. Told me the names of my wife, kids, your wife, your kids, our addresses, our individual schedules, where the kids get on the school bus, our license plates, every damn thing but what kind of toilet paper we use."

Lovich made a rough sound.

"Then," Amanar said, "he said that you and me had to be on that seaplane or he'd kill the kids in front of us, after he raped everyone."

"Did . . ." Lovich's voice dried up. He swallowed several times and tried again. "You believe him?"

"What choice is there? You think either of us can stand against weight like Temuri?"

"Shit," Lovich said. Then he repeated it like a litany.

"I'll pick you up in five."

"Shit," Lovich said.

Amanar punched out and started packing.

52

Mac and Emma rolled separate carts down the marina ramp and over sprawling dock fingers until they reached *Blackbird*. When the wind had begun to ease shortly after eight this morning, they had divided chores and gone different ways. She had picked up some quick supplies while he went to the chandlery on some mysterious captain's errand.

Emma waited until she was certain they were alone before she asked, "Your cart looks like a fishing line factory threw up."

Mac looked at the pale green, unruly mound of plastic netting that was trying to crawl out of his dock cart. "Close."

"Anyone we know get hurt?" she asked drily.

"So far so good."

"Mac, what the hell is in your cart?"

"Plan B," he said. "Or maybe I just missed my yowie suit."

"Your what?"

"You probably know it as a ghillie suit," Mac said.

Emma wondered what a sniper's camouflage outfit had to do with the mess in Mac's cart.

"Partner," she said, "you should know that I make chowder out of clams."

"Mmmm, clam chowder" was all he said.

She ignored him and concentrated on loading supplies aboard *Blackbird*. She kept on pretending he didn't exist until he reappeared in the cabin after stowing the explosion of net in one of the yacht's many lockers. He took a last bite of something that smelled like a septic tank, then stuffed greasy fast food wrappers into the trash.

Buzzers told Emma that he was getting ready to fire up the big diesels. One engine turned over and began to purr. The second followed. The muscular throb of power vibrated through her in a wave of sensation she could get addicted to.

"Want anything more to eat than whatever it was you stuffed in here?" she asked, opening the trash drawer.

"You."

"You had me last night, and then some. Dawn was . . . a whole new experience."

"Same here. A woman like you gives a man a real appetite."

"For grease?" she asked, dangling a food wrapper between two fingers.

"For more. And then more."

Emma dropped the greasy paper and looked into Mac's dark eyes. She knew that honesty was dangerous.

She pulled the trigger anyway.

"You're the only civilian I've ever been in bed with who knew what I was and what I was doing," she said. "No lies, no games. Truly naked. Incredible."

"Like sex without a party hat."

She laughed briefly, almost sadly. "Never done that."

"Neither have I."

Silence stretched, a sensual tension that was as tempting as it was hazardous. They didn't have time for what both of them wanted to try.

Dangerous sex.

She forced herself to turn away and check the engine temperatures. "Getting warm down there."

Mac blinked. "You didn't just say that."

"Say what?" she asked absently, wondering why one engine warmed up a bit more quickly than the other.

He tried to come up with an answer that wouldn't involve getting naked. A cell phone rang, saving him from having to think.

"Mine," she said, patting the pockets of her cargo pants.

"Yours," he agreed huskily.

"Good morning, St. Kilda," she said into the phone.

"What's happening?" Faroe demanded.

"The wind is down to fourteen knots and supposed to continue dropping to five. Or ten, depending on your weather guesser."

"Anything new?"

Emma doubted that Faroe wanted a roundup of who did what and with which and to whom last night. Much less how many times.

"We're leaving Discovery Harbor," she said. "Other than that, nothing new."

Faroe cursed. "Wish they'd pull their finger out and get on with it. Our clock isn't getting any longer."

"We're aware of that."

And she wished she wasn't. Wished she was Jill Normal getting up with Jack Normal for some Normal daily life.

No such luck.

"We found out through back channels that Temuri crossed into Canada at Blaine, Washington," Faroe said. "They lost him. Haven't found him yet."

"That you know of," Emma said crisply.

"I hear you five by five, but Alara is the only card in our hole right now."

"Now *that's* a visual."

Faroe ignored her. "Our system didn't detect any calls to you or Mac last night," he said.

"Correct."

"Chatty, aren't you," Faroe muttered. "Anyone there but Mac?"

"No."

"Demidov's account number went back to accounts used by the KGB."

"Which no longer exists," Emma pointed out.

"Same people, same accounts, new organization name. Information and extortion are very profitable. Ask the former KGB/present oligarchs who do it for a high-flying living in Russia."

"Shocked here. Just shocked."

Faroe laughed, a sound as weary as she was beginning

to feel. The clock in her mind never stopped running, even when she lay tangled up with Mac. A look at Mac's face told her that his clock was counting down along with hers.

They understood each other too well for such a short time together.

We're in trouble, Mac.

Wonder if we'll live long enough to enjoy it.

"Lovich and Amanar didn't turn up for work at Blue Water Marine today," Faroe continued. "As they're usually unlocking the door bright and early, at six-thirty or no later than seven, Grace called the Blue Water office at official opening time. She was told a 'family emergency' would be keeping them busy for 'an unknown amount of time.'"

"If those boys are smart, they're headed for Ecuador," Emma said.

"We're checking outgoing passports. Rather, Alara is. She can do it faster than St. Kilda."

"At last, something she's good for."

Faroe grunted. "St. Kilda will be picking the wheat out of her chaff for a long time. It will work out to our benefit."

"If you're lucky."

"Make us lucky."

The line went dead.

"Well, he's in a sweet mood," Emma said, putting the phone back in her pocket.

"Waiting is the hardest part of the game," Mac said. "It's the first thing a sniper learns and the last thing he forgets. First to flinch eats the first bullet."

"You talk sweeter in bed."

"That's because you taste . . ." Mac's voice faded as he listened.

Somewhere close by, a seaplane droned toward landing. The sound grew closer, changed direction, went away, then started getting louder and louder.

A shadow flashed over *Blackbird*.

Mac and Emma grabbed for the binoculars at the same time. He was closer. He went outside and stood deep in the shadows thrown by the cabin in the morning sun. Swiftly he put the glasses to his eyes and focused.

"Single-engine DeHavilland Beaver," he said over the waning engine noise. "It's flying out over the forest, turning . . . damn, that's not a downwind leg setting up for landing. They're coming back over the harbor for a better look."

"Get under cover!"

"No need," he said. But he stepped back into the cabin without losing the plane in the binoculars. "Anyone who cares enough to kill me would know that Faroe could be up here, running *Blackbird*, before the last echoes of gunfire died."

"Sweet-talking man," she said through her teeth.

Mac smiled beneath the binoculars, watching the plane grow bigger and bigger.

A quarter mile away and closing fast, the aircraft leveled off at about one hundred feet above the forest. Even without binoculars, Emma could see a man in the co-pilot's seat. His face was turned toward them, but his eyes were concealed behind what looked like a camera with a telephoto lens.

Mac tracked the plane like the trained sniper he was. He

read off a single letter followed by the five-digit registration number he could see on the tail of the plane.

Emma scribbled down the identification code and read it back to him.

The plane wagged its wings at them.

Hello, good-bye, screw you.

Without removing the binoculars, Mac flipped off the aircraft.

"Friends of yours?" Emma asked.

"More like yours."

"Agency?"

"I'd take money on it."

She grimaced. "I wonder why they waited until now? They must have known about us before we did."

"Good question," Mac said.

"Maybe. And maybe we're wrong in our assumptions, they just discovered us, and are here to help."

"That would make life easier, which means it ain't gonna happen."

Emma hoped Mac was wrong, but didn't think he was. She flipped open her phone, hit Faroe's speed-dial number, and began talking, knowing that every call was automatically recorded. She started with the plane's tail numbers.

"Type of plane?" Grace asked when Emma was finished.

"Single engine, dry- and water-landing gear, DeHavilland Beaver. Don't know the age. White plane, with a blue-green wavy stripe on a diagonal over the fuselage. They made two passes and wagged their wings at us. Mac flipped them off."

"One hand or two?" Grace asked absently.

"One. The other was busy holding binoculars."

"Your man is reminding me more and more of Joe. Stand by."

"Standing by," Emma said. Then, to herself, *My man?*

It was a heady thought.

Grace wasn't gone long. There weren't nearly as many aircraft registrations as there were for land vehicles.

"As my husband would say, oh shit, oh, dear," Grace muttered. "You sure about that tail number?"

"Repeat, please," Emma said, switching the phone to its external speaker.

"Was the tail number real or a guesstimate?" Grace said.

"Real," Mac said. "What's up?"

"Nothing good," Grace said. "The registration comes back to a company called Greentree Aviation at Boeing Field in Seattle."

Emma looked at Mac, wondering if he understood. The look on his face told her that he did.

"Back when I was in special ops," he said, "I rode Greentree aircraft a time or two. Those pilots have balls."

"The CIA has never been short on *huevos*," Grace said, using the slang of her childhood.

"They're certainly hanging them out for God and man to see," Emma said. "That's unusual."

"Inevitable," Mac said. "From the moment Demidov showed up."

"Yeah," Emma agreed, disgusted. She'd really been hoping to be left alone to answer questions for St. Kilda and the razor-tongued Alara. "Well, at least we know who three of the locator bugs you found belong to."

"St. Kilda put two on *Blackbird*," Grace reminded her. "Redundancy in the face of fragile technology."

"Then I'm betting the CIA did, too," Emma said.

"That takes care of the five we found," Mac said. "Two St. Kilda, two CIA, one Russian."

"I'll call the instant I have anything more," Grace said.

"Wait," Emma said, "is Canada in on the game?"

"All our information says no," Grace said. "What are you going to do?"

"Head north," Emma and Mac said together.

"Like fucking lemmings," Mac said under his breath.

Emma felt the same way.

And she was tired of it.

"St. Kilda can track us by our special phones, right?" she asked Grace.

Mac looked at Emma, smiled, then started laughing. When it came to tactics, partnering with her was like looking in a mirror.

It was time for the other side to work blind.

"What's the joke?" Grace asked.

"Can you find us by our phones?" Mac asked.

"Yes."

"Good," Emma said, watching Mac. "Because in a few minutes, *Blackbird* is going stealth."

53

A single locator says *Blackbird* hasn't left Discovery Harbor," One said. "The other locator is dead."

Tim Harrow looked at the hard, well-built man known only as "Team One" or "One." The other team members were also known by a numeric designation.

Don't ask.

Don't tell.

"One" was the leader of the team of five that had met him at public docks connected to a small, deserted resort/campground. The nearby, popular Blind Channel resort obviously siphoned off all the business. At this time of year, the ratty public docks were ignored. In any case, most cruisers were in their winter docks by mid-September. Harrow's team had told him that fall weather was notoriously unpredictable in northern B.C.

It was hard to believe that today. Steady breeze, a few

clouds, water like blue glass with artistic ripples here and there to keep things from being boring. Ringing it all was the endless mixed forest, green on green.

"Thank you, One," Harrow said. "Let me know the instant that changes."

"Sir."

The man went back to his team. Part of the team was aboard the *Summer Solstice*, a sixty-foot power boat. The rest was in the Zodiac that served as the larger boat's tender.

Harrow had no doubts about the competence of the team. He'd never met a group of better conditioned, smarter men in his life. Seasoned, too. All of them looked to be in their mid-thirties.

Or maybe they're in their twenties with a lot of mileage on them, Harrow thought. *Hope this assignment doesn't pile on more.*

What the hell are Emma and Durand doing on Blackbird? *Polishing the decks with their tongues?*

Harrow pulled out his special cell phone. Good satellite signal. He punched in Joe Faroe's number.

"Who are you?" asked a male voice.

"Emma Cross used to work for me," Harrow said.

"I care about that because . . . ?"

"She's working for you and St. Kilda Consulting now."

Silence.

"Look, Faroe," Harrow said impatiently. "*Blackbird* is sitting dead in the water in Campbell River and I want to know what the hell is going on. The clock is running hard. You know it. I know it. Cut the bullshit."

At the other end of the connection in Rosario, Faroe

kicked back in the uncomfortable motel chair and thought hard. Part of him and all of Steele had been expecting this.

And most of Faroe had hoped they both were wrong.

"What do you want?" Faroe asked.

"*Blackbird* at the coordinates I'll give you. And I want her there fast."

"If you don't get what you want?"

"St. Kilda Consulting is out of business. Permanently." Harrow listened to the silence stretch. "Look, we're taking over the running of the op. Help us and you're golden. If you get in our way—"

"Yeah," Faroe cut in, "I heard you the first time." He paused, thought of Alara, and wished he felt better about cutting in a third party. Or was it a fourth?

"Faroe?"

"Give me the coordinates," he said curtly. "Then call me back in ten minutes."

As soon as Harrow gave the numbers the connection went dead.

Faroe, you son of a bitch, you're everything your file told me to expect.

54

Seymour Narrows was behind them. It had been a treacherous surge and boil of cold green and nearly black water sucking around *Blackbird*. They had powered through the rough, heavy currents and tidal whorls without waiting for slack water, something that many pleasure boats couldn't or wouldn't do.

It had been an exhilarating ride. Once Emma had realized that Mac was watchful rather than worried, she had enjoyed the feel of *Blackbird* meeting conditions that changed from second to second. She was discovering that she liked challenging water.

"I keep thinking the boat should feel lighter after you off-loaded all that junk," Emma said.

"Locator bugs don't weigh much."

"Still . . . Do you think they're waterproof?"

"I think the plastic bag I tacked below the edge of the dock will get wet whenever a big enough boat goes by."

"But until then," she said, "the bugs will send reassuring signals of *Blackbird* tied to the dock in Discovery Harbor, Campbell River, B.C."

"Too bad it isn't true. That was the most fun I've ever had in Discovery Harbor."

She didn't hide the grin that spread over her face. "No wonder yachting is so popular."

Mac made a sound of strangled laughter. "Never heard it called that before."

"My turn," she said, reaching for the wheel.

"You said that last night."

She gave him a sideways look. "Turn about and all that."

"Did I complain?" He turned the wheel over to her.

"Is that what all the groaning was?"

"So I'm noisy. Sue me."

"I'd rather take you to the stateroom and—" she began.

Both their cell phones rang.

"I'll get mine," he said. "Let yours go. This water can shove you around before you know what's happening."

Emma eyed the deceptively calm surface of a huge circle of water nearby and kept both hands on the wheel. After the openness of the Strait of Georgia, Discovery Passage was like running upstream against a cold, deep, muscular river.

"Mac here," he said into his phone.

Emma's phone stopped ringing instantly. She didn't like thinking about what might be important enough for St. Kilda to light up both of their phones at the same time.

"Faroe. Is Emma nearby?"

"Yes," Mac said.

"Put your phone on speaker. It will save time."

"On speaker . . . now."

"Okay. You both hear me?" Faroe asked.

"Yes," they said together.

"A man called Timothy Harrow—" Faroe said.

"Oh shit," Emma said.

"—called. I guess Emma knows him," Faroe said.

"We worked together when I was new to everything spooky," she said. "We worked real close for a few months, but he didn't wear well."

"It took about thirty seconds for me," Faroe said.

"You're a man. If he'd been a hot woman, I wouldn't have been in the same room with him for longer than it took to say good-bye."

Faroe laughed.

Mac shook his head.

"Did good old Tim tell you anything we didn't already know?" Emma asked.

"Nope," Faroe said. "According to him, we have no need to know."

"Okay. This really is an official cluster," she said. "What little gems did he share with you?"

"Harrow, who never admitted to being with the Agency—"

Emma made a rude sound.

"—told us that it's all very hush-hush, Canada isn't in on the whisper circuit, and there could be some heavy lifting ahead. So St. Kilda is supposed to shut up, get down with the opposition, and report every little fart and burp to Harrow, who, by the way, is now running this op."

Emma shook her head.

"Bullshit," Mac said.

"He's high on the crap quotient," Faroe agreed. "But he's in charge."

"*What?*" Mac demanded.

"I'll bet Harrow made an offer St. Kilda couldn't refuse," Emma said. "Like Alara."

"Pretty much," Faroe said. "When Steele told her about the new player, Alara started speaking in foreign tongues, and I'm betting she wasn't describing flowers. Steele stuck to Urdu, which means we're well and truly in the toilet, and someone is fondling the flush lever."

"Can we trust Harrow?" Mac asked her.

"Depends," Emma said. "He's real far up the feeding chain, not like I was. I was a regular mushroom—kept in the dark and fed horse apples. I got tired of it and left the Agency."

"If Harrow is high on the food chain, I don't trust him," Mac said.

"That's my boy," Faroe agreed. "Steele is the only Big Man In Charge I trust, period. And some days, I wonder about even him. He's had a rough day or two. We had a rescue operation go south. Everyone got out alive, but not without blood. Shit happens and all that."

"Emma, would you trust Harrow as a working partner?" Mac asked.

Silence, then, "He knows where a lot of bodies are buried, and he's buried a few on our side. If I had a choice about trusting him, I'd keep him in front of me."

"But we don't have a choice," Mac said. "And we don't trust him."

"Amen," she said beneath her breath.

"You can be as touchy-feely as you like with him," Faroe said, "but he's giving the orders. He made that deadly clear."

"What does he want?" Emma asked.

"You and Mac at the following coordinates, and he wants it all yesterday."

Mac wrote while Faroe read numbers.

"Oh," Faroe added. "He thinks you're still in Campbell River."

"We are," Emma said instantly.

"I've been chasing electrons," Mac added.

"Any luck?" Faroe asked. "I hear they're quick little buggers."

"I've caught enough that we can be at Harrow's coordinates between one and two this afternoon. More or less."

"Depending on weather, and we won't know until we get there, right?" Emma added.

"Harrow is going to have a litter of green lizards," Faroe said.

"Sweet. I'll make a video and put it on YouTube," she said.

"Does Steele care how we deal with Harrow?" Mac asked.

"Short of getting caught committing murder, no," Faroe said. "What do you have in mind?"

"If I tell you," Mac said, "St. Kilda Consulting will be responsible for my actions. If I don't tell you, then you have a rogue agent causing you grief, and really, who can blame you for what you can't control? It's called deniability. The Agency should understand."

Emma gave Mac a sidelong look.

"Don't get caught," Faroe said, and disconnected.

55

Dragging chain behind it, *Blackbird*'s anchor dropped out of sight in the cold green water.

"I can't see any docks," Emma said.

"We're more than a crow-flying mile from Harrow's co-ordinates."

"I'm pulling out my chowder recipe and wondering how small I'll have to chop a tough clam like you."

The look in Emma's eyes told Mac that he could tell her what he had in mind, or find a new first mate.

"If I don't tell you—" he began.

"That's bullshit, Mac. Just bullshit. I'm with you all the way to the guillotine."

He blew out an unhappy breath. "The only thing we have that everybody wants is the *Blackbird*."

She nodded.

"We're going to hide her before I go—"

"We," she said curtly.

"—to meet Harrow."

"News flash. The Agency has more than one satellite in orbit. No matter where we park *Blackbird*, the Agency geeks will be able to count the hawseholes on this baby's stern."

"That's where the yowie suit comes in."

"How is putting you in a ghillie suit . . ." Her eyes widened. "Jesus, Mac. You really think we can hide *Blackbird* from the Eyes in the Sky?"

"I think we're going to try. You have a better idea?"

Emma smiled, then she laughed out loud, a full belly laugh that made Mac join in.

"We're crazy, you know that," she said when she had her breath back.

"Or maybe we're the only sane ones in the asylum."

"Chilling thought. So you bought enough netting to make a ghillie suit for *Blackbird*?"

"Not one that I'd trust my life to."

"But one that's good enough for government work? A lunch-hook job, as it were."

"Yes."

Not knowing whether to laugh some more or shake her head, Emma followed Mac out onto the deck. The air was cooler here, the quality of the water seemed different, and the forest mix had changed—only a handful of leafy trees against an endless brocade of mixed evergreens.

Well, not endless, she thought wryly.

Beyond a decorative ribbon of forest perhaps fifty feet deep along the waterline, the rugged land rose in a stark scenery made of stumps, rock, and dirt—hallmark of recent logging. The green waterline ribbon hanging over gray rock cliffs made the newly exposed dirt look naked, almost embarrassed.

"It may not be pretty," Mac said, "but the industrial harvesting means that tourists won't be coming up here for a few years."

His voice came from the flying bridge, yet way to the stern, rather than the bow, as she expected.

"What are you doing?" she called up.

"Launching the dinghy."

A gust of wind made the green ribbon of trees sway. Water lifted and whispered against rocky bluffs and sheer, high cliffs.

"Wait," she said. "I want to learn how."

"Sure. I don't mind missing our mandated time and putting Harrow's knickers in a twist."

"I'm not that slow," she said, bounding up the stairs.

"No, but his, um, knickers are easily twisted."

"I thought you didn't know him."

"I know the type of person who wears thin after a short time," Mac said.

Wind gusted, held, gusted again, then settled to a steady rush of air over land and water. *Blackbird* swayed lightly.

Mac showed her the electric swing-arm controller that would lower the dinghy into the water. With easy motions, he put the dinghy's lifting straps in the steel ring at the end of the arm's steel line, released the dinghy restraints, and talked Emma through the process of launching the dinghy.

"RIB?" she asked. "As in military usage?"

"Rigid, inflatable boat."

"Gotcha."

She was a quick study. Before the dinghy was all the way down, she had a feel for the changing dynamic of swing arm and wind. The dinghy met the water with a delicate splash.

"Good," Mac said. "Now bring in the arm so I can tie the dinghy to *Blackbird*."

Emma looked over the edge of the upper aft deck, waited until the dinghy was tethered, and asked, "You want to take it off the lifting tackle now?"

"Yes. Give me a foot of line."

The lifting arm spit out a bit of steel cable, Mac unhooked the tackle from three rings on the dinghy, and told Emma to bring it up.

"Slow!" he said, ducking the swinging, heavy snap rings at the end of the lifting tackle.

"Sorry."

"No problem. When the cable is in, unhook the tackle and stow it in the box to your left. Then—real carefully—pull the controller plug out of its socket and stow the controller on top of the straps for now."

Emma struggled a bit with the trio of straps and the heavy snap ring on the lift arm, but got everything put away as Mac wanted.

"Ready," she said.

"Put on something with long sleeves and legs. Gloves, if you have some. We've got some brush to cut before we're done."

She looked over the side. Mac was loading an ax, a pruning saw, a big reel of green netting, and a bunch of spare netting into the dinghy.

"Now what?" she asked.

"We back *Blackbird* in there."

He pointed over his shoulder at a small indentation in the shoreline close to where they had anchored. The little "dog hole" was nearly concealed by the buffer of trees and brush that arched out over it like a lanai.

"It won't fit," she said flatly.

"Like I said last night, trust me."

She shut up.

For a minute.

"Is that hole deep enough?" she asked.

Mac's laughter floated up.

"MacKenzie, get your mind out of your pants!"

"Don't worry, babe. I can multitask. The water next to the rock face is thirty feet deep. More than enough 'hole.'"

"Whatever you say, Captain Babe."

"Change clothes, then come down here and hold the dinghy while I back *Blackbird* into the hole."

Emma heard the big engines fire up while she pulled on long pants and a long-sleeved T. By the time she stepped out onto the deck, Mac had the pod control in his hand and was heading for the bow. He worked the foot pedal to ease out anchor chain and backed *Blackbird* with the pod control at the same time.

He wasn't kidding about multitasking, she thought.

"Bring the dinghy forward as I back us in," he said, without looking away from the stern of *Blackbird*.

"Aye, aye, sir."

And she meant it. No sarcasm, no joke. The man was damn good with a boat.

She dragged the dinghy alongside *Blackbird* in the water until she was at the bow. "This is as far as the dinghy goes."

"Good. I'm backing in."

Mac touched the throttle, let off, touched, let off, until *Blackbird* slowly, carefully, backed into its rocky berth. Tree limbs, saplings, and springy, low-growing brush gave way, then flowed back over the boat like water. When the swim step was about ten feet from shore, he put the pod controls in neutral and dumped a hundred feet of anchor chain down on the bottom to hold the boat.

Then he waited.

"It's a jungle up here," Emma said, looking at the enfolding vegetation. "Tell me nothing is poisonous."

"Nothing is poisonous," Mac repeated dutifully.

She wasn't reassured.

"I'm going to put out a stern tie," Mac said. "Bring the dinghy back here."

Emma started to ask what a stern tie was, then shut up and brought the dinghy back. She watched while he put a reel of line on the stern rail, pulled the dinghy around to the swim step, grabbed the line, and stepped aboard the dinghy. A shove had it moving to the end of its long tether, which got Mac ashore.

He scrambled up the steep, rocky rise only until he found a good boulder to pull the line around. Then he brought the free end back to one of *Blackbird*'s stern cleats and tied off the reel end of the line on the opposite stern cleat. When that was done, he ran midship lines to nearby trees, tied off, and called it good.

Wind rushed and sighed and combed the trees. Pushed at the boat. Pushed harder, from a different direction.

Blackbird didn't wander.

"I wouldn't recommend trying this on your own," Mac said finally. "This is an emergency kind of setup."

"Is this an emergency?"

"Yeah. I'm fed to the teeth with being a mushroom."

"I'm right there in the dark, spitting out shit with you," she said.

"Good. Then you won't mind helping me make a yowie suit for a yacht. You want to handle the pruning knife or the weaving?"

"We'll trade off."

Mac nodded. "Help me string the netting."

56

Tim Harrow paced the empty public docks. He thought about calling St. Kilda and chewing out whoever answered, but he didn't. He'd already yelled at Joe Faroe, started to yell at Grace—who disconnected—and fielded calls from his own boss, who he wished he could disconnect.

No one was happy.

Blackbird had fallen completely off the scope.

Rogue agents, my ass, Harrow thought savagely, even as he appreciated the ploy from a strategic viewpoint. St. Kilda Consulting could throw up its hands and deny all responsibility.

It was what he would have done if he'd been in Steele's place.

That didn't mean Harrow enjoyed having it done to him. He was fresh out of that valuable commodity called deniability. The feeling of a cold wire noose tightening around his balls made him twitchy.

He picked up the binoculars hanging around his neck and scanned every bit of water he could see.

Nothing but wind and currents. Not a boat. Not a seagull. Not even a clot of seaweed.

Not one damn thing to hide behind.

Nothing to take out his frustration on.

Nothing to do but wait for something that might never happen. And listen to the cracking sound of his brilliant career falling in lethal shards around him.

57

After a few minutes at the helm of the dinghy, Emma was in love. The fifty-horsepower outboard made the little craft fly. The controls were easy, intuitive, and wicked quick. The faster she went, the quicker the boat responded.

"Now I know why SEALs love their Zodiacs," she said over the sound of the outboard.

"Just keep an eye out for logs," Mac said.

He stretched, yawned, and leaned against the back of the padded bench seat next to her.

She watched him from the corner of her eye. He looked utterly relaxed as he watched the shoreline. Twice he pointed her toward the proper passes and channels. If he was antsy about not being in control, it didn't show.

Smiling, she settled in to enjoy the ride. She had worked with men who were too insecure to let a woman be in command. Tim Harrow was one of them. But in his case, it wasn't a gender issue. He simply didn't want anyone of any sex to be in control but him. Her competence and independence had rubbed Harrow raw.

Mac saw those command qualities in her, appreciated them, and took them as signals he could relax a bit.

If they hadn't spent much of the night finding out just how many stellar ways they fit together, she would have thought that Mac simply didn't notice the physical, sexual differences between them. But he did.

Oh, yeah. In the best possible ways.

Last night had been an eye-opener for both of them.

She guided the speeding dingy into a channel that was marked by a head-high metal day-marker. The water ahead of the bow began to dance in the afternoon sunlight, as though stirred by a giant swirling school of fish. She slowed the boat, trying to read the water.

Mac pointed out a course that took them closer to the day-marker.

"Are you sure?" she asked over the sound of the outboard.

He nodded.

As she turned away from the roiled water, a whirlpool appeared and widened into a wildly spinning wheel of water revolving around a central vortex.

"Whoa," she said. "That could ruin your day."

"Sure could."

"Why isn't it marked on the chart?"

"The rock that spins out that whirlpool only does it at the strongest tides," he said. "The rest of the time this place is just garden-variety Inside Passage water."

"But how did you know?" She tapped the little nav computer perched up and behind the wheel. "The chart doesn't give you a hint."

"I learned the hard way."

He worked the computer, dividing the small screen. The left side showed a nav chart. The right side showed what was below the boat.

"When you're new to these narrow byways and channels," he said, "you check the tides and currents, and watch the water and sonar for big rocks or other bottom structures that can roil the water above. But you still get surprised."

She smiled. "Who knew? I always thought yachting would be easy to the point of boredom."

He noted the light in her green eyes and the eager tilt of her chin.

"You really like this," he said.

"Nope. I *love* it." She grinned over at Mac and patted the dinghy's steering wheel. "Mine."

"Yeah, I got that feeling."

"You're feeling right."

His laughter was drowned out by the engine as the dinghy skipped through a narrow slot and shot into a wider channel. He pointed toward a rocky outcropping about five miles away.

"Wake me up before we go around the headland," he said.

"Will do."

She drove the twelve-foot dinghy with flair, skimming down the channel like a crazed water bug. She liked everything about being in control of this particular transportation, especially the speed.

Best of all, Mac wasn't upset about being busted down to first mate. Quite the opposite. He had kicked back to take one of the power naps all people in demanding professions learned to use for recharging.

There were a few signs of humanity on the long channel. A deserted cottage, floats marking crab or prawn pots, a workboat headed for somewhere else at top speed, a fisherman looking for a late salmon. Enough for local flavor, but not so much that Emma felt crowded.

She was having too much fun with the zippy little dinghy to notice that she was tired. Camouflaging *Blackbird* had been a grueling experience, complete with scratches, welts, and sap from the fresh greenery they had weaved through the netting. The camouflage wouldn't hold for more than a few days—at most—but all they needed was a chip to bring to the Agency poker table for a few hours of play.

Blackbird was a very big chip.

58

Shurik Temuri watched the signal on his cell phone screen, turned up an inlet, and scanned the shoreline with his glasses. Though the signal was clear, he couldn't see *Blackbird*.

He braced the fishing rod upright against the gunwale, a silent explanation of why someone would be out in a little boat, going nowhere in particular. Then he engaged the outboard engine and eased up the inlet.

He was almost past *Blackbird* when he realized that he was looking at a camouflaged boat.

Carefully Temuri maneuvered closer until he was right on top of *Blackbird*. If he hadn't been so impatient, he would have appreciated the skill and hard work that had gone into making the boat all but disappear. As it was, he was simply pleased that no one was aboard.

Even seen through binoculars, the couple in the red

Mustang suits and speeding dinghy had been unmistakable. He didn't mind killing, but he did object to unnecessary fuss. Much better to find *Blackbird* empty than to have to empty her himself.

Just in case the captain and first mate came back too soon, Temuri checked his weapon. As always, it was ready, waiting. His knife cut and slashed through netting and greenery. He boarded *Blackbird* from the swim step.

The back door was locked.

Temuri used his foot on the glass. Noisy, but fast. Soon he was inside the cabin. Quickly, thoroughly, he went through the boat, collecting what he needed. The cash was a happy surprise. He stuffed it in his pocket without counting the bills.

It finally was time to end the game.

59

Occasional spray felt cold on Emma's face. Wind and tide combined to make a nasty little chop on even the most protected water. Nothing dangerous, but there was enough splash that she was grateful for the fitted Mustang suit Mac had insisted that she wear. If nothing else, the waterproof gear covered nearly all of the scratches on her. Gloves took care of the rest.

And Mac looked so male in his red gear that she kept wanting to take a bite out of him.

The rocky outcropping came closer like a video on fast forward.

"Showtime," she said over the outboard's noise.

As though he hadn't been snoring two seconds ago, Mac came fully alert, ready to rock and roll. He lifted the water-proof binoculars he wore around his neck.

"Go up and around," he said. "I want to eyeball the setup before we commit."

"So do I."

Mac directed Emma around a small island and down a tiny, shallow channel. She watched the nav screen to maintain her bearings. She'd discovered that it would be easier to get lost in the tangled waterways of the Inside Passage.

"Slow to a crawl," Mac said.

She cut back and went around the point at the slowest speed the dinghy could manage. She could just make out a deserted resort with a single public dock tucked back into a cove at the head of a narrow side channel. At the end of the channel, a stream cascaded in a sheet of froth into the bay, making a rushing sound that rivaled the wind.

Mac lifted the glasses and examined the area thoroughly.

"You see Harrow aboard?" she asked.

"The yacht has *Summer Solstice* painted on the stern," Mac said. "Plus a black Zodiac that's too military looking to be a yacht tender."

"A SEAL team?"

"Or something like it," he said. "I can see two ripped dudes in T-shirts, khakis, and Glocks out on the deck of the big boat, another equally ripped dude in the Zodiac wearing a dive suit. Whoa, there's a big guy in khakis and a wind jacket with what looks like a machine gun underneath."

"Sweet."

"Yeah. I'm touched. They're all watching the main channel. I guess they're expecting to see *Blackbird*. A fifth man just came out on the deck. He's a good-looking city type in a dress shirt, no tie, expensive slacks, and leather boat shoes."

"Blond?" she asked. "Short, sleek hair? Mouth like the sharp side of a blade?"

"Yeah three times."

"Meet Tim Harrow."

"I believe I will. Take us in at about eight knots."

Emma powered up on the outboard. The dinghy ran quietly toward the little marina. The men on the big boat glanced in their direction, then turned back to their posts, still watching for *Blackbird*.

Or most of them did. The man in the wind jacket kept watching them.

"So Harrow brought a team with him," Mac said. "Spec Ops, no doubt."

"I'm shocked."

"No awe?"

"I'm not planning on going mano a mano with them."

Mac gave her a dark, sideways glance. "You want to take the lead with Harrow?"

"No. He could teach slippery to soap. He knows that I'm not good-cop material, and you look like the hard-ass you are. We'll double-team him."

Mac smiled grimly. "Even if I looked like Peter Pan, Harrow likely has my file memorized. He hasn't gotten so high on the food chain at the tender age of forty-one by being stupid."

"Good thinking. Which means I don't have to convince you that a Langley suit is as dangerous as a sack of live grenades with loose pins."

"You don't miss your old work much, do you?"

"Do you?" she retorted.

"Not since I met a certain smart-mouthed brunette."

She shot him a look, saw that he meant it—and more—and smiled. "Same goes."

The man in the wind jacket was tracking them through binoculars. Harrow came over, took the binoculars, and scanned the little dinghy.

Emma waved.

"Busted," she said to Mac.

She sped up and swiftly approached the public dock. Following Mac's instructions, she eased way back on the power, turned the wheel, and shifted into neutral for the landing. The dinghy slid in broadside, losing forward momentum just before meeting the dock.

Emma managed not to look surprised, but she knew she'd just had a serious bout of beginner's luck.

He winked at her. Then he swung up onto the aged planks with an ease that told the waiting men Mac's file hadn't lied—he would stand toe-to-toe in any fight they offered. If anyone had really studied his file, the men also would know that Mac was too smart to go looking for a brawl.

Mac tied the dinghy's bowline and held one of the side straps against the dock so that Emma could simply step up from the dinghy's gunwale onto the weathered wood planks.

Tim Harrow vaulted down from the yacht and strode toward them. The man in the wind jacket followed about ten feet to the rear, on Harrow's left. The other two waited thirty feet back along the dock. The man in the Zodiac stayed put.

A loose guard, Mac thought. *They aren't expecting us to be violent.*

He agreed with their assessment.

Mac didn't fancy the odds of taking on the shadow's Uzi with only a rigging knife as a weapon. Even without the gun, the man moved like the highly trained fighter he was. The other men were equally light on their feet.

Equally deadly.

Even Harrow moved well. For a desk flyer, he kept himself fit. He had put on a blue wool blazer before leaving the boat, but hadn't fastened it. The gun in his shoulder harness flashed in and out of view. As he approached, Mac saw the telltale crease in his smooth hair that indicated he was wearing a nearly invisible com unit.

Like a street walker jiggling her assets, Mac thought sardonically. *Letting everyone know who has what.*

"You're late," Harrow said to Emma.

"Chasing electrons eats time," she said.

"If you don't believe us, ask your tech specialist," Mac offered.

Harrow gave him a sweeping look, then concentrated on Emma. "Our locator says you're still in Discovery Harbor, Campbell River."

"Your locator is. We aren't."

Harrow's blue eyes narrowed. "One of your problems, Cross, is that you've never been as funny as you think you are."

"Could be your sense of humor," Mac said.

Harrow shot him a cold look. "Your problem, MacKenzie, is that you don't have a sense of humor at all."

"Yeah, I never learned to laugh at the sight of blood and flying body parts."

"Where is *Blackbird*?" Harrow demanded of Emma.

"Why do you care?" she asked.

"Don't fuck with me."

"No worries," she drawled. "I don't like sloppy seconds."

Color blazed along Harrow's high cheekbones.

Mac discovered his sense of humor. He laughed out loud. Then he bent and brushed a lover's kiss along Emma's neck.

"Ease up, babe," he said too softly to be overheard. "He's going to stroke out on us."

"I'll savor the possibility."

"You still don't get it, do you, Cross?" Harrow said with icy calm. "No matter how you swing that sexy ass, at the end of the day I'm still boss. You aren't."

"You missed the part where you tell her that she's in trouble and all you want to do is help," Mac said.

Harrow shot him a surprised look.

"I took Advanced Interrogation 101," Mac said. "The first rule is that it's never your cock on the line. Just the opposition's. Otherwise you lose control of the interrogation."

Harrow took a slow breath and nodded curtly. "I'm glad you're on our side."

"Won't work," Emma said. "He graduated Divide and Conquer at the head of his class."

"You always were too—" Harrow began.

"Quick for you," she finished. She looked at Mac. "Tim and I have radically different views of the world and the people in it."

"Talk to me," Mac said.

"That's just one of the many things I love about you,"

she said. "You listen. Tim, however, is 'on' all the time, a handsome icon of the modern warrior diplomat, with skills and instincts that are both smooth and honed. We dated for a time, were engaged for two weeks. Then I walked in and found him polishing his desk with an associate's naked ass." She shrugged. "We got un-engaged real quick."

"No harm, no foul?" Mac asked, cutting across Harrow's attempt to talk.

"Pretty much. I was mad for, oh, half an hour. Then I was relieved."

"So Harrow is a walking, talking nation," Mac said. "He doesn't have friends, he has interests."

Emma laughed with delight. "Nailed it. And him."

"If you're finished with the lame comedy routine," Harrow said, "we'll go aboard the *Solstice*, get comfortable, and talk."

"No," Mac and Emma said as one.

"This fly ain't strolling into no spidery parlor," she added.

"We could be overheard out here," Harrow said impatiently.

"If you're worried about somebody lurking on that little islet over there with a parabolic microphone, forget it," Mac said. He jerked a thumb over his shoulder. "The sound of the cascade trumps any listening device."

Harrow put his fists on his hips, bringing the shoulder harness into full display as he got in Mac's face.

The shadow wearing a wind jacket and an Uzi drifted closer.

"Listen, ass clown," Harrow said, "I don't have time for this. I don't even have time to beat the truth out of you."

"Good job you brought a team," Emma said. "Mac would mop the dock with you and you know it."

"Think of the splinters," Mac said, shaking his head.

"Mmm, I am."

"Before you do a grenade imitation," Mac said to Harrow, "understand that we're not going anywhere with you and you're not going anywhere with us. And the dude in the dive suit isn't going to plant any cute device on the dinghy, or we're going to whistle up a seaplane to fly us out of here and leave you with your thumb up your ass and your balls swinging in the breeze. Are you hearing me?"

Harrow glanced reflexively toward the Zodiac. He could just make out the black hood of the diver who had slipped into the water. With a muffled curse, Harrow pulled a hair-thin mic out from behind his ear.

"Abort dive," he said in a clipped voice.

A disembodied voice replied, "Say again."

"Abort."

Emma watched as the diver came up out of the water and rolled back into the Zodiac with a casual display of strength and coordination.

"I've got you outgunned," Harrow said to Mac.

Emma smiled. "We have *Blackbird*. You don't."

60

Let's cut the bullshit," Harrow finally said. "We need to get a locator on *Blackbird*."

"Not going to happen," Emma said.

"Joe Faroe assured me that St. Kilda would cooperate," Harrow said with an icy kind of neutrality. "He knows they can't afford the kind of trouble I can cause."

Emma met his eyes calmly. "Is it as big as the trouble that would come down on you if the sovereign nation of Canada discovered the CIA was running a covert op in its territorial waters?"

"We're not running an op," Harrow said.

"Exactly," she said crisply. "You *were* running an op of some sort, maybe along with the FBI, and then things jumped the border. So now you're relying on a private proxy, St. Kilda Consulting, to get the job done."

"You have no need to know," Harrow said.

"Think of it as a need to survive," Mac said.

"Mac and I have our asses on the firing line," Emma said. "If we get caught with whatever prize everybody is chasing, we might convince the Canadians we were good guys investigating an international smuggling operation. *Might*."

"But the odds are that we'll draw a long prison sentence," Mac said. "That probably would depend on what goods we were caught with."

"So tell me, Tim, what we're going to go to jail for," Emma said.

"You want me to believe you don't know what you'll be smuggling?" Harrow laughed without humor. "Not going to happen."

"Mules don't have to know what's on their backs," she shot back. "What difference does it make? They're just dumb muscle."

Harrow stared at them.

"Right," Emma said. She turned to Mac. "About that seaplane."

"You really don't know what's going on?" Harrow asked in disbelief.

"Now you've got it," Mac said.

"Bloody, buggering hell," Harrow said in disgust, proving that he was an internationalist when it came to language. "This is a three-star cluster. What *do* you know?"

"You first," Emma said.

Harrow hesitated, then shrugged. "I was told that there was an old op, one that began years back, before the present administration."

"Sweet," Mac said under his breath. "Feasible deniability, all present and accounted for. Public theater in an off-Broadway opening, soon to be in D.C."

Harrow ignored him. "We didn't want to use drugs to pay our secret allies, or arms, because there was a huge political downside if the press found out. And when the presidency changes hands, so do secrets. For our covert allies, any diamonds that aren't Russian goods are automatically suspect on the market."

"How could anyone know the difference?" Mac asked.

"Russian diamonds have a very faint green tinge," Emma said. "Not enough to be noticed by anyone but a real expert."

"Our allies didn't want to be carrying bales of American money around in satchels, either," Harrow said, "so we sent them some embryonic currency."

"What—" Mac began.

"You gave them printing plates?" Emma cut in, startled.

Harrow nodded. "They were old. Not good for more than a few hundred passes before they would be too worn to use."

Emma waited, listening very carefully to what Harrow said. Or more important, what he didn't say.

He stopped talking.

"Who were your dollar allies?" Mac asked.

"Georgia. The Ukraine. A few of the '-istan' governments."

"So you were bankrolling insurrections," Emma said.

"Can we help it if a few old printing plates go missing?" Harrow asked, shrugging. "It was years ago. Shit happens."

"Fascinating and all that," Emma said, "but what does it have to do with *Blackbird*?"

"The op went south. Russia got hold of the plates and began minting new hundreds. A lot of them."

"Where did they get the good paper to go with the plates?" Mac asked.

"Same place they get truckloads of blank passports," Harrow said. "They hijacked what they needed. Now they're trying to smuggle tens of millions into the U.S. to leverage some financial deal that will at best break a few hedge funds and at worst drag the economy into another Great Recession. If that happens, the party that doesn't believe in war anywhere will be in control, which would please the hell out of our enemies."

"Our economy eats billions and looks around for a real meal," Mac said. "What good is a few million?"

"Spoken like a true warrior," Harrow said. "You flunked advanced economic manipulation, didn't you? A few hundred million can be a lot of leverage, but I don't have time to explain calculus to a kindergartener. All I want is *Blackbird*. Here. Now."

Mac and Emma looked at each other.

"Keep talking," Emma said. "I'm having trouble envisioning a multimillion-dollar yacht being used to smuggle currency."

"Abkhazia," Harrow said in a clipped voice.

"Suspicious tribes, clans, and gangs," Mac said. "Fallout of the FSU. Criminal Central for Middle Europe. Specialty, counterfeiting. Pounds, euros, dollars, whatever sells. And they're good at what they do. Very good. They damn near put Lithuania's economy under. It's war without firing a shot."

Harrow studied Mac, then nodded. "Your file didn't mention that you spent time there."

"Spent time where," Mac said without inflection.

Harrow nodded again. "Warlords, *mafiya* chieftains, and the bitter ends of corrupt bureaucracies all got together to act like governments and get rich fleecing the peaceful, stoic, or stupid. No matter how you look at it, Russia 'taxes' or runs most of the various criminal enterprises within the Russian Federation."

"Crime is where the money is," Emma said.

"Exactly," Harrow said. "Our best estimate is that the Russians either have taken over or are in a power struggle with the Middle Europeans over the hundred million dollars that is somehow connected to *Blackbird*. This isn't the first load they've run into the U.S.," he admitted. "It's just the first one we've found out about in time to do something."

"A hundred million bucks at a crack," Mac said. "Even in hundred-dollar bills, that's a big pile of green."

"A million C-notes," Emma said, doing the math in her head. "That's a hundred thousand bundles of a hundred bills each."

Mac smiled slowly at her, then said to Harrow, "I've been all over *Blackbird* looking for your damn bugs. I didn't see a good place to hide that much paper."

"Fuel tank," Harrow said.

"Those bills are going to stink of diesel," Mac said. "Hard to pass skunky bills."

"Not if you build a sealed trap to hide the money inside the tanks," Harrow said.

Emma didn't know about fuel tank dimensions, but she did know about stacks of currency. She'd used a few suitcases of payoff money in her time.

"So," she said, "the Agency says *Blackbird* is the mule of choice for a currency-smuggling gig."

"That's what we *believe*," Harrow said. "Dollars may not be as sexy as diamonds, but they're a hell of a lot more convertible into sheer leverage in the marketplace."

Mac didn't know what Harrow or the CIA really believed, but he knew that counterfeiting was the story they were passing out.

"Considering that you provided the plates for the counterfeiters to work with," Emma said, "discovery would be seriously embarrassing for some high-up people. Career fatalities all over the place."

Harrow let out a long breath. "I told them you would understand."

"Where's the handover supposed to take place?" Mac asked. His voice was like his face, neither understanding nor skeptical.

"We're not sure," Harrow said. "We have information that the goods are coming off a container ship onto a fishing boat off the Pacific Coast somewhere between Port Hardy and Prince Rupert. The fishing boat will come south and make the transfer to *Blackbird* at their leisure, somewhere in a quiet cove. God knows the Inside Passage is full of deserted places."

"Can't argue that," Mac said. "Especially after summer."

"When is it supposed to go down?" Emma asked.

"In the next few days," Harrow said.

"Was Tommy yours?" Mac asked, his voice as unreadable as his face.

"Tommy?" Harrow looked confused.

"The dead man on the rez," Mac said.

"Oh. He was the Bureau's. That's why they were unusually territorial about the case. I looked at the file. Nobody owned Tommy but the last person to put crank or a bottle in his hands."

"Lucky for you Tommy died," Emma said. "It gave you a ticket aboard *Blackbird*."

Mac had been thinking the same thing.

"Maybe," Harrow said, shrugging. He narrowed his eyes at Emma. "Tommy was whacked by someone, but it wasn't the Agency or the Bureau. We would have been happier with him in place."

"Huh," Mac said, a word as neutral as his expression.

"But we're in place now," Emma said. "What if we don't want to play nice with you?"

"Even if St. Kilda Consulting wiggles out by playing the rogue-agent card, you and your ex-hotshot captain become international fugitives with serious money on your heads. Award paid on proof of death." Harrow shrugged. "Doubt if you'd last real long."

It wasn't a threat.

It was a fact.

"Where is *Blackbird*?" Harrow asked again.

"You don't trust us to play nice?" she asked.

"I don't trust anyone."

"Especially not the man in the mirror," Mac said very softly.

She didn't argue.

"We need a locator and a data recorder aboard," Harrow said, "and we're going to get them. Cooperate or I throw you to the bounty hunters."

"Who killed Tommy?" Mac asked flatly.

"I told you. I don't know. Why do you care?"

"Collateral damage pisses me off."

"Throw a fit on your own time. Are you in or out?"

Mac looked at Emma.

They exchanged a long silence.

Then she turned to Harrow and said, "In."

61

Taras Demidov divided his attention between his cell phone screen and Lina Fredric.

Both required watching. His two coordinates were no longer closing with one another, which was making his boss crazier than usual. He had kept making and countering his own orders, until finally Demidov quit following them. He was waiting for two like orders in a row.

As for the woman, Lina was restless, wanting to go back to her safe little life. Demidov didn't understand the desire. The grave was safe. Life was for taking risks. Lina had become too soft for anything but death.

Demidov's boss might be crazy, but he didn't have a soft impulse in his body.

"Don't worry, little bird," Demidov said to her. "This will all be done in a day or two. You'll be taking fat fishermen out on the water again, and I'll be another name you've forgotten."

Her expression said everything she was too frightened to voice.

"Why would I kill you?" he asked practically. "You could be of use again. A smart man plans ahead."

"And you're a very smart man," she said, her voice empty.

"I live. Others died." He shrugged. "That is smart enough, yes?"

His cell phone chimed softly.

A text message appeared on the screen: TARGET ON MOVE. INTERCEPT TOMORROW. NEW COORDINATES TO FOLLOW.

62

It took Harrow an hour to cover each bullet point that had been passed down the chain of command to him. In that time, Mac remembered all over again why he didn't miss bureaucracies. The sheen of impatience in Emma's eyes told him that she felt the same way.

Finally the repetition of the obvious irritated even Harrow. He waved them off and stalked back toward *Summer Solstice.*

Silently Mac untied the dinghy and stepped aboard. He was carrying a waterproof, spun-metal case that was no bigger than his palm. Inside, nested in foam, were several impressive bugs.

Harrow reluctantly had agreed that Mac could put them in place. The fact that everyone hadn't scrambled for the Zodiac when Emma and Mac left told him that at least one of the bugs was already live. Probably all of them were.

"Firewall it," Mac said.

Emma gunned the inflatable away from the dock. In seconds they were flying, little more than the engine's prop in the water.

"They'll catch up," she said over the engine. "That Zodiac they have goes like stink."

"Make 'em work for it."

The meter on the chart plotter's electronic screen quickly climbed to thirty knots.

"You're really pissed," Emma said, reading Mac better than either of them expected.

"I thought Harrow or one of his hires pulled the trigger on Tommy."

"Doubt it," Emma said. "Tommy made a better puppet than we do."

"Yeah. Damn it."

"This fast enough for you?" she asked.

All Mac said was, "Why didn't you question Harrow about any Russian involvement? The SR-1 Vektor isn't something everyone uses. Other guns are more available, cheaper, and more reliable—unless you know how to tape the safety in the off position."

"One, Harrow wouldn't have told us. Two, the dumber he thinks we are, the more room we'll have to maneuver."

"They'll throw us away faster than a used condom."

"You think?" she asked sarcastically.

She swerved the dinghy around some rocks, instinctively using a gentle touch at high speed.

"Did you believe Harrow?" Mac asked.

Emma thought for a moment. "He's a gamer by nature

and training. He could have told the truth, but only if he thinks we'll believe it's a lie."

"I hate spooks."

"Me included?"

"You're an ex-spook. Hate has nothing to do with how I feel about you."

In that moment, Emma did something she'd never been able to do in the past. She took Mac at his word.

"Same goes," she said. "Tim is different. If he doesn't think he has better cards than you do, he won't play the game."

"What about you?" Mac asked, looking over his shoulder.

The Zodiac was behind them, hauling at least three passengers at high speed.

"I like to keep paranoids like Tim comfortable," Emma said. "That's when he gets sloppy."

"How did he get sloppy with you?"

"By banging one of his office staff on the side, but only after he was convinced that I trusted him completely. He forgot that I had access to his expense accounts and travel vouchers, as well as hers. The second time they spent a weekend in adjoining rooms at the same hotel, I went to confront Tim on the subject. He was busy at the time."

"Polishing his desk."

"Oh yeah."

"Harrow's an idiot to screw around on a woman like you."

"Thanks." She smiled widely. "In truth, he didn't get nearly as much out of me in bed as you did. And vice versa."

Mac ran his knuckles lightly over her cheekbone. "It was really good. Especially the vice versa."

They skipped along through tidal races and down channels, retracing their earlier track. This time she didn't see any other boats.

The whirlpool was gone, too.

Mac glanced over his shoulder several times. The dinghy and the Zodiac were both blazing over the water, but Harrow's boat had more muscle. It was slowly closing in. No surprise there. The Agency could afford to play with really expensive toys, both human and machine.

"You know what bothers me most about this whole goat-roping?" Mac asked as he pulled out his cell phone.

The gods were with him. There was a satellite overhead.

"Speak," she said.

"Everybody wants us to succeed. The FBI could have blown us out of the water, but only gave us a smack on the butt. Ditto for Demidov," Mac added. "The same doubled for Harrow and his handlers."

"No mystery there," she said. "This is the kind of game where everybody has cheats in place except you and me."

"That's what I was afraid of. All we have is a hole card everyone knows about."

"*Blackbird*."

Mac pushed the button that would give Faroe a scrambled call.

Emma drove while Mac gave St. Kilda a summary of what had happened. By the time he was finishing up, she was coming off the power, picking a way through the rocks that guarded the entrance to the bay where *Blackbird* waited, concealed.

"We did a really good job," she said. "I don't see the boat."

Mac's dark eyes raked the shoreline. Then raked again. "We are so fucked."

Blackbird was gone.

63

Emma stared in furious disbelief toward the rocky niche where they had hidden *Blackbird*. Nothing was there now but a tangle of freshly cut evergreen boughs, random pieces of forest, and a pile of gillnet washing idly against the rocky shore.

"Is Faroe still on the line?" she demanded.

"Can't you hear him swearing?"

"Over you? Not likely. Tell him to send a seaplane, money, and some good binoculars to the coordinates where we met Harrow."

"It's a long shot," Mac said.

"Do we have a better one?"

"The Agency lost a damn fine officer when they lost you."

Emma was too angry to appreciate the compliment. With *Blackbird* gone, she and Mac had to start over.

And the clock simply didn't have that much time left on it.

Mac was speaking quickly into the phone, watching her through narrowed, black eyes. He was no happier than she was.

"While you're at it," he told Faroe, "get Harrow off our butt *now*. If we're being watched, we don't want to give away the whole game. We've lost too much ground as it is."

A pause, then Faroe said, "Grace is on it."

"She has maybe three minutes before our raggedy-ass cover is completely blown."

And it was Mac's experience that when cover was blown, body parts quickly followed.

"Call me when you know something useful," Faroe said.

"Like how many ways we've been screwed?" Mac asked.

The connection was already dead.

Now the Zodiac was less than a half-mile away, its whine of power increasing with each second.

Emma didn't look up from the dent in the shoreline where *Blackbird* had been concealed. But not well enough. She hissed a word through her clenched teeth.

"Not your fault," Mac said. "Obviously I missed a locator bug."

"It's a big boat." She started working over the little nav computer as she spoke. "Without a sweeper, it would be impossible to secure. Faroe knew it. That's why he didn't crap all over you. St. Kilda took a calculated risk. We lost."

"You think Faroe sees it that way?"

"Yes. He's not running around now, trying to cover his ass. It was his call to leave the bug sweeper behind. It was the right call, as our little strip-search proved. If there's a slap coming down, he'll take it."

"That would be . . . refreshing."

She laughed without humor. "It surprised me, too, the first time it happened. But if he thinks you've been careless, God help you, because the Devil is rubbing his hands in glee."

The sound of the Zodiac's massive outboards swelled like an approaching aircraft.

"I should just wave them over to us and throw in the game," she said, her voice rich with disgust.

"But you won't."

"No. Not while there's still a chance, however *pinche*."

Mac recognized the Southern border slang and nodded. "I feel the same way."

Two hundred yards away, the Zodiac suddenly altered course. The craft heeled over and sped off in another direction.

"Just another whale-watching boat gone chasing a new orca spotting," Mac said.

"Harrow doesn't call off easily. Wonder what Grace said."

"Yeah, I'd like to have heard it. That's a no-assing-around kind of woman." He smiled grimly.

"She's a former federal judge."

"Must have been hell on the bench," Mac said.

But they weren't really listening to each other. He was focused on the fading sound of the Zodiac. She was frowning over the nav computer.

The black craft roared up a different channel and vanished. The men aboard were pros. Not once did any of them look toward Mac and Emma.

"How much time before the seaplane arrives?" he asked.

"At least an hour. It will probably be flying up from Rosario or Seattle, maybe farther north if we're lucky. The CIA has more assets to call on than St. Kilda."

"Then we have time to take a look around."

She shrugged. "Can't hurt and we might even find something."

"Elephants might fly."

"Thought that was pigs."

"Pigs are easy," he said.

Any other time she would have laughed. Now she just guided the little boat closer to the place where they had left *Blackbird*.

"At least we know odds are good it wasn't Harrow," Mac said. "He was too eager to co-opt us."

"Which leaves Demidov."

"Or the mysterious, stupidly rich owner who was going to contact us somewhere along the way on this Inside Passage snipe hunt."

"If he exists," she said.

"Plenty of stupidly rich exist. Temuri might be one of them."

"Why would he steal his own boat?"

"Good question. I'll ask him the next time we see him."

While Emma motored them closer to the clutter of beached and tangled debris, Mac watched through the binoculars.

The gillnet camouflage floated in the rocky niche like

the empty cocoon of a giant insect. Lines that had secured the boat dangled uselessly in the water. Two of the lines were already beginning to unwind where they had been slashed through, removing their whipped ends.

"It looks like somebody just cut the net loose, peeled it back, cut the lines, and motored away," Mac said. "Ten minutes work, at most."

Emma's cell phone went off. It wasn't Faroe, which left Harrow—unless somebody else had squeezed her number out of St. Kilda. She cut power and answered.

"What," she said curtly.

"Do you expect me to believe you've lost that fucking boat?" Harrow yelled.

"Believe what you want. *Blackbird* is gone."

Harrow's response told her that he had been hanging out with sailors long enough to expand his salty vocabulary.

No news there, she thought bitterly. *At least half of his team are probably SEALs. Why have water specialists if you don't use them?*

"Get that goddamned boat back and do it fast," Harrow snarled, "or I'll hang your ass so high you'll think you're walking on the moon."

"We're working on it," *you stupid strutting bureaucrat*, "which is more than you can say," she said. "We'll be airborne in an hour. I'm already plotting search grids. There aren't that many places nearby where you could hide a boat as big as *Blackbird*. Get your satellite recon techs on it. We'll see who finds her first."

She ended the call.

"That was fast," Mac said, still studying the debris.

"I don't have to take his abuse anymore."

"I hope Harrow alerted Border Protection in the San Juan Islands," Mac said without looking away from the binoculars. "If they've already loaded the currency, or whatever the goods are, *Blackbird* could be running for international boundary waters right now."

"You're back to sweet talk again."

"Pushed to the firewall, *Blackbird* can do close to thirty knots on decent water," Mac said. "If the captain is willing to risk running at night, he could be across the international boundary and headed for Seattle by dawn."

"Do you want to look at the crime scene or keep depressing me?"

Mac started swearing, a toneless stream of words that made Emma wince.

"What now?" she asked. "Did you find a nasty-gram in a floating bottle?"

"Oil slick ahead."

Emma pulled the throttle back to idle. "Will it hurt the dinghy?"

"No. It's the death cry of a blackbird."

"Mac—"

"The bastards sank her," Mac said bleakly. "A fuel slick is a ship's grave marker."

"What?"

He pointed toward the plume of the fuel spill. "See that?"

"Yes. Smell it, too."

"Follow the slick back to its source." *And pray that I'm wrong.*

She traced the slick, saw that it led toward the mangled camouflage netting, and said, "You want to get closer."

"Yeah." He reached past her and began making the little nav computer sit up and do tricks. "Don't worry. The slick is no worse than what you find near a fuel dock in a commercial marina."

"Beautiful."

"Go slow. I want to watch the bottom. This could be just a smokescreen. If we think *Blackbird* is here, we won't look for her anywhere else."

Emma idled forward, following the rainbow sheen of fuel to its end, maybe fifty yards from where *Blackbird* had been concealed.

Mac watched the display. The sonar gave a garish, two-toned picture of the uneven, rocky bottom. Emma crisscrossed the area, amazed to see that only a few yards away from where they had concealed *Blackbird*, the bottom went from seventy feet deep to three hundred.

"Cliffs above water usually mean steep drop-offs below," Mac said, when she commented.

"You really think *Blackbird*'s still here?" Emma asked, glancing over the side.

Not that she could have seen bottom, with or without the shimmer of fuel. The green water was rich, nearly opaque with plankton.

"Either that or there's a petroleum pipeline running right under a nameless little dog hole, and while we were gone, the line just happened to pop a leak."

"Not likely," she said.

"No, it—wait. Go out of gear."

She put the shifter in neutral and watched Mac. He gave her some terse directions and watched the wildly colorful screen. The dinghy doubled back on its course, then turned again, and again, painting images of the bottom on the screen with each yard of motion.

"There," he said, pointing at the screen. "Bloody bastards. She was a good boat."

She stared at the bright colors. It was hard for her to translate them into anything useful. But that was why people hired experts.

"You're sure," she said. It was a statement, not a question.

"She's sitting on her keel in one hundred and fifty-four feet of water." He stabbed the screen with one index finger. "That's the top of the cabin, twenty feet above the waterline— if she was floating. What I've had you doing is the equivalent of flying over her from bow to stern."

"Guess we'll need that seaplane just to get home."

Mac grunted.

Emma started to say something, shook her head, and tried again. "Why? Why would anyone sink millions of dollars' worth of new yacht?"

"They didn't need her anymore."

"If the smugglers found out that the Agency was closing in, it's possible that they buried the evidence and ran. But . . ."

"But that doesn't explain *Black Swan*, the missing twin."

"Yeah," she said unhappily.

She thought hard, fast, silently offering and rejecting explanation after explanation for the scuttling of *Blackbird*. None of the things that made sense gave her a smile.

"Maybe Demidov got impatient," she said finally.

"Would we?"

She sighed. "No. Maybe they're planning to salvage her and start again. A different way of hiding her, as it were."

"A ship that has been on the bottom is pretty well ruined. You're not going to just float her, pump her out, and take off."

Emma stared at the deceptively beautiful rainbows in the slick. The most likely conclusion made her stomach clench. She looked at Mac.

He looked as grim as she felt.

"You're thinking what I don't want to think," she said.

"I'm not real happy about it, either."

"It's a crazy idea. Premature. Unsupported."

"And it fits the facts as we know them," he said bleakly. "You can paint over almost every color hull but black."

"I didn't know that."

"It comes as a surprise to a lot of people." He shrugged. "You want to call or should I?"

"I will."

She dug out her phone, hit speed dial, and braced herself to tell St. Kilda some really bad news.

64

Alara sat in Steele's office as she had for hours, talking on her phone, trading favors, calling in IOUs, bribing, threatening careers, and looking more exhausted with each lost minute.

Steele didn't look any better. St. Kilda had been combing through its own mazes, searching for something—a hint, a tone of voice, a choice of words, something done or undone—anything that would indicate that someone knew more than he or she was telling.

Nothing had come his way.

"Deputy Director of Operations on line four," Dwayne said to Steele. "Two other calls standing by, but they're just lower-level screamers."

Steele nodded. He paid Dwayne very well to sort out important calls; at times like this, he was worth double his salary.

"Switch Duke to my phone," Steele said.

Alara's black eyes narrowed as she focused on each nuance of Steele's expression and words. The image of a dying city haunted her, slicing her soul with the knowledge that her children's children had inherited a world gone mad.

But when was it ever sane? she asked herself bitterly.

She had four advanced degrees in global history. She was no closer to answering the sanity question than she had been as an eager student whose mind was on fire with the beauty and complexity of the world's cultures and history.

The complexity, at least, remained.

Even the beauty, sometimes.

Without realizing it Alara shook her head. She had lived too long knowing too much—and not nearly enough.

Steele watched her as he listened to Duke. If her eyes had been open, he would have thought she was warning him against talking to the CIA's Deputy Director of Operations. But her eyes were like her past, closed.

"Duke," Steele said finally, "I give you my word that you have everything we have. More. You know what originally kicked this avalanche off the mountain. St. Kilda doesn't, which places us at a real disadvantage."

"You're in a tough place," Duke agreed. "We all are. This kind of investigation is difficult in the extreme. People won't, often *can't* by the very description of their office, say anything until there is agreement that it's necessary to reveal highly, *highly* sensitive secrets. Decades of careful placement of agents and officers is at stake."

"If you make Seattle's memorial big enough, your explanations might fit on the plaque."

"Damn it, Steele. It's not only our people at risk. Our allies—"

"Will pass the hat for the plaque," Steele said. "So will our enemies. When it comes to sharing real information, there's little difference."

"We have sat intel people working 24/7," Duke said. "Problem is, there's a storm moving down the northwest coast from Alaska. It's already hammering the Queen Charlotte Islands. Northern Vancouver Island will feel it tomorrow, but the clouds are coming in right now."

"I'm certain your satellite intelligence technicians are capable of penetrating a few clouds."

"Whether or how much is classified," Duke said.

Steele bit off a particularly vicious oath. It seemed that the only thing unclassified about this steaming pile of shit was the finger-pointing.

"Look," Duke said, "I've given you all that I can and more than I should. Tim Harrow's diver confirmed that *Blackbird* is on the bottom. He and the team are standing by for any hint, however unlikely, of *Black Swan*. Another team has joined them. They are highly specialized and so secret that I'm the lowest ranking officer who knows of their existence. Every sign of *Blackbird*'s scuttling is being mopped up."

"The environment thanks you."

Duke swore. "If I could get away with giving you men and material, I would. But until you give me a *Swan* sighting, my hands are tied. You sure your agents haven't really gone rogue and are playing for the other team? You know it happens."

"Unlike you, I'm very certain of my employees."

"Hackers, then."

"I'll note your suggestions for the feasible deniability file."

"Steele, if I . . ." Duke's voice died.

There was nothing to say.

Both men knew it.

65

Emma lowered the binoculars for a moment and closed her eyes to rest them. Both she and Mac had been in the air, staring through binoculars since dawn. She had seen some breathtakingly wild places—evergreens clinging to rocky cliffs, moss in more shades of green and brown than she could name, water both fresh and salt, calm and roiled, colors of gray and silver and blue impossible to describe.

Then there were the boats. Some small freighters or tankers, cruise ships shifting locations for the winter season, fishing boats, crabbing boats, prawning boats, sailboats, tugboats, log barges, freight barges, inflatables, rowboats, skiffs, power cruisers both dainty and extravagant. She and Mac had examined everything that could float and a few that shouldn't have.

They hadn't seen anything that looked like *Blackbird*.

Mac hung up his cell phone and spoke through the headphone link to Emma. "Steele says Harrow has at least two planes working south, covering Seattle and the San Juan Islands. Faroe wants us to stay north of Campbell River in case *Black Swan* is still up here somewhere under wraps."

"But—" Emma began.

"The problem is," Mac continued, "she could appear anywhere, because she could have been hidden anywhere from Southeast Alaska to the B.C. coast above Vancouver Island."

"Wouldn't that cause a stir? That's an expensive boat to be left for months at a time."

"It's not unusual for summer yachties to leave their boats stashed in safe ports up north for the winter, fly out to Florida or Mexico, and fly back in the spring or summer. Some people hire transit captains to bring their baby north to south and back again."

Emma digested that as she tried to ignore the growling, low-frequency grind of the big radial engine sitting a few feet in front of her. Even with the headset to dampen the bone-deep, droning roar, she felt like she was inside a metal coffin that was being beaten with baseball bats.

She hadn't liked small planes before she stepped aboard this one. Now she respected the sturdy DeHavilland for its ability to rise and fall with the terrain and wind, and land in hair-raising places; but she still didn't like it.

"Give me a boat any day," she muttered.

"What?" Mac said.

"It's noisy in here."

"Try the engine room of *Blackbird*, when she was running."

"No thanks."

"You sure?" he asked. "I have extra ear protectors." *Or had.*

"The pilot must be deaf."

"Only in the lower ranges."

The pilot was a man of indeterminate age and complete control of his airplane. Whatever his per-hour rate was, he earned it.

"There's Chatham Point," the pilot said over the intercom, pointing ahead through the windshield at a bright, white-and-red-striped lighthouse on a finger of land. "No noncommercial black, approximately forty-feet-long hulls on the water that I can see. I'll make a lower pass to be certain."

Mac put down his binoculars. He'd learned that the pilot's eye was so good it was almost eerie, reflecting a combination of expertise and a sixth sense. He could tell the difference between a forty- and a fifty-foot cruiser at a thousand feet.

The plane banked, drifted lower, and circled as though looking for a place to land.

Emma scanned the water through her glasses.

"Anything?" Mac asked.

"Nothing we want." She sighed and lowered the glasses. "The Inside Passage is an extraordinary, beautiful maze. And maddening. Did I mention that? You could lose an armada down there."

The radio crackled.

"We'll need to refuel soon," the pilot said. "You want me to do it at Campbell River or Port Hardy?"

"Port Hardy," Mac said. "We're going to give the far northern stretch another look."

"Roger Port Hardy."

Emma listened, put the binoculars back to her eyes. She refused to let despair creep over her as she watched the countless, intricate waterways of the Inside Passage and listened to the clock ticking relentlessly in her head.

We'll find Blackbird's *twin.*

We have to.

66

The seaplane splashed down fifty yards off the breakwater that protected the boat basin at Port Hardy. In choppy water, the plane taxied to the aviation section of the fuel docks. The pilot went to work filling the plane's tank and cleaning the windshield just like a ground-based gas jockey.

Emma called Faroe as soon as her hearing returned to normal.

"We're refueling in Port Hardy," she said quietly, relieved to be free of the hammering engine sounds. "No joy so far."

"Frack," Faroe muttered savagely.

"Frack?"

"I'm holding Annalise. No F-bombs allowed."

Emma smiled, reaching for the sane and normal. "Someday soon, she's going to ask her mommy what 'F-bomb' means."

"Yeah, and by then her big brother will probably have taught her ten other nasty words, right, sweetie?"

Annalise cooed.

"She's the only joy on my end," Faroe said. "If Harrow's searchers have had any more luck than St. Kilda has, he's sitting on it."

"I hope he gets hemorrhoids. Mac says we've covered all the back ways up to the Queen Charlotte Sound and back down to twenty miles below Campbell River."

Mac reached for the phone.

Emma gave it to him.

"Mac, here," he said. "I gather you've come up as empty as we have."

"Double handful of F-bombs."

Mac shook his head. "As far as we can tell, no *Blackbird* twin has turned off through the Thurlows or gone sneaking around the back side of Quadra. Do you have any contacts other than Harrow and Alara?"

"Steele knows Harrow's boss."

"Twist his nuts," Mac said.

"Already done. No go. Until everyone at the top of the feeding chain is dead-solid certain that Harrow can't get the job done before the bad news sails into Seattle, we're stuck up north sucking the Devil's, uh, thumb."

Annalise burbled in the background.

Mac smiled despite the anger, fear, and sheer frustration raging beneath his calm surface.

"If the Agency lets it all hang out in public," Emma said impatiently, reclaiming the phone, "everyone's lifetime of experience, decades of effort, overt and covert contacts, and international knowledge in general is in the sewer or dead by execution. If the top of the food chain keeps a lid on *Blackbird*, they might survive, and with them whatever ops and covert sources they have running outside this one particular op. For them, it's not just careers at stake. It's actual human lives overseas. Until they're certain there's no other way out, they'll zip it and keep it zipped. This can't be news to anyone with the IQ of a pile worm."

"Doesn't mean I have to like it," Faroe shot back.

"Did somebody ask you to?"

Faroe said something Annalise wasn't supposed to hear. Then, "You sound like Grace."

"Thank you."

There was the rush of Faroe releasing a long breath. "Sorry. Last few hours, my AQ is off the charts."

"AQ?"

"Asshole Quotient."

He disconnected.

Emma looked at the phone with a bemused expression.

"What?" Mac asked.

"My boss just apologized. To me."

"Savor it," he said absently.

She followed his glance. He was watching the fuel dock where boats orbited like moths waiting for their chance in the flames.

"What?" she asked.

"Having a 'duh' moment," he said.

"Speak."

"Assume *Swan* came off a compliant containership somewhere between Southeast Alaska and the northern tip of Vancouver Island."

"Where we are now."

Mac nodded. "When I picked up *Blackbird*, she had about enough fuel to make Rosario, if I trusted the sight gauges."

Emma cocked her head and listened.

"But I know better than to trust anything coming right off a containership," Mac said, "so I got some reliable fuel aboard before I ran to Rosario."

"That's where I met you. At the fuel dock."

He turned and smiled. "Sometimes a man gets lucky. Real lucky."

"So does a woman. Which leaves us with a probably thirsty *Swan* somewhere between way north and here."

"Port Hardy is a magnet."

"Why?" she asked, looking around at the unassuming little harbor.

"First reliable fuel—"

"You keep mentioning 'reliable,'" she interrupted.

"Some places don't sell enough fuel to keep their storage tanks clean."

She started to ask another question but didn't. The intricacies of good diesel fuel weren't her problem. Yet.

"North coast of B.C. has some of the first reliable fuel after crossing Queen Charlotte Sound from Alaska," Mac said.

"Or being off-loaded from a containership at sea. Is that possible, by the way?" she asked. "Off-loading at sea?"

"Depends. If the weather is decent, and the containership's deck crane operator is mostly sober, you can off-load a boat like *Blackbird* pretty much where you want to. Takes maybe half an hour."

"What about all the outfitting that was done in Rosario?" she asked.

"They've had a year to work on *Swan*. They could have done it in pieces without making any waves at all."

"But no matter what," she said, "if *Swan* was off-loaded north of here, she would likely make a call at Port Hardy?"

Mac nodded. "I'm going to talk to the fuel jockey."

She fell in step beside him. "If Port Hardy is such a magnet, what makes you think anyone would remember a single boat?"

"The opposition made a mistake when they stole a beautiful, black-hulled ship. She's memorable."

"And can't be painted over."

"Nearly impossible. Besides"—he shrugged—"despite being a magnet, the amount of traffic Port Hardy sees isn't spit compared to Port of Vancouver or Elliott Bay. The farther north you go, the smaller civilization becomes, until a handful is a crowd."

"We're grabbing at straws, aren't we?"

"Depends."

She sighed. "Next to what we have, straws look like logs."

"Pretty much."

Mac and Emma closed in on the lean woman who was giving orders while a younger man pumped fuel into boats as fast as the fat, heavy hoses allowed. Emma let Mac engage the woman—the owner, as she quickly pointed out to him—in talk about grades and purity of fuel, virtues of gas versus diesel, various filters, taxes, taxes on taxes, licensing fees, environmental fees and restrictions, fishing restrictions, the silliness of sailboats in a place when the wind was rarely constant, and the weather. In between words, the owner was directing her dockhand.

By the time Mac and the owner got around to yachts coming and going, Emma was having a hard time swallowing all her yawns.

". . . and a black hull. Seen anything like that?" Mac asked.

Emma snapped into focus and mentally reviewed the past few sentences. Mac had been describing *Blackbird.*

The owner removed a grubby fishing cap, scratched through an explosion of silver hair, and said, "Matter of fact, the cousin you're asking about came through here around dawn today. Made such a fuss, I opened the fuel dock early."

"Yeah?" Mac said idly, but his eyes were like black ice. "He have his wife with him?"

"Didn't see her. There was another man, though. Maybe it was a different boat."

Mac shrugged like it didn't matter. "Sounds like my dear old cuz. He takes buddies fishing a lot. Leaves the wife behind. Pisses her off, I'll tell you."

The owner laughed. "That explains it. He spent a lot of time on his phone. Didn't look like he enjoyed it. In fact, he was heading home real quick, taking the shortest way."

Emma sensed Mac's sudden intensity, but nothing showed on his surface.

"You mean he's going down the outside?" Mac asked, shaking his head. "Damn fool. Weather is tricky this time of year."

"I said something about that. He just kept on buying charts from the Brooks Peninsula all the way to Bamfield. I didn't have any for farther south. One of the men, the taller one, was screaming about not piloting the whole west side without charts, and the other guy said they'd pick up the rest in Tofino, since they were going to have to fuel there anyway."

Mac was too busy clamping down on his control to make a polite and casual reply.

Son of a bitch!

Nobody had expected anyone to take on the Pacific Ocean in autumn in a *Blackbird* twin designed for the very different waters of the Inside Passage.

The owner shrugged. "Man's captain of his own boat. I just put fuel on board and rang up the sale."

"He never was real good at listening," Mac said.

"He's got a sound boat underneath him, for a yacht." The owner stepped away for a moment to flip on a fuel pump. "They figured to run close to twenty knots, be home in eighteen hours. I looked at the numbers on a big chart and it came to seven hundred kilometers, give or take."

"He's shooting for Seattle?" Mac asked. "All at once?"

The owner laughed. "Yeah, his wife must have put fire up his butt. He wasn't entirely stupid, though. He listened when I told him to head two-hundred-seventy degrees for twenty minutes, long enough to miss the big reef out there, before he headed south."

Mac remembered the reef. Just one of the many treacherous features of the beautiful, wild stretch of ocean that thundered along the west side of Vancouver Island.

"I saw him make the turn a little later," the owner said, tugging her cap down with an automatic gesture. "He was throwing a bow wave like a customs cutter on a hot run. Made my kidneys ache to look at it." She sighed. "That's why I got out of the crabbing business in Alaska. Didn't have the kidneys for it."

"Seattle in eighteen hours. Wow," Emma said. *It will take an airplane to catch them.*

"Big storm coming, too," the owner added absently, looking around the fuel dock. "Guess he plans to beat it to Seattle. Hope he makes it."

Mac and Emma looked at each other, wondering the same thing.

Would it be good or bad if Blackbird's *twin sinks?*

Suddenly the owner loped off to help an old yacht that was making hard work of landing at the fuel dock. Apparently the captain was single-handing the boat.

Mac took Emma's arm and urged her back to the seaplane. She hurried along beside him.

"Did I understand that correctly?" she asked in a low voice.

"Lovich and Amanar are taking the outside route. Stupid bastards."

"Why? It fooled us."

"*Blackbird* wasn't built for ocean storms," Mac said simply. "She can take swells in decent weather, even lousy weather, but without a stabilizer, the crew will get hammered real good. A big enough wave over the beam could blow out all her side windows and sink her."

"God." Emma swallowed. "Is that likely?"

"She's well built. Lovich and Amanar may be greedy, but they're good captains on the water. Their spines will hate them, and their stomachs will be slamming against their brains, but without bad luck they'll get through."

"What is Tofino?" she asked.

"A port about three-quarters of the way down the west side of Vancouver Island."

"Reliable fuel?" she asked.

"Yes," Mac said.

"Can our plane reach Tofino before Lovich and Amanar refuel?"

"That's the easy part."

Emma didn't ask about the hard part. She already knew.

67

Emma searched the Pacific Ocean beneath her through binoculars. The slanting light and broken clouds—and her weary eyes—made shadows that looked like black-hulled ships.

At her side, Mac searched between the plane and the ragged black line of shore. Waves that surged rather than broke against cliffs flashed white against the darkening land.

She saw a shadowy black hull, lifted the glasses enough to rub her eyes, and focused again. The hull was still there.

Then it wasn't.

With fingers that wanted to tremble, she refined the focus. The silhouette of a ship settled into the clear viewing field of her binoculars. She wanted to use the computerized zoom feature, but was afraid to lose contact with the shadow in any way.

"Mac."

The huskiness of her voice brought every nerve alive in him. "Here."

"About two-thirty. Out to sea. When you find it, zoom in."

He found the ship quickly, zoomed in. "Hello, *Blackbird*. Or *Black Swan*. Aren't you a beauty."

"ID positive?" she asked.

"Unless someone built a triplet, that's our baby."

The certainty in his voice was as unmistakable as the elegant silhouette sliding down the side of a wave.

"Want me to circle?" the pilot asked.

"No," Emma and Mac said as one.

"Just keep on like you're flying in to one of the remote resorts on the west side," Mac said.

"When we're out of sight of the boat, go straight to Tofino," Emma added.

"Roger."

The plane kept on a course that angled slowly away from the boat. Before it was out of sight, Emma was on her special phone.

Grace answered immediately. "Anything?"

"We found a ship identical to *Blackbird* going down the west side of Vancouver Island," Emma said.

"Thank you, God," Grace breathed. "Above or below Tofino?"

"Above."

Grace sighed more thanks into the phone. Then her voice became precise, efficient. "I have permission for you to repossess a ship of *Black Swan*'s description."

"Repo? As in steal?"

"Stealing is illegal. Repossessing is part of a legal process."

"Um, right," Emma said, feeling an absurd kind of laughter tickling her throat. "So we go to the local cops and—"

"We'd rather you didn't," Grace cut in. "The insurance company paid off *Black Swan*, which means that they legally own the ship if and when it is found. However, it would be a much smoother ownership transition if you simply hijack the bitch and run for the border."

"Possession being nine-tenths of the law."

"Faroe knew you would understand."

Emma laughed.

"We've arranged for a rental car," Grace continued, "and silent water transportation."

"Come again?"

"Kayaks."

Emma made a strangled sound.

"According to your files, both you and Mac have some past experience with them," Grace said.

"Past being the operative word."

"Would you rather do an underwater approach? In the dark?"

"Kayaks it is," Emma said, remembering the look of the water north of Nanaimo. "Unless Mac objects."

"He won't. This kind of kayak is easier to get into and out of than diving gear. The rental car papers, necessary personal items, cash, and repossession papers will be at the airport."

"We're on a float plane. Water, not paved runways."

"Joe assured me that your plane does solid as well as liquid landings," Grace said. "Call Steele when you control *Black Swan* masquerading as *Blackbird*."

"What if—"

"Then call me."

Grace disconnected.

68

Lina Fredric paid the truck driver in cash, then watched as he racked the fuel hose after refueling the boat. Fuel in Port Renfrew was by arrangement only, and trucked to the water's edge; rather like an undeveloped country or a step back in time. The tourist-oriented waterfront was the most modern element of the town. The rest was mostly shacks, rocks, evergreens, water, and the sense of a vast ocean waiting beyond the rocks guarding the harbor.

The boat Lina had rented from the friend of a cousin of a friend—or perhaps an enemy, considering the dirty interior—was topped off and ready to run. Except for having a bigger kicker and extra fuel cans lashed inside the stern gunwale, the boat was essentially like the *Redhead II*, with all the benefits of speed and drawbacks of a boat run by anyone with the cash to rent her.

At least the chart plotter worked. Because most users of

the boat had been sport fishermen chasing salmon, radar wasn't required. In the dense fogs that haunted the west side during summer, pleasure fishermen stayed within view of shore, or went out in packs following someone who had reliable radar.

"Well?" Demidov prodded.

Lina stepped down into the boat. "There is a light for night running, if you insist. I can't recommend it. We have no radar."

Demidov looked at the screen of his phone. "I'll guide us."

Right into a tanker, she thought sourly.

But she was through arguing with Demidov. As far as he was concerned, he had his orders, he had her, and the boat she had scrounged up was fueled and ready to go. Discussion over.

"Do we leave now?" she asked.

He looked from the numbers on his phone to the paper chart he had found aboard the *Sea Tiger*. The scow was more like an alley cat than a tiger, but he'd had worse transportation in his career. The van in Rosario came immediately to his mind. At least the slops bucket on the boat could be emptied overboard with each use.

"We have an opportunity for food," Demidov said. "Is that pub still open?"

"Partially. It seems that some people will endure any kind of weather to avoid crowds. Hikers and kayakers, particularly. The fact that it's after the first week in October and the weather is dodgy . . ." She shrugged. "It keeps the summer mobs away."

Demidov glanced around. Crowd wasn't a word he would

have thought of in the same sentence as Port Renfrew. It was the end of the road. Literally. Like the car they had driven here, the town had a weary, hard-used air. He had parked the vehicle in an empty lot with keys inside. If someone wanted to steal the car, Demidov wished him luck. There was almost no petrol in the tank.

"Bring back enough food and water for a day," he said.

Without a word, Lina climbed onto the dock and went in search of provisions. Like loose wiring, she clicked in and out of touch with reality. Constant fear was numbing.

Except when it wasn't.

69

The evening air was cold, damp, with an edge that told of winter rolling down from the Aleutians. The harbor itself was slick and quiet, a black satin that reflected pieces of the pastel sky when the clouds and local lighting allowed.

The wide, blunt, plastic kayaks bobbing gently by the rental dock were a scuffed-up red. The color didn't worry Mac or Emma. At night, red disappeared easily into black, which was why many emergency crews preferred a neon kind of yellow-green.

Mac watched the pocket harbor of Tofino with the same binoculars he had been using since dawn. Only one fuel dock was still open. It was a fairly large place with an attached store and chandlery. For someone needing fuel and charts, it was a magnet.

Emma prayed that the store and fuel would draw in *Black Swan* or *Blackbird*, whichever nameplate was on the boat.

She had a legal document that allowed them to repossess *Blackbird*'s twin. All they had to do was sneak aboard and take over the ship.

Yeah, right.

But that was the best plan anyone had come up with. Certainly the only one that had a chance of keeping a lid on all the need-to-know-only possibilities that *Blackbird* was the center of.

She lifted her own binoculars and focused on the gloaming beyond the chain of islets and rocks that protected Tofino from the open ocean. If her memory still worked, another element had been added to the scene.

A spot on the horizon had become a black-hulled ship.

"Mac."

"I see her. Damn, but she's a pretty boat."

"Too bad she's gone over to the dark side."

He smiled grimly. "We're about to take care of that. Come on. By the time we get in position, Amanar and Lovich should be fueling."

Emma lowered the binoculars and saw Mac frowning at the kayaks.

"Problem?" she asked.

"Guess what's the most dangerous form of watercraft on the ocean, including personal watercraft and aircraft carriers?"

She looked at the fat kayaks. "Don't tell me."

"Okay."

"Is that why Faroe put a roll of duct tape in your gear? To keep these afloat?"

"Handcuffs," Mac said.

Emma blinked. "I thought that was what the dental floss was for."

He laughed.

She maneuvered into her plastic tub. There was no spray skirt to keep water out, but her clothes were designed to keep her dry. Dark, one-piece, fitted, stretchy, the special gear was warm and almost as waterproof as a dive suit. Neoprene gloves, reef shoes, a dark knit cap, a delicate headset, waterproof belly bag for personal gear, and a flotation harness completed her outfit.

Mac stretched against the black waterproof gear he wore. The length was good, the reef shoes fit, and the shoulders were too tight. He was glad no one had thought of waterproof hoods. They pulled all but the shortest hair and made your scalp sweat. The small backpack and flat flotation harness he wore were simply there, like a wristwatch, unnoticed until needed.

He eased into his kayak and looked at Emma. She was poised, waiting for him, double-ended paddle at the ready. A wind riffled over the smooth harbor. Though the water was warmer than in the open ocean, the wind smelled like winter.

Mac and Emma paddled slowly away from shore, waiting for old, unused reflexes to assert themselves. By the time they had crossed the little harbor, neither of them had to think about every shift and motion of paddle and kayak.

They paddled quietly toward the fuel dock, skirting anchored commercial fish boats, moored freight barges, and the occasional yacht. As they reached a long-line troller that was tied off to a buoy, *Blackbird* roared up to the fuel dock, leaving the kind of wake that threw boats around. The smaller boats tied to the transient mooring around the fuel dock got the worst ride.

"Idiot," Mac breathed into his headset.

"I like what that fish captain yelled better," Emma answered softly. "Not sure I caught that last reference, though."

"Something about a chainsaw enema."

"Yikes. They grow 'em mean out here."

"Flop some of that bullwhip kelp over your bow," Mac said. "It will help to ride out the wake."

She dragged a strand of kelp as thick as her arm over the bow just in time for the first two-foot-high wave. Before the last of the wake stopped throwing the kayaks around, *Blackbird*'s twin was being tied up at the dock. Amanar stood on the dark swim step and passed a stern line to the attendant while Lovich leaped out and strode toward the store like a man on a mission. He ignored the surly shouts from people who didn't approve of his wake or his landing speed.

"One down," Mac said very softly.

"One left on the boat," she said.

She dumped the kelp off her bow and followed Mac toward *Blackbird*. With every dip of her paddle, she willed Amanar to step onto the dock, leaving the boat empty. It had been a long, hard ride from Port Hardy. Surely the man would want to stretch his land legs during refueling.

Mac checked *Blackbird*. The dock attendant had already handed one thick delivery hose up to Amanar, who was positioning it near one intake. The attendant trotted back to the pumps and flicked it on. Soon the hose was humming with fuel being pumped into the thirsty *Blackbird*.

"Figure about twenty gallons a minute," Mac murmured. "Figure twenty minutes, if they're topping off, twice as long if they're running low. A little extra time thrown in for counting all the cash. Twenty-three minutes, minimum, unless the attendant goes slow to punish them for the rude landing."

"Plenty of time for a silent approach," Emma said softly, "if Amanar gets the hell off the boat."

"Big if. Those two might not be trained, but they're meaner than the average boat jockey."

It didn't take long for the port tank. Amanar grabbed the hose, shut the fuel port, and moved the hose to the starboard tank intake.

"That was fast," she said.

Mac was silent.

Emma looked at his outline. Relaxed, motionless, waiting for whatever happened next.

Sniper at work.

I don't have the patience to be a sniper, she thought. *I'd rather kick Amanar's butt overboard and get on with it.*

Or is that the "Coastguard Cocktail" talking?

She had taken the two pills Faroe had included in her belly pack gear. The first pill relaxed the long muscles of the gut so seasickness wasn't an issue. The second one was speed, pure and simple. It cut through any mental fuzziness caused by the first pill.

And made her a bit edgy.

She waited quietly anyway. The fuel dock was well illuminated. Other boats were within calling distance. Some had cabin lights on.

Damn, I hope Grace's decoy works, she thought.

Emma reached for her cell phone in the waterproof belly pack and waited next to Mac, two shadows among the deepening shadows of Tofino harbor sliding into night.

"Breathe," Mac murmured through his mic. "Slow and easy."

Emma realized that she had been holding her breath.

Stupid newbie mistake, she told herself.

She breathed, slow and easy.

By the time the refueling was winding up, she was almost as relaxed as Mac. As the fuel hose left *Blackbird,* Emma hit the send button on her cell phone. If the insurance company didn't call the dock number as arranged, it would be a lot harder to get aboard. And it wouldn't be real silent.

A buzzer sounded above the door of the fuel dock office. The attendant trotted inside and picked up the phone on the second ring. He spoke for a moment or two, then called out, "Anyone named Lovich here?"

"*Go,*" Mac said.

70

While Lovich walked from the lighted chartroom that was part of the chandlery, Mac and Emma paddled out from behind the cover of the troller. They saw Lovich take the phone with an impatient movement.

Then Emma kept her head down, away from any illumination that might make her eyes light up like an animal's along a dark road. Mac was doing the same.

Damp air carried noise very well. Lovich's voice came in staccato barks.

"—hell you talking—"

"Stupid son of a bitch, you're crazy if—"

"—think I'm as dumb as—"

Emma guessed he would descend to the level of chainsaw enemas real quick.

"Amanar!" Lovich finally yelled. "Get over here and talk to this—"

The rest of his words vanished beneath the sound of a cabin door slamming aboard the yacht. The stern gate leading to the swim step opened with an oil-me screech and then closed. Hard.

Emma held her breath. A glint of gold along the boat's side caught her eye. Warily she looked up. If there had been any doubt about the boat's identity, the nameplate removed it.

BLACKBIRD.

"Do you believe in resurrection?" she asked very softly into her mic.

"No. Death and lies? Oh yeah. I believe."

Mac was glad that they didn't need to worry much about being absolutely quiet. Amanar was thundering over the dock like a buffalo, Lovich was screaming curses, and everyone in the harbor who could hear was riveted on the mouthy newcomer at the fuel dock.

For Mac and Emma, the black hull of the yacht provided a perfect screen from the action on the dock.

"Faster," he said and dug his paddle deep into the water.

She tried to keep up with him, but his upper body strength was easily three times hers. By the time he reached the swim step, she was thirty feet behind.

Mac's kayak tenderly nudged *Blackbird*'s hull. With one hand he reached out and caught the three-foot-tall chromed rail at the edge of the swim step. When he was certain of his grip, he let his paddle slide away into the water.

Emma glided close enough to touch him.

"Shove my kayak toward the middle of the harbor," he said very softly into his mic. "Send the paddle after it."

Before she finished dumping the excess gear, he grabbed the chrome rail and levered himself onto the swim step as easily as a gymnast mounting flying rings. But she knew that it wasn't easy. It was a wrenching exercise in naked strength.

No way, she thought. *I can get up on the swim step by myself, but it's going to be messy.*

"Hey, Spiderman," she said in quiet disgust to her mic. "You going to beam me aboard?"

"You're mixing your superheroes."

"I figured it would take two."

He made a low sound that could have been laughter. Then he caught the bow of her kayak and drew it alongside the swim step, holding her steady.

"Send your paddle toward the middle of the bay," he said.

She aimed her paddle on top of the water and shoved it off into the darkness.

"Now grab my wrists," he said.

She locked her fingers around his wrists and felt his own hands clamp around hers. Without being told, she drew up her knees. Before she could take a breath, he lifted her clear of the kayak and steadied her on the dark swim step.

"Good?" he murmured.

"Yes. Go."

With a lithe movement, he levered himself over the gunwale and its rail. Then they locked wrists again. He brought her aboard with barely a brushing sound. It was certainly a lot quieter than the squeaky gate would have been.

Mac touched her lips and his own in a gesture asking silence.

She nodded.

Both of them duck-walked along the port side of *Blackbird*, keeping themselves out of sight of the dock.

In the background, Amanar joined his cousin in a cussing duet. Whatever the insurance agent was telling them, they didn't want to hear it.

Mac reached into his small backpack and pulled out a folding knife. He thumbed it open and gave it to Emma, handle first.

"Stay down." His voice was a bare thread of sound. "When I give the signal from the bow, cut us loose at the stern."

She looked at the knife's serrated blade, then tested its edge very lightly with her thumb. The wicked little teeth tugged at her skin, nearly drawing blood. She nodded approvingly.

Mac touched her elbow, then scuttled across the aft deck, keeping his head below the gunwale.

On the dock, Amanar began repeating himself at a higher volume. Anything that wasn't stone deaf would know what he thought about the size of the caller's brain and gonads.

At the starboard rail, Mac straightened a little and ran, head low, to the bow.

Emma glanced again through the stainless hawsehole toward the fuel dock. Her breath stopped when she saw Lovich glance in the direction of *Blackbird*.

If he saw anything out of place, he didn't point it out to Amanar.

Mac looked at the bowline and wanted to curse along with the cousins. *I knew this was too easy.*

Unlike the stern line, which led directly from the inside

cleat through a hawsehole and from there to the dock, the bowline had been looped back on itself through the hawsehole. It was under too much tension to work free.

Mac needed the knife he'd given to Emma.

From the stern, she watched as he grabbed the line with both hands. She could sense the effort as he tried to pull in enough slack to back the twisted loop off one horn of the cleat.

No good.

The shouts from the fuel dock were getting fewer and further between.

They're winding up, she thought. *Time to go.*

She crouched low and duck-walked toward the shelter of the salon. Once there she straightened enough to move fast. Within seconds she was crouched beside Mac in the shelter of the bow. She passed over the knife handle first.

Swiftly he laid the blade to a taut portion of the mooring line. The braided nylon was under strain, holding the yacht to the fuel dock. The knife passed through the heavy line like it was cold butter. When there were only a few threads left, he handed the knife back to Emma.

"Same for the stern?" she breathed.

"No. Clean through. I'll signal."

There wasn't time to argue about a cut line splashing into the water near the dock or sawing a boat free before the engines came on. Emma just scuttled back to the stern the fastest way she could.

Mac followed as far as the pilot house door. He stayed out of sight of the dock as he checked the electrical switches in the panel next to the wheel.

Emma went back to her position at the stern hawsehole and watched through the glass door of the salon toward the pilot house. Wind swirled, shifting, pressing *Blackbird* against the dock rather than pushing her away.

Mac raised his head long enough to check the settings at the helm.

"Cut," he said.

She started cutting, only to find out that it wasn't as easy as the bowline.

The stern tie was slack.

Mac stood up behind the wheel, knowing that the motion would betray him to anyone watching. If nothing else, the computer screen was bright enough to backlight him. He glanced over his shoulder to see how Emma was doing. The lazy curve of the stern line told him what was wrong.

Desperately she tried to take up the slack in the line with one hand and cut with the other. It worked, but she was barely halfway through the thick line.

"Hey!" Lovich bellowed across the dock to *Blackbird*. "What do you think you're doing?"

Time's up.

71

You need us!" Lovich shouted. "You can't just—"

Blackbird's engines roared to life, drowning out Lovich.

He started to run toward the boat, but the fuel attendant grabbed him and demanded to be paid. When Lovich struggled, other men ran from nearby tie-ups to help the dockhand. *Blackbird*'s boat-tossing arrival hadn't won Lovich any friends in the harbor.

"Stop cutting," Mac said. "Wait for my signal."

Emma yanked back the knife.

It was the only warning she had before *Blackbird*'s stern swung hard away from the dock, only to slam up against the restraint of the stern line. The braided line vibrated with tension.

"Now," Mac said.

Emma laid the serrated knife against the shivering line. It leaped apart beneath the blade.

"Go!" she said before the cut line splashed into the water.

As Amanar ran past Lovich and the angry dock attendant, the underwater side-thruster growled. The stern of the *Blackbird* jumped sideways a few feet, then yards.

"Clear," she said. "Go. Go. Go."

Amanar stared at Emma, shook his head sharply in disbelief. "You!"

He started to lunge for her, then realized that the stern swim step was already too far away from the dock. If he tried to leap for the boat, he'd be swimming real quick. He windmilled for balance, found it, and saw his best chance.

Blackbird's bow was still held to the dock.

The aft side-thruster snarled while Mac slammed as much power as he could against the stubborn nylon threads.

Amanar ran toward the bow, balanced on the dock's bull-rail, and leaped for *Blackbird*'s chrome railing. With a strength born of desperation, he swung his body sideways, scrambling for purchase on the varnished wooden cap of the gunwale. One foot slipped and almost spun him loose. His second foot and both hands barely kept him clinging to *Blackbird*.

As desperate as his cousin, Lovich shook off grabbing hands and sprinted for *Blackbird*.

The last threads of the bowline snapped.

"I'll handle Amanar," Mac said. "Come up and take the wheel."

"No time. Lovich is almost here."

Mac slapped the controls. *Blackbird* shuddered sideways, farther from the dock with each second.

Emma didn't wait to see Lovich learn that the boat was

too far away. She sprinted for the bow, where Amanar still struggled to throw his weight aboard rather than hanging off the rail over the water.

The diesels roared as Mac poured on the power. Big propellers bit into the water. *Blackbird* surged out well away from the docks, but he had to fight for control. Despite the obvious health of the engines, this version of *Blackbird* wasn't as responsive as the previous one had been.

Staggering to keep her feet against *Blackbird*'s unpredictable changes in direction, Emma closed in on Amanar. He had hooked one foot over the cap rail and was slowly levering himself up to safety. He saw her, dismissed her as a threat, and kept trying to get the majority of his weight aboard.

"We're repossessing the boat for its original insurer," Emma said clearly. "If you stick to that story when you get ashore, you probably won't go to jail."

Amanar saved his breath for inching his weight onto the rail.

A knife sliced through the lace of his deck shoe, his most secure hold on the boat. His footing shifted and the shoe spun away into the dark.

"If you let go before *Blackbird* gains speed," she said calmly, "you'll survive the swim. Either way, you're letting go."

"My family!" he snarled. "He'll kill them!"

Amanar released one hand from the rail and grabbed for Emma. She ducked back, then leaped forward before he could recover.

The knife blade flashed in the harbor lights.

Amanar screamed and dropped into the black water. Five seconds later he surfaced, cursing and shouting loud enough to be heard over *Blackbird*'s engines.

All Emma understood was "Temuri will kill you!"

He'll have to catch me first, she thought.

As Amanar started swimming toward the fuel dock, she opened the door to the pilot house and slipped inside behind Mac.

"You always play with your food?" he asked, steering and tugging off his gloves at the same time.

"I didn't know he was stupid to the bone."

"Huh. What was that about Temuri and family?"

She frowned. "Something about killing them. And me."

"That would explain it."

"What?" she asked, stripping off her gloves.

"As crooks go, Stan and Bob aren't even close to Temuri's league," Mac said. "But if their families are being held hostage, both cousins would do whatever they had to however they could to keep their families safe."

"I'll mention possible hostages in my report," Emma said.

Her fingers worked over the waterproof belly bag that was fastened to her waist. Her phone was in there somewhere. And her head itched beneath the knit cap. She had never gotten along well with wool.

Mac's hands worked over switches and buttons, changing the readouts on the nav chart, depth sounder, and engine to what he was familiar with. One of the trim tabs was set oddly. He started to change it, felt the boat stagger, and quickly returned the starboard setting to its previous position.

Something in the galley rattled, then settled.

"What was that?" she asked.

"Trash can. Those boys love their beer."

The radio spit static, then words.

"Don't touch it," Mac said quickly. "We listen, but we don't answer."

Emma scratched beneath the snug-fitting cap. "I told Amanar that we were repossessing the boat. If he gets smarter by the time he swims to the dock, he'll go with that story."

"Maybe," Mac said.

"I hope St. Kilda is able to help the cousins' families."

So did Mac, but all he said was "Not our part of the op."

"How long will it take to get us to U.S. waters?" Emma asked, finally freeing her phone.

"This version of *Blackbird* is more sluggish than ours was. No wonder they didn't want to push her past twenty knots." He frowned. "Tell St. Kilda more than two hours, less than three."

"Gotcha." Emma punched her favorite cell phone button and stretched her neck, trying to relieve the tension that had built as they stalked and then stole *Blackbird* from the fuel dock.

"Report," Faroe's voice said in her ear.

"We have another *Blackbird*. We suspect that Temuri or someone working for him is holding Lovich and Amanar's families as hostage for the men's good behavior. They were running *Blackbird* when we took her."

"Wait," Faroe said.

Emma scratched her head, then yanked off the cap. No need to disguise her profile any longer.

Within twenty seconds Faroe was back on the phone.

"St. Kilda will do what we can for the families," he said. "Where are you?"

"Hauling ass out of Tofino." She rubbed her scalp. "We didn't pull off a total sneak, but no one got killed and so far I don't see any lights behind us."

"Radio traffic is quiet, too," Mac said, loud enough to be picked up by her cell phone.

"But someone might want to tell Canada that ours was a legal seizure rather than an act of piracy," she added.

"The insurance company is working through layers of bureaucracy as we speak," Faroe said. "How long until you get to U.S. waters?"

Emma made a startled sound as *Blackbird* shifted and surged with the feel of the open water beyond the rocks at the harbor mouth.

"What?" Faroe demanded.

"The ocean is a lot bumpier than the strait," she said.

"No shit. When and where will you cross into U.S. waters?" Faroe repeated.

"Where do we cross to the U.S.?" she asked Mac.

As she spoke, she put the phone on speaker and held it toward him.

"Juan de Fuca Strait," Mac said, without looking away from the dark water ahead. "Somewhere between Neah Bay in the U.S. and Port Renfrew on Vancouver Island. Two hours, maybe three."

"You check the weather?" Faroe asked.

"What good would that do?" Mac said. "We sure as hell can't go ashore again in Canada."

"Storm coming" was all Faroe said.

"I can feel it in the waves," Mac said. "That's why I'm heading for Juan de Fuca rather than trying to put ashore anywhere near Cape Flattery, which is closer. The water around Flattery will be too damned rough. Graveyard of many a good ship, and this version of *Blackbird* is a bit of a pig."

"Why? What's different?" Faroe's voice was hard, demanding.

"Answering that is on my to-do list," Mac said. "After I find a handy freighter to hide behind and keep us off coastal radar."

"Call when you have something new."

Faroe disconnected.

With one hand Emma grabbed on to the overhead handrail that ran the length of the salon. She used the other to stuff the phone back into its waterproof home.

Mac pushed the radar's reach out to maximum and studied the echoes on the screen. As he'd hoped, there were big boats plying the shipping corridor down the west coast of North America.

None were close.

This *Blackbird* had the same electronic setup as the other one. He called up the vessel identification function on the computer and studied the specs of the first three ships that were heading south. Two were going faster than he wanted to push this incarnation of *Blackbird*. He set an interception course with a tanker that was traveling at about eighteen knots. It would take at least an hour, but once he got on the far side of it, he would be screened from coastal radar.

Hell, if it gets any rougher, the swells will conceal us most of the time anyway. Unless we get really unlucky, we'll slide by.

The Canadian government didn't have even a handful of ships stationed on the west coast that could handle big weather safely, much less comfortably. Too much coastline, too few machines, money, and manpower.

All he needed was decent luck.

Mac glanced at Emma. "You doing all right?"

"A little buzzed."

Mac nodded. He'd taken the Coastguard Cocktail before he'd learned he didn't need it. Some of the people he'd gone through training with had been sick no matter what meds they had.

Thank God Emma isn't one of them.

So far.

The water ahead would test any meds.

72

Emma had her legs braced wide and knees flexed, but she still had to use the overhead handrail that ran the length of the cabin. It was a rough ride to the radar shelter of the tanker, but once in place, *Blackbird* would be at a better angle to the waves.

"I used to think this was for hanging towels," she said.

Mac's smile gleamed blue-white, a reflection of the computer screen. They were running stealth, no lights but those on the electronics.

She watched another black mountain rise up out of the darkness, felt *Blackbird* climb, then slide down and down and down into the trough. The ocean didn't have anything in common with the Inside Passage except saltwater.

"If you need a bio break, better take it now," Mac said, watching all the engine readouts, the charts, and the compass. "We're at the grinding point of the weather system.

The ride is going to get worse when the wind switches to southeast. Then we'll really be in for a slog."

She staggered and grabbed on with both hands as *Blackbird* lurched suddenly. Cold water slashed against the front windows, a wave breaking over the bow.

"*Going* to get worse?" she asked. It looked bad right now.

"Oh yeah." He never looked away from the darkness beyond the bow. "Use the head now. Later you might be on your hands and knees."

Clinging to overhead or stair handrails every foot of the way, Emma stumbled toward the downstairs head. When she ran out of rails, she braced herself on walls in the narrow hallway. It was dark belowdecks, but she knew where the head was. The layout was the same as the first *Blackbird*.

Both stateroom doors had been locked in the open position. A tiny night light gleamed in each of them. The beds were bare except for a small duffel on each. No suitcases, man bags, or grocery sacks. Lovich and Amanar had been traveling light.

The door to the head was almost closed. As she struggled to open the swollen wood sliding door enough to lock it in place, a sour smell flowed out.

Ugh. What is it with men and toilets? A guy can be a world-class marksman and still miss a toilet when he's standing right—

Something surged up out of the darkness and slammed her against the sink. Her head banged into polished granite, then banged again, harder. She kicked and elbowed as dirty as she could, but the blows to her head had made her dizzy.

"Emma?" Mac asked. "Did you fall? Are you all right?"

She felt a knife against her throat.

A man's voice growled into her mic pickup. "Hear me, Captain, or bitch to die."

Mac recognized Temuri's voice. Time slowed as the icy clarity of battle descended.

"I'm listening," Mac said flatly.

"Move boat. Seattle. Do wrong. Bitch die."

"I don't trust your word," Mac said. "I want to see Emma up here, alive and unhurt. Now. Or else I run this boat aground and hell can have the leftovers. You hearing me?"

He caught Emma's hurried translation, then an explosion of invective. Mac smiled savagely. Shurik Temuri was furious.

And Emma was alive and well enough to translate.

"Temuri doesn't like your first offer," she said.

"It's my only one. If you get hurt, I'll sink the fucking boat."

She didn't have to ask if Mac meant it. The sound of his voice was enough to make sweat freeze on her skin.

Apparently Temuri was hearing the same thing.

While Russian erupted in Mac's earphones, he dug out his cell phone, hit the speed dial, and jammed the phone inside the neck of his tight weatherproof suit, close enough to the mic that at least one side of the conversation could be overheard.

"Where are—" began Faroe's voice.

"Listen," Mac cut in.

The phone went silent.

"Temuri is listening," Emma said tightly. "He's just not liking what he hears."

Mac doubted Faroe liked it any better.

"Then Temuri isn't listening real good, is he?" Mac drawled. "He has my only offer—you alive and unhurt or all of us dead when I sink this boat."

Mac almost felt the intensity of the silence coming from the phone jammed into his suit. He hoped St. Kilda was listening hard. On ops like this, postmortems were a bitch.

He didn't plan on being one of the dead on the dissection table.

"We're coming up," Emma's voice said. "He says to tell you he'll cut my throat first, then gut you."

"Your throat, then mine. Got it."

He listened intently to the sounds of two people moving awkwardly up the narrow stairway and into the main salon. Until he knew what kind of hold Temuri had on Emma, Mac could do nothing but follow directions.

And wait for an opening.

Just one.

Mac knew how small the odds were of catching someone like Temuri off guard. He didn't care. Concentrating on how many ways things could go to hell was stupid. Hell wouldn't help him.

A single opening would.

"Does Temuri need a light?" Mac asked. *I could blind the bastard.*

"No. No lights." She made a sound that was close to a gag. "Back off, Temuri. You're going to kill me by accident." She repeated the words in Russian.

Mac thought of some seriously painful ways to kill Temuri.

Two figures stumbled into the salon. The computer

screen gave everything a ghostly blue-white glow. The light was just enough for Mac to see that Temuri was using Emma for balance. One hand was buried in her hair. The other held an open folding knife that had the subdued polish of use.

It was close to her throat. Too close for rough seas.

Emma had a livid bruise on one cheekbone and on her forehead. Lines of blood that looked nearly black in the light ran from various knife cuts on her cheek and throat. Only one of her hands was free to grab the overhead rail for balance. Her right arm was twisted up behind her back so that Temuri could hold her wrist and her hair in one big fist.

He doesn't leave much room for me, Mac thought. *He'll cut her throat before I can take one step away from the wheel.*

The smell of vomit came off Emma and Temuri in waves.

At first Mac thought she had been sick from the increasing roughness of the waves. Then he realized it was Temuri.

Some people didn't adjust to big water. They got sick, then sicker, and kept throwing up even when their stomachs were empty of all but bile and nausea.

It smelled like Temuri had spent a lot of time puking.

Mac wanted to smile. Seasickness didn't kill you, but it sure made you want to die. Being in the calm of Tofino harbor had revived Temuri. Enough bad water would put him down again.

Mac hoped it was soon.

"Seattle," Temuri growled.

"Seattle," Mac agreed.

"Move fast."

"Whatever," Mac said, pushing the throttles up. "Just keep that knife away from Emma's throat."

Temuri moved the blade maybe half an inch.

Mac knew it was as good as he'd get.

She took in air more deeply, no longer worried that a simple breath would slit her throat.

A burst of Russian.

"Temuri wants you to run for the international line," Emma said.

"I am."

"He wants a more direct course to Seattle. Closer to shore."

"He'll get it," Mac promised.

The coastal route was indeed shorter in distance, if not in time. Closer to shore the ocean bottom came up hard, doubling the size of the swells. If you got too close, reverberation from waves that hit cliffs and washed back turned the water into a cauldron of triangular waves. Razor waves.

It would be hell on the passengers.

Silently Mac widened his stance, prepared to absorb the beating *Blackbird* would give anyone stupid enough to take the wrong course. He put the controls on autopilot.

And waited for a decent break.

73

Alara paced like a caged cat.

Steele wished he could join her.

Both of them listened to the open line Mac had left between himself and Faroe.

Nothing human, just the liquid hammering of water against glass, the skid and roll of loose equipment.

Alara's cell phone hummed. She listened and broke the connection.

"Harrow and his teams are in place. They're a thousand feet inside the international boundary line in Juan de Fuca Strait," she said tightly. "The weather is growing ugly. Gale winds predicted."

Silence. Then Alara's hand smacked hard on Steele's desk.

"Why doesn't he make a move?" she snarled.

"He's waiting for an opening that won't kill Emma."

"If Temuri is still in control when *Blackbird* crosses the line, Harrow's teams will sink her."

"I know."

She looked at Steele. His eyes were gray, his mouth thin.

"We don't have a choice," she said.

Steele didn't answer.

Alara didn't speak again.

74

A wave crashed hard over *Blackbird*'s starboard bow. Water foamed gray and silver in the thin moonlight that penetrated the massing clouds. Even though rain hadn't begun, the ship's three windshield wipers moved furiously to clear the forward windows after each wave broke. And they broke all the time.

Emma and Temuri lurched sideways, held from a fall only by her hand wrapped around the overhead handrail that ran down the center of the salon ceiling. She groaned and said something in Russian.

Temuri's response was blunt. *"Nyet."*

"I can't hold both of us with one hand! My wrist . . ." She sagged and flinched.

Her fingers slipped.

The knife drew more blood.

"Watch it, Temuri," snarled Mac. "Another cut like that and we're all going to the bottom."

Emma repeated it in Russian as she struggled to balance herself and Temuri's much heavier weight.

Waves hit *Blackbird* one after another, sending the ship wallowing from side to side like an egg rolling in a bowl.

Even in the dim light of the computer screen, Mac could see that Temuri was turning green. He had a fine sheen of moisture on his face.

Cold sweat, Mac thought. *It's about time. If one of those big waves catches us wrong, the side windows will blow out.*

And Mac would let it happen. He and Emma were wearing float harnesses. Temuri wasn't. Those were better odds than they had right now.

Temuri said something guttural to Emma. She moaned as he freed her right hand. She shook out her arm. With agonizing slowness she raised her fingers toward the rail.

Then she twisted and slammed her elbow into Temuri's neck. He managed to take most of it on his jaw, but lost his balance. He yanked savagely on her hair. The knife jerked.

Mac's kick deflected the knife before Temuri could cut Emma's throat. As she rolled free and came up on her feet, Temuri shifted the knife to his other hand and lunged for her. The hard side of Mac's hand slammed against Temuri's shoulder. Mac had been aiming for the neck, but a wave had interfered.

With a grunt, Temuri sliced the knife toward Mac.

He fell, scissoring his legs, and took Temuri down. In seconds they became a grunting, cursing, kicking, slashing pile of intent to kill. Being knocked around by the boat and each other didn't leave any room for finesse. Biting, kicking, gouging, they grappled under the dinette for control of the knife, which had become slippery with blood.

Another wave sent both men rolling between the sofa and the dinette.

Emma dragged herself to her feet, braced herself, and watched the straining men like a snake waiting for a chance to strike. She managed a hard kick to Temuri's kidneys before the melee moved out of her reach.

It wasn't enough.

Mac was losing the battle. His right wrist and hand weren't working. Adrenaline had suppressed Temuri's sea-sickness. In a few minutes Emma would be left alone to deal with an assassin and a gale-force storm.

With a desperate heave, Mac changed positions with Temuri and locked his thighs around the man's thick neck. Pain slashed across Mac's left thigh and hip. He tightened his hold and wrenched with every bit of his body.

Mac felt as much as heard Temuri's neck snap.

Emma grabbed the bloody knife as it skidded over the floor. Automatically she closed the weapon and stuck it in the pouch she wore around her waist. She didn't need to check Temuri for a pulse. She had heard the crack of bone and tendon.

Her headset lay on the floor. Mac's headset wasn't far away. She grabbed for them while he kicked Temuri's body to the side and staggered to his feet.

"You—okay?" Mac asked, breathing hard.

"Some cuts," she said, pulling on a headset. "You?"

He ignored her question. "Take the wheel off auto. Steer into the waves."

He locked his left hand into Temuri's hair and dragged the body to the back of the salon. As he let go of Temuri, a big wave slammed into the boat, sending *Blackbird* reeling. Reflexively Mac tried to brace himself and nearly passed out when his injured wrist smacked the edge of the dinette. He tried to bite back a hoarse sound of pain, but wasn't entirely successful.

Temuri might have been slowed by seasickness, but he had been as vicious a fighter as Mac had ever gone against.

"You're hurt!" Emma cried.

"Keep on my intersection course for that tanker," he said, pointing to the radar overlay on the chart.

Every breath was a fight for Mac. Every heartbeat was a stab of pain. He had to take advantage of adrenaline while he had it in his system. Bracing himself with his legs and wedging his back into a corner behind the pilot seat, he used his good hand to yank out the cell phone that was gnawing on his neck.

"Temuri's dead," he told Faroe. "We're banged up, but nothing fatal. I'm heading out into the shipping zone miles offshore, but something's wrong with *Blackbird*. I'll see if I can find out and get back to you."

"Anything useful on Temuri's body?" Faroe asked.

"Haven't had time for treasure hunting."

"Don't throw him overboard until you do."

The sound Mac made was too cold to be a laugh. "Wasn't planning to. As soon as I wrap my wrist, I'm going to the engine room to check some things."

"You can't use your right hand," Emma called out, loud enough for Faroe to overhear.

"If I find anything," Mac said into the phone, "Emma will call."

"What happened to you?" Faroe demanded.

"Broken wrist."

"Shit."

"The left one works fine."

Mac disconnected. He didn't need Faroe to add to the distraction of the pain pulsing through his arm with every heartbeat. Adrenaline was a primo painkiller until it wore off.

It was wearing off.

75

We've got to splint that wrist," Emma said.

"Steer."

"Splint. You're no good to anyone if you pass out from pain."

Mac couldn't argue with that. There were bones grinding in his wrist, and each time it happened, the pain wrenched his stomach and blurred his vision. He'd had compound fractures before, so he knew it would get worse. A lot worse.

The stab wounds in his left thigh had joined the chorus. Temuri hadn't gone down without exacting a blood payment. Mac was still paying, and would until he could get stitches.

That was one son of a bitch who lived up to his advance publicity, he thought unhappily. *And I've lost more of my edge than I realized.*

But his willpower was still intact.

He eased out of his small backpack, yet still almost blacked out when one of the straps snagged his wrist. He hissed a savage word between his teeth.

"I'm putting the wheel on auto," Emma said.

"Not yet."

"At least wear these so we don't have to yell." She slid his fragile-looking headset into place and spoke softly. "Can you hear me?"

"Yeah."

It was more a rasp of sound than a word.

Mac's backpack made a small thump when it hit the floor. He put his foot on it and yanked at the waterproof opening with his good hand. After a few moments he threw a med kit and a roll of duct tape on the pilot seat.

"Remember the machine space?" Mac asked.

"Where the tools were on the first *Blackbird*?"

He breathed through clenched teeth and ignored the agony that was his wrist. "See if there are tools down there now."

"If I'm looking for splints, I'll be happy to do it. If you're planning a spot of boat repair, forget it."

"Splints," he agreed finally, and reached for the wheel. "If you see ear protectors lying around, put them on."

Emma slid out of the way, pulled a small flashlight from her belly pack, and went to the middle of the salon. She held on to the overhead rail while a wave of dizziness surged through her. Her head felt like it had been slammed into an anvil.

Think about something else. Like getting home.

She hesitated, then left the tiny headset in place. If the noise bothered Mac, he could take off his own.

Temuri's body lay at the far edge of the hatch. She could open it without having to touch him. She bent, tugged the hatch up, and was almost blown back by the unbridled thunder of the diesels. If the door had been installed between the machine space and engine room, obviously the cousins had left it open. With a grimace, she secured the hatch and eased down the steep, built-in stairway, clinging to something every inch of the way.

At the bottom she saw ear protectors dangling from a clip, grabbed them, and shoved them on over her smaller headset like oversized earmuffs. The bruise on her forehead rewarded her carelessness with blinding pain, but the assault of sound diminished to a bearable roar.

Sacks and satchels of tools lay scattered around. Either the cousins were messy, or the *Blackbird*'s wallowing had tossed things about. Probably both.

Staggered by the occasional jagged spurts of pain from having had her head banged against the sink, she began crawling carefully from bag to bag. Soon she had a selection of tools that might serve as splints. She emptied a small satchel into a larger one, filled the smaller one with her choices, and headed upstairs.

By the time she scrambled out of the space and closed the large hatch, Mac had found the best line for taking the waves and cut the speed back a few knots. As a result, the boat had settled down into something resembling the other *Blackbird*'s usual grace.

Mac was pale, sweaty, drawn. Somehow he had put a

compression bandage around his thigh. The heavy elastic was already dark with blood.

Emma knew he was going to feel worse before it got better, but there was no help for that. The wrist had to be splinted. She peeled off the heavy ear protectors and set them on the pilot seat.

"There's a shot of something like Novocain in the kit," Mac said hoarsely.

Emma reached for the small red zipper case. It was already open and messy, like Mac had been sorting through it. Despite the surging waves and her throbbing skull, she found and set up the numbing shot quickly.

"I'll do it," he said.

Before she could argue, he grabbed the syringe and shoved the needle into his broken wrist. She braced him when his body shuddered in pain, then took the empty syringe when he was finished.

Sweat ran down his face.

"Tell me when it's numb," she said roughly. "I'll steer."

"Splint it now or I'll do it without your help."

Emma choked back her protests. Mac knew more about field medicine and the engine room of any ship than she did. If what they both feared was true, there was no time to educate her. He had to do the work himself.

Teeth clenched until they ached in time with her pulse, she measured the tools against his injured wrist. She selected two wrenches and wrapped them into place. Duct tape was good for more than handcuffs.

He kept steering. And sweating.

She was sweating, too.

"I'll make a sling," she said, turning away.

She pulled Temuri's knife out of her belly bag as she went to the back of the salon and turned her little flashlight on. She knew that she'd probably have nightmares about Temuri's open eyes staring at death, glassy in the cone of her flashlight, but that was for later.

Right now she needed his shirt for a sling. She leaned down and went to work with the already bloody knife.

As the worst of Mac's wrist pain let up, the knife wounds in his left side felt like they were on fire. He'd already put a compression bandage on the thigh wound. The other one was on his hip, too high for anything close to a tourniquet. He knew that the steady blood loss from the wounds would bring him down, but he didn't know when.

Mac forced himself to concentrate on the readouts and settings on the console behind the wheel. It didn't take him long to confirm that the starboard trim tab was locked down on maximum. The port tab wasn't being used at all, which meant that something on the port side of the boat was heavy enough to require a lot of compensating with the opposite trim tab.

He fought a wave of dizziness and nausea. He would rather have been wrong about *Blackbird*'s bad trim.

But he wasn't, so he went through the tools remaining in the little satchel by touch. As he'd hoped, a telescoping rod had caught Emma's eye. Holding the wheel on course with his right thigh, he put the rod between his teeth and clamped down.

Emma reappeared with stinking strips of Temuri's shirt. Silently she knotted them into a rough sling. She arranged it on Mac and eased his wrist into place. Since he didn't pass out during the process, she figured the numbing shot was working. Or maybe it was the steel tool clenched between his teeth.

He spat out the rod, caught it, then placed it carefully in the sling.

"Take the wheel," he said, grabbing the big ear protectors from the seat. One-handed, he fumbled them into place. Like Emma, he didn't bother removing his own communications headset first. "Keep the same angle into the waves."

She slid by him and took over steering. She didn't have his instinctive understanding of waves and bow angles, but she could keep *Blackbird* keel side down.

She hoped.

"I could use some headlights to see what's coming," she said.

"Why not call the Canadian Coasties while you're at it? I don't even have the running lights on."

Whatever she might have said in reply was drowned out by the blast of engine noise as Mac heaved the hatch open and secured it. He put all his weight on his left hand and dropped into the machine space. Taking a chance, he flicked on the engine-room light.

On his left thigh, blood gleamed against his black waterproof gear and ran down his leg to the floor. More blood than he'd hoped, less than he'd feared. Either way, it was what it was.

He limped down the passageway between the two diesel engines that were identical to the ones he'd checked out in the other *Blackbird.*

One-handed, it took him three times as long to go over the engines. The fact that they were hot didn't help, but being below waterline at least minimized the boat's motion. Not that he didn't burn himself more than once. Compared to what he'd already been through, the burns were nothing.

There was a slight leak from one of the packing boxes connecting the starboard engine with the pod drive. He caught a drop of the fluid, smelled it, tasted it. Saltwater from the cooling system. It was the kind of minor leak that came with new engines and usually fixed itself.

He went to the bulkhead wall and inspected the fuel manifold, a complicated set of high-pressure lines, gauges, and switches. Diesel engines weren't as simple as gasoline, since diesels had a constant return flow of unused fuel. The gauges and levers told him that everything was working as expected.

There were no big blocks of lead or gold or anything else heavy strapped along the port side of the engine room. The extra weight had to be in the port fuel tank itself.

The big stainless-steel boxes of the fuel tanks were painted white. They were equipped with brass fittings and sight gauges that gave a direct measure of the level inside. The starboard engine registered full. So did the port.

He rapped his knuckles against the metal sides of each tank, but couldn't be sure of anything through the ear protectors. He pushed against the metal of the starboard tank with his left hand. It gave ever so slightly, just as he expected.

But the port tank was like trying to flex a steel girder.

He dragged himself back to the manifold and studied its

scheme again. It took him too long to figure out what was wrong because his eyesight kept going dark at the edges. But enough blinking and squinting told him that the lines that returned unburned diesel from the engines had been rearranged. The fuel return from the port engine had been rerouted to the starboard tank.

No wonder it didn't take them long to refuel.

He limped heavily to the machine space, selected a wrench, and went to work on the inspection port welded to the top of the port fuel tank. By stretching and balancing on his good leg, he could peer into the tank just enough to see red diesel fuel sloshing around.

And bang his head a few times, making it ring along with the insidious dizziness that kept trying to bring him down.

With a savage curse he pulled the telescoping rod out of his sling. There was a magnet on one end for retrieving tools that fell into the bilge. He didn't need the magnet, but he needed the extending rod. After a few misses thanks to waves rolling the deck beneath his feet, and his own eyesight taking holidays, he got one end of the rod in the inspection port. He hit the button that released the sections.

The rod went only six inches below the level of the fuel in the "full" tank.

Mac leaned against the tank while he closed the inspection port. Sweat made the wrench slippery. So did blood. A wave of dizziness nearly sent him to his knees.

Got to check the wiring harness, he told himself.

Another round of dizziness forced him to admit that he could check the wiring harness and pass out in the engine room, or he could climb back into the cabin and steer until he passed out.

Wrong answers.

He fumbled some pills from his pocket. He'd really hoped to delay taking them. The false energy of chemicals didn't prevent blood loss, and had never worked long for him anyway, but he had no choice. He had to stay on his feet until they reached the border.

He put the pills under his tongue and let them melt.

In less than a minute, a wave of adrenaline roared through him, burning away the darkness that kept trying to shut him down. That was the good news. The bad news was that when the chemicals wore off, he would crash. Period. No exemption for emergencies.

He was hoping he would last more than an hour.

Experience told him it would be less than half that.

Mac limped slowly toward the wiring harness. Like arteries, the wires took power from the fuel-driven heart of the ship. He wiped sweat out of his eyes, noted without interest that he must be bleeding somewhere on his head, and began tracing wires according to function. Knowing there had been modifications to the port tank made him distrust anything he couldn't see for himself.

Leaning heavily against any available support that didn't burn him, he studied the reinforced blue rubber hosing and individual metal fittings of the fuel injection systems. Electronically controlled diesel engines operated at very high pressures. The connectors and hoses were notorious for leakage.

These metal connectors were bright, shining in the hard

fluorescent light. Just right for a new boat. Yet the longer he looked at the hoses, the more he thought something was wrong.

Even with the chemicals sleeting through his blood, it took him several minutes to realize what his eyes were seeing. Two of the hoses were a lighter shade of blue than the others. It was a subtle difference, but real. Since the engines had been installed at the same time, the tubing should be precisely the same.

Two of the hoses had been changed out.

Mac wiped his eyes, cursed the scalp wound that bled like a faucet into his eyes, and followed the two hoses. One led from the fuel distribution manifold to the generator that was mounted on a platform between the big diesel propulsion engines. The second ran from the manifold around to the back of the starboard fuel tank.

Why? There already are hoses in place for fuel supply and return on the generator.

He forced himself to concentrate on each detail. The hoses looked like fuel lines but one of them was connected to the output line of the generator, not the fuel system. He squeezed the line. It didn't feel right. No humming tension of fuel under pressure.

Why?

It made no sense.

Mac staggered to the machine space and dragged a satchel of wrenches into the engine room. He fumbled out one wrench, found it didn't fit, and tried another. By the fourth wrench he'd found a winner.

Carefully, fighting dizziness and the constant lurch and

roll of the deck beneath his feet, he went to work on the connector at the generator end of the circuit. After a minute it gave way. He unthreaded it and slid it back down the blue hose.

It wasn't a fuel line. It was a heavy-gauge electrical wire.

With growing dread, he followed the wire. It was tied into the electrical circuit that ran from the generator to one of the starter batteries.

A different kind of adrenaline slammed through Mac.

Fear, pure and simple.

76

Emma worked to hold *Blackbird* close to the course Mac had laid out. It took more strength than she'd expected. The waves seemed bigger, steeper, pushed up rather than rounded. As Mac had warned her, the wind was backing toward southeast, changing everything.

And the radar was getting flakey. Once in a while it returned an odd blip off to their stern, just at the edge of the radar's reach. Sometimes the echo was there, more often it wasn't, making it more a tease than a threat.

Or maybe it was just the meds and the fact that a big freighter was closing with them that had her edgy. On the radar, the ship's echo looked like an island. She hoped that Mac returned before *Blackbird* and the freighter collided, but she didn't change course.

The waves were all too real, too threatening. She didn't need to search the radar for more trouble.

Behind her the hatch door slammed down.

"Mac?" she asked.

"Minute."

His voice was harsh. He limped heavily back to Temuri's body and began an awkward, one-handed search. When he was finished, he hadn't discovered anything more sinister than money and an old black comb. The passport was Canadian, in a name that wasn't Shurik Temuri.

With a long, relieved breath, Mac pulled himself to his feet and limped heavily toward the stairs leading down to the staterooms and head. He paused only to check *Blackbird*'s speed, direction, and radar. The freighter was coming along nicely, soon to provide a moving screen.

A bit of orange flashed at the most distant radar ring. Hanging on to the console, he stared at it.

"Death echo," he said.

"What?"

"One of my team . . . used to say that. Shouldn't . . . be there."

Emma took one look at Mac's face and said, "Lie down before you fall down. I can run *Blackbird*."

"Gotta search rooms."

She started to ask a question, then bit her lip. "There are small duffels in the cabins. Take the wheel. What am I searching for?"

Instead of answering, Mac eased himself down the stairs. It wasn't pretty, but he didn't add to his injuries. He went through empty drawers like a kid looking for Christmas. Then he emptied out the small duffels. His breath hissed at a flash of silver in the dim light. Very delicately he began to take apart the small package.

A ham sandwich.

Wrapped in tinfoil.

He didn't know whether to laugh or swear, but he did start breathing again. He sorted through the rest of the belongings. Like Temuri, the cousins hadn't brought anything aboard that would raise a border guard's interest.

The effort made his hands clammy with sweat, but he climbed back into the salon. He tossed the partially unwrapped sandwich on the pilot seat.

"At least we have food," he said, breathing hard. "Lovich's wife doesn't believe in plastic."

"You're weaving on your feet," Emma said. "Lie down."

He tossed the ear protectors on the pilot seat and repositioned his headset. "Got a puzzle."

Her hands flexed hard on the wheel. Neither of them could afford to waste energy arguing. She concentrated on keeping *Blackbird* on the compass course he had given her.

The freighter took up an unnerving amount of the radar screen.

Mac leaned against the pilot seat. "The port fuel tank is bogus. Whatever is inside isn't paper. Too heavy."

She didn't question his conclusions. Ships were his expertise, not hers.

"Two choices," he said. "Solid gold. Lead shielding."

A chill swept over her, making goose flesh rise.

"I'd like to go for gold," he said, spacing his words for

breath, "but I found some heavy wire cabling inside a fake fuel hose."

"Jesus," she breathed. "A bomb. It's already wired?"

"Yeah." Mac braced himself and frowned at the compass. Still on course, and too rough. The wind must be shifting.

He started to fade, then felt the chemicals kick in again. They wouldn't keep him on his feet much longer.

"The good news," he said, "is that I didn't find a timer or a radio trigger. This could be a fancy head-fake. Show how easy it is. Humiliate Uncle Sam and the Georgians at the same time, and raise terrorist aspirations around the world."

"Or not." Her voice was clipped.

"Or not. I'd give my left nut for a Geiger counter. Until we know if the guts are in place, we can't—"

"Take the wheel." She grabbed the med kit.

Automatically Mac began steering. "What are you doing?"

"That sandwich gave me an idea. Do you have a comb?"

"Temuri does. Left rear pocket."

Emma grimaced. A minute later she came back with Temuri's comb and a bundle of long, dark hairs clenched in her fist.

Mac started to ask about the hair, then shut up. Sure as hell, Temuri didn't have any more use for it.

"I need your serrated knife," she said.

"Backpack."

She fished the knife out one-handed, snagged the foil-wrapped sandwich, and went the few steps to the galley. She unwrapped the sandwich, used it to hold down the long hairs, and set the foil in the sink. Then she went head-down in the trash. Metal clashed as she shook the container. She found several cans that were fairly round. Apparently one of the cousins didn't need to exercise his manhood by crushing beer cans.

Her belly pack yielded dental floss. The med kit had some thin tape.

She attacked a beer can with the wicked, serrated edge of Mac's knife, sawing off the top.

"You'll ruin the blade," Mac said.

"Better the blade than your left nut."

He opened his mouth, then decided to shut up. It was hard to disagree with her on that one.

Mac concentrated on getting *Blackbird* into position to use the big ship as a radar shield. It was making good speed. Almost too good. The oddly laden yacht would be working hard to get into place and vanish into its radar shadow. But it had to be done. The closer they got to the populated southern portions of Vancouver Island, the more likely an encounter with Canadian Coasties became.

Especially if Lovich and Amanar were too angry or stupid to take the out Emma had given them.

Despite the boat's roller-coaster ride, Emma cut herself only twice—once on the ragged edge of the can, once on Mac's knife. Neither cut interfered with her work. Nor did the relentless throb of her headache. As she finished each piece, she put it in the galley sink for safekeeping.

By the time she was ready to assemble her experiment, the sink held two one-inch squares of foil with a hole in the center, a length of dental floss, and the butchered beer can.

Carefully she cut and laid out thin strips of tape from the med kit.

Now came the finicky, time-eating part.

She picked up a hair from beneath the sandwich and went to work. The motion of the boat didn't make her job any easier. Neither did the pounding in her head that made her want to close her eyes. But she finally managed to tie a knot, then two, then two more. With grim intensity, she concentrated on assembling the unlikely device.

Twice she had to start over.

"Yes!" she said as the last bit of tape finally went on.

Mac glanced over and didn't see a reason for her cheer. Unless half of a beer can was something to howl over. Or maybe he just wasn't thinking straight. His head felt like it belonged to someone else.

I should put the steering on the joystick.

Oh, yeah. Real bright, Mac told himself. *You know the joystick so well, you'll pitch-pole us first chance you get.*

And he was getting the chance about every five seconds.

He felt reality begin to slide away from him. Deliberately he rapped his cast against the wheel. Not too hard. Just hard enough for the pain to clear his head. The wake-up trick wouldn't work forever, but he didn't need forever. Just long enough to get *Blackbird* home.

Mac realized Emma had been calling his name. "What?"

She held up the half of the beer can she had worked on. He squinted, blinked, and saw that she had used Temuri's hair to tie two squares of tinfoil to the strand of dental floss she had stretched over the open end of the can.

"What . . . is that?" he managed.

"A backcountry Geiger counter."

"One of us is crazy."

"Wait," she said.

Quickly she rubbed Temuri's comb over the cloth on her leg, then touched each foil square. The pieces of foil jumped apart and dangled separately on nearly invisible tethers of human hair.

"Static electricity," Emma explained. "If we introduce a source of radiation, the squares will lose their charge and fall back together."

He stared at her in confusion.

"Do you think I went through Temuri's pocket and yanked some hair for kicks and giggles?" she asked. "We had a field course in nuclear physics at the Farm. A senior scientist from Oak Ridge taught us how to make a radiation counter. I never really thought much about it again until I saw that sandwich."

Mac shook his head hard, trying to clear it. For a few moments the world came back into something like focus.

"We can look for radiation . . . with tinfoil, hair, and a comb?" he asked.

"Don't forget the floss and tape."

"Judas H. Priest."

Emma ignored him, put on the ear protectors, and opened the hatch. She fell as much as used the steps to get down, but landed on her feet, head ringing like a fire alarm. She lurched into the engine room. The first pipe she tried to use as a handhold was burning hot. She patted around until she found one that wasn't.

Crouching low, she moved the makeshift Geiger counter slowly back and forth over the port fuel tank. The foil squares didn't fall together. She leaned in and ran her crude detector in back of the tank as well as around the sides.

Nothing.

Either the tank is clean or my cut-and-tape toy isn't working.

Both engines revved hard. *Blackbird* lurched sideways, ripping the pipe out of her hands and throwing her off balance. She went down on her hands and knees, barely avoiding the hot exhaust stack next to the port fuel tank.

The detector fell in the bilge.

"You okay?" Mac asked through her headphones.

"Who knew that yachting was a full-contact sport?" she groaned.

"The radio is full of official chatter. Coasties are out. We have to get to the freighter before we show on anyone's radar."

She heard the strain in his voice as he wrestled with the wheel, trying to hold his course and still meet the oncoming waves safely.

The engines made a continuous avalanche of sound.

Carefully she fumbled beneath the port fuel tank for the detector. Despite the spinning of the shaft leading to the propeller, she managed to grope around until she found the can. Gently she pulled it toward her. But not gently enough. The two pieces of foil had touched, releasing their charge. They hung limply on their tethers. Useless.

She reached into her belly bag for the comb and began rubbing it fiercely over her clothes.

The engines thundered around her, working harder than ever.

"It's a Canadian Coastie," Mac said. "Looking for a yacht that called in with engine failure. At least that's what they're putting out for the public. Hang on!"

Mac was yelling into his mic. He knew what an engine room was like, especially at full throttle.

"No," she said loudly. "Cut power. Cut power! Go out of gear. I might have something, but I have to go beneath the port propeller shaft to be sure. We've got to be sure!"

At first she thought that Mac hadn't heard her. Or was ignoring her. She started to call out to him, to explain.

The port engine's RPMs fell off fast. The starboard engine revved to the top of its range. Mac was compromising—she could crawl around the port side without being beaten up by moving parts, but the starboard side was working flat out.

Above her, Mac battled the ocean. "Go!" he yelled into his mic. "If *Blackbird* doesn't meet these waves right, the salon windows will blow out. Tell me when you're clear. Hurry!"

"Copy that."

Emma clawed her way into position with the newly charged detector in one hand. The propeller shaft leading from the port engine was no longer spinning, but she would be thrown against a burning hot engine if she lost her footing. Completely at the mercy of chance, balance, and Mac's skill, she bent lower. Breath held, she edged the beer-can device into the space beneath the port fuel tank, careful to avoid touching the metal bottom.

There wasn't much light beneath the tank and sweat was running in her eyes. Impatiently she swiped her face against her arm. Blood and sweat. She'd hit her head again, but her eyes worked fine. The foil leaves danced on their threads like leaves in a breeze.

Until they collapsed.

Emma stared in horror, not wanting to believe. Deliberately she created more static with the comb, charged the leaves, and held the device beneath the engine again.

The tinfoil squares fell together.

She lunged to her feet and bolted up the machine room steps, slamming the hatch door behind her.

"I'm clear!" she yelled into her mic.

But she wasn't.

No one was.

77

Before Emma careened up the stairs and slammed the hatch back down, the port engine had thundered to life again. *Blackbird* hesitated, shuddering under the blow of a big wave. Water squirted in where a salon window hadn't been tightly closed, but the window itself stayed intact. Foam and black water sleeted across the deck.

One-handed, able to rely on only one leg, Mac fought the wheel. It was better with both engines working together again, but it wasn't easy. Blood mixed with sweat ran down his face. He glanced at her.

"So it's hot," he said.

She grabbed the overhead rail. "Yes."

The boat shifted as the wave it was climbing dropped. Lights shone through the rain and spray, filling up most of the view.

"Mac, that's—"

"A big bastard," he said, looking away from her. "We're in its radar shadow. Not close enough to worry the captain. Just finding a bit of shelter from the wind, now that it has backed around."

Mac's voice sounded like a stranger's, rough and blurred. He cracked his splint against the wheel, shuddered, and came into focus.

The motion of *Blackbird* had changed. It was more of a continuous climb and push from the stern. They weren't quite riding the freighter's bow wave, but it felt a bit like it.

"What—"

"*. . . vessel out of Tofino, heading . . .*"

The static made it almost impossible to understand.

"The Canadian Coasties didn't spot us," Mac said mechanically. "In a few minutes they'll pass between the freighter and shore going north. We're about half an hour from the border. If there's anything you have to know about taking *Blackbird* home, ask now."

She could barely hear him. His voice was nothing but a harsh whisper.

"I'm good," she said, "but you—"

Emma grabbed the wheel as Mac slumped back against the pilot seat. He kept on sliding, thumping down until he was stretched out on the wooden flooring between the sofa and dinette.

Quickly she bent, found the pulse in his neck, yanked off a sofa cushion and wedged it beneath his feet. There was no time to do more. The motion of the ship had become erratic.

Blackbird had fallen off the sweet spot.

Clenching her teeth, she took the wheel and tried to hold the yacht on course. No matter how hard she worked, she couldn't get the bow headed in the right direction at the right time. The ride became a brain-bashing, stomach-wringing, arm-yanking roll, lurch, climb, lurch, roll, fall, lurch, until the world was nothing but the scream of wind and hammering of waves.

How did Mac do it with only one hand?

Amphetamines were good, but not that good, especially when fighting injuries and blood loss. Mac had done what he had to so she could play Geiger games. Now he was paying the price.

So was Emma. Even without the relentless throbbing of her headache, she simply didn't have the skill to get enough speed out of *Blackbird* to cling to the freighter's radar shadow longer than a few minutes. She turned up the volume on the radio and listened, listened, listened. . . .

The Coast Guard vessel she couldn't see on the radar apparently couldn't see her either. Nobody hailed her.

Using every bit of her strength and concentration, she held to the freighter's radar shadow as long as she could. Finally she was forced to cut speed a little, then a little more. It was the only way she could begin to control *Blackbird*'s stubborn wheel.

She thought about the joystick and discarded the idea as quickly as it came. *If it would have worked, Mac would have used it.*

The big freighter pulled away, leaving *Blackbird* alone on a lightless sea.

She fumbled her cell phone out. The screen was cracked

and the battery was low. It would have to do. She couldn't leave the wheel long enough to get Mac's. The ride was easier now that she had cut back speed, but it wasn't that easy.

She punched a button.

"What's up?" Faroe's voice demanded.

"*Blackbird*'s hot, wired to blow," she said tersely. "Mac is alive, but down. Amphetamine crash and blood loss. I'm going to head straight out to sea, deepest water I can find, and—"

The sudden crackle of the radio overrode her words. "*Black Swan, Black Swan*, switch to six-four."

The call repeated several times.

"It has to be Demidov," she said to Faroe. "No one else knows about *Blackbird*'s twin."

"Find out what he wants."

Numbly Emma fumbled with the radio until she had switched channels. "*Black Swan* here. Who are you?"

"Someone who understands the radiant core of your problem," Demidov said.

Beautiful. Just fucking beautiful.

She hissed out her breath between her teeth, then put an edge of hysteria in her voice.

"You do? Then help me! Mac slipped and knocked himself out and the water's awful and I keep throwing up and I have to steer and I don't know how!"

The last words were a definite wail.

"Be calm," Demidov said. "Angle the bow east, toward shore. I'll meet you and bring you in. Everything will be fine. Just do as I tell you. In fifteen minutes you'll see me."

"R-really?" Emma asked, throwing in a sniff.

"Of course. You're only fifteen minutes from safety. Come to me. I will help you."

"Oh, God. Thank you, I'm so—" She banged her fist against a window, yelped, and bashed the radio on the wheel. "Damn this cord! It keeps—"

Emma switched to an inactive channel and let the microphone dangle from its cord. "Okay, we're alone again."

"Do you believe Demidov?" Faroe asked.

"Do I have a choice other than going toward shore?" she asked in her normal voice. "Obviously Demidov has a locator bug aboard *Blackbird*. We have to assume that he also has a radio trigger for the bomb."

Silence, a curse. "Agreed."

"I can't outrun a radio signal," she said. "If I head for deeper water and Demidov hits the button, likely at least one freighter will be taken out with us. Same thing if you call in the Coasties who almost caught us."

"Agreed."

"But if I go toward shore, there's at least a chance I can catch Demidov off guard. Each time we've been in contact with him, I've been in arm-candy mode. He thinks I'm dumber than tofu."

Faroe grunted.

"If I can't get the job done," Emma said, "you and Harrow will have time to set up an ambush and take *Blackbird* out before Demidov gets to Seattle."

"What makes you think Demidov will wait until then to pull the trigger?"

"He wants a big American city to hold hostage, not a

nameless hunk of Canadian coast. Publicity is the whole point of ops like this."

"Can you disarm the bomb?" Faroe asked.

She laughed a little wildly. "Can you beam bomb techs aboard?"

"Do you know how to sink *Blackbird*?"

"Hit a big rock. No rocks around here. I'm miles off-shore."

"Can you launch the dinghy?" he asked.

"Alone? In this water?" She laughed again, then stopped. She really didn't like the sound of it. "Even if I could, and I somehow managed to drag Mac aboard, my fifteen minutes would be more than gone. Then Mac and I would get one hell of a sendoff."

"How long has Mac been out?"

"Not long enough to recover," she said flatly. "He's lost too much blood. If he hasn't already gone into shock, he's headed there on a fast train. I've done what I can, but somebody has to be at the wheel all the time."

Faroe said something blistering.

She laughed oddly. "Good-bye, Faroe. It was fun while it lasted."

"Wait! What are you going to do?"

"Find out if Demidov is a soldier or a mercenary."

And scream.

She really wanted to do that. But if she started, she didn't think she would stop.

78

Emma strained into the darkness. If there were any lights out there, she couldn't see them through the hammering rain.

The radar didn't have a problem. It showed an endless gold mass stretching across the western half of the screen. Occasionally, just at the edge of the inlet where the waves weren't nearly as big, she saw a separate flicker that was Demidov's boat.

Death echo.

"Okay, Mac. We're going to see if we can't make that name come true."

She picked up the dangling microphone and switched to 64.

"Hello?" she asked raggedly. "Anyone there?"

"*Black Swan?*" came the instant answer.

Demidov.

"Here," Emma said. "What s-should I d-do? The waves are b-big and the rain and Mac—" Her voice broke. It wasn't difficult to sound shaky, a woman in over her head, at the edge of drowning.

"Turn the wheel toward the light I'll show you."

"S-sure . . ."

After a few moments, she saw a faint flicker, like a flashlight whose illumination was being blotted out between waves.

"I s-see you," she said in relief.

"Very good. Be calm. You will be safe. When you get close, we'll go farther into the harbor, where it isn't as rough."

Emma made a panicked sound and let the hand microphone drop and dangle noisily, banging against the console.

She'd heard all she needed to.

"This is it, Mac. Wish us luck."

Silence answered her.

Waves humped up beneath *Blackbird*'s stern, but rarely came apart in a thunder of foam anymore. The swells pushed the boat toward shore with a surge and a swoosh, almost like surfing. She kept *Blackbird*'s speed up, but was careful not to overrun the waves. Childhood boating on the Great Lakes had taught her the dangers of dropping off a wave too fast and burying the bow in the water. It was a sure way to flip a craft end over end.

Kayaks could recover.

Blackbird wouldn't.

Mac lay on the varnished teak floor, half-wedged beneath the dinette, unmoving except for the boat's motions.

"Mac?"

In the past thirteen minutes she'd called his name many times. He hadn't answered then. He didn't answer now.

The only way she knew he was still alive was the continued, slow ooze of blood onto the polished teak floor.

She talked to him anyway.

"Faroe keeps calling. I suppose I should answer, but really, what is there to say? It either works or it doesn't. If it does, he can fire me at his leisure. If it doesn't . . . well, it won't be my problem anymore. Or yours. That's all I'm really sorry about. You didn't get a vote. You deserve at least that. You're a good man, MacKenzie Durand. The best. I waited a lifetime to find you."

Mac didn't answer.

She didn't expect him to.

Windshield wipers kept the glass clear for about one second. She looked down at the radar screen that overlaid the nav chart.

"Won't be long now. That echo is less than half a mile away. No lights showing but for the flashlight popping in and out. We don't even have that. We're an accident waiting to happen."

She laughed.

The sound made her skin crawl. She swallowed hard, fighting to keep it together for a few more minutes.

A wave began breaking sooner than she'd expected. She pulled back on the throttles, then speeded up as another swell arrived. This close to shore the waves were losing any rhythm. Rollers slammed into cliffs, reverberated, and sent part of their force back out to sea, meeting incoming waves.

Sometimes this had the effect of smoothing the water. Sometimes it made everything worse. Most of the time it was just an unpredictable mess of conflicting forces.

The echo on the screen came closer, closer, closer.

"*Black Swan! Black Swan!* Steer to the right of us!" Demidov yelled through the radio. "And slow down!"

Emma jerked the wheel as though to avoid the boat she still couldn't see with her eyes. Abruptly she pulled back on the throttles. That should make whoever was aboard the other boat feel better.

For about five seconds. Four. Three.

Two.

"Turn more!" the radio screamed.

One.

Now.

She jerked the wheel back toward the other boat and slammed the throttles to the max. *Blackbird* heeled, then roared forward. The radar echo leaped closer. On the next sweep it would merge with *Blackbird*.

"So what are you made of, Demidov?" she asked. "Will you die with your bomb like a soldier or jump and swim like a mercenary?"

Blackbird lurched, a horrible sound came from the bow, and something holding a flashlight spun aside, then vanished beneath the wild water.

No more sounds came from the radio.

She slowed *Blackbird*, turned back toward the open sea, and searched the radar and the water as she retraced her course. All she saw was the pale outline of a boat.

Upside down.

She firewalled the throttles and headed back out to sea, angling so that she could meet the waves and still put Vancouver Island behind her, racing for the international boundary, expecting each second to be her last.

Just a few miles.

Just a few.

After several miles she relaxed her grip on the wheel; if Demidov had carried a radio trigger, he wasn't using it. There were no ships in sight, no one else at immediate risk. The international boundary was close.

Fingers shaking, she punched in St. Kilda's number.

"Emma?" Faroe asked, a prayer in his voice.

"I sideswiped Demidov's boat. It flipped. I didn't look for survivors. I firewalled it. Now I'm several miles west of something called Port Renfrew. If you can't reach me, call the Canadians. Mac needs help *now*."

"Keep on your course. We're closer than any Canadian boat. You'll hear a helicopter real soon. Stay on the phone. Someone will give you instructions."

"Send a medic down the rope first. Mac needs . . . needs . . ."

"We're coming, Emma. We have you on radar. Hang on."

Emma wrapped her hands more tightly around the wheel.

And hung on.

79

Emma put her hand on Mac's forehead as though reassuring herself that he was still alive. He put his good hand over hers and gently squeezed. She was sitting on a long couch in his small home. He was stretched out, his head in her lap. Her hand went back to stroking his hair, soothing both of them.

A gun was stuck muzzle down between her hip and the couch.

A knock came from the front door. Emma lifted her hand and reached for the gun.

"Heads up, mice," Faroe called, "the cat is back."

"It's open," Mac called.

"I have company," Faroe warned.

Emma flipped the safety off. "And I have my Glock. Come in soft."

Alara entered first, her hands visible. Empty.

Faroe followed and closed the door behind him, shooting the deadbolt from habit.

Emma put the safety on and shoved the gun back in the sofa.

Alara's dark eyes went from Emma's vividly bruised face to the splint on Mac's wrist. His stitches were hidden beneath his loose pants, his bruises largely concealed by his beard.

Neither agent looked good.

"Even though you were cleared for any radiation problems, you should have stayed in the hospital," she said to Mac.

"Don't like them."

Alara nodded. "So I've heard." She looked at Emma. "You were as smart as your mouth. You have my gratitude."

Emma's lips tightened. "I'd rather have answers."

"Ask."

"Is Demidov alive?"

"His body was recovered this morning," Alara said. "He died in a boating accident caused by stupidity—he shouldn't have been out on the water in bad conditions."

"Was he driving the boat that flipped?" Mac asked.

"Lina Fredric, born Galina Federova, was the captain. Thanks to the survival gear she wore, she lives," Alara said. "She is being debriefed by Canadian and American interrogators. She claims that she was forced by threat of death to help Demidov. I believe her."

"Lovich and Amanar?" Mac asked.

"Back in the U.S. We are still debriefing the man who was holding the families hostage." She looked at Faroe. "St. Kilda barely left enough of him intact to question."

Faroe smiled thinly. "Don't terrorize children on my watch."

"Where is *Blackbird*?" Emma asked.

"I don't know," Alara said.

"Bullshit," Mac said.

"I do know that the experts quickly dismantled the standard explosive part of the bomb," she continued as though he hadn't spoken. "Mac was correct. The initiator was wired through the fake fuel hose to very powerful conventional explosives, which would have in turn scattered the fissionable materials. It was crude, effective, dirty, and would have detonated."

"I'd rather have been wrong," Mac said.

She looked at him for a long moment, nodded, and said, "The radioactive part of the bomb is taking longer to deal with. Our people did find the locator bugs that were installed within the very hull at the time the ship was built."

"Bugs? Plural?" Emma asked.

"Identical, too," Faroe said. "Russian. Bulky, tough, and long lived. They only transmitted every twelve hours."

"My head hurts," Emma said. "Make it easy on me."

Alara laughed. "Ah, if only. Like most covert disasters, the postmortems on the *Blackbird* affair have barely begun. I do know that the op was old. It began years ago when we doubled an agent. The man was well connected with the Russian government as well as the *mafiya*. Originally it was a currency sting."

"Still hurting, here," Emma said.

Mac took her hand from his hair and kissed her palm. "So Harrow was telling a form of the truth."

" 'A form of the truth.' " Alara smiled. "I will remember that. The currency in question was used to buy the contents of an orphan nuclear source—an abandoned lighthouse in Kamchatka. As the op evolved in Russia, it became a game of embarrassing the Georgians. We informed the Georgians, who decided to let the op go—and then swoop in at the last minute and embarrass the Russians."

"How did the U.S. feel about it?" Mac asked.

"We collected intel every step of the way," Alara said.

"You could have stopped it at any point."

"I? No. I wasn't informed until the last minute, when *Blackbird* was identified as the twin of *Black Swan*, the primary pawn in the op."

Silence.

"Eventually," Alara continued, "Grigori Sidorov took over the Russian end of the op. He decided he'd rather destroy an American city and blame it on the Georgians. After all, the Georgians had left a nuclear calling card—a rudimentary dirty bomb—in Moscow once, simply as a warning. Why would anyone doubt that they would do it again as payback to the U.S. for not supporting their government more boldly?"

"What was in it for Sidorov?" Emma asked.

"Power, of course. And a kind of patriotism. According to our intel, Sidorov wasn't entirely sane."

"No shit," Faroe said under his breath.

"He grew up in the ruins of the former empire and was obsessed with making Russia powerful again, with himself as a kind of peasant tsar," Alara said. "Demidov was his employee."

"Grigori Sidorov," Emma said. "Last night, I saw that name in an online blog where present and former State Department types weigh in."

Mac nodded. "You read the blog to me. Something about a *mafiya*-style execution—no head, no hands, lots of torture. Heavy betting on who would come into power now."

"I heard that, too," Alara said blandly.

"Just somebody sending a message," Faroe said. "Break the nuclear rules and die the hard way."

"Who dropped the hammer on Tommy?" Mac asked.

"According to Lina, it was Demidov," Alara said.

"Why?" Mac asked.

"Our best guess is that Sidorov wanted to delay the op long enough for an important enemy to arrive in Seattle on international business. The man couldn't be killed in Russia. Sidorov had tried several times."

"Take out a city, take out an enemy. A twofer," Mac said. "Son of a bitch."

"Some people should have been killed at birth," Emma said.

"Unfortunately," Alara said, "we don't know which ones until it is too late."

Silence expanded.

Emma looked at Mac. He shook his head.

"No more questions on our end," she said.

Alara nodded and turned to leave.

"You okay?" Faroe asked Mac and Emma.

Mac took her hand again. "We're good."

"I'll check back in a few hours," Faroe said.

"We're fine," Emma said.

"Tell it to Grace."

The door shut behind Alara and Faroe. Emma let out a long breath. So did Mac. He rubbed his cheek against her palm.

"Did I thank you for saving my life?" he asked.

"You saved mine first. No way I could have taken Temuri down."

"You know what they say about saving a life. . . ."

"What?" she asked.

"That life belongs to you."

"So we belong to each other?" she asked.

"Sure do."

Emma touched Mac's lips with their intertwined fingers and smiled.

"Works for me."